CU00894415

Souls That Rule

Earth Divine

Dyran Kincaid

Copyright © 2023 Dyran Kincaid
All rights reserved
First Edition

Fulton Books
Meadville, PA

Published by Fulton Books 2023

ISBN 979-8-88731-655-0 (paperback)
ISBN 979-8-88731-678-9 (hardcover)
ISBN 979-8-88731-656-7 (digital)

Printed in the United States of America

To William, for teaching me what courage is
To Z, for teaching me what love can *be*

CONTENTS

The role of God is to Be. He is omniscient, omnipotent, and indivisible. His will is eternal and absolute. But when God must break anew to combat the sins of evil, and thus, becomes an example of the flaws he once reigned supreme over, he now is no different than Man. He now is an example of what God once was. He now is vulnerable to the men and demons who seek the title of The Almighty for themselves. He now is no longer God. Who then, shall become known as the New God?

—Unknown

CHAPTER 1

Break Anew

A mysterious man wearing strange clothing stood still, allowing a light breeze to roll over his shoulders as it whistled through the trees and drifted over the hills, which watched over a small suburban neighborhood in the distance.

As the man watched, he noticed that the breeze came and went periodically, ever so often leaving everything calm and still. But the man also noticed that every time the breeze departed, if even for a moment, his mind was interrupted and left stranded in a wasteland of idle thoughts.

In fact, his mind was both an oasis of paradise, reassuring his distant allies but also a source of calamity for his enemies, which lurked in the nearby shadows.

The man turned his neck, shutting his eyes as he tried to remember something of particular interest—or at least something important enough to retain his concentration for the time being. It was a memory of a previous life, one that did not belong to him but was just as important as anything he considered to be among his most treasured possessions.

It was only when the man was able to focus his attention back to the sight in front of him did he now notice that the absence of the breeze made his body feel cool. But for some reason, the fact that he *knew* the breeze would return at some point, no matter how long it took, created a sense of warmness and familiarity that most had come to take for granted in recent times.

Some things, after all, would only be temporary. Some things would be lost to time, and others lost as a victim of war and destruction.

And most of that was the man's fault—or so many claimed.

The man raised an eyebrow, suddenly sensing something in the air that did not match the tranquility of the peaceful afternoon. He had an innate ability to sense disturbances in the many worlds around him.

The man looked up above and peered into the atmosphere, scanning everything above him as far out into the horizon as he could see. A perceptive individual would notice that a storm was coming. It was a storm that would bring with it the revelations of destruction and creation alike, an unavoidable combination of death and rebirth that a prophet referred to as the Apocalypse.

The man knew that when the storm finally arrived on that fateful night, the reservoirs created from the rainfall would claim the very hills he stood on now. He anticipated that the craters produced from the forceful strikes of lightning would destroy everything, leaving nothing behind but a permanent ruin of catastrophe, whisked away by the powerful winds that would seek to uproot and disturb the peace and tranquility the man enjoyed at this very moment.

The storm's destruction would be ingrained in nature and a part of all the lives of those fortunate enough to survive, a permanent reminder of how tentative peace was for those who meddled with it everyday.

The man shifted his attention from the neighborhood in the distance and was now looking down at a large house that appeared as if he had been purposefully secluded from society. It was shrouded by trees and rested on its own hillside—quite a way away from the nearest city.

The man began walking, moving between vantage points on the hill for moments at a time, watching the same exact spot from different angles. He knew with confidence that no matter how fast or careless his movements were, he remained hidden even in plain sight.

Then as the breeze rolled over his shoulder, the man adjusted his posture, rolled his neck around, and looked some more. He was patient. He was observant. Nothing slipped past his view. He even had eyes in the back of his head.

The man then focused his attention on a square window in the house, surprised to see that the curtains had not been strewn apart yet.

The man looked up at the sun, staring directly into its fiery center, feeling no discomfort looking into what he used to think was a beautiful sight.

Yeah, it was almost time for the day to start.

Just a few minutes more, the man thought to himself, *and then the curtains will finally be pulled apart. Only then can I put the tremendous power I've acquired over the years to the test. I alone shall decide the destinies of all who live in this wretched wasteland we call "reality."*

The man stood tall, his eyes leering toward the house in the distance once more. The stillness of the air had suddenly turned into a whisper as the breeze returned.

Then without a single trace—not even making so much as a whisper—the man *disappeared* into thin air, allowing the breeze to flow uninterrupted once more, blowing the grasses in the direction of the house secluded from society.

*****

Over the hills and hidden between the trees, no one could predict what went on inside the single secluded home resting on the hillside. It was an orderly house with a seemingly ordinary family but one with an extraordinary situation. No one knew who they were or what they were ever doing. As a result, they never bothered to explain themselves to the world around them.

But the world would find out soon enough.

A woman flipped a switch on the stove, turned a knob to increase the heat to *high*, and placed a pan on the heated circle, allowing the oils in the pan to slowly gloss the pan to its edges. The woman promptly left the stove and turned her attention to a blender which sat next to a coffee machine on the countertop. In one fell swoop, all the ingredients she needed were dropped in the blender and finely mixed until she got the color and thickness she wanted.

With a careful maneuver, the woman poured the liquid in two sparkling glasses, making sure with absolute certainty that both glasses had even amounts of liquid, and she gently placed them around a dining table alongside plates and utensils. Then the woman returned to the kitchen and began to brew herself a cup of black coffee with four packets of sugar and a tablespoon of milk to go alongside with her breakfast. Her routine was the same every day.

As the woman returned to the dining room, she paused for a moment, listening to the background noise as something in one of the upstairs bedrooms rustled around. For only a fraction of a second was she tuned in, attentive to every intricate sound that followed.

She heard nothing. Perhaps it was still too early in the day?

With one hand she drew back the cloth on a window next to the dining room table, bringing sunlight in the quiet house.

When she noticed that the pan on the stove was hot enough to begin using, the woman cleared her throat, preparing to get the attention of the two other individuals living in the house.

"Boys! It's almost time to eat!" she yelled into the large house before plopping a couple of eggs into the stove alongside some bacon.

The upstairs bedroom was still silent. The woman waited for a few seconds before she downed her last gulp of coffee and poured herself another cup.

*****

When Lance heard the voice yell from the kitchen, he opened his eyes, staring directly at the ceiling above him. He had already been awake for quite some time now.

Lance turned in his bed, rolling on his side. He noticed the bed next to him had been unnaturally still all morning.

"Chase"—the word trailed off as it bounced off the walls— "dude, are you seriously still asleep?"

But Lance already knew the answer to that question.

Still, Lance knew his brother would suddenly spring up with a burst of energy as soon as the sweet aroma of cooking food found its way to the bedroom upstairs.

But today was different. Chase was unusually quiet, and Lance was unusually attentive today.

The only thing Lance noticed was the sound of dishes clashing against one another and the electronic beeping of appliances downstairs. As usual, there was nothing going on outside their home, and there was nothing strange happening downstairs.

So what was this bizarre feeling? Did it have something to do with Chase and Lance being *different*?

Lance tossed the thought out of his mind. It was almost time for breakfast, and he was getting hungry.

He was becoming impatient. He turned and propped his head up with his arm and turned to look at his younger brother, Chase, in a bed on the opposite side of the room.

But Lance never ate without his brother. And while it wasn't exactly uncommon for Chase to sleep in, Lance still couldn't help but feel that something was off.

Lance turned to look at his alarm clock that read "6:03 a.m." It was a little later than Lance liked. He rolled to his other side and grabbed a book lying on the bed and opened it to where he last left off and began reading. Lance wasn't an active reader, but this book had been especially important. He was told by his caretaker that reading this book would be his biggest responsibility while growing up. Lance's job was to study it front and back, learn each and every page, discover the trivial themes and connections made within it, and understand it well enough to "reproduce" its contents for his caretaker…or whatever that possibly meant.

Without much consideration as to why, Lance knew well enough why he'd been told to do such a thing and with the amount of emphasis placed on it. It was simple.

It was because Lance and his brother were among a race of a powerful alien species known as *Rasrims*.

Rasrims were indeed beings from another planet. However, Lance and his brother had been raised as Humans and taught how to behave like them. They even looked like Humans. But more importantly, their jobs, either as Humans or Rasrims, was to ensure that the Humans prevented themselves from destroying the earth, an issue that had become increasingly significant within the past decade.

Lance flipped a page. He had been a fast reader. Soon enough and he'd finish the book.

The book had been titled *Water: A Rasrim's Guide to Using 1 of the 9 Elemental Prowesses*. It was, no less, a book designed for individuals like Lance to learn how to begin using their powers, a thorough guide, as if the topics mentioned in the book were every day, household topics and not highly controversial.

Lance found that odd. After all, how does one create a guide to teach aliens about…themselves? Was the author also a Rasrim? They would have to be, right?

But what Lance found even stranger was that the book didn't really exist. If you searched for this book online or in a bookstore, you would suddenly find armed police officers or even the military at your front door or elsewhere. To anyone's surprise, these individuals wouldn't have the book, but they were definitely as interested in finding it as you were.

Lance knew this. He figured it out the hard way. It was only thanks to his clever thinking and profound knowledge of technology and the Internet that he managed to avoid these individuals all together. But that doesn't ignore the fact that he *knew* he was being looked for and that this book, or rather the topic, was the reason why.

Upon doing more careful investigations, Lance learned that he and his brother had the only books of their kind. What was strange about this was that both he and his brothers' books appeared to only be the first books of an entire *series*, both dubbed "1 of 9," and both of these series were imaginably tailored to his and his brother's respective "abilities."

Lance also learned that the author was a person by the name of "E. Rior," but this wasn't a real person. "Rior" wasn't even a real last name nor had it ever been used as a pseudonym or pen name for any writer in history.

Lance returned his focus back to his book. After a few more minutes of skimming through the pages and making sure to jot down the important sections in his head, Lance grabbed his bookmark and placed it into his book before he closed it and sat it down on a nightstand next to his bed.

Lance sat back in his bed, deep in thought. He took a deep breath before slowly releasing it.

"Am I ready? I'm not a Human. I look like one, think like one… but it's time for me to realize who I truly am, right?"

The words flowed out of his mouth, less as a question and more as an indicator of anticipation.

Several thoughts flashed through Lance's mind, all of them contradicting one another. Why was he reading a book about his "supposed" abilities instead of actually using them? Was it because of how dangerous they were? Maybe he would be caught and killed by the same armed individuals who searched for other Rasrims on Earth?

Lance held his hand up in front of his face, inspecting it as if he had never seen his own hand before. They looked the *exact* same. There was no difference yet. Soon, he believed his powers would manifest and give Lance a multitude of abilities, including being able to manipulate the structure of his body, starting with his *hands*.

Well, according to this "E. Rior," that was.

But Lance only looked harder, focusing hard. Something was bound to happen. Lance's body would be undergoing changes soon. He knew that his eyes and his hands would be the site of these changes. But he still saw *nothing*.

Lance suddenly peered over at his brother Chase and nearly laughed aloud. Chase had been sprawled out, lying across the width of his bed more than half of his body hanging off the side of the bed. He looked like an absolute moron.

Lance looked back down at himself, focusing on his hands again. He thought about bringing this up to Chase, but he stopped himself.

This wasn't something he should bring up to Chase just yet.

Lance sighed. He rubbed the back of his head and then finally sat up in his bed.

Instead of wanting to read, Chase would pull these stupid stunts around the house involving fire, even going as far as trying to pull a prank on Lance after losing an argument. It didn't end well for Chase as Lance had been a step ahead of him everytime Chase tried to prank him by sabotaging them, rendering all his tricks and pranks useless. It was because of this, and without even knowing it, that Lance had saved the house from being burned down several times.

Of course, their caretaker got involved every time but never seemed to get angry or frustrated with the boys for playing such dangerous games in the house. Lance felt that she was secretly encouraging it, but he could never prove it.

Lance took a breath and opened his book again.

Their caretaker had told them not too long ago that reading was one of the best things they could do. She said, to be specific, that it would "strengthen their minds" while teaching them how to live on Earth. Lance could understand that. But he also understood a lot of things that went unsaid too. He had already made the connection that he shouldn't be able to process what typical Human behavior was or how to recognize it without thorough Human interaction and exposure to interpersonal relations. But Lance was a hyperanalytical thinker and excellent problem solver. He could read situations and make profound observations about seemingly anything with no problem.

Lance was observant and innovative, which was likely how he would describe all of humanity from the things he read in history books.

He modeled himself after what he believed the "perfect Human" was: smart, strong, bold, and innovative in the face of adversity.

By no means was Lance perfect, however. He was perceptive enough to know that Rasrims were not Humans. While he understood that Rasrims and Humans shared a number of physiological traits like skeletal structure and bodily functions, he knew that as a Rasrim, his species evolved in a totally different fashion compared to Humans.

For one, it was very rare for Rasrims to exhibit the same emotions that Humans did. Rasrims at large, for example, were sociopathic creatures who relied on their individualized traits and characteristics to achieve the things they needed to. They didn't need societies or "packs" to hunt or to protect themselves.

And Lance was the embodiment of this idea. He was a lone wolf but one always trying to learn from his and other people's mistakes.

Of course, this meant that Lance was by no means a conversationalist but instead a very observant practitioner of science and deductive reasoning. He likely spoke twenty words a day, and he never made small talk unless it was with his brother who needed to be reminded *constantly* to do things. Lance preferred to listen more than he did to speak, and this was mainly because his mind was so rampart with thoughts and ideas that attempting to divert his attention from sorting all that information would drive him crazy.

Now his brother Chase was an entirely different story.

Chase was the opposite of what most Rasrims were. He was perhaps more Human than most Humans were themselves. He was kind, compassionate, and understanding. Chase was sensitive to others' emotions.

If Lance were able to read others' thoughts and make calculated decisions based on inference, Chase was able to read emotions and connect to others internally.

But this was a problem, Lance told himself.

He knew that Rasrims were not supposed to be empathetic creatures. They were meant to be strong, persistent, and powerful creatures with the ability to defy nature itself. What sense did it make, therefore, to care about the very thing you were destined to conquer and permanently alter?

But this was how Rasrims behaved on their home planet, Osamos. Was Earth any different? Did it matter how Rasrims interacted with a completely foreign environment? Were they meant to conquer this planet as well? And what about the people? Did it matter if Rasrims even care about the race of sentient creatures roaming freely on this planet at all?

And if not, did that mean there was a possibility that there were Rasrims lived on this planet who hoped to conquer the Earth and destroy the Humans living on it? Would Lance ever meet these Rasrims? Was he one of those Rasrims without even knowing it?

Lance suddenly paused on his reading. He remembered *that* day. He remembered that exact conversation word for word and all its accompanying details. It was only now that Lance found that conversation strange. It was a conversation he had overhead, which was the reason he *knew* so much about Rasrims in the first place. To be frank, it was a conversation he was not meant to hear.

Whom was *she* talking to that day? And what was she—

A movement in the right jolted Lance's body, freezing him head to toe, turning him as stiff as ice. Lance's eyes flashed to the site of the movement. After looking for a moment, Lance cursed himself under his breath, shaking his head.

The sun finally inched over the tallest section of the hill, causing a beam of light to flash across the wall. It had happened too suddenly and caught Lance's attention.

Lance yawned and put his bookmark back in his book. He was restless and had only just woken up.

"All right, Chase. Get up. You overslept *again*," Lance said as more objects in the room became lit up by the sun, revealing a pile of dirty clothes and junk in front of Chase's bed.

Lance stopped, looking at his clean, organized area and then back at Chase's. Had Chase's side of the room gotten bigger and more full of junk?

"And your side's a damn mess, clean it up!" Lance blurted as he tossed a sock he had he only just found on his bed at Chase's exposed head.

Chase wrapped himself up in his blanket and rolled his body back into bed completely, groaning as he did. Lance thought he heard Chase say something too but wasn't entirely sure.

Lance swung his legs out of his bed and reached over, sifting through some clothes that didn't belong on another floor before he settled on the missing match of one of Chase's musty socks and picked it up with his thumb and index finger. He nearly gagged as he caught a whiff of the smell, tossing it as it landed perfectly on Chase's head.

Chase groaned but hardly moved, clearly still knocked-out. He pulled the covers over himself some more, muttering something in his sleep.

Lance realized that Chase wouldn't be getting up anytime soon. Instead, Lance walked over to the window and pulled the bedroom curtains apart, letting more rays of sunlight into the room. This seemed to do the trick as Chase suddenly yawned before sitting up half-awake.

"Mornin', Lance." Chase stretched his arms out with his mouth wide open.

Lance turned back with a smile on his face.

"Are you talkin' in your sleep again, or are you actually awake now?"

Chase laughed and rolled on his side, closing his eyes as if he were going back to sleep. "Well, I *must* be dreaming. Especially after that stupid fight we had." Chase yawned again and stretched his legs out across his bed. "You know I won, right?"

"Not a chance. There's no way."

"Oh please! Of course I did!"

The boys stopped for a moment when they heard what appeared to be the sound of laughter coming from downstairs in the kitchen.

Chase and Lance looked at the door, paused for a moment, and then looked back at each other.

"She's up, too, huh?"

"Duh! She's always up this early!"

"Wait, really? I guess I wouldn't know." Chase yawned.

Lance shook his head. *Unbelievable*, he thought to himself.

There was a brief pause between the two, who looked at each other with blank stares.

"I still won that fight you know."

Lance rolled his eyes. "The only way you won that fight is if you produce fire in your hands right now. Can you do it? No!"

Chase groaned, irritated. Suddenly, he balled his hands into a fist and began punching the air jokingly.

"I'm telling you, I *can* do it! It was happening *just* like this, I swear!"

"Yeah right! I tried to do the same thing a million times and nothing happened!"

"That's because you can't control Fire Risima, but I can!"

"Not yet, you can't! Idiot!"

"And *when* I show you I can, you'll be strutting around this house like a clown, all mopey again. That's what happened the last time I proved you wrong!"

"I was only trying to figure out how you managed to fix the TV before I could, that's all. It wasn't even all that complicated!"

"So why were you so angry then?"

Their voices trailed off as the sound of dishes clanged against one another. The lady downstairs grabbed a sponge and began scrubbing a pot in the sink, listening to what she could.

"Because I was thinking so hard! You know how I get when I—"

The lady turned off the sink and grabbed a towel, wiping her hands and the area around the sink, leaving the marble looking shiny.

She carried two plates of food lying next to her to the dining table and set them next to the glasses and then brought over a smaller plate of food and set it in front of her coffee.

She smiled to herself. Breakfast was almost finished.

Then she cautiously turned to face the stairs. She shook her head as she eavesdropped on Chase and Lance's conversation.

"Well, how about this! If you can prove that you can get that TV to work without its battery, I'll give you a hundred dollars right now!"

"You don't even have a hundred dollars!"

"Remember last month? When we cleaned the entire deck after *someone* set off a paint bomb, which missed horribly, which *then* caught on fire?"

"W-well! I, uh, well, I—"

"Yeah, exactly!"

The lady downstairs grinned to herself and returned to the kitchen to finish the last of the breakfast preparations, thinking to herself.

The boys frequently had fights in the house, but they were never anything serious. It was just as two twin brothers would normally fight, but these two were different from other twins. The first difference was that boys enjoyed it and never took grudges or allowed anything to stay in their heads for too long. They only had each other for company and understood that no matter what happened, they were always brothers first. They had learned that their kind back on Osamos took the bond of families seriously.

The lady thought to herself for a moment, resting her hands on the warm countertop.

She frequently thought about a question that someone in particular had asked her once, a long time ago:

> *Do you know just how little we actually know*
> *about Rasrims and the universe, let alone our own*
> *friends and families who are Human?*

The lady paused again, looking outside the window above the kitchen sink.

She bit her lip, deep in thought, frustrated with herself. Of course she knew. She likely knew more than anyone, and she knew that was a serious claim for anyone to make. But that was the issue: she knew far too much and was forced to keep it all a secret, and this would reveal to be her biggest mistake in the near future.

In fact, not a single person even knew that she was here now, illegally taking care of two Rasrims and putting her and the boys' lives in jeopardy.

She didn't have a family of her own. Her parents had been killed when she was fourteen, and she wasn't left with grandparents, aunts, uncles, or siblings, so this was the only family she ever had and would ever have. On Earth, she was completely alone with no one to trust or ask for help despite her massive amounts of knowledge, technology, and experiences that she hoped would one day turn into a legacy to be passed on to. But this: the fact that no one knew all of this but that it was also all *true* was the sole reason she was still alive.

The woman lifted her head.

She understood the risks. She had calculated them herself. She knew what she signed up for—she designed the plan herself and did what she had to do in order to ensure Chase and Lance's safety even before they were born. She knew how dangerous and powerful the boys would become. And she knew that once they became full-fledged Rasrims, there would hardly be anything in the universe that could stop them from achieving whatever they set their minds on.

She only accepted the risk of raising two Rasrims as her own because she was the only one who could address the consequences of making such a decision.

The Humans on this planet were no longer capable of protecting themselves. They were hell-bent on war and destruction, chaos and control.

If she could do the impossible, if she could somehow manage to program a race of creatures to live and recognize Humans as their own flesh and blood while maintaining their inherited legacies, they would grow up with the uniquely special perspective that neither Humans nor Rasrims had, which was to *defend* world instead of wanting to *destroy* them.

The only question was, Should she tell them the *truth* about who she really was?

The lady scanned the kitchen, making sure everything was where it needed to be, that all the food was prepared, and that the table was set.

Yeah. Everything looked good. They boys would enjoy it. That was for sure.

The lady rocked her head slowly, making sure she was content with the preparations.

As far as the "universe" was concerned, she didn't care about the things she knew or was ignorant to—that didn't matter now.

The lady pushed a set of glasses up to her eyes.

Once she had discovered the existence of Osamos over two decades ago, she wanted to figure out as much as she could about the planet: its mass, climate, ecosystem, wildlife, geography, atmospheric pressure, radioactivity, and magnetic properties... She quickly learned everything she could. But once the "basics" were taken care of, she turned her attention to the inhabitants of Osamos more seriously when she discovered a recurring theme in the properties of

Osamos. Unlike Earth, which with time introduced evolution and began influencing the actions, behavior, and appearance of the planet, she discovered that Osamos and Rasrims emerged at the same time and, as a result, influenced each other directly and to a much larger degree than Humans did to Earth. She figured out that Rasrims protect Osamos with their abilities, shaping and redirecting unfavorable conditions that would end up risking their lives or the integrity of the planet. The abilities of Rasrims granted them godlike powers, such as being able to redirect asteroids, manipulate great seas, and prevent their planet from producing serious volcanic activity.

And of course, she knew that the Rasrims had the ability to use these powers on each other, unafraid to destroy one another or an entirely separate species if it risked Osamos's safety.

She learned so much in such a short amount of time that she eventually possessed enough knowledge to become as dangerous as Rasrims themselves were, down to being able to replicate and utilize all of their abilities on command.

But she never tried to before. She never needed to.

But after a long, excruciating journey, she had found herself taking care of the two boys. According to a Rasrim she had met long ago, Chase and Lance Kolorio were destined to become some of the most capable beings in the universe. They had been beings who had "descended from the Gods of a Higher Order" or something like that, whatever that meant. It sounded like nonsense, but then again, so did the initial discovery of Osamos.

Olivia Elementa, whom her boys referred to as Miss E, didn't care about anything except them since the very day they were born. She didn't care about what challenges or threats she would receive from anyone, Human or Rasrim. She was willing to risk her life if they were ever exposed or threatened, and she reminded herself of that every day. Chase and Lance were *her* universe. They were all that mattered to her. And to the boys, she was the most important thing to them. She knew that.

But weren't Humans like that too?

Miss E placed three sets of utensils next to each of the plates of food. There was only one more thing to do. She noticed that as she set down the last set of knives and forks, she had clanged the fork on the plate, causing Chase and Lance to become quiet in their room, postponing their argument.

Chase got out of bed, suddenly aware. "Didn't I hear you say something about breakfast a few minutes ago?" He walked over to the foot of his bed and then began looking through a pile of clothes for a T-shirt he seemed to like wearing more times than what was acceptable.

Lance swung his legs out of his own bed and then got up, slipping on a pair of slides. "It's Wednesday. Today's 'Wednesday Waffles.'" Lance scratched the back of his head. "I still think having certain food on certain days is weird."

Chase slowly turned and looked at Lance, eyes wide open. "Oh my god, wait! It really is, isn't it?"

"Yeah. You know how dry Miss E's humor can be."

"No, not you! The waffles! It's really Wednesday! We're having waffles today, dude!"

Lance nearly gagged. "A—are you kidding me?"

"What? No! You *just* said it was Wednesday, and something else I wasn't paying attention to. But waffles! I was waiting all week for this!"

Lance couldn't believe his ears. "You know, if you don't hurry up and clean your side, you'll only be licking a plate of syrup."

Chase sucked his teeth. "Yeah right! You hardly eat anything! Half a bowl of cereal and you'd gag," Chase fired back before leaving the room, heading into the bathroom just outside the door.

Lance muttered something under his breath, rubbing the back of his head again. Were waffles really *that* serious?

Lance walked to his corner of the room and looked out his bedroom window, looking down at all the rolling hills and calm grasses surrounding the house. Lance had never quite learned to appreciate what living in such a house meant, nor had he experienced everything outside of the house he wanted to see either, including places some would say aren't worth visiting or, in another sense, had "no value."

Lance never understood how to place value on anything. Although he had learned from his caretaker what being poor and rich meant, there would be some time before Lance truly understood the difference between physical value acquired through appraisal and the personal value attributed to something you either liked or loved.

Lance scratched his head, thinking to himself.

He knew one thing, though: The trio was rich. Miss E had loads of money. And while Lance never bothered to ask her how much she really had and how she got it all, anything Chase and Lance wanted they got, within reason, of course. But these were two aliens from another planet. How could subjecting them to the concept of wealth and indulgence impact their development in a foreign area? It was something that Lance had figured out Miss E *might* have been testing, but his suspicions were never confirmed. Lance found everything about his living situation to be bizarre. There were too many things that he wasn't being told, and this was especially true after Lance tried researching Miss E herself. What did he find? Nothing. Absolutely nothing. Like the author E. Rior, the woman known as "Olivia Elementa" did not actually exist.

With age, Chase and Lance learned that they had the freedom to do almost anything they pleased. The two boys had the entire house and then an additional five acres of land to use however they really wanted to.

Their only rule was to not destroy the entire place.

Miss E also told them once that when they finally gained mastery over all their abilities that they would only ever have one job, and an important one at that. Miss E emphasized the importance for Chase and Lance to use their abilities to protect humanity, no matter what.

That too, as painfully simple as it seems, always played in Lance's mind like a record on repeat. Why were Chase and Lance *here* on Earth, in this house, with these lessons, sworn to protect the Human race? What sense did it make taking them from their own planet and raising them here? And why were they not yet able to use their abilities?

Lance stopped himself. He didn't know anything about their home planet, Osamos. He didn't even know another Rasrim aside from Chase. After all, when it came down to it, Lance had no real way to even know for sure if he truly *was* an alien or not! Rasrims and Humans looked the same. They spoke the same. They had the same features, the same emotions, and seemed to enjoy the same things.

How was he supposed to—

Lance stopped, forcing himself to relax. He remembered to breathe, slowing his racing mind down to a more reasonable level.

He put his hands in the pockets of his sweatpants and left his window.

Only then did he realize Chase had still been in the bathroom.

Lance cleared his throat. "Yo! How much longer are you gonna be in there?"

Lance didn't get an answer.

He sighed, carrying himself back to his bed, and plopped on it.

Back to staring at the ceiling again, Lance thought to himself.

This was Lance's daily routine. He was always stuck in his mind. He was always asking himself the same questions, producing the same ideas, and then shutting himself down the same way. He never once had the opportunity to "apply himself" like he felt he ought to.

After all, what exactly would he do?

Lance knew that he and Chase were special. They were intelligent, strong, and sociable. They had already learned a ton and were constantly fed new information to disseminate and build into new ideas.

Then again, what sane person with *this* amount of money would go to this length to keep them stored up in a house?

Lance tried to relax. He was doing it again!

His only option was to wait until he knew for sure.

He opened his eyes again, finding his hands floating above his face. He looked at them. He looked at the palms of his hands closely. He balled his fist. He opened them again and turned them around. And then they dropped to the sides of his bed.

He had to wait until he could see for himself what kind of powers he really had.

Lance turned in bed. He thought about how the day would go. It was midsummer, which meant it would be a good day. Every summer day was a good day.

Lance decided to get out of bed, attempting to escape his mind. He began tidying his stuff, rearranging some books on a shelf and folding up clothes.

At 6:30 a.m., a watch on the nightstand next to Lance's bed began ringing. Lance walked over to it and picked the watch up. Lance had built the entire watch himself. He had learned at a very early age from Miss E to be as productive as he could be and that Lance would be an excellent crafter. That same day, she came home with some tools and supplies but also several catalogs from hardware stores and asked Lance what he had seemed interested in. She had told Lance that they would work on some projects together, but Lance had been intrigued by what he had seen. It was the first time he had seen so much of…stuff outside his house. Computers, tablets, circuits, robotics, holograms…you name it. From that day, Lance had dedicated hours building as much as he possibly could.

Lance strapped the watch on his left arm. He held it up to his eyes. When he looked close enough, he could faintly see the reflection of himself and caught himself looking into his own eyes, looking deep into the light blueness his eyes produced.

After what seemed like hours, Chase finally got out of the bathroom for Lance to use.

As Chase came back into the bedroom and before Lance left the room, he very *casually* asked Chase for perhaps the tenth time this morning to clean his side of the room, gesturing to the visible "line" dividing the room thanks to Chase's neglect. And Chase, very casually in return, suggested that he would, but Lance knew better.

Lance closed the bathroom door and turned on the faucet. He opened one of the bathroom cabinets and removed his toothbrush and a bottle of toothpaste, surprised that he didn't have to go looking for either one today.

While they were too young to appreciate it, Chase and Lance lived in a beautifully maintained large house with three stories, complete with five bedrooms and three and a half bathrooms. It was certainly a lot of room for two kids, and Lance often wondered why they needed an extra two bedrooms. Chase and Lance enjoyed turning them into pillow forts and played all sorts of games in them and in the rest of the house. Miss E never seemed to care. She knew that noise wasn't an issue, and whenever something was broken, Lance had always offered to try and fix it. But when this wasn't possible, Miss E had it replaced the next day. That being said, the two boys were careful not to break anything, and especially not in the bedrooms. Miss E told the two boys—jokingly of course—that she may end up taking in more Rasrims at some point to keep them company. But then, as Lance remembered that conversation, they were given another very serious conversation about what to do if strangers were over the house. This didn't happen often, but when it did, Chase and Lance simply stayed in their rooms or went into the basement to watch TV. They were obedient and respected Miss E's wishes, but they didn't quite yet understand the severity of getting caught. They had never been in trouble before but were still taught discipline. Their responsibilities were keeping the house clean. Miss E had been clear about what other children had to do, and when Chase and Lance could understand this, they had been more aware of their presence and behavior in and around the house. Since then, the house was always clean—never a speck of dust or dirt present anywhere. So with the exception of the bedroom, the boys and their caretaker had no issue keeping the house and the yards nice and neat.

When the boys wanted something to do, they usually played somewhere in the three open floors of the house, be it in their rooms, the basement, or outside in the yard. They were never concerned about people seeing them out in the yard, as the lawn had been big enough to keep the house secluded, with several large trees barricading the perimeter of the land. When it was too cold to go outside or raining, the boys went into the lower level of the house, which they had called "the basement," but the truth was, they weren't allowed to go into the actual basement of the house located behind a door and down a deep flight of steps in the lower level. That area of the house was considered off limits after their caretaker told the boys that there had been a flood that left mold all on the walls and that the entire area needed to be "remodeled."

Lance turned the faucet on and spit out his toothpaste and rinsed off his toothbrush. He turned the water off.

"A flood, huh? But when she told us that, the last time I remember it raining was a few weeks before that."

Lance brushed his hair back, using nothing but a little water to get it back into the shape and style he always liked.

Lance recalled that around that time that he saw Miss E take several trips with several types of tools down to that area by herself, but the boys had left it alone since then. Neither of them even knew they had a basement until Lance accidentally stumbled across the secluded room leading into it, located on the wall on the far corner of the lowest level. It wasn't that it was hard to see, but the lower level was just one of those areas you didn't bother wandering around as much as the first two levels. This often made Lance wonder if there were other secret rooms or anything their caretaker had hidden from them in general.

Chase and Lance never disobeyed the few rules they had. But what bothered them the most was the fact that they lived in such a large house with a ridiculous amount of land despite hardly ever going into the suburbs or the city to explore. They knew what was out there. Chase had been a huge fan of movies, and Lance was nothing short of a young scientist, frequently surfing the Internet for projects to read about. They had learned a lot on their own and only wished they could see and learn more by exploring the world.

After taking a trip beyond their yard one day, the boys had discovered a nice spot on a corner leading into the nearest town to them where kids their age had gathered every day. At the same time in the morning, Lance realized, those kids would all board a yellow bus, disappear for several hours, and then all get off at the same place from the same bus at the same time. That intrigued Lance.

One day, he mentioned it to Miss E, careful not to explicitly state that he had gone past the perimeter himself. She ended up explaining to him that he had discovered a stop for children going to something called *school*. Lance remembered that when he had brought Chase along with him, that he had nearly tried to get on the bus himself to see what all the commotion was about.

And then they got caught by Miss E.

Fortunately, they weren't in too much trouble. Miss E understood the boys' curiosity and told them that they were never be punished for being curious or wanting to explore. However, they were reminded that even if they were ever allowed anywhere past the perimeter to *never* tell anyone who they were.

Once Chase and Lance practically got on their knees and swore to her that they wouldn't, she very reluctantly gave the boys permission to travel to the city and explore it.

As the boys got older and when their house became dull and boring, they took more time traveling throughout the city. But the boys had never taken trips longer than a few hours at a time. But in order to make the most of their trips, they tried their best at finding things to do for fun without drawing attention to themselves. There was actually a good bit to do in the town and especially late at night, but Miss E had given the boys a rule to be back home by six every night…and slowly eased off on it as time went on.

Even so, the boys only really went out in the mid-afternoon. They had discovered a movie theater, a bowling alley, a fitness center, many different parks, several places with delicious kinds of food, and many more different types of stores selling different things such as toys, games, tools, and electronics.

Nowadays, the boys usually only went shopping for food and materials to repair things around the house or to experiment on various technologies like holograms or biotech such as prosthetics or "Bioflesh," a relatively new type of drug that could speed up the recovery time for physical wounds by over 100 percent. The boys didn't play with toys or anything most kids their age did. They still wanted to have fun and simply turned their heads to science or physical training to have their thrills and excitement.

Using some of these materials and technologies, Chase and Lance developed some new skills and hobbies. Whenever they weren't doing chores or periodic work around the house, Lance was in the bedroom staying on top of cutting-edge technology, trying to jumpstart his way into mastering Risima. He hoped to accomplish this by experimenting with the symbiotic-type relationship that Rasrims had with the environment and if there was such a way to replicate or otherwise reverse-engineer it for amateurs or "Non-Rasrims" to do so as this would be their only hope at using it. Chase, on the other hand, wanted to figure out if there was a way to wear "all of his outfits at once" by using Risima particles to manipulate the fabrics of his clothing. These were two incredibly advanced ideas for boys who could hardly even use their powers, but it showcased one of the boys' abilities that had already manifested, their genius level IQs and surreal talents to bring uniqueness and innovation to a variety of situations—including what would soon be considered their intense physical training.

But it especially manifested in Lance. With a hyperathletic physique and an astonishing IQ of 210, Lance proved himself to be a genius-level innovator and versatile engineer since the age of four. He was capable of tearing complex machines down to basic components, could analyze people down to their innermost selves, and was an expert at pinpointing weaknesses in structures. He was physically strong and durable and liked to design technology to help him learn more about himself as well, including devices such as his holographic watch—the very one he had been wearing now—which monitored his brain activity and heart rate.

The strange part was only Lance actually knew how the thing worked, and he never bothered to tell Chase nor his caretaker about what it actually did beyond its superficial functionalities.

Lance's profound interest in technology saved the trio a ton of money and also taught the boys unique skills that their caretaker knew would take them a long way—superpowers or not. For example, when the washing machine miraculously stopped working, Lance ordered a few new parts and completely redesigned both the washer and dryer himself in just a day and for fun. In fact, he even created a way to reduce shrinkage in clothing almost completely, even able to revert clothing back to their regular size and shape after being shrunk. This saved them about $800, and the idea, their caretaker suggested, could have made them multimillionaires overnight.

But this never happened, and nothing like it would never happen. There would never be a time where Chase and Lance or even their caretaker would become famous despite their several reasons for deserving it.

Obviously, to Lance, this made sense. And this was simply because *not every adventure Chase and Lance had ended well.*

In fact, the reason Chase and Lance had temporarily stopped going into most of the town and spent more of their time inside crafting and teaching themselves new skills due to was a disaster they had been a part of. It was one that either could have left the two dead—or exposed them as Rasrims, both just as bad as the other.

It was still early in the afternoon and Chase and Lance had just left the park. They took a few baseball gloves and baseballs to play catch in it. Afterward, with some of the money they had saved up from doing chores, they decided to buy sandwiches from a nearby deli they had come to enjoy.

As soon as they had left, they had noticed a commotion going on. They left the deli and found the center of the commotion only around the corner out in the middle of the street. Maybe six or seven police cars and vans had gathered with dozens of armed men holding rifles and several helicopters in the sky, focused on one individual in particular. They seemingly appeared from out of nowhere.

This particular individual's body had been faintly glowing a light greenish color. His eyes were also the same color. He had been over top of something, shielding it, looking at everyone around him with fierce eyes, forcing them to stay away.

He had been a Rasrim. And he had accidentally revealed himself when he decided to protect a child from being hit by a car who wasn't paying attention.

But the police didn't care. This was at a time when too little information about Rasrims had existed. Society had already declined into a state of paranoia, fearing that the Rasrims would attempt to kill innocent people or destroy the world and had transformed communities to ostracize and prevent even the word *Rasrim* from being spoken from peer to peer.

But this Rasrim had done the opposite—something that would change both the boys but also the entire world for good.

Lance remembered looking around and stopping to see what he had done. Did he attack someone? Maybe he had been fighting with another Rasrim?

But what Lance found was an object that looked like a large rock or boulder had been stuck in the middle of the road. When Lance looked closer, he realized that it seemed as if a section of the street had risen up and created a barrier of rock and asphalt that spanned the width of the street. But there was too much of a crowd to see everything.

But Lance could barely catch a glimpse of what else was in the middle of the street: the car that had nearly hit the kid with the driver slouched over, his head lying motionlessly on the steering wheel, the entire front of the car smashed in where it hit the barrier of rock. The damage that the car sustained put it beyond recognition.

The Rasrim had been pleading to allow him to leave peacefully, saying he had done nothing wrong and only saved a life.

Chase and Lance had noticed that they could understand what he was saying. But that was only because the Rasrim could speak English. He had been crying, holding the child in his arms as if he were proving that he had only been trying to save him. The boy, on the other hand, had been unharmed. But his face had said it all: He had been but terrified.

Then as someone walked by Lance and accidentally kicked his baseball and a glove across the street, Lance realized that Chase was in the crowd, trying to get a better look himself. He looked like he wanted to help, but there was no time for that. There was nothing either of them could do, but Lance knew that Chase was too stubborn to admit it. Lance cursed himself and pushed through the developing crowd, nearly shoving others to the ground to reach Chase. Before too long, Lance was able to grab a hold of Chase and pulled him back by his shirt out of the crowds as the others moved forward. Chase had been yelling, fighting back, trying to rush forward but was unable to overpower Lance.

"Why are people moving forward?" Lance revealed himself shouting into the chaotic theater of the crowd.

Lance remembered that he had nearly gotten Chase out of the crowd completely before it happened.

He only wished he was able to pull Chase back sooner.

Unexpectedly, a gunshot went off, the sound deafening which filled the entire air with smoke and the smell of gunpowder. But then Lance remembered hearing what sounded like a massive explosion combined with a loud cracking sound as the ground around the Rasrim ruptured, sending shock waves and rubble across the entire city. Several people in the crowd screamed out, and Lance took cover.

The explosion that everyone had heard created an earthquake, which sent chips of debris into the air, leaving the entire crowd to either fall to the ground or left struck by debris from the attack.

Lance remembered rolling out of the way before a chunk of rock the size of his head crashed into the ground next to him. But Chase didn't fall. He had been perfectly fine.

Chase had started running straight toward the Rasrim and the child, and Lance shot up right after him once more.

The Rasrim had prepared to attack again. Lance didn't have a chance to see how he had done it. The heat of the moment and all his adrenaline had kept his mind focused on Chase.

Lance remembered feeling a tingling sound in his ear, and his head jerked to the side, leaving him staring at one of the armed members of the Anti-Rasrim Force holding their weapons up, ready to unleash hell against the Rasrim.

For only a fraction of a second did Lance look, but Lance had seen and remembered *everything*—down to what they had looked like, how tall they all were, down to the fibers on each and every one of their uniforms and then the various weapons cradled in their hands.

Almost on cue, time slowed down around Lance.

Lance was confused, but quickly, he noticed the commotion of the ARF gunmen prepared to engage the Rasrim in the street.

To Lance's surprise, he could see every movement the ARF guards made, down to the most precise movements, time moving one one-thousandth that of what it normally did.

Lance took notice of the closest man to the action and watched as his index finger twitched as it just barely began squeezing the metal trigger of his gun.

Lance watched as the explosion occurred. Lance remembered seeing a purplish gas exit the gun along with the reddish fire of the explosion and that the bullet had a dark purple center on its hull, spiraling forward toward its target. Lance's eyes followed the path of the bullet as it exited the gun and watched as it crashed straight into the Rasrim's head, missing the child he had been holding by inches.

The Rasrim, at the same time, had closed the palm of his right hand tightly into a fist and made contact with the ground as he began to slouch backward, unleashing his ability to the fullest.

It was just as Chase reached the Rasrim that another earthquake went off. Its power was truly terrifying. The earthquake completely obliterated the truck and any vehicle in the immediate vicinity, flung Chase and other civilians to the ground and through buildings, and smacked Lance into the ground as if he had been launched into the air and struck with a sledgehammer, knocking the wind out of him and nearly causing him to black out.

Luckily, Lance's undeveloped abilities saved his life. After regaining his senses and fighting the dizziness in his head, Lance was somehow able to climb to his feet, but he became stiff as he realized how dire the situation had become.

His eyes turned, scanning the area, his head still spinning, his adrenaline pumping, and his senses confused as chaos and fire consumed the area around him entirely. Lance could only stare in terror as the panic and chaos began to unravel. Cars were on fire, entire buildings were crumbling, and blood and rubble riddled the streets, painting the once peaceful town with permanent damage that would haunt its inhabitants forever.

Lance fell to his knees, dust and grit all on his face and in his mouth. He could hear the sound of women and children screaming—the chaotic shrill of sirens and cries of pain from civilians as the town fell into utter despair.

Lance had slouched over and banged his hand on the floor. Only now did he notice Chase been doing the same, not even fifty feet from where he was, watching the horrified look on his brother's face that was mourning over the body of an innocent boy, whose skull had been cracked open, lying in the center of the crater while the town around him crumbled into ashes.

The official news report was deliberately delayed to allow officials to place their own spin on the event. "The Rasrim attacked the city, going after a family, killing a total of 130 people, wounding hundreds more." But Lance had known better. There were even more deaths than that on that day and all because of that poor boy being caught in the wrong place at the wrong time. Lance had walked away with a scrape, and Chase had somehow not had a single scratch on him. Even so, the injuries weren't what mattered to Lance. It was the fact that some Human somewhere had decided to lie about what occurred here only to make the already tense Human-Rasrim relations that much more unstable.

Lance couldn't stop thinking about *that* image: the fear on the boy's face, the anger in the eyes of the police officers, the determination of the Rasrim to defend himself and the child. It was just another example of something that played in Lance's mind on repeat with no end in sight.

Lance felt chills go down his spine. Was he going to make people feel like that if they found out about him? And what would happen if—

Lance stopped when he heard a knock on the door.

"Dude! Are you okay in there? I forgot my brush. Can you bring it out when you're done? I'm starving. Hurry up!"

Lance's eyes were wide open. He had been staring mindlessly into the sink as water poured out the faucet and down the drain. Lance's eyes squinted. When did he turn the water back on?

Lance looked up in the mirror and noticed that his eyes seemed to be a lighter blue color than he normally did. He was probably imagining it.

"Uh hello? Are you in there admiring yourself? I hear the water running. I know what you're doing! No, wait, are you trying to use your powers again?"

Lance sighed and turned the water off.

"Idiot!" he exclaimed as he opened the door and forced Chase's brush into his arms.

Chase stood there, aloof, his facial expression nothing but confused.

Lance folded his arms. "Well, go on. Get lost!"

Chase smiled and gestured to his brush. "I needed this first. Thanks!" he said as he went back into the bedroom. "I didn't mean to interrupt you!" a sarcastic voice said through the walls of the bedroom.

Lance turned around, facing the bathroom again. He sighed once more. "No...thanks for that," he whispered to himself.

As Lance finished up in the bathroom, he tried his best to forget about that incident and think about breakfast instead. After all, who knows what Miss E had in store for them today?

As Lance rounded the corner into the kitchen, he was greeted by his caretaker, who was waiting for him at the dining table to begin eating.

"Well, good morning, young man!" Miss E beamed.

Lance acknowledged her. "Good morning, Miss E!" he replied in a calm tone, always careful with what he said and how he said it. Lance always spoke his words clearly. He didn't necessarily speak with manners but with intention. He always spoke as if he were tasked to respond, not as if he were engaging in conversation. And he was never ambiguous and disliked sarcasm when he spoke to anyone other than Chase or especially Miss E.

She had learned when Lance was younger that he had spent too much time in his head and developed a tendency to avoid conversing with others, relying on his creations and projects to speak for him. As a result, his mannerisms became crisp and no-nonsense. This helped Lance keep his mind focused at all times. If he ever needed to divulge his time to pick a more curated choice of words, he was wasting precious time to process more important things.

29

But this never mattered to Miss E. She always enjoyed talking to Lance. He was always insightful.

"Up all night reading again, I'm sure?" she asked Lance down at the dining table next to where Chase usually sat. Miss E had been on the opposite side of the table, her back facing the windows in the dining room but facing the kitchen. And this was their everyday arrangement.

Lance sat up in his seat. "Yeah, I got a decent bit covered earlier this morning."

Miss E nodded. She tried to act surprised even though she wasn't. Lance was never the type of person who needed reminders or motivations about anything, although it was difficult to call him a "self-starter." He was more independent than most his age, but he seemed to have a tendency to allow his impulses to overcome his intuition. Sometimes in the middle of an activity or even when eating, he would get up and go work on one of his projects as if he had suddenly been programmed to do so.

The first time this happened, both Chase and Miss E had been upset, thinking that Lance had been bored. But he explained to them that he had what he felt was a burning impulse to try something new with whatever he was working on and didn't want to forget it. Miss E knew that this was only half the truth, though. Lance had an excellent memory. Even if he had an idea for something months ago, his only issue was a matter of acquiring the necessary tools and resources first. Or perhaps, the intelligence necessary to begin it seriously.

He was always off in his own world, which proved that Lance constantly had millions of things on his mind. He spent hours sorting and shuffling between all his thoughts.

Ironically enough, the only things that tethered him to reality were the seemingly impossible creations too advanced even for an alien from another world he enjoyed researching and picking apart.

Was that a bad thing? Miss E shrugged, not satisfied with her initial, instinctual answer.

"Oh, really?" she presumed. She wanted to engage Lance in a way that kept his interest and allowed him to continue generating ideas. "So by now you know the differences between 'streaming' and 'infusing' Risima Energy?" she asked. Then Miss E turned and gestured to the dining room entrance when Chase walked in, still looking half-asleep.

"Sure," Lance simply replied, grabbing his fork and knife.

He knew what Risima Energy was. But what was the best way to recap what Risima was?

"Risima" was the main component for a Rasrim being able to begin utilizing their powers and abilities. It was like the motherboard for a computer.

Without it, there would be no way to synthesize naturally occurring particles and compounds into a form that could be manipulated without the presence of another substance or particle, which he also learned long ago was the basis of chemistry. Risima itself was also a naturally occurring Energy, but it was present almost everywhere in the universe, although Lance had reasonably suspected that only Rasrims had the ability to locate it and use it properly. To a Human, this would be no different than experiencing a change in climate, temperature, or pressure. In instances where more Risima was being used, it was apparent that *some* external force was responsible, but no Human had the ability to identify the links between Rasrims and Risima without the assistance of technology.

And even then, it was extremely difficult.

Lance began to answer Miss E's questions but briefly stopped as Chase plopped into his seat and rested his head on the table while letting out a low groan. "Already with this? Can't we just eat?" his muffled voice said.

Lance ignored him. He turned himself back into the inner workings of his mind, focusing on his thoughts.

"Well…'streaming' Risima Energy is when energy within oneself becomes compatible with another energy present elsewhere in the universe, connecting it back to the Risima Energy located within the Rasrim. It's a two-way connection with Risima present on both sides of the equation. For example, it could be depicted as a Rasrim summoning Water Risima and 'streaming it' in order to shrink or expand the size of a river or using Earth Risima to create a pillar of rock or other materials and so on."

Lance stopped for a moment, his eyes beginning to wander into space.

"That's great, Lance. Now can you think of an everyday example of streaming fire? This could be helpful for Chase."

And then Chase perked up, looking at Lance. "Hey! You better get this right!"

Lance put a hand on his chin and thought for a moment.

"I guess an everyday example might be streaming Fire Risima into wet clothing in order to dry it, couldn't it? Would save us some money too, after all," he joked on Chase's behalf.

Miss E smiled and gave Lance a little applause.

"Amazing. Perfect example, Lance. Now what about infusing Energy? Chase, think you can take this one?"

Chase looked down at his plate of food. Then he looked back up at Miss E.

"Wouldn't...I mean, couldn't you somehow infuse Energy to cook food?"

Miss E made a humming sound, indicating that Chase hadn't been completely correct.

Chase sighed. "Okay. Well I *do* remember Lance saying something about infusing Risima Energy. Compared to streaming Energy, *infusing* Energy is like gathering Energy inside an object in order to make it more powerful by fortifying its properties with the properties of Risima Energy. That's basically how Rasrims attack, right? You stream then infuse to attack. You could also infuse to store and maintain more Energy. Wait...then why couldn't you infuse Energy inside a waffle and heat it up?"

Miss E stopped him.

"Well, yes, that's correct, Chase, but if you were to infuse Energy inside of food, you would be eating both Fire Risima and your food...and I don't believe that would taste good at all."

Chase's eyes widened as he looked at his waffles a little closer, moving his head away from it.

Miss E seemed reassured. She had enjoyed Chase's sense of humor.

She continued, beginning to cut her omelet in half. "Infusing Energy will combine the natural states of the energies in question. On the other hand, if you *streamed* Fire Energy toward your waffle, you would *then* be heating it up. It would be like bringing a flame to it except you are in control of that flame entirely. But in most cases, you'd likely end up burning your food." Miss E took a bite of her omelet, noticing that Lance had been deep in thought, lost in space, staring at his food with his fork and knife in hand. Miss E knew that once she finished her point, he'd snap back into it, so she ignored it for now.

"With that being said, Rasrims can both stream and infuse Energy to attack enemies. But you won't see a Rasrim infusing Risima Energy in order to attack. You would see a Rasrim stream their Energy in order to attack and then infuse Energy in order to *defend* themselves from other sources of Risima Energy or to prepare to transfer Energy for a completely different type of situation. Fortifying oneself or even a building from a Fire attack with Water Energy would prove much more effective than trying to counter it by throwing any other element back at it. That's not too hard to understand, is it?"

Lance nodded. Then he began cutting his waffle.

"Oh. I didn't realize that. So you're saying that infusing Energy could be compared to starting up a generator, while streaming Energy would be like plugging the generator into a machine in order to power it," Lance said. He got a nod of approval from Miss E, who had been finishing her omelet.

Lance rested his utensils on his plate. He had thought of something else.

"So say two Rasrims were fighting where one was streaming Energy and the other was infusing their own Energy. What would that look like?"

Miss E wiped her mouth with a napkin. "Well," she began, "I believe that the Rasrim who was streaming Energy would be looking for openings in his opponent's defenses. If he was using Electric Risima to attack, for example, he would try to channel fast, powerful electric attacks at his enemy or *stream* electricity into his environment in order to move *faster* than he normally could. If his opponent was also using electricity but this time infusing it, he would be building up large amounts of Energy to release in one large attack or to accumulate enough Energy to defend from an attack that under normal circumstances could prove fatal. Of course, when you infuse Electric Risima, your body also begins exhibiting properties of electricity, which could be fatal in and of itself even for some inexperienced Rasrims."

"Wow! Seriously! So you actually *can* move as fast as lightning? I thought you were joking about that!" Chase exclaimed.

"Oh, god, no. I was *not* joking about *that*," Miss E said while laughing.

"But hold on!" he then suddenly said as he began counting on his fingers.

"Water, Fire, Electricity, Earth, Wind, Death, Riora, Ultima, Stellar. These are the nine Elemental Prowesses. I know that. But is there a difference between them when you stream and infuse them?"

Miss E nodded. "Great question! I'm very glad you asked, Chase. That's what I'll be teaching you today! But we can't do that on an empty stomach, right?"

Chase's face suddenly turned gray as his stomach growled. Lance and Miss E laughed.

"Food! That's the most important thing—how could I forget?" Chase beamed before practically stuffing his face with waffles. Lance had a look of disgust on his face.

"And he's asking you if it's possible to move as fast as lightning?"

This was how mornings for the three were. They weren't a coordinated family, but everything happened in an ordinary fashion, which included the three of them being together. Therefore, nothing ever happened without at least one other person knowing what was going on.

"I wanted you to help cook this morning, but I knew that you were reading earlier. You only have a few chapters left, right? So were you studying those core concepts?" Miss E cut her waffle in half and ate a modest piece with only a drop of syrup on her waffle.

"Not really, I made stops and took notes. And I keep rereading the first chapter. I think I understand how to use Risima. I just—" Lance stopped again. He sighed to himself.

"I just *don't* know how to do it. I thought by messing around with electrons 'n' stuff that I'd figure it out, but I haven't yet."

Miss E noticed that Lance had seemed down.

"Why do you think you've been unable to?" his caretaker asked.

Lance shrugged.

"I need to understand the basics better first. No point in learning advanced techniques when I can't even stabilize my Energy."

"Yeah. That's true! But I think you're almost there," she replied. "Chapter 11 will be interesting, as you'll soon find. I'm hoping you can reach it by Friday."

"Why? Are we learning something new then too?"

Miss E shrugged, hiding a slight smile on her face. "Not exactly. You could call it a hands-on exercise, I suppose."

"You mean…?"

"Yes. I do. You two are ready to try and use Risima yourselves for the first time."

Chase put down his plate, still chewing. "Mwmh—whait, rwheally?" he said with his mouth full.

Lance tried his hardest not to laugh and make it even worse. That was Classic Chase.

Lance's eyes slowly drifted over to the window out at the yard, noticing that the sun had been completely up now.

"Well then, I can't wait to see what we make of it." Lance said with a renewed attitude.

Today was going to be a good day, he told himself.

Chase and Lance were both ten years old and would turn eleven in the winter. Both Chase and Lance had similar features, but they were incredibly easy to tell from one another. Chase had bushy dark-brown hair and a rounded face that looked nice with a smile on it. It suited his bubbly and easygoing personality. To top it off, Chase's eyes were a fiery-red and brown color which occasionally looked like they were on fire. Chase swore he could change the way they looked depending on what he was doing or how he felt, and he was never denied for it. After all, the eyes were extremely important for Rasrims and being able to effectively use Risima.

Lance, on the other hand, had silvery-gray hair that had black and blue hues to it. It was all blended well and looked like he had simply had it dyed, so he was never questioned about it. However, this color or hair was incredibly uncommon even for a Rasrim, and Miss E had trouble deciding what it had meant. To go along with it, Lance had a set of deep-blue eyes and a sharp face and less rounded chin. Lance had been told that he had always seemed angry or bored with such a face. It didn't help that he was always caught in his own mind or messing around with electronics.

But Lance didn't care too much about his appearance. Aside from Miss E's suggestion that Lance get his hair twisted or braided into thicker strands—a suggestion he ended up taking on his eighth birthday—the only thing Lance did to aid his appearance was to sport a headband to keep most of his hair up so he could see better. That was Chase's idea. Chase was much better at coordinating and picking out outfits, and so he allowed Chase to own that.

Olivia Elementa, on top of that, had long, beautiful brown hair that went down to her mid back. She always kept her hair nice and clean. She wore glasses with a metal-black trim which were square, which gave her an intelligent demeanor. But she was most definitely qualified for the look.

Olivia enjoyed cooking, arts and crafts, interior designing, and of course, teaching. An expert in the medical field and several different subfields of science including biology, robotics, botany, chemistry, and physics, who also studied economics, literature, and even a few foreign languages, it wasn't clear to the boys what Olivia's profession was or what she even liked to do in her real "free time." No matter what she did, she always stayed productive however she could even if that meant spending her time with Chase and Lance. But whatever she did, it was obviously enough to keep them living comfortably.

When Miss E began formally teaching the boys different things, starting with how to read but later much bigger and more advanced topics such as algebra and motion energy, the boys wondered why she wouldn't allow them to just go to a public school.

But her response was always the same. She didn't want to "risk" them exposing themselves just yet. She explained to the boys that society wasn't ready to learn about Chase and Lance even if they managed to convince everyone that they were Humans.

Miss E enforced a strict schedule for Chase and Lance, which involved improvised academic lessons that spanned from 9:00 a.m. to 2:00 p.m. every weekday. Miss E tailored activities for the two of them to complete based on their skills they already expressed but also the traits they were soon to develop. Chase was more of a visual learner, and while this was also true for Lance, he needed a hands-on approach to fully grasp the concepts of various topics. He was much better at learning something by disassembling it under the wise and careful guidance of Miss E and proved to be a quick study even when things didn't work out so well. Chase struggled in math. He was great with his hands but preferred to do more free-hand work in labs, such as building circuits and messing around with chemicals for fun, but never had the itch to take the time to thoroughly learn what he was doing as he was doing it. However, he excelled at history and could produce hypotheses and assessments of individuals and their motivations to a point that even impressed Miss E, an individual who had studied more than her fair share of history and the sciences for years. It was a trade-off that paid homage, again, to the boys' shared interests but also their personally distinct differences as twins. Lance enjoyed math and science, and while he also seemed to have the most randomly assorted memory that could possibly exist, able to retrieve large swaths of information across various topics, he struggled at returning to the core concepts and basics of individual topics as he was a very "go-getter" individual who stayed on top of innovation as if there was no other option. And never ask him about when famous individuals were born or when bills were passed. He would always ignore you and direct it toward Chase instead.

Despite all this, Chase and Lance worked well together in every subject. Where one underperformed, the other usually excelled, and this was how they remained vigilant in their studies. The only topic they both struggled on was...psychology.

Beyond the anatomy and applied sciences of the brain—both chemistry and physics—Chase and Lance could not understand the various psychologies of Humans. Studying Freud, Nietzsche, and even Plato and Socrates, the two boys could recite information and even correctly identify instances of their references in modern society, but Chase and Lance were stumped when they were asked to compare the psychology of Humans to the collective goals and work of Earth as a whole. They had a much better job at finding concessions and fallacies in the work and logic of how Humans interacted with the Earth compared to how their brains functioned.

For example, Lance knew that the Rasrim brain served a similar evolutionary function like any other vertebrate found on Earth. However, the Rasrim brain, at some point in history, branched off from where the Humans had first begun developing their own civilizations. While the Human brain evolved to consider empathy and love to build communities much more than aggression and fear as the need for hunting and survival diminished with new technology, Rasrims never lost these evolutionary traits, and their societies reflected that much. It did need to be taken in consideration that the wildlife on Osamos was much more predacious than on Earth and that animals on Osamos could also use Risima to fulfill their needs for survival. And as a result, the average Rasrim was dauntless and careful. They did not use or wear flashy colors or travel in large groups. A maximum of two Rasrims was the norm when traveling the planet. They did not put value on precious materials nor status in social life, although it was a very intelligent species with a more advanced communicative system than seen on Earth.

Olivia learned through many years of survey and study that the average Rasrim did not necessarily "care" for another Rasrim.

Rasrims merely assumed that they all could fend for themselves until it was absolutely certain that their lives were in danger. But this was because Osamos was a planet constantly engaged in a war with other species—and so prioritizing one's own life and abilities trumped over maintaining the masses.

Rasrims were not invested in each other's social lives and preferred minding their own business in times of peace. Their social groups mingled but did not intertwine. There was simply too much chaos and danger from Osamos's environment and from external threats to meander throughout the planet as carelessly as one could on Earth. Rasrims did train and eat together on occasion—especially in familial units—but they never developed close relationships through these activities.

Rasrim children were taught the importance of the self as much as the collective whole. One child never took away from another. And while they did not default to "helping" or providing for one another, they surely did not do the opposite. Rasrims had families and communities and enjoyed engaging in recreational activities, but they weren't as extensive as the ones on Earth.

Much more of their time was devoted to honing their skills in order to coexist with the beings on Osamos known as the *Demiurges*, or powerful creatures who controlled aspects of the environment with their insanely powerful Risima abilities. These beings were different from the "monsters" of Osamos, who were, unlike the name suggested, much, *much* weaker beings who fought with the Rasrim population and Demiurges in order to *become* Demiurges. It was an unending cycle of war and evolution that the Rasrims found themselves taking charge over.

Perhaps this was why, instead of children using social tendencies to decide friend groups and explore sexual behaviors, they bonded together over their dominant elements and used this method when deciding the partners they took and even the activities they enjoyed doing. For instance, Water Rasrims were excellent swimmers and stayed near the coasts to grow crops and tend to the environment. Earth Rasrims were phenomenal builders and were experts in crafts and science. Fire Rasrims were hunters and enjoyed traversing the planet to fight various monsters. And Electric Rasrims were most suited at exploring life outside of Osamos entirely.

Rasrims were also far advanced in space exploration, arguably billions of years compared to Humans and even their most advanced achievements in space. For example, in early 2035, NASA successfully developed a colony on Mars, which currently has a population of 204 but an estimated sustainability of a few thousand. NASA has also worked alongside intergovernmental agencies to develop a massive space program known as the StarCraft Development, which researches space weapons such as hypersonic weapons, particle accelerators, and gravity bombs and also developed the technology necessary to transport objects at the speed of light. But like noted earlier, these achievements were merely laughed at on the realm of Risima, as all these weapons could be defeated by even the weakest of Risima abilities, whereas traveling at the speed of light had been accomplished several times by Electric Rasrims—and even others such as Fire and Death Rasrims.

As a result, the Rasrims eventually revealed to the Humans at one of the few meetings they had that there were indeed several other planets with unique life. And a few of them even had their own unique powers which Osamos had to defend against time and time again.

The idea of Rasrim-Human neurology was one of the first things Olivia studied in college. She had made her own theses and made top-notch scientific breakthroughs in the study of biology and psychology as it stood, so these things all made sense to her... because she was the one who discovered it. She had been the sole Human expert on Rasrims and even other beings in the universe—and she had been the only individual capable of designing weapons and technology that had the ability to harm them—not even the best and brightest minds from NASA or MIT came close to her level of expertise.

While Olivia thoroughly enjoyed teaching Chase and Lance nearly everything she could about anything they were interested in, she never told the boys *that*.

She remembered that the same day she introduced Lance to high-tech technology for the first time, he had spent hours learning everything he could about it to the point that he was able to disassemble and reassembly it entirely on his own.

Of course, the thing that Olivia had given him was a holographic tablet she wanted him to use to learn with.

But she wasn't upset. He had definitely learned *something* with it when he took the tablet apart and completely redesigned it into his watch, which he cleverly told Miss E was so he could "learn anything, anywhere."

Olivia laughed to herself, thinking back to that day. Nowadays, every phone, computer, tablet, and even some materials used in infrastructure had "H-chips" in them, which allowed users to access holographs on virtually everything…quite literally. But it wasn't quite yet available to "wear" as an accessory even years after Lance figured out how to make it himself, which was why Olivia knew that Lance was special from an early age.

In any case, a holographic phone could pull up hundreds of holographic screens on top of its physical one to do anything you wanted. One screen could play music while the others could maximize their displays by up to 1,000 percent to display an accurate map of your surroundings for easy-to-use navigation. Storefronts used holographs to create representatives to speak to passers-by to sell products. Warning signs automatically appeared on an individual's phone when an obstacle was in the way or when a thunderstorm would occur. If you had your phone set to notify you of things such as the release of new music, clothing, or games or perhaps told your phone what you wanted to eat that day, a hologram would appear in the direction of whatever point of interest you set it to. The best part was, they were designed to be completely transparent in order to prevent obstruction and make usage while navigating, including driving, totally safe.

In any case, Miss E knew how talented they both Chase and Lance were and the number of accomplishments they would make in their lives whether on Earth as a Human or on Osamos as a Rasrim.

The two boys were extremely smart and had already developed their own traits, skills, and hobbies despite only being ten years old.

Chase and Lance were maturing much faster than she had expected, and that meant that it was only a matter of time before they were truly able to begin their lives.

And that, despite Olivia's initial prediction, was a terrible thing she hoped would never come but knew she couldn't prevent.

Olivia stood up, putting her dishes on top from another before pushing her chair in, watching as Chase and Lance had fun with one another as they ate their breakfast, talking about everything from holograms to movies and their lessons. They enjoyed their lives no matter what the day called for, and Olivia was responsible for making sure that never changed.

Even when the time for their lives to truly begin came hurtling toward them like she was warned it would in the very near future.

Olivia smiled at her two boys.

If she could continue having days like this, she would give up anything to preserve it.

CHAPTER 2

Emergence

For most families, breakfast was the time for families to prepare for the day ahead of them. They would make coffee, walk the family dog, prepare last-minute arrangements for work and school, and of course, eat breakfast before parting ways as they did every day.

But for the Kolorios, breakfast was the time they talked about everything involving supernatural abilities and the universe. It was also the most time they spent together throughout the entire day.

The conversations the three had during breakfast were full of intriguing ideas, science, mysteries, and topics that probably didn't belong in a household, most especially during breakfast.

But Miss E enjoyed when Chase and Lance pinged their curiosity on her own beliefs, although she feared that their curiosity would soon begin to punish them as much as it would ever reward them. Chase and Lance were nothing short of curious and far-reaching individuals. Their conversations spanned on and on about theories about Risima even though some of them were less spectacular than others.

Chase, for instance, went on and on about how cool it would be if he would one day learn the abilities of an Electric Rasrim, saying how much faster it would make his cleaning chores go by after being assigned kitchen cleaning duty. Lance, on the other hand, only pestered Chase, poking holes in his logic, saying that mixing cleaning with electricity while washing dishes was "stupid." And although he certainly had a point, Miss E had pointed out that Lance was incorrect, explaining how using Risima Energy was too intense of a practice and that it was unlikely for someone to even want to use such abilities while doing chores.

But Chase and Lance jokingly disagreed, and that morning, the three were locked in a debate about which powers would make household chores and other "annoying things" more manageable.

Only last week, Chase had brought up that he swore he had used Fire while it had been drizzling only a few days before. He claimed to have been walking back home with Lance when they had been caught in the rain and challenged him to a race to see who could make it back the fastest before the rain came down any harder. Of course, Lance agreed with no hesitation, but during the heat of the moment, Lance had been aware that while they had been running, raindrops had instantly evaporated as they hit Chase's body.

Unfortunately, Chase had lost that race, which was why Lance didn't notice, but for the rest of the day, Chase had been trying to reproduce the effect from running around the front yard in the rain to taking fully clothed showers to pouring entire buckets of water over top himself—all to Lance's amusement—but couldn't do it again.

It had been a funny occasion, and the two continued to joke about it when they fantasized about their abilities and saving the world.

"Instead of pouring buckets of water all over yourself and my nice hardwood floors, you should try getting your heart rate up," Miss E lectured him.

"Maybe while you were running, you were infusing Energy within yourself to prevent yourself from getting exhausted. It's the same thing as eating."

Chase looked like a scholar, nodding along with her as she began to use sophisticated terms and make obscure references to scientific experiments.

But he had been completely lost.

Finally, Miss E concluded her lecture. "You know, as a Fire Rasrim, you can retain Energy much more than you will expel in a variety of physical situations."

And Chase had been amped ever since. For the next couple of days, Chase had begun exercising in all sorts of different ways, trying different things from push-ups to running more laps to even trying out a few martial arts to "channel" his Energy as he had said. He had taken it seriously too and on occasion would begin producing steam from his body after exercising for several minutes without rest. And the steam had been *piping* hot. The steam that Chase was producing had started to melt objects in the house, especially anything made of plastic, and a special area in the "basement" had been designated for Chase's workouts for this reason.

But it was only then that Miss E realized what was going on. That day, only a week ago to this day, Chase and Lance had finally unlocked the first threshold, which contained their massive arsenal of powers and abilities.

Soon enough, Chase and Lance would begin exhibiting the properties of Fire and Water without even realizing it. Olivia's job, therefore, was to teach them how to navigate this threshold without becoming lost or without getting themselves or another person killed…without even realizing it.

The next day, Miss E found Chase in the basement while he was in the middle of one of his workouts and only right before he began reaching the point of exhaustion. But Chase didn't notice Miss E as he was on the ground in a plank position, concentrating on his form with his eyes closed. But that had hardly mattered as only seconds later, she noticed steam rising from the droplets of sweat on Chase's forehead.

At once, Miss E interrupted Chase, startling him and causing him to fall to the ground.

He quickly rolled over to his back and sat up, facing Miss E with a startled expression.

"H—uh? Yeah?" he puffed. But suddenly, a small flame popped on Chase's right shoulders.

Chase noticed it right away, but instead of panicking, he only looked at it cautiously from the corners of his eyes. He looked for a moment, confused as to why he hardly felt it. And then he slowly faced Miss E, who had also refused to react in any extreme way.

"Hey, uh, I'm on *fire*! I'm not imagining this, am I? I don't even feel it!" Chase roared. And then Chase let out a confused sound as he noticed the flame had begun shrinking.

Miss E snapped her fingers, holding back a large smile as she remained focused. *This is it*, she thought to herself. She had suddenly begun moving and talking fast, keeping Chase's attention and speeding his heart rate back up. "Stand up, quickly! Don't focus on it right now. Just pay attention to me."

And Chase stood up immediately, ready for anything.

Miss E knew that this next part would confuse Chase. To be frank, it was nothing more than a hypothesis that she had developed and only now thought to test.

"Throw a punch at me! Go!"

Chase's eyes instinctively flickered from the flame to Miss E and back. "Huh? You said hit you?"

"No! Just throw a punch at me in the air! Go!"

Chase scrambled his body as he tried to remember how to use his hands and feet. He quickly assumed a fighting stance and threw a punch at the air with his right hand.

The flame on Chase's shoulder disappeared, but instead, a small fiery explosion occurred in front of Chase's knuckles. The fire quickly disappeared into smoke and dissipated into the air.

"Well then!" Miss E said. "Look at that. I mean, you just streamed Fire Risima!"

Chase tried to say several words at once, unable to say what he wanted to.

"Slow down, Chase. You need to focus! You can't stream Risima when you're flustered, only when you're concentrated."

Chase's head dropped, and he let out a sigh.

"Yeah. Right. No, you're right," he said.

And then Chase's entire body exploded with Energy; his fiery attitude came alive. "But I mean! Did you see that? Did you see?

46

There was, like, *fire* right in front of my fists!" Chase began punching the air again, repeatedly throwing out his right hand in the same motion.

Miss E shook her head. "Try it again!"

So since that day, the three of them decided on a new routine.

Only two days later on a dreary Friday afternoon, Miss E gathered the boys in the living room and asked the boys if they felt they were old enough to start training themselves. And while she knew she was asking too obvious a question, Chase and Lance assured her with extreme confidence that they wanted to. But they weren't quite sure of what it was they needed to do.

She told Chase and Lance to start off easily by learning how to defend themselves, and they were intrigued as to why. Chase found it insulting. Seeing as how could create flames by punching the air now, he only felt as if he should learn how to throw better punches. Lance, on the other hand, when he learned of the truth, simply told Chase and Miss E. that he had already learned how to defend himself.

Of course, Chase took this as another insult. In order to prove Lance wrong, Chase decided to prove Lance wrong the best way he could.

Right then and there in the living room, Chase unleashed a punch at Lance. And while he didn't intend to, Chase had created *another* explosion when he threw the punch, which occurred only six inches in front of Lance's face.

But Lance saw *all* of it coming.

The punch, alongside the explosion, missed Lance entirely, and Lance countered Chase's attack by throwing a well-placed punch into Chase's stomach, causing him to yelp out in pain and slowly fall to his knees, clutching his stomach.

"See?" Lance said, dropping his hands. He thought nothing of it. "I slipped your punch. It was too slow. And that's the reason you can never hit me when we fight!"

Chase muttered something, trying to get his breath back.

"Jerk," he finally wheezed out. "I thought we just agreed I was going easy on you..."

47

Lance scoffed, "We didn't agree to anything!" He exclaimed, trying to stay serious and not laugh.

Miss E, on the other hand, had noticed something that neither of them had themselves. Both Chase and Lance were using Risima Energy, using only trace amounts of it present in the air and elsewhere but enough to accomplish a noteworthy task.

Had Chase landed this lunch, he could have severely injured Lance. And if Lance had been Human, he may have died.

Miss E kept her expression cool, but she understood that at times like this she needed to act more like a mother and less like a teacher.

She placed her hands on her hips. "First off, don't fight in the living room! If you break something, you *will* fix it, okay?" she exclaimed.

Lance scratched the back of his head.

"But second," Miss E stood tall and pushed her glasses up to her head and then placed her hands back on her hip.

"You *both* used some of your powers. And while I am certainly impressed, I just can't believe that *this* is how it's happening," Miss E scoffed, folding her arms and she leaned on her left foot. "Well, I'm not surprised. I guess this is just considered natural. But it's too natural. I don't want this to be the way things are if—" She began talking to herself.

Chase groaned as he stood up and interrupted her. "Did you say 'both'? If we're talking about powers, other than Lance having the power to be a massive d—"

"Watch it, Chase!"

"Erm, to be a massive jerk, I just don't know what else he could have possibly done."

Chase stretched his shoulder out, swinging it around in a circle. "And with water? You can't fight with Water Risima, can you?"

Lance shot a mean look at Chase.

Miss E perked up. "Well, Lance certainly did."

"I did? How so?"

"Really? You don't know how? Well, think about it, Lance!"

Lance was lost for words. He felt as if he only dodged a punch. It was all he did!

And then it slowly began to hit him.

When Lance dodged the punch, he felt his body maneuver out of the way in an incredibly smooth fashion. It was as if his entire body loosened up and moved in one synchronized motion like his joints as free-flowing as water. But he only guessed that this was his quick reflexes in action. Lance had good instincts and had always been interested in martial arts, so he began studying various techniques across several disciplines and felt he had already mastered a thing or two.

But Miss E was right. This was a little more than martial arts.

Lance spoke up. "Yeah. I do know what happened," he suddenly announced.

Chase had been lying face down on one of the couches in the living room, hands still clutching his stomach.

Lance gestured to Chase. "I used Water Risima to shift my body when Chase was throwing the punch. I *became* water, didn't I? I don't know if that's considered streaming or infusing it, but I most certainly felt *something*. I just don't—"

Miss E interrupted him. "Don't ask me! Trust yourself, Lance. What did you feel just then?"

"Nobody's asking me how I feel…," a muffled voice said in the corner of the living room.

Lance thought for a moment. "I felt loose. I felt quick and agile. I felt flexible but powerful at the same time."

"When you were dodging his punch, you mean?"

"Yeah. Oh! You know what? I didn't become water, but I *felt* it!" Lance's body language and facial expressions resembled a sort of "aha!" moment.

"It told me how to move and where to throw my punch! The movements were all me, though. That means I streamed it," Lance said.

"Good!" Olivia replied. "So let's recap. You streamed Water Risima to figure out how best to dodge Chase's punch and hit him back. Is that right?"

Chase lifted his head. "Yeah, ouch! Thanks again!" And then he dropped it back into the cushion.

Lance waved Chase off, still trying to think his thoughts through.

Lance was beginning to get irritated. Miss E had known the truth and wouldn't confirm Lance unless he had known for sure. She had done this intentionally. Lance would never walk away from a situation unless he was absolutely sure about it, and Miss E knew that by refusing to tell Lance anything, he would have to figure it out one way or another.

But he would never ask her for help. And this was what irritated Lance.

"I did both. I streamed water in order to better control my movements. It felt like I was able to move in anyway I wanted to."

That gave Lance an idea. Perhaps if he were ever in a life-or-death situation against an experienced fighter, Lance's Water Risima could be more of a useful tool than he had realized. And the best part was, his opponent would never suspect he had been using Water Risima.

Lance continued speaking.

"The Fire from Chase's punch should have hit me even if his punch didn't. But because I temporarily developed the properties of water, I was able to move much quicker than a Human could while defending myself from the properties of Chase's Fire Risima when he attacked me, which is considered infusing Risima. Yeah, I did both!"

Miss E gestured herself in a way that indicated she agreed with Lance.

But this was merely Lance's cue to continue.

Lance rubbed his chin. "I also used Water to pick my strike. Water is everywhere. Rasrims can sense and direct their energies and attacks by using Risima Energy as guides. But…I'm not totally sure why I knew to punch where I did."

"It's because when you streamed your Energy, you subconsciously made an important decision: to go for the gut, which meant you weren't intending to hurt Chase."

Miss E stood tall. "Lance, don't lie to yourself. What went through your head when Chase punched you?"

Lance breathed in through his nose.

He knew it. She *had* known the truth. But how?

"I thought that the punch was slow. I saw it coming."

"You saw *everything* as it was happening. You mapped out Chase's entire body and, from there, directed your Energy in the best way to defend *and* attack at the same time, and I bet you know why too!"

Lance relaxed a bit.

"Chapter 3 of my book says that Water Energy is not a good Element for Rasrims to fight with. It's more of a tool than a weapon. You only use it to set up more potent attacks."

Then Lance began to get frustrated, remembering what he had read. "It explicitly says in Chapter 3 that it's best served as—"

"'Improvisation' per the user's interests.' That's what it says, doesn't it?"

"I knew it—you read it too!"

Miss E disregarded his statement, although it had been true. "Is that what the book says or not?"

Lance began to stammer. "Y-yes! But if I can use water like this, I don't see why it's regarded as such a weak element! I could use it for all sorts of things! I've been trying to for weeks!"

Miss E nodded. "And when you two are ready, your powers will become your greatest strengths. But whether you use them as weapons or not is entirely up to you two, as Rasrims."

Miss E reached out and placed her hands on Chase and Lance's heads.

"But for now, recognize what your strengths and weaknesses are. You two have already been using your abilities and without noticing it! That's *real* power. Don't ever forget this moment. In the next coming weeks, your powers will begin developing at a rapid pace. In the meantime, I must prepare you for the pain that will come along with it."

Miss E smiled as passionately as she could, hugging Chase and Lance tightly.

"But let's eat for now. I'm sure you two are hungry."

*****

Chase and Lance enjoyed their breakfast. It was a brisk morning but a peaceful one.

Only occasionally were their mornings disturbed by things happening in the city. Even then, they welcomed whatever any day would bring them. After *that* incident, Lance began telling himself that he would devote much of his time learning as much as he could to prevent Chase or anyone else from ever getting hurt.

And the feeling he had that day, that burning motivation in his heart, that was something that Lance would *always* take seriously even if that meant sacrificing his life in the end.

Miss E reached out to grab something lying in front of her plate. It was the receiver for the TV screen. Miss E flicked her thumb up on the indented pad in the center, and a light flashed from the receiver to the corresponding screen on the wall, which as of now had nothing on it whatsoever. Suddenly, a light-blue holographic screen materialized on the wall and produced a picture, instantly playing what station it had been tuned to, which happened to be the news station.

Miss E hardly watched the news during breakfast. That was something Lance did more often. Even so, it wasn't uncommon for her to put something on when she was having a slower morning. And she didn't even really "watch" TV; she just had it on to listen to in the background.

Chase swallowed a large piece of his waffle, stopping for a second to not choke, pointing rapidly at the TV the entire time. Lance tuned in.

"Quick! Turn it up a bit!"

Miss E looked up at the TV and turned it up, pressing a button on the small plastic receiver, but she paused for a second to read the headline afterward, her hand still hovering above the receiver. The headline made the three of them freeze, unable to come to terms with what they were reading.

BREAKING NEWS: US GOVERNMENT
REPORTS FIRST SUCCESSFUL SPACE ASSAULT
AGAINST RASRIMS WITH 6 CONFIRMED KILLS.

At first, it seemed Miss E had tried to produce some sort of comment, but she had stopped herself several times, her eyes glued to the TV, her entire posture indicating that she was analyzing the screen.

Chase struggled to find words himself. But all Lance could think about were those who had been killed.

"T-they killed Rasrims! The war is real! It's happening!"

Chase desperately searched for an answer from either Lance or Miss E. But neither offered an explanation, not even a thought.

"But how?" was all Lance's voice could produce. "Isn't it insanely difficult to even locate Rasrims in space, let alone kill them? There's no way there's already weapons that can fight against Rasrims in space, right? How is this possible?" Lance was sure that his caretaker's expression would give some sort of answer, but he was wrong. In fact, Miss E's expression said that they both had more questions than answers available. But then Lance shook his head, his mind lost, wandering.

"This isn't good news," Miss E's voice mumbled at some inaudible decibel.

But almost as if she had lost interest, she changed the channel and quickly turned away from the TV.

And then, as if it were scripted, she took a slow sip of her coffee, offering no insight or additional remarks whatsoever.

Lance couldn't help but watch her curiously. What did she know about this? Why was she being dismissive all of a sudden?

It was Chase who decided to take the shot. "Do you know anything about that, Miss E?" he tried asking.

But her face had shown no emotion. She didn't seem nervous, nor did she take any more time to think about it.

"No," was all she said at first.

The two kept watching her, waiting to get more insight, hoping that they would.

Miss E glanced up from the table, briefly trading looks with the two boys before she turned her attention back to her coffee.

"But as you know," she finally began, "Osamos and various militaries on Earth have been planning to go into war with each other for quite some time."

"Yeah, we know that!"

"What you *don't* know is that the world is pressuring our country to announce they will join and potentially lead the effort. It's been nothing but a political nightmare that has now spiraled out of control."

Miss E sighed. She took off her glasses and wiped them clean before sliding them back up to her eyes.

Chase raised his arms as if he were trying to say he was confused.

"But that's total BS! They're definitely a part of it!"

"Yes, Chase. That's correct."

She sat her cup of coffee down on the table.

"But understand that the entire world has its hands tied with what it hopes is an opportunity to learn from. What do we do now? Will Earth or Osamos launch another attack? And if so, how hard? Should Humans eliminate the Rasrims on Osamos entirely or just the threats that exist? How can we even search for where to hit the Rasrims and with what weapons do we decide to build to use against them? Or do we take the scientific approach and research the Rasrims instead?"

Miss E picked her cup of coffee back up and sat back into her chair, swirling her cup around. "And even *those* situations have their own catch-22s. Nothing can be done without a tradeoff that results in the loss of life on either side. Any wrong move made by our leaders would end in a disaster, to say the least. World economies would collapse." Suddenly, Olivia took a pause, a serious look on her face. She knew something else, something *extremely* important that she had been leaving out.

There was a special group of highly trained individuals within the American government that tasked themselves with studying and replicating the abilities of Rasrims, all carried out with extreme secrecy.

This group had been called the *Advanced Experimental Sciences Division*. It was likely one of the most funded, most knowledgeable, and most powerful Government Organizations in the entire world.

For example, it had recently succeeded in sending a team of scientists to Osamos and back using some of the most advanced technology on the planet, *all in complete secrecy*. No one in space nor any other government on Earth nor the Rasrims on Osamos had ever gotten wind of the AESD's activities. How they were able to pull off daunting missions like this was anyone's guess.

That was, except for Olivia.

She knew that the AESD currently had what it took to kill Rasrims from both space and on their home planet with high rates of success with access to the most important information in history, and now having the ability to conquer planets, the Division entered a secret agreement with the leaders of countries from all over the world to discuss its sole ability to defend an attack from the Rasrims and made a case for gaining access to even more resources and technology to continue doing so. However, the AESD had warned these leaders that only its group had the capability to achieve such a task and that if the Rasrim Space War turned into a Ground War here on Earth, the AESD would lead the charge against Osamos and gain power comparable to control over the entire planet, and these leaders reluctantly gave their support.

The AESD would then have the authority to assume command of the entire planet's collection of military might and resources alongside each country's entire defense budget and black book, a coalition of resources she had inside information on.

Olivia knew that this coalition, when it finally was cleared of all the political red tape, was to be called the Ground States' Union Military, which would effectively replace the United Nations and become a weaponized force of shared scientific information between countries of the world. The AESD would use their power to not just defend the planet but to destroy Osamos entirely.

The reason Olivia knew all of this was because *she* was the leader of the Advanced Experimental Sciences Division since it was founded in 2021.

And she was only twenty years old then.

All the talks Olivia had in the headquarters of the AESD were top-secret and off-book. She had been originally briefed by an underling that the Ground States Union Military would be created to be an official organization that worked diplomatically with the United Nations to become its official weaponized arm against alien threats and terrorists. Olivia took an interest in the idea and suggested that GSUM become a more offensive unit that incorporates tactics used by the AESD's more covert operations instead of a diplomatic punching bag that could only use military action and strike back once threatened and wiggled its way out of political discourse involving 183 member nations who all had radically different ideologies and agendas.

While this idea was incredibly favored by her peers and underlings, it proved to be a terrible mistake.

As tensions arose, the AESD changed course and now modeled the GSUM to become a puppet-organization secretly funded by the AESD, which would take orders directly from Olivia herself and give little room to outside debate, even from the likes of the president.

Along with several other ideas, Olivia promptly shut it down, only to have it and everything else resurface after a drastic change in fate.

Olivia had been the first person on Earth to figure out how to replicate the properties of Risima on command after taking a voyage to Osamos that lasted a few years shortly after becoming the leader of the Division. As many would imagine, why the leader of such a powerful group would risk their own life in such an operation was foolish and reckless, but she had been the only person capable of surviving the trip and getting what she needed undetected.

But to her surprise, she had been betrayed by other members. The other members of the AESD were planning on killing Olivia when she returned and taking whatever information they could from her to create their own clone of a Rasrim to experiment on and potentially use in wartime efforts. It was a plan that had been suggested by a senior member of the group in the Division's earliest days but one that Olivia had shut down every time, leaving no room for debate. Of course, once she had left, there had been no other person to prevent such an atrocity from becoming reality.

Knowing that her cover had been blown, Olivia changed the mission entirely. It now no longer mattered if Olivia remained hidden on the massive planet or not. She had an even better idea.

But even with a new plan in mind, Olivia encountered an inexplicable mystery that changed everything for good.

When Olivia had been living on Osamos, hiding out in the vast jungles of Osamos, using its cool and moist climate to survive, she had been caught and confronted by a strange individual who had been concealing his identity but had information regarding the attempt on her life. This individual was not Human, and although Rasrims and Humans had physical similarities and even at times resembled one another perfectly, this individual had an aura that suggested he was something even more dangerous than a Rasrim.

Olivia, a very cautious person herself, forced the individual to prove himself.

And then the individual did something that Olivia still couldn't explain to this day, something that brought her extensive awareness of Rasrim abilities into question.

This individual had the ability to communicate using telepathy. To prove himself to Olivia, the individual used his ability to steal the thoughts of her co-workers while they had been discussing their plans, somehow streaming their voices and even what they had been seeing into Olivia's mind on the spot. She could see everything they were seeing all at the same time. Their words were blended, but Olivia's mind automatically sorted and processed everything that was being said into coherent sentences. Even their thoughts were displayed into Olivia's mind.

Seeing that Olivia was lost for words and visibly disturbed, unable to truly understand what just happened, the man disappeared into thin air without a trace, leaving nothing behind but a very confused Olivia left stranded within Osamos while still trying to piece together a plan to prevent her assassination and prevent two entire planets from destroying each other into oblivion. To only make matters worse, she had no idea she was about to be thrown into another situation that would only make things even tighter to manage.

But it was one situation that gave her a unique opportunity to defeat two birds with one stone. But neither of her stones had known any of this nor did they realize how much pressure rested on their shoulders.

Miss E lifted her eyes and returned to her senses when she noticed Chase and Lance arguing about something. Although she was still deep in her own thoughts, she knew that Chase and Lance would require her input at some point.

Plus, she just liked listening to them talk.

"But these are their first confirmed kills! Not just planning, not just arming, but actual deaths!" Lance shouted. "They were literally warned not to attack Osamos! So why start now?"

Miss E interrupted Lance, something about the previous mark leaving her unsettled. "They won't be getting anymore," she said with no immediate insight.

Lance looked like he was rolling over his words. "Seriously? But wouldn't they be even more aggressive going forward?"

Olivia actually produced a quick smile, although it was probably more of a mocking gesture than anything else.

"You would think so, and some here definitely will think so too. But the illusion is—and what the Union will soon realize—is that the Rasrims are masters of disguise." Olivia paused for a moment, recounting her own experiences with dealing with them. "They have, well, the entire *universe* and all of its massive amounts of Energy to use as weapons. What I don't understand is why"—she stopped herself, as if she were beginning to figure something out—"whether or not the king will *actually* launch a counterattack or not."

Lance squinted. "Well, shouldn't he?"

Miss E looked down at her knuckles as if there were crumbs on them.

"That's enough for this morning. We'll let the news simmer and see what developments are made throughout the day. For now we need to prepare for your training. Today's a big day for you two!" She quickly changed the subject, leaving the table and carrying her dirty utensils to the sink.

Olivia realized that she had practically dropped her own bomb on them just now. But that was for a very important reason, and one she still didn't understand. She looked at the time on the stove.

She couldn't believe her eyes.

It was right on the dot, down to the second.

This entire day had been predicted almost a decade ago with astounding accuracy, down to the conversations that Chase and Lance would be having.

Was she even allowed to be impressed with herself, knowing that she remembered after all these years?

An even bigger bomb had been dropped on Olivia. She was specifically instructed to wait for this day to come, for this very *moment* to occur, that everything would change. That the ball would be in her court, which was a clever euphemism to say everything now relied on her and that she had better do her job well. Or else.

"Finished yet? How was it today? Enough cinnamon for you?" she asked.

Following Olivia's nonchalant response, Chase nodded happily instead of answering and helped himself to another glass of juice.

Lance, on the other hand, sat still, watching syrup drip off his last waffle. He couldn't help but think about the news.

He thought to himself for a moment.

If Osamos decided to fight back, how bad would it get?

Lance had seen some of the news, but now it was practically impossible to find anything on the subject as the various governments of Earth produced an amendment at a United Nations Summit, penalizing anyone for possessing footage or information of Rasrims, titled "The Alien Accords" cleverly enough.

But in the footage Lance did get a chance to see, he had seen Rasrims fight not just Humans but strange monsters of sorts too, using Fire to blast them away or summoning mountains of rock to separate them from larger foes. They worked well together, utilizing their various powers to do all sorts of things seemingly impossible.

And in an effort to prove Rasrims weren't dangerous, videos began surfacing showing Rasrims using their powers to rebuild roads or put out wildfires. But it all still looked like something straight out of a movie, and this was probably why it was decided to not completely hide the Rasrims' existence—that was long since impossible to do at this point—but to keep them at a distance to observe and eventually attack.

Lance once estimated that only roughly 30 percent of the population knew anything about Rasrims beyond the fact that they were a real alien species. He could tell this by searching the web and secret forums and platforms hidden deep on the Dark Web. And chances were that if people *did* know about the Rasrims, they found them "cool" or "godlike" instead of dangerous. Otherwise, there was simply too much disinformation or misleading articles about the aliens, some as much as downplaying the existence of them all together— even though the planet that harbored Osmaos was now visible from Earth itself and way too easy to identify compared to the moon.

Lance caught a glimpse of the news before it was turned off, and it stayed in his mind well after.

A reporter stated how the Rasrims were toying with the Humans' space defense program. They were simply entertaining the idea of a war with the less-advanced Humans until they eventually succumbed and asked for help. But this never happened. Even some of the most liberal lawmakers on the planet were weary of "aliens," especially ones that confessed they could destroy the Earth if they wanted to.

That set Lance's mind off. It was obvious to Lance that the Rasrims on Osamos could destroy the entire Earth. Having the ability to control the environment didn't stop between person-to-person interaction just because.

"Miss E, have Rasrims ever fought in other wars before? How much power does the strongest Rasrim actually have?"

Miss E sat her cup down. She seemed to be a little relieved.

"The strongest? Ha. Well, that one there is a question in itself. Rasrims don't measure themselves based on power but Energy projection."

Lance crossed his arms. "You mean how many things that they're able to control?"

"Or how many controllable things they can *reach* with minimal effort."

Lance's eyes slowly widened. That made a lot of sense.

"And the strongest one can reach an entire planet, can't he?"

Miss E remained quiet for a bit. She folded her hands on the table.

"The strongest one can reach several galaxies, Lance."

Lance's stomach dropped. Was that some sort of bad joke, or was she being serious?

Chase's mouth was left hanging open with his head crooked to one side.

"A galaxy? No! C'mon!"

Miss E remained expressionless, remembering the look on her face when she had learned the truth herself.

She was looking down at her cup of coffee. It was time for a refill.

Oliva cradled her cup. "Rasrims are powerful, Chase. I mean, what do you expect?"

"If you told me that the strongest one could destroy a building, I would've said the same thing. But a frickin' galaxy? You're talking billions of buildings, millions of planets! I mean, when you say that, you mean this galaxy too, right?"

"Well, yes," she replied, her tone almost too plain as if it was obvious to her.

"And you're just going to say it like you aren't impressed or shocked or *scared*? Seriously!"

It was then Olivia got up from the table and took her cup to the counter where the coffee machine was.

She placed her cup underneath the machine on a small tray and pressed a flashing blue button on the machine. Slowly, steaming hot coffee dispensed from the machine and slowly refilled her cup.

Olivia stood at the counter, resting her hands on the sides of it.

"Boys, I thought I said that was enough for this morning."

"But, Miss E! Seriously! You can't tell us all of this and expect us not to press on! We know practically *nothing* about any of this compared to you," Chase pleaded. He turned and looked at Lance with a desperate face.

"We all start somewhere, don't we? Even if that means merely asking questions." Olivia replied to the two.

Chase and Lance looked confused and unsatisfied, but they allowed her to continue talking.

"Today's the day," Olivia announced. Her tone had been bitter, almost regretful, and she sucked on air in her mouth as she said it. But her face and body language suggested that she had been excited, perhaps nervous even.

"What?" Lance asked, feeling the Energy Olivia had been resonating.

Olivia turned to face the sink and poured the remaining coffee down the drain and rinsed her cup out.

"Fire and Water." She cleared her throat. "Today's the day you two learn to control it."

She turned to face Chase and Lance. She had caught them off guard. Chase looked like he was about to drop his plate.

"Are you two done?"

"Y-yes!" Chase snapped.

Miss E snapped her head toward the sink, and then walked past Chase and Lance, heading toward the stairs.

"Drop your dishes off and follow me. We've got to get this started soon. It's *time*," she said with a sense of urgency in her voice.

Miss E led the boys down to the lower level, taking the staircase down to the bottom-most floor and out into the open area that had been designed as another eating place in case close friends or other company had been over for dinner.

Chase and Lance stopped behind Miss E, who had been showing them her back as she observed the room.

"What was with this urgency all of a sudden?"

"Do you two understand how different you are from the vast majority of people you will ever meet?"

Chase and Lance looked at each other, confused.

"Yeah, time and time again we learn how special we are. I mean, I've seen it for myself. And that one incident...," Lance trailed off.

Chase seconded that. "We know that we have powers and that we could be dangerous. But that doesn't make us all that different, does it?"

Miss E didn't answer right away.

"When I show you two what's behind these doors, you *will* be different. But you must own up to it. It's for the sake of the planet. You two can handle that, right?" But they didn't have a choice anyways.

Of course, without a real reason to object, Chase and Lance agreed in unison.

Miss E obliged, still facing the doors in front of her.

"This house is not an ordinary house. It has tricks and secrets you will never find anywhere else, not even on Osamos," Miss E said, her eyes focused on Chase and Lance. "I spent time working for different companies and learned several different things about architecture. This entire house was designed by me, specifically, and for one reason." And then she sat back, allowing the boys to come up with something to say.

Lance had an idea, but he wasn't sure. "Why?"

Miss E looked at him. She talked slowly.

"It was for you two for this very day." She turned around and faced the door, waving the two boys over as if she had a sudden change of mood again.

Chase looked at Lance with a lopsided face. "Huh? What the hell was that?" he mouthed, before following Miss E.

But Lance didn't move just yet. And then it hit him. His eyes lit up.

"It's been here all along?"

Miss E stopped at the door. She looked at the two. "What's been?"

"This house isn't just a 'house,' is it? It's also a secret facility!" Lance said.

Miss E looked directly at Lance, offering no emotion or sense of hesitation nor confusion. That was important for the time being. "Yes, Lance. It is."

Chase stopped in his tracks. He turned to look at Lance, but he only shrugged, offering no other explanation.

"You mean to tell me that you knew this all along?"

"Think about it, Chase. We're Rasrims! The person in charge of us knows everything about us!" Lance gestured to Miss E. "And she's a scientist too! It was only a matter of time that she would start experimenting on us, but we're hated everywhere. Where else could we go?"

"Woah, slow down there, sir," Miss E held up her hand, grabbing Lance's attention as she interrupted. "I am not going to experiment on either of you! Why would I do that?"

"Then what then?" Lance asked back.

Chase watched the exchange, almost feeling weary inside. Did Lance not trust her?

"I already told you. You two *must* learn how to control your abilities. You two are tasked with the protection of Osamos and Earth alike, and it's my job to get you there." Miss E put her hands over her eyes and then wiped sweat off her forehead. Her voice got low.

"I don't ever want to see you two get hurt. But understand that once you two learn to control your abilities, the world will change again."

"'The world will change again?'" Lance questioned. "And what do you mean by that?"

Miss E held her position. She wasn't a fan of pointless bickering or arguments. "What I mean by that is that *things* will change when the world is exposed to you and your talents. And when it does, there will be nobody out there to sort through the chaos except you two."

She pushed her glasses up to her face. "I know that something *big* is coming. You two will experience trials and tribulations that I personally cannot attest to. It isn't my position to even guess but simply acknowledge. All I can do is guide you until you're able to make those decisions on your own."

"Then why did we wait so long to figure all of this out? You have a whole place somewhere in this house where you're supposed to turn kids into superheroes or something? It doesn't even begin to make sense! And we're just supposed to go along with all of this like it's a game?" Chase exclaimed. He raised his arms in confusion. "That doesn't make any sense!"

She stood tall, pushing her glasses up to her face.

"Understand this then, Chase: I am *both* a scientist but also your guardian," she said sternly. "I've done an unhealthy amount of research and spent a stupid amount of money on protecting you two! This is *no* game. It's very, *very* real."

She looked at Chase softy, trying to better emphasize her emotions.

"I know it doesn't make sense. But it *will* when you two experience the pains and hardship lying at every corner in your journey from here on."

Miss E turned toward the basement and opened the door.

"I can't protect you two forever. I can't even offer you the same warm smiles I've been giving you once you experience the *truth*. Your perception of everything will change. While I still have time, I want to prepare you two up as best as I can before any of us begin to make regrets and mistakes beyond repair. Can you at least understand that?"

Chase didn't answer. He had been stubborn. He felt as if he was owed an explanation more than anything else.

Miss E paid little attention to Chase's uncertainty. She knew he would understand.

Even reaching that level of awareness required blood, spit, and misery. It would be just like it was when she was in their position a very long time ago.

Miss E cleared her throat, stepping in the basement, determined not to waste another moment.

"It's time you see for yourself what really awaits you two as Rasrims."

CHAPTER 3

Perfect Practice

Miss E seemed almost anxious as she led Chase and Lance toward the stairs leading to the basement.

She tried her best to ignore the boys' obvious hesitation toward her, remembering that it was part of a grand calculus that needed to succeed.

She promptly opened the plain, ordinary white door tucked away in the corner of the lower floor and flicked on a light on the wall inside the door.

With no hesitation, Miss E took the flight of stairs down. At first, the boys resisted, understanding they were about to break the one serious rule they ever had, but both Chase and Lance had taken mastering their abilities even more seriously. After a quick glance down the steps and a curious sniff of any potential odors—which there weren't any of—Chase took the stairs down, and Lance slowly followed behind, feeling anxious on the inside.

Where was she taking them that they hadn't already been to? This *was* their house, after all! Why would there even be a need to hide an entire room or perhaps a whole 'nother floor from them?

The two found Miss E standing at yet another corner, placed squarely between two plain walls that had been completely bare. It seemed inconspicuous to say the least.

Lance looked around, not sure what to think. He expected a room full of scientific goodness, automatic lighting systems revealing perhaps robotic suits or displays of computer monitors surveying various things.

But it was an ordinary room. Even the light switch was old, contrary to the rest of the house which had state-of-the-art light systems that detected movement and responded to sounds.

Lance observed the room again. He could vaguely smell metal in the room as if it had been heated up and molded into the room. He was familiar with the smell. The room had seen some modifications recently. Lance frowned. Something wasn't adding up.

"I thought there would be more stuff—you can't teach us anything here!"

Miss E had been waiting for that comment.

"So you don't notice anything odd about this room?"

Chase looked at a corner in the basement and elbowed Lance. "'Tis is nothing but a box of dust and cobwebs," he whispered to him, trying not to laugh.

But Lance did.

"You know, it's actually pretty clean. Strangely clean like there's been—"

"Oh, shut up! I mean, there's nothing here! The only odd thing about it is that there *isn't* anything odd in it!"

But Olivia didn't say anymore. Instead, she briefly rubbed her hand on the bare wall and then flicked a light switch on it.

The three stood and watched before, suddenly, a panel in the wall opened up, retracting into the floor, revealing an elevator behind it.

Lance whistled, although, he admitted that the sight was surreal. Chase, on the other hand, was wide-eyed and frozen in place. But Miss E seemed strangely removed from the sight, as if it were nothing new to her.

"C'mon, give me a break! You both play with high-tech space toys that not even NASA knows exist. You can't be surprised to see something like this, can you?"

Lance shrugged. "True. Well, I mean. I didn't *know* that before just now but still true."

Chase ignored that. "But you have a secret underground facility? In our own home? Hey, Lance, didn't we just watch a movie with some secret room hidden in it?"

"No?"

"Yes, we did! Like two weeks ago! It was one of those badass spy movies! It had hidden compartments, cool gadgets, all that stuff! You think that's what this is?"

"Wait, did we really?"

Chase sighed.

Miss E gestured to the elevator with her arms. "Whatever the case is, *this* is the real thing! But it really is just an elevator. I know tons of people who have elevators in their homes."

"Do they live in hotels or something?"

"Some do, sure!"

Chase crossed his arms, still in disbelief. But he was a horrible liar. Underneath all that, he was surging with excitement.

She waited for the boys to move.

"You should, uh, go first," Chase whispered to Lance.

Lance looked at Chase. Chase looked back.

"Are you seriously scared right now?"

"No!" Chase pushed past Miss E and stood in the elevator. And then he shuddered.

"Secret compartment? I'm in a secret compartment in the basement of my own house... What the actual—" Chase stopped.

The sound of creaking metal as Miss E stepped into the elevator made Chase jump.

"Lance, you're up."

Lance tried his best not to overthink it, but wasn't this when you were *absolutely* supposed to overthink?

He took a step forward. Then he took one last look at the room he was leaving behind.

Once he stepped in, Olivia pressed a few buttons on a panel on the elevator.

It had been completely electronic. Lance noticed the design of the panel as well. For some reason, he could tell that it had been fitted with a high-tech security system, and he could even *feel* the Energy that the entire elevator ran on. He simply understood that the whole setup required a ton of electricity to run.

Lance thought to himself, *But he was certain there wasn't any Water Risima involved in it. That was odd.*

Miss E began to talk as the elevator moved.

"I didn't mean to hide this from you two, but once you see what this all really is, I hope you understand it by then," she said.

She yawned. She seemed tired suddenly.

"I only had contractors build this elevator system and carve out the room below. Everything else I made entirely by myself. This is secret stuff. It was designed for you two."

Chase shook his head. "Is there a teleporter down there? I'm sorry. I just have to know. No! Wait, we're learning how to use our powers…so that means—" Chase said in a humorous tone.

"Snap out of it, Chase! This is no game."

"I'm sorry! I mean, there's a friggin' secret compartment in our house! I mean, there's gotta be—"

And then the elevator stopped. The overhead lighting changed to a bluish color, and the doors slid open in a dramatically slow fashion. It took a moment for the boys to rest their eyes easily on the sight beyond, as suddenly, there was too much to look at.

Lance was the first to step out, paying no attention to the steps he took as he looked around. He couldn't even bring himself to make observations, struggling to understand what he was seeing. The room must've been the size of a football field, maybe more.

The first thing he noticed was a large central platform in the very center of the room in the shape of a circle with a set of computers within it, showcasing futuristic technology that included tubes full of a light-blue liquid with particles flowing within it, spreading out across the entire room in overhead pipes. The room had smaller sections marked off everywhere, some with red paint, others with blue or yellow paint. They all seemed uniquely different, with control panels on just about everywhere in the room to control the layout of the room. The walls were clustered with those pipes containing the strange blue liquid while other areas were completely barren and plain with nothing on them except light-gray paint.

Lance looked to the side of the room, his left marked off with yellow paint. There was a machine built into a desk with all sorts of equipment and tools categorized neatly in transparent boxes and shelves next to it. It looked to be a workbench that seemed to suit a variety of purposes.

"What is that?" Chase exclaimed, quickly taken aback by how his voice traveled in the room.

He ran up to the center of the room and examined the computers in it.

"Wait, you're telling me this whole place is for training? This computer screen here says the room can change its environmental settings, atmospheric pressure, and even simulate battle terrains like on Osamos?"

"It can do a whole lot more than that!" Miss E raised her voice in the vastness of the room. "So why don't I give you the official tour?" she asked, also focusing her attention on Lance, who was poking around at the workbench.

"I see you're looking at where I believe you'll spend most of your time, no?"

Lance couldn't believe what he was seeing—multitools with high-powered lasers built in for soldering and welding, thousands of tools you would find in a high-tech repair shop, sophisticated computers with AI for logging data…

"What is all this? I've never seen equipment like this! I mean, the workbench alone looks like it would have cost you millions!"

Miss E's head tilted to the side.

"Yeah, that sounds about right. But what's any amount of money when you're tasked with raising two Rasrims? Anything's possible!"

Lance watched as Chase pressed a few buttons. He watched as the far-right corner of the room began changing everything around. It had created small cubicles within itself about the size of a batting cage. The cubicles seemingly appeared from nothing, a wisp of the light-blue light present as the entire room moved in almost holographic way. In fact, the entire room was full of this color; a misty-like aura spread throughout it.

"Wait a second. Is this light some of that new 'Meta-Presence Matter' I've been hearing about?"

Miss E was impressed. That was something most people weren't even familiar with yet.

"Yes, it is. Very good eye," Miss E said in a pleased tone. "It's nanotechnology. It runs on a specialized type of Energy that can shape itself and materialize to produce all sorts of unique objects with attention to detail. It's what I would consider the next step of 3D print technology. But—" She caught Lance's eye, who had begun to understand what she was saying. "No one else knows that this particular model of its existence yet. It is a *very* special device that must be taken care of. It goes without saying that no one should ever find out about this technology. If they find out about it, they find out about *you* too."

Suddenly, the light glow of the Matter-Phaser swirled around an area within the room, beginning to shape itself into a particular figure. Lance watched closely, his light-blue eyes reflecting the light he was seeing.

"Woah…," Lance said to himself as a tall, metallic creature had been summoned in the place of the Phaser.

"I started naming these 'nano-phase machines,' or NPMs for short!" Olivia beamed.

Lance walked up to the machine, examining it from top to bottom. While he imagined the render would have flaws in its design, it was nearly impossible to know that this was a machine made from liquid nanotechnology and not something constructed in a factory instead.

But was intrigued Lance the most was the level of detail the nanotechnology could construct. He no doubt knew that a machine constructed even in seconds could perform all sorts of tasks and even be modified on command. But he also couldn't find any brands, names, or anything that suggested that these parts had been imported or been modeled after designs of hardware parts that already existed.

Everything in this room had been improvised and original designs. It likely didn't exist anywhere else on the entire planet.

Lance looked at Miss E. "You designed all this stuff by yourself, didn't you?"

Miss E pushed her glasses up to her eyes. While she had every right to be, she wasn't impressed with herself. Even though she had been an accomplished scientist in dozens of fields, she wouldn't be satisfied until Chase and Lance were successful and able to complete their own journeys.

"Yes, I did," she simply replied, "but I already told you that I designed everything in this room."

Chase had been out of the earshot of the conversation, but she had smiled when she noticed him playing around with the NPMs.

She continued talking to Lance. "That machine was a work in progress ever since I graduated from high school, and that was…a long time ago. Try messing around with it. And don't be afraid to get a little rough with it! The Center Console is what you must absolutely be careful with." Then she looked at Chase and shouted to him, "Feel free to completely wreck any NPMs that you create, assuming you remain a very safe distance away from the center console…seriously! These were designed to withstand the effects produced from outbursts of Risima Energy."

But then she held up a finger, turning back and speaking to Lance again. "However, there is an *obvious* limit to that. The accumulation but also redirection of Risima Energy consumes a large radius of space. That means that as your efficiency grows—"

"So does the potency *but also* the possibility of discharges," Lance finished. "I remember reading that. And conveniently enough, the best way to learn how to use Risima, per the book, is in a controlled area where its effects can be monitored. Words of a scientist, no doubt."

Olivia noticed Lance had been on the floor attempting to take parts of the robot apart. He had been successful in reaching the core of the robot's hardware. Lance noticed that instead of wires, there were thin metallic poles that emitted the same color as the matter-phase technology flowing throughout the interior of the robot.

Then Olivia noticed that Chase had created his *fifth* NPM in another part of the room. He had already found the receiver that had been programmed to perform the same functions from the Center Console and even managed to configure how he wanted his machine to operate. From the appearance of the NPM, Chase somehow managed to find some of the preset designs the NPMs were able to create, managing to use the receiver to create a small mobile robot no larger than a dog to be assembled by the center console.

She watched as the machine went to attack Chase using a slow forward-moving punching attack. She nearly winced as it almost hit Chase, but he had simply thrown his own punch back, managing to produce a small explosion of Fire like he had learned to do. The punch destroyed the face of the machine, rendering it into melted metal. The machine fell to the ground, unable to continue operating.

Chase held two thumbs up, giving his "audience" a slick smile and a look of accomplishment.

Miss E sighed, trying her best to hold in a laugh.

"As you can see, part of this experience is not just to teach you how to use your powers but also to teach you how to control your output of Energy."

Miss E looked at Lance with a very serious look. Lance almost didn't notice it as he was still trying to figure out the ins and outs of the NPM.

"Using Risima Energy isn't an easy task. I know that much. But with the amount of time and money invested into the tech in this room, I hope I can ease that pain as much as possible." She turned and used her shoulder to gesture to the robot that Chase had defeated.

"Check that out," she said as the robot suddenly dematerialized into the same blue Energy before disappearing altogether.

"That is...so damn cool!" Chase yelled.

Determined to see for himself, Lance ran over to the Center Console, too eager to see what the phase machine could truly do. "Here, let me have a go!" Lance cheered, hopping into one of the four chairs at the console.

At first, his eyes and hands hovered over the vast buttons, controls, and screens, taking it all in. He studied the layout closely. Then in one confident sweep, he began pushing and moving all sorts of controls, eager to see what the console was capable of.

First, the cubicles turned into two large platforms that spaced themselves out evenly from each other that began to slowly rise off the ground until it was about ten feet off the ground. Between the two platforms was a gap in the center of them.

Then by pressing a series of buttons on a black keypad, entering some numbers in a list provided on it, Lance created two more robots, which apparently would have an estimated durability of carbon fiber. For some reason, a vast majority of the options were tailored towards conflict. Was that international?

The combat-oriented NPMs stood still, placed in the middle of both platforms.

Lance applied the atmospheric pressure mode and watched a thin black veil drop from the ceiling around the outlines of the cubicles before it tightened itself and then disappeared altogether.

"What was that?"

"It seemed like a barrier."

"But it disappeared!"

"It all uses nanotechnology," Miss E explained. "Keep going. You'll be in there yourself soon!"

Lance pressed an initiator, and a whirring sound was heard as the robots collapsed to the floor. They had been programmed to respond to external stimuli similarly to how a humanoid being would, and so, they propped themselves upward to fight against the pressure of being smacked against the floor.

After a while, the robots gradually became strong enough to withstand the pressure of the room, more blue light shining in their bodies as if the blue light was giving them more energy.

"You can turn that feature off if you want to. Otherwise, hardly anything would stop 'em. Well, unless you use too much Energy, but not even I know how to do that...*yet*," Miss E said.

Chase sprung up from his spot. "Hey! Let me try that out!"

He ran over to the cubicles but stopped when he ran face-first into the barrier, the transparent grayish light appearing that had separated space between him and the cubicles behind it.

"Did you already forget that was there?" Lance laughed.

"Nah. I just wanted to test its strength! But can you disable it… please?"

Lance snickered and shook his head before he disabled the gravity zone and the barrier.

Afterwards, as Lance crossed where the barrier was, he noticed a small indication on the floor in the shape of a straight line where he believed the barrier would be when activated. Doing a quick estimate, Lance knew that the training section of the room was about five hundred feet in length and width, more than a good size.

Lance instinctively looked down at his hands. Then he perked up as Chase started to speak.

"Miss E, without being able to use our powers, what good would all this room do for us?" It seemed Chase read Lance's mind.

But Miss E remained quiet and resorted to showing off a sly smile. Had she already had everything prepared? She pressed a few buttons on the center command. Lance watched her hands move gracefully as she operated the area with wisdom, almost as if she had designed it all herself. Maybe she did.

Lance held his balance as the entire room shook a bit, taken off guard once more. Not even the matter phaser had moved the room this much. What could she have done now?

Chase and Lance looked beneath their feet as the ground above opened, revealing a much larger platform, which was split off into two sections within the training area.

An even deeper level beneath the floor?

Chase hopped back as his cubicle began to move backward, shifting its size. Lance looked down and almost panicked as he realized the blue light had replaced the solid material of the floor he was on. At first, Lance thought he would fall straight through as it seemed the block he stood on had simply disappeared, but he quickly realized an Energy had surged throughout it, taking over its physical properties in order to modify it in all sorts of ways, such as height, durability, and even more miniscule ways such as details and color.

Lance observed as he realized a large area of blue suddenly appeared. Was it more of this Energy? He took a few steps closer, mesmerized by how clear and with such a deep blue color the area was decorated with.

But then Lance laughed aloud as he realized what he was looking at. It was a pool of water. A large one at that.

He took notice of Chase, staring at a large red and black box which looked hefty in its size.

"There you have it. Obviously, the pool is for you, Lance, and the blast chamber for you, Chase."

A pool and a blast chamber. Water and Fire. They were designed to literally hold the respective elements for Chase and Lance. *What an interesting idea*, Lance thought. But what were Miss E's intentions? How could they use these things to train their powers?

She pressed a few more buttons, and the blast chamber released the lock on its heavy metal doors. It gave off a presence of hot air, which immediately heated up the room by a substantial amount.

Chase hadn't moved yet. He seemed, strangely enough, content, neither anxious nor excited like he was deep in thought but already reassured of what he wanted to do.

Miss E left the Command Console in "manual stationary," or in other words, in a position that it could be used with unless an individual was present on the console floor. It was a safety precaution, one of the several that she had installed just in case.

She stopped next to Lance.

"Chapter 4 of your book should reveal that training in the environment of a Rasrim's natural element would be the best and most efficient way to master the first of their elements," Miss E began.

Lance nodded.

"Right. But I assumed this would mean the ocean, perhaps."

"So what? Wouldn't a pool work just as well?"

Lance chuckled. "Well, I don't know. It just seems…elementary to me."

"You're just learning. These are baby steps, Lance! We learn to walk before we run."

She turned to Chase. "Hey," she called out to him, "feel the heat already? I'll give you a warning: It's set to two thousand degrees, which is typical for young Fire Rasrims to begin us—"

"Wait, *two thousand?*" Chase shrieked.

"It shouldn't be all that hot for a Fire Rasrim!" Miss E exclaimed. "I was saying that many Fire Rasrims hardly notice such a temperature."

"Yeah, uh, that's cool and all, but you *really* want me to go in that thing when it's *that* hot?"

Olivia didn't move. She wasn't worried one bit. She stepped into the training area and placed her hands on her hips.

"The best way for either of you to learn your elements is to submerge yourself into a place where the element resonates most purely."

Lance nodded. Chase, on the other hand, hadn't been paying attention.

"That would probably be an ocean for you, as you already observed, Lance, and likely a, well, a volcano for you, Chase. And most volcanoes have an average temperature of around tw—"

Chase's eyes shot open. "Wait, a *what?*"

Miss E sighed. "I get that exposure to such extreme elements seems intimidating, but I shouldn't be the one more encouraged than you two are. These *are* your natural environments even if you've been taught to live and learn as Humans."

Chase and Lance looked somber as if they tried to consider the truth in that statement.

"Besides, this is *nothing* for Rasrims! That's what I'm trying to say. Instead of meandering our way up at elementary paces, I'm going to put you into a situation where I'm confident you'll be able to jumpstart your way into managing Risima."

"So we're taking it down a notch to learn how to maintain stimuli," Lance said.

Chase blew a raspberry. "But you *really* think that puttin' me in a car-sized oven is taking it down a notch?"

"Precisely. The idea of this training exercise is for you to learn how to communicate with the environment and *feel* what it's like to use your elements in the natural environment."

She turned back toward the Command Console.

"I have monitors that gauge the variables of both the pool and the chamber, including temperature, pressure, oxygen levels—you will be safe at all times. I can adjust these levels if I suspect you two can't handle it, but I assume the opposite will be true: you'll need higher pressures and probably early on."

Chase put his hand over his head and paved around, laughing nervously to himself.

Meanwhile, Lance looked at the pool, almost as if he were underwhelmed. "I'll just be in water, though. How difficult can it really be for me?"

Miss E gave Lance a sarcastic look and laughed. "How long can you *really* hold your breath, Lance?"

That stumped Lance. "Oh, uh…"

Miss E gave a thumbs up, her over joyous scientific side emerging. "You'll both do fine! I'll be watching the whole time!"

For some reason, the way she had been so confident made it all seem *worse*.

She waved over to Chase, trying to break him out of his nervous pacing. "That chamber there is state of the art. It knows what conditions your body works under. At a calm state of being, you should be able to handle what I have it set to. But as you take more Fire Energy in, I'll have to *increase* both the heat and the pressure exerted on your body, okay?"

Chase laughed nervously. "Yeah…right! There's nothing wrong with a little extra pressure when your life flashes before your eyes…," he replied sarcastically.

Miss E sat down at the Command Console and initiated the barrier. But Lance turned back quickly.

"Why'd you do that?" he asked, poking the barrier that now kept him inside the training area next to Chase's blast chamber.

Miss E shrugged, which Lance knew was supposed to be funnier than mean anything.

"Oh, right. Lance!" she shouted. "Your task in there is quite simple: *Don't drown*. I haven't been swimming in years!"

This time, she had been joking.

Lance's face turned gray. "W-what's that supposed to mean? Do you *think* I'll drown?"

Miss E found Lance drifting in his mind. "Just don't ignore your instincts. If something feels wrong, trust it," she answered. "Otherwise, I want you to stay in there for as long as possible. The longer you're in there, the better you'll be able to begin sensing Water Risima!"

Lance looked up and around the area surrounding the pool, tracing the outline he could find on the floor. If he looked hard enough, he realized that he could barely see a trace outline of the barrier.

"*Trust Risima*. It will find you and communicate with you. When you're focusing hard enough, you'll be able to isolate Risima from *everything* else. You'll find out for yourself what that means soon."

An indescribable feeling suddenly motivated Lance, telling him that this was it. He hustled over to the pool and wasted no time as he stripped off his shirt and took a breath. He knew that he could spend a long amount of time in the pool. He had done it before for fun. This was no different, right?

Looking into the pool and through the crisp, dark-blue water, Lance could tell it had a depth of about twenty-five feet. There had been no markings anywhere on the pool deck otherwise.

As he stood there, watching the clear pool water slowly slosh around, Lance began to remember a conversation he had had with Chase and Miss E one day. What did she say again?

Lance curled his toes over the edge of the pool, trying his hardest to remember but also concentrate at the same time. Was he anxious? Did he think he'd fail at conjuring and mastering Risima? No. Lance was more than prepared. This was his time.

Lance closed his eyes and promptly jumped into the pool—pencil-diving down straight to the bottom. He didn't want to waste any more time.

The pool had been icy cold, just how Lance liked it. He immediately felt relieved as Lance's feet touched the bottom of the pool. At the same time, a memory popped into his mind.

When you surround yourself in your natural element, you'll first need to establish an equilibrium between your body and your environment, a place where you can feel both your blood and air flowing in and around you at the same time. This way, isolating the location of Risima in your body for the first time becomes easier to do.

Lance's feet completely touched the bottom of the pool. He placed them flat before he moved to sit straight down on the floor of the pool.

You should have realized by this—I mean, you must meditate in your element's naturally occurring environment in order to feel its presence and begin streaming it into your body.

Lance was fully relaxed. He was focused. He found a comfortable position and maintained it, only allowing the swishing water around his body to enter his mind before that too left his thoughts. His mind was blank. But then one more thought crossed his mind.

Once you've found that position, that neutral, calming position, begin to focus on your element. You are a Rasrim. You can use the environment's Energy as your own so long as you respect the environment and abide by your body's limits.

Lance's hands were steady. He held them tightly together over his legs. He straightened his back, flexing his neck muscles, holding his head straight before he relaxed his entire body at once.

Then almost immediately after, Lance felt a tingling sensation that started in his *eyes* before it traveled throughout his body. It lingered around his heart. He could feel Energy in his chest. This was Risima's Energy.

*****

Chase shut the doors of the blast chamber, pulling the heavy metal doors toward his body, the creaking sound of the doors unpleasant to listen to.

Chase felt strange locking himself into an oven. But the feeling had bothered him more than the heat inside the oven—which oddly reassured him.

Then he heard what he believed to be a splash from outside the chamber. *Lance is already beginning*, Chase thought. Once again, he felt like he was losing a race that he had created but he refused to admit had existed.

Chase turned and tried his best to focus his attention on the chamber. It had a grooved inside but was completely bare. There had been no decorations other than the scorching hot red metal inside of the chamber. The ceiling of the chamber lowered as you traveled further inside of it. It seemed smaller from the outside, though. Chase figured the box was about thirty feet long and wide.

Chase laughed to himself. It was *pretty* hot in the chamber, he realized. Just a few weeks ago, it had been ninety-nine degrees, the hottest Chase had ever experienced, but it was over three times that hot and gradually increasing as the minutes went by. He felt it was crazy that Miss E had confidence in the idea of such a thing. A Human would have been dead from the burns and exhaustion by now. He *knew* that.

But Chase wasn't even sweating. He actually felt good. He knew that with a Fire Elemental Prowess, he would be immune from the effects of fire such as being burned or getting too hot.

Now it was time to make Fire Risima truly his to use. He had been waiting for the opportunity for as long as he could remember.

Chase realized what Miss E had told him and Lance about meditating in their elements' "natural environments," and Chase had even read a few chapters in his own book. Of course, Chase hated reading and gave up on it after only a week or so. He thought being made to read about something he couldn't do was pointless and stupid. But now he got his wish. Whether or not he succeeded was entirely up to him. He almost wished he had kept his reading up.

Chase slowly sat down on the floor, making sure that nothing bizarre would happen as he did so. It wasn't as hot as the room had been. That meant the floor had been made of a different material than the walls. But Chase couldn't help but feel strange sitting inside of an eerie heat chamber deep underneath his house. The thought was unsettling yet, for some reason, exciting at the same time.

After only a few minutes of what Chase *thought* was deep meditation, he grew irritated. *This is a waste of time,* he thought to himself. He was pouting, crossing his arms with his head turned in disgust. "Lance is probably already creating water spears in that pool. Meanwhile, I'll be in this thing roasting like a turkey!"

But then Chase shook his head, reminding himself to focus. He shouldn't think like that. It wouldn't help. Even if Lance had already found his element, Chase would be more than behind if he left the chamber without some evidence of being able to use his own element. He wouldn't let Lance have that over him.

He didn't like to meditate. Lance almost did religiously, once in the morning and then again before bed. And that was *before* he was even told to!

Chase didn't fret any longer. Instead, he remembered how Miss E had taught him how to meditate. It was terribly simple, although its benefits were rewarding.

The blast chamber creaked, hot air blasting Chase in the face. That proved his point, although no one was around to witness it.

Well, it was probably better than having to hold your breath in a pool. That calmed Chase down a bit.

The hot air he sucked in was still, surprisingly, refreshing.

He exhaled, the breath he let out much cooler than the air he took in. Chase allowed any and every thought he had to invade and leave his mind as they pleased. He thought about the fights he and Lance had, the various bets that Chase made with Lance, and their disparaging test scores. He remembered every lesson he had been taught, every activity he did, and how each of them went. It wasn't even about the results as much as it was the idea that he always went up against Lance at everything they did—sports, video games, chores, even odd things like eating. Everything was a competition.

Having an older twin brother, one who was naturally good at everything, wasn't easy. It was difficult for Chase to find his own calling when it seemed that Lance had already long since explored and gotten bored of it all. After all, Lance *also* had designed high-tech machines like AI software, holographic screens, and complete *junk*, Chase joked to himself.

But then Chase felt a little embarrassed. What was left for him to actually be good at? Something that he could understand better than Lance?

Chase eventually told himself to relax. These thoughts were meaningless. Was it getting hotter or colder in here? Chase couldn't tell, although he knew it wasn't the same temperature as just a few seconds ago.

Then his mind went blank.

At first, Chase saw nothing. He thought he got light-headed or dizzy for a moment. But then a brilliant light of orange and red appeared in Chase's mind. Chase focused on it, not realizing what it was.

The flame in his mind grew larger and brighter. He could feel the heat from the flame. His body had gotten extremely hot. He could feel it burning inside of his body, giving his body a new sense of Energy that he had never felt before.

Chase heard something in the chamber. It sounded like a *poof* as if a flame suddenly sparked. Then he felt a hot presence on his shoulder.

He had noticed this same exact feeling again since the very first time he practiced throwing punches with Miss E.

And then Chase's entire body felt kinetic as if a warm aura had eased his muscles and soothed his joints. But it wasn't until Chase's shirt began withering away and specks of ash trickled onto Chase's legs that he figured out what the feeling was.

Chase's entire upper body had been engulfed in fire.

Chase nearly broke his concentration, but he forced himself to remain calm. He knew that he was safe. Fire *would not* bother him, he told himself.

But if the fire started to bother him, Chase would simply take his shirt off and go back to meditating. After all, he felt like soon he would be able to reproduce this feeling he had now felt twice.

That had to be Fire Risima. Not just the intense heat but the fiery feeling that Chase had felt with every breath. It had been coursing throughout his body, making him feel like he could burst into a flame at any point.

Chase returned to the image in his head. At first it looked like a dancing flame, a small wisping ball of fire swirling back and forth. But then it started to resemble a person. Chase hadn't recognized this individual. He was tall. He himself was on fire too. Then Chase saw a dark crimson red line blaze across the person's body, traveling up to his neck before it reached his head. His eyes glowed crimson red.

Then an explosion occurred inside Chase. It was a burst of Energy that frightened Chase. The feeling of Risima was an incredible force; it made the body feel as if it could suddenly erupt with power. But the feeling was all too familiar. Chase remembered feeling this same sensation during that incident. Perhaps Risima Energy truly was everywhere. He moved ever so slightly, but that made his connection deeper. The Energy within Chase burned hotter.

Once Chase's connection with Fire Risima reached a level he was certain he never felt before, his shirt suddenly exploded in a spontaneous combustion of embers and ash, combusting into a massive flame that was so bright Chase could see orange light filing in through the lids of his eyes. He could feel the ash from his shirt scatter down his chest and back.

But it didn't hurt. It didn't bother Chase one bit, although he was sure he was completely on fire.

Chase tightened his position and took another deep breath in, the hot air from the fire traveling into his lungs.

He gritted his teeth as he felt a tremendous Energy awakening in him before, finally, he was sure he had it. He had found Fire Risima in and around him. He was now controlling it.

Chase focused on his flaming body. By focusing a great deal of his thoughts on the fire, taking shallow breaths as he did it, the fire began to burn bigger and hotter.

Chase felt the fire spread to the rest of the chamber. At this point, he could hear it dancing on the floor of the chamber.

Then Chase took one big, deep breath before straightening his body, and almost as if he had roared inside his body, he forced any and every presence of Energy he *thought* he had felt on the fire.

But Chase could sense he was overdoing it. Without knowing for sure how to begin drawing in but also really easing Risima Energy in the proper way, Chase was going to overexert himself. And that seemed to be the case.

At once, the entire chamber went dark. Chase paused. What just happened?

The chamber began to cool. The fire had disappeared from the walls, leaving no light but the molten-red metal walls.

But the presence in Chase's body remained. In fact, it was much more potent than it was before.

Chase opened his eyes slowly, not sure what to expect.

He made a sound. He had felt brand-new, but he noticed that the fire in the chamber was extinguished completely. Maybe he reached a time limit?

Chase's ears twitched when he heard a sudden knock outside the chamber. He didn't move.

"Chase?" He heard a muffled voice outside. Chase had to focus hard to make out the distorted words.

The voice called out again. "Chase, are you okay? Your vitals went blank! Is everything okay?"

Chase looked down at himself and froze. His entire body was scorching red, the air around him sizzling with Energy. If he touched anything made of paper or plastic, he'd instantly destroy it.

Chase studied the palms of his hands. They were still pulsating with Fire Risima. Chase still hadn't let go of the Energy in his body. He had only focused and emphasized on it more the entire time.

He flexed his wrist, emphasizing a great deal of this Energy in the region of his hands, and a small flame appeared in the center of his palm. Chase shook his head.

"Unbelievable…"

Chase tried to focus as much Energy as he could into his hand, but he stopped suddenly as he felt a sharp pain flash throughout his head and especially in his eyes. They started throbbing.

He winced and held his head, aching in pain. His body cooled off, and the Energy in his body disappeared.

"Chase! Hold on, I'm coming in."

Chase lifted his head, remembering something.

"No! Yeah! I'm all good. I'm all right!" Chase shouted through the chamber.

He heard Miss E relieved on the other side.

"Dear goodness. Hold on, I'm coming in!"

Chase stood up and faced the door, still clutching his throbbing left eye. He didn't realize Risima stung so much. He let go and looked at his hand.

His entire hand had been covered in blood!

Chase could hear his blood sizzling as it trickled down his face, boiling as droplets hit the molten-hot floor. He wasn't sure what to think! What was that pain? And why were his *eyes* of all things bleeding? But why did the Energy in his chest disappear? He felt fine until he tried to conjure the Energy into his hand, but until then, there had been no problems with it!

Chase felt around, trying to summon the Energy once again, but he couldn't. And now, he was beginning to feel sore.

"Damn!" Chase angrily slammed his bloody hand against the heavy tungsten door in front of him. But he froze in place, staring at the door, completely petrified as he realized he had put a large dent into the door of the chamber.

He took several tiny steps back, in awe. It was only then that he looked around the chamber to see how warped and damaged the interior of it was from the fire. How strong was that fire?

The door on the blast chamber fought from being opened, getting stuck at the hinge next to where Chase hit it.

"It's stuck, and the emergency release hatch failed along with all the other systems. I can't believe I didn't hold on," the voice outside said.

Chase grabbed the door and pried it open. With hardly any strength, he had almost torn the door off its hinges.

Miss E stood at the entrance, holding her arms in front of her face as she leaned back. "Phew! It's hot in here all right!" she shrieked.

But she looked at Chase and greeted him with a warm smile. She noticed that his shirt had been burnt to a crisp, but his jogging pants and shoes were otherwise unbothered.

"Chase, your eyes...!" Miss E's expression was bright and full of surprise.

But Chase swatted the air, more concerned about his *arm*.

"Oh, yeah. They're fine. I don't know why they're bleeding." Chase dapped his eye with the back of his hand, blinking hard. "I think some ash got in them or something. I dunno."

Seeing that Chase was in a completely livid and pumped state, Miss E nudged him. "It seems like you had a blast in there, huh?"

Chase frowned. She could not have been serious.

"Wow. That one was *so* good. You're on fire...," he said dryly.

But almost as if a surge of excitement possessed his body, Chase suddenly turned toward her and burst with Energy. "Hey! I had it! Like, I did it! I had this weird feeling in my chest—it was hotter than the chamber was. It was, like, an electrical force or something—I dunno—but my shirt exploded, then the fire in the chamber got hotter, and then..."

Miss E rubbed the area above Chase's eyes softly.

"You overexerted yourself."

Then she rubbed his head, causing Chase to make a weird face.

"But I'm very proud of you, Chase. How do you feel now?"

"Fine! But I just can't seem to find that same Energy again."

Chase held out his hand and strained, trying to focus Energy in his body once more. Miss E watched carefully, studying Chase's *eyes*. They were glowing red, the color in his irises a sharp and vibrant color, flowing with what Miss E knew was Risima Energy. That was a sign Chase had indeed begun tapping into his papers. But Miss E was still curious.

Her attention turned to the blast chamber.

Chase had destroyed the interior of the blast chamber and demolished his shirt completely—things that should be able to withstand heat equivalent to that of the *sun's* surface. But Chase didn't know this, that both the chamber and his clothing had been designed by Olivia for this very occurrence.

She stepped back, pondering.

"Chase, when your shirt first caught fire, what were you thinking about?"

"Huh? You mean when I was meditating?"

"Mhmm."

"Oh, uh…," Chase began. "Oh! Well, I actually remember seeing a dude when I was meditating."

"A man?" Miss E asked the question as if something had been wrong. She bit her lip. "What did he look like?"

Chase sighed. "He was tall. That's all I remember. He looked like something out of a fantasy movie or game. I think he was wearing armor or something. I don't remember too well. He reminded me of a knight or an ancient king even."

Miss E looked at Chase from the corner of her eyes, deliberating on something she hoped wasn't true.

"Was he…no. Never mind," Miss E said, waving her hand. "Was there anything else you remember?"

"I saw fire too. A *lot* of it. Then again, the man was on fire too! I could've sworn I saw red eyes and everything. It wasn't too clear, but that's definitely it!"

And she agreed.

"Perhaps it also could have been—" But she stopped herself again, resorting to a sigh instead.

"What's wrong?"

"Oh, nothing. I was just trying to figure out exactly how much power you gave off in there, that's all." Miss E crossed her arms. "Maybe your power output was linked to whatever you were visualizing, yeah?"

Chase gestured to the center console. "Didn't you say you had radars installed?"

Miss E straightened herself. "That's the thing. The power index was so potent it fried the sensors within the blast chamber. I'm going to go out on a limb and say that the estimated amount of power you generated whenever that 'explosion' occurred could have definitely destroyed the entire chamber and maybe even the house. I think even—"

"*What?*" Chase exclaimed, his eyes glowing an even brighter red.

Miss E laughed nervously and patted him on his shoulder, slightly irritated that Chase had conjured even more Risima Energy upon hearing this.

"*Maybe* I should stop there."

"No, finish, please! I'm sorry. You said I had generated enough power to destroy the house?"

"And several large buildings, potentially." She winced.

Chase choked. "No way..." Miss E could tell this had impressed Chase. She wanted him to be more encouraged but not *enthused*. That was an important distinction in the realm of Risima.

"You passed today's test, Chase. I want to congratulate you now before saying that from this point on, our training will focus a large part on honing and mastering what you experienced today."

Chase nodded, trying not to overreact out of enthusiasm. "Yeah. I think I've got a solid grip on how Risima works now!"

"Already? Just like that?" Olivia thought to herself. She cleared her throat. "Fire Risima is a rough power to fully master. It's a very destructive Energy—it is extremely powerful, even for an amateur powerful and can be used in all sorts of ways. There are several layers to mastering Risima, whether it be Earth, Wind, or Fire. This is only the very beginning of your blooming."

Miss E turned to look over her shoulder toward the pool. "But understand this, Chase: The power resonating in your body comes with a toll. I won't give the whole 'With great power comes great responsibility' speech. I think you already know that much."

Chase shook his head seriously. "Yerp!"

Miss E continued. "*But* also understand what your body will demand of you in your pursuit to mastering Fire. You must train hard. You have to imagine a flame in your mind and how you *want* that flame to behave."

Chase was confident with himself. "Right. Gotcha!"

But Miss E wasn't finished. She emphasized her next point carefully: "You *must* stay sharp—and *focused* on that flame. And you must stay calm whenever you decide to stream your Energy, okay? You need to understand that as a Fire Rasrim, *you* have the ability to control a dangerous part of nature without any help or anyone to hold your hand. There will be no one to tell you how to use your powers." She took a breath.

"All I can do is guide you there. Do you really understand the importance of all this?"

"Yes. Well, I think so," he said, scratching his head, "but…what would happen if I didn't do all that?"

Olivia thought to herself for a moment, trying to phrase her thoughts.

"Without a clear mind when using Risima, you will *never* be able to control it properly."

Chase squinted. Sure. That made sense. But did it mean anything beyond that?

Olivia took a deep breath.

"Every time you attempt to stream or manipulate Energy, you have the potential of misdirecting its traversal due to a variety of factors. It could be a bad estimate of distance, an obstacle in your way, an opposing force colliding or clashing with yours, or even bad temperament."

Chase rubbed his chin, nodding slowly.

"I'm following so far."

Olivia continued.

"When this happens, you will be manipulating Energy that you have not fully taken control over, which leads to a *discharge* of Risima energy, which you *cannot* control. Discharging Energy is dangerous. You could unwillingly lose control of yourself and destroy everything around you. In some cases, discharging Risima can even be fatal."

Chase's eyes slowly began to grow wide, his mouth hanging open.

"*Fatal*, you said?"

"You *cannot* afford to discharge Fire Energy out in public without any exceptions. I will take it upon myself as both a teacher but also your guardian to train you as best I can to ensure you can control your powers before you learn the hard way what a serious discharge looks like *and* feels like."

Chase gritted his teeth. He had already done that in the chamber. *That* was why his eye began to bleed.

Fortunately, bloody eyes were only the very beginning of a discharge.

Olivia realized she had been a little harsh. She suddenly had a bright smile, one that made Chase feel warm inside. "But I trust you, Chase, and I always will. You have a fiery spirit, and so it's only natural that you were born with the abilities you have. I will never doubt you or your capabilities."

Chase looked down at the ground, trying to hide his smile from Miss E.

He needed to be serious right now.

"I will do my best to master Fire and keep my power under control." He lifted his head and looked at her directly. "I promise you that."

Miss E slowly nodded. She looked relieved. She clapped her hands and then folded them.

"Good!" And then she instinctively turned to the pool again, trying to remember something else she had forgotten. They had both stood there for a moment, staring at the surface of the pool water.

Miss E. glanced at Chase and then walked over to the pool as if to signal to him that it was Lance's "turn."

Chase scratched his arm. "Uh, right! I forgot all about Lance."

Chase skipped beside Miss E, who had been watching her step as she inched closer to the pool.

Together, they stood as close as they could to the edge of it, looking down into the water.

"So how long has he been in there, like ten minutes?"

Miss E turned to Chase. Her expression was neutral.

"You were in that blast chamber for fifty minutes. Lance was in the pool for an hour."

Chase felt a jabbing pain in his gut. He felt as if he lost his ability to breathe.

"A-an hour? How?"

Miss E sighed. "Lance is…well…" Miss E rubbed the back of her head. "It's Lance. He's on his way."

"But he didn't do what I did yet, did he?"

"Not quite." Miss E's eyes focused on Lance. She noticed that the water beside Lance had been a darker shade of blue than the rest of the pool. It was as if Lance had created an aura around his body. Miss E put her hand on his chin and observed more of the pool.

She peered into the water with an analytical expression, taking notice of the water level, and even the waves forming within it.

"I see…"

But Chase had been paying close attention to her reaction.

"What's that?" he asked.

"Lance found Risima shortly after he got into the pool. He's getting a feel for Water Risima. I *think* he's using the pool to infuse what Energy he can to study how it's impacting his body."

She peered closer into the pool, but was cautious not to get too close, just in case.

"That's just a guess, though."

"Right. Yeah. That's what he would do alright."

She began biting her lower lip. But as Olivia began to think about Chase's experience, she couldn't help but think that something very similar might happen with Lance. "But I haven't seen him actually *stream* Water Risima from within the pool."

Miss E began making her way back to the center console, making sure to quickly wink at Chase, who couldn't help but anxiously stare into the pool at what Lance would soon do. "Unless he's hiding something from us, you've got him beat there!"

Chase closed his eyes and celebrated a small victory in his mind, holding his fists up triumphantly.

Once the two were seated at the center console, Chase watched as Miss E began typing keys into a prompt that had been analyzing Lance's vitals.

"Because I'm having Lance hold his breath, I need to monitor his brain's activities to make sure he won't suffer any brain damage."

Chase sat back in his seat, dazed. "Jesus," he said under his breath. Chase had to take a moment to understand how serious this all was. If setting himself on fire didn't do that, knowing that Lance was in this much danger certainly did.

He lifted his entire arm and pointed to the screen, concerned when he saw a graph with fluctuating readings on it. The highs and lows of this particular graph made Chase think that it was the pressure or PSI within the pool, but he certainly hoped it wasn't Lance's heart rate or oxygen levels. "He's okay, right?"

But Miss E simply pointed to a few more graphs, certain that Chase already knew that answer.

"Lance's vitals are lower what I anticipate they would be. It's difficult to really understand what a Rasrim's vital signs mean because their bodies are always interacting with the environment."

Miss E took her glasses off and wiped them with a cloth she always kept with her.

"I'm still figuring out how to measure the vital signs of a Rasrim. I mean, I never had the opportunity to study the internal anatomy of one, but with what I know, I can make *very* safe and reasonable assumptions. With that being said, I'm more than 99 percent sure that Lance is fine."

She put her glasses back on her face and then paused.

Suddenly, she burst out into laughter. Chase jumped in his seat, shooting Miss E a frantic look as if she were crazy. "What?" he said, but Miss E kept laughing, which made Chase begin to laugh as well.

"Hey, what's so funny?"

Miss E pointed to a graph on the far right side of the monitor.

"I just realized—*your* blood pressure, oxygen level, and heart rate were off the charts, Chase. I didn't know what to think at first. I was honestly stumped. I mean—well, I figured out that by being a Fire Rasrim, your body will naturally accelerate the rate that it can do almost everything it does. Your heart rate was an astonishing *220 beats per second*, that's...that's just unheard of!" She pointed to a chart displaying Lance's heart rate in large, red print.

"Now look at his chart."

Chase rolled over his words as he inched closer to the screen. He looked at Miss E.

"Thirty-one beats per minute? Is that—!"

Miss E placed her elbows on the console and folded her hands. She looked confident.

"He's completely fine. His brain is functioning normally, and there are no other signs of concern. He probably has never been this relaxed before in his life," Miss E scoffed. "Maybe that was a stretch. Who knows?"

She crossed her legs, relaxing herself.

"Lance has gone into 'Zen mode.'"

Chase squinted his eyes.

"What? Zen mode? The heck is that?"

"It's a mediation technique that Buddhist monks use to control their breathing, slow their heart rate, and relieve stress and pain from the body."

Chase looked confused.

"That sounds like a power, all right. So it's Risima?"

"Far from it! It involves *no* Risima Energy whatsoever to accomplish! When you're injured or in a stressful situation, slowing down your heart rate by taking deep breaths and relaxing your mind can make a *huge* difference."

Olivia gestured to the pool.

"And by being in a pool for *this* long, it goes without saying that you need to conserve your oxygen by keeping your heart rate down to a minimum."

Miss E tapped the screen. "That all being said, Lance hasn't even noticed he's been in there for this long."

Chase had to admit that was cool. "And he hadn't done anything yet? What's he waitin' for?"

"I think I'll give him another thirty minutes."

"So how long can most Water Rasrims hold their breath?"

Miss E looked up at the ceiling. That was a good question.

"Water Rasrims don't have to 'hold' their breaths. In fact, some Rasrims don't need food, oxygen, or water to survive at all. Of course, by living on Earth, you've just trained your body into *thinking* it does."

Chase suddenly looked excited.

"So I might be able to hold my breath forever? Of course, I'll still *eat*, but——!"

Olivia laughed aloud, clearly thrilled by the sudden interest by Chase.

"I'm not sure, Chase! It's different for every Rasrim and *their* ability to connect to nature."

Olivia turned her attention back to Lance.

"Of course, we're finding out in real time whether or not Lance does, but I'm allowing him time to see how far he gets."

Miss E sat straight and pulled up to the desk, studying the pool intensely.

"If Lance does what I'm *expecting* him to do, I'll give him another hour."

*****

Lance's body was beginning to feel extremely cold after the first twenty minutes. He had been counting the seconds in his head as they went by, although he never stopped to consider how crucial of a feat it was. In other words, he simply knew but didn't want to care.

Lance had long since felt Risima's presence in his body, although he was unsure about what he wanted to do about it.

Lance knew he could stay in the pool a while longer before he had to worry about oxygen. His lung capacity wasn't the problem. Lance was more concerned about what effect this exercise would have on his *brain*.

As Lance sat still, allowing the water around his body to flow freely, he continued keeping his mind busy and off the prospect of oxygen or stress. He knew he had felt comfortable in the pool, but that was far from the beginning of his task at hand.

Lance had a few options: He could leave the pool now knowing he *could* sense and possibly conjure Water Risima.

Or, Lance thought, he *could* begin using Water Risima right here and *now* within the pool.

Lance moved his hands from a resting position from his legs to a more central position in front of his chest, folding his hands and resting them calmly. He could once again feel the flow of Water Risima in his body, and then could stream it outward into his environment. That was straight from the book.

Lance remembered another important piece of text from his book. It read, "Risima is present within the environment, but it is only available to stream and infuse once it interacts with the individual who wishes to manipulate it." Lance knew that this meant that he would have to first feel Risima flow into his body before he could wish to use it externally. That meant, within the pool, even though he was always surrounded by water, he would have to find a balance between the Energy flowing within the water and the Energy in his body before either of them could begin communicating with one another.

Lance relaxed himself, keeping a calm, steady mind. He focused on nothing but the *idea* of Water Risima, referencing the feeling in his chest that flowed to his limbs, his mind, and then a small area around his body. He could sense the Energy there—he had already begun streaming Water Risima, although it was too insignificant to do anything with now.

This was just the starting line, Lance told himself.

It was time to begin the marathon.

With one continuous motion, not even thinking about his actions, Lance shifted his hands, opening his palms and placing them together. Rasrims could better interact with Risima using physical movements. As a result, running, fighting, or being able to move limbs in stationary positions were all supplements to feeling for Risima Energy.

Then he streamed the powerful, clustering feeling of tension— which was Risima—from his chest to his palms, focusing on the Energy's new resting position, almost like flexing the muscles in his chest and then steadily flexing his shoulder and forearm muscles in a continuous motion. It was dormant...calm. That was good.

Lance began focusing more Energy. He summoned more Risima Energy into his chest, drawing in more of the Energy from the pool water into the storage of Water Risima within his body.

The way Lance would explain this process was especially ironic. He was essentially building a small fire by taking small pieces of fire kindling and wood and adding it to a small flame. As he added more pieces, remembering to stay calm and focused, the fire would slowly grow bigger and brighter.

As for the feeling in his body as it related to the pool, Lance knew that he could control the pressure of the water in the pool, its temperature, and even at this point, create small waves and torrents of water around himself. But this still wasn't what he wanted. He needed to know whether or not he could actually "feel" Risima when he used it.

Lance centered his focus on his hands, pouring the Energy generating within his chest and defusing it to his hands. Already, he had noticed a difference. The pressure on his body was already immense, but now it had turned into a torrent of tremendous force.

The water in the pool began to sway, waves forming at the surface like in a tidal pool that crashed into the sides of the pool, spilling onto the deck. But Lance wasn't moving at all.

Lance's palms were beginning to tremble. He managed to create a vortex of Risima Energy in the balls of his palms, but the force was incredible. The energy started to push his palms apart as water began to rush in and condense together, the Risima Energy ripping water molecules from the pool into its own gravity of Energy. The pressure was increasing, and bubbles began to form in the pool, raising the temperature from seventy degrees up to ninety-two degrees Fahrenheit in just a few seconds.

At this point, Chase and Miss E's full attention was focused in the direction of the pool. They had seen the water move but at first simply thought nothing of it. But now the water was swishing in a frenzy, looking almost like an ocean experiencing a storm.

"Is Lance doing that?" Chase asked. He was hoping Miss E would shake her head and explain that it was simply a simulation for Lance to experience, but her few seconds of silence troubled him.

"Yes," she finally replied after observing the waves forming in the pool. "Lance is already beginning to use Water Risima."

Chase sighed, slouching back in his chair, tapping his finger on the deck. He was annoyed. Again! Lance had already beaten him at something he was *sure* he had finally performed well in.

But he decided not to complain.

He looked over at the pool, watching as a wave, this one several feet over the edge of the pool, crashed onto the deck, spilling water onto the training grounds.

"Maybe I should turn the barrier back on," Miss E said as she began pressing buttons. "I honestly didn't expect this much to happen today."

"It's just water," Chase mumbled.

Lance removed his palms from each other. He had felt more than Water Risima Esnergy. He could sense the entirety of Risima. He could even begin to sense Risima in the concrete and vinyl the pool was made of and even in the warm air above the pool. At first, he thought this was normal.

His concentration was at its peak. He had the essence of Risima, literally, in the palm of his hand. But now it was time to begin using it.

A surge of water formed around Lance's right hand, putting great pressure on his entire wrist.

Lance opened his eyes.

He had formed a cyclone of water around his hand. He raised it to eye level, observing the swirling pattern of Risima that manipulated the water around his arm, which Lance himself had imagined in his head. He watched it, intrigued by the small, lively patterns of particles that he had been able to observe even now in the pool. They looked like small orbs of white and light blue crystals that moved in all sorts of ways but followed the flow of Energy that Lance had wanted it to. Could Humans also see these patterns? Lance wondered.

Lance directed the Energy from his right hand to his left hand, which took a great deal of concentration to do without disrupting the existing Energy in his body.

The water in the pool had distorted itself, causing even larger, more ferocious waves to form and swish around in the pool.

Lance knew he was making a mess of the pool deck. But that wasn't important. He'd handle that in just a moment. Besides…if he could accomplish what he wanted, he just hoped that Chase or Miss E weren't standing next to the pool right now.

He then tried imagining a sphere of Water Risima in his left hand and, as it did, watched as it spiraled around in a circular motion, careful to note the relationship between Lance's concentration and the stability of the cyclone he was creating. Then he released the sphere into the water and observed it. Sure enough, with no additional Energy supplying its formation, it simply disappeared into the water, leaving Lance unable to distinguish the particles he had just been manipulating from the ones of the unbothered pool water.

Interesting, Lance thought to himself. He had noticed that there was a slightly lighter section of blue in front of him, surrounding his body. He tried to focus his Energy on that instead. The veil of water around his body was Lance's externalization of Water Risima or, in other words, the first step to streaming Risima. For a Rasrim like Chase, this would look like steam coming off his body. For an Electric Rasrim, this would be him or her creating fields of electrical Energy around themselves.

But for Lance, it was a thin blue aura of water that magnified his ability to gauge his surroundings. Lance could feel the presence of water all around him—both in the pool and even outside of it.

Closing his eyes again and emphasizing more Energy on this veil, Lance was able to "communicate" with other areas of water.

If he tried hard enough, Lance could sense a small pond of water near his house in a park he had frequented. He could feel clouds forming far in the sky above him, the water condensing within them.

If Lance focused *really* hard, he could feel several tiny locations of water scattered around him, dripping down from one spot to larger accumulating sources of water in an area below.

It didn't take Lance long to realize that he had even had the ability to sense water transpiring off plants, dew on the trees and grass, and mist in the air.

Now was the time, Lance thought. He wouldn't have much more Energy to sustain this.

Lance focused Energy into the corner of a pool, drawing Water Risima from that area of the pool to himself.

At first, Lance strained himself. He felt a jabbing pain in his left eye and winced. He wasn't doing it right.

Then Lance relaxed. He would try it another way.

This time, he started from his body, creating another small area within his chest to focus on, and streamed Water Risima from his body into an area just right in front of him. Sure enough, a small surge of water appeared, encapsulated in its own "veil," which Lance controlled. This was finally it: This was what streaming Risima was all about!

Lance directed his ball of Energy outward. It surged out, taking the shape of a thin line, the thousands of tiny particles receptive to Lance's energy. As Lance concentrated harder, utilizing the fact that he was unable to breathe—stockpiling all the mental energy he amassed to stay focused—he began imagining that the ball of Water Risima would suddenly swell in size and increase in power dramatically. But Lance quickly learned how imperative it was for Rasrims to understand their limits while also having the stamina required to manipulate Risima Energy. Lance's control over Risima was noticeable and becoming more proficient by the second, but he found the pressure on his body to grow immensely as he tried streaming more Water Risima into the pool. The ball of Water Risima began to grow unstable, causing a tremor to disrupt the tranquility of the pool. Lance was beginning to discharge Water Risima. But fortunately, he knew exactly how to approach this.

"No!" Lance urged, reminding himself that discharges were avoided when the user could restabilize Risima, "I need it to be calmer."

And so Lance closed his eyes once again, keeping his focus centered on the ball of Energy he had just created. Even with his eyes closed, Lance could still *see* his Energy. In actuality, he could feel its presence and map out his surroundings as a result. It was similar to using *echolocation*, another concept his book had taught him, but Lance had accidentally stumbled across this. He wasn't supposed to know about this until he got to Chapter 9.

Lance laughed to himself. So what? he asked. He was handling it just fine now. And that was an "advanced" technique, apparently.

Then Lance got serious. It seemed he only discharged the first orb because he was being careless. But he was still underestimating himself.

He streamed Risima without overexerting himself. He tried his best to reduce the pressure on his body without losing his concentration on the Risima he had begun controlling.

But Lance understood that this was proving to be challenging. It required him to draw even more Energy from his body. He wasn't strong enough to do so yet.

But he kept on. There was no point in stopping now. But then he had an incredible idea.

The veil of Energy in front of Lance...

What if he absorbed the Energy from this veil and streamed more Energy out into the environment in quick succession, gradually piling energy together in order to create one much larger concentration of Energy at the same time? By doing this, he would only need to alternate between infusing and streaming energy without having to exert any more Risima into the pool; he would then only need the willpower and endurance necessary to control this amount of energy at a constant interval.

Well, there was no harm in trying...except possibly drowning. Could Water Rasrims even die from "drowning"? Lance used the Water Risima he had since infused and, in small quantities, shot small streams of Energy into the pool, all the while visualizing what he was doing in his mind.

Then Lance imagined flinging the Energy outward, using them to stick to the corners of the pool before. *Four corners, four balls of Water Risima*, Lance thought to himself. Now it was time for the hard part.

At once, Lance connected the balls of Water Energy all together, using one additional string of Energy to do so. He opened his eyes to watch what happened. They shot across the pool seemingly ignoring friction as they left, forming streaks of Energy that stretched from each section of the pool before they met and converged at a center. After he took time to analyze what he had just accomplished, Lance reached his hand out and tried to pull the Energy back into his hand.

Obediently, the water retracted into Lance's hand, every individual particle he had taken control of found his body in an instant, almost as if they teleported to him. He could feel the Water Risima traveling back into his body.

Lance tried, once again, to stream Water Risima into the entirety of the pool to control it all, but somehow, he had messed up. The Energy he had formed suddenly dispersed outward, exploding all at once. The particles moved like bullets, spreading out all over the pool, disrupting the pool so much that the tremors cracked the material outlining the bottom of the pool. The force was tremendous; it knocked Lance backward, moving him out of his position, causing the water in the pool to splash out, at least a few gallons spilling out.

Lance fought with the discharging Water Risima, using all his strength to take the pressure. He had nearly gasped instinctively, but he forced himself to stay calm and not expend any more oxygen out of shock. "It definitely isn't twenty feet deep *now*," Lance joked to himself.

But it worked. Right before the explosion occurred, the water sloshing restlessly like it was an angry ocean in the middle of a storm suddenly came to a halt—like all of the water turned into a solid. The waves ceased. The water in the pool was all being converted into Water Risima but under Lance's control. It was water that Lance could use to do a variety of things, including absolutely nothing and instead ceasing all movement entirely.

Lance had partially succeeded in that, but he had realized something.

He had been *infusing* Energy to do this. He remembered the distinction Miss E made to him earlier. She had said that infusing Energy was redirecting it within oneself to release it all in one steady motion. Lance had done that to control the pool's violent rocking. But why did he fail when he tried it the first time? Was it too much for Lance to handle?

Lance promptly shut his eyes. It was time to find out.

Lance slowly maneuvered his body to rise from the bottom of the pool, using his arms to keep himself in place without floating to the surface. He did this as he continued infusing Water Risima, practicing how to change the amount of energy he wished to draw in and how to choose different areas he focused on streaming to. He then, and only then, noticed how tired he had become. He wanted to take a breath, to suck in as much air as he could and relax his burning muscles, but couldn't. Not just yet.

Instantly, his body became like a magnet, attracting and accumulating all of this as Water Risima swirled around Lance's body, meeting at a position in front of him in his right hand.

Streaming, Lance thought.

Then he slapped his palms together. The Energy surged throughout the pool before Lance began drawing Energy from the pool into his body.

Infusing, he said to himself.

Finally, he exploded Energy outward, streaming Water Risima from his body into the pool.

Lance understood that his options were limited when it came to using Water Risima as a weapon. Unlike Fire, which could, even with the most basic usage, unleash debasing attacks with fireballs or concentrated beams, or Earth Risima, which could create earthquakes or launch large projectiles from objects, projectiles made from Water Risima were much less powerful with the same amount of energy. However, Lance had several unique ideas about how to bypass this setback. By taking control over all the water in the pool and imagining something similar to what he would see during a tropical storm or hurricane...

Suddenly, a cyclone of water formed, spiraling down to Lance, almost as if a tornado had spawned, disturbing everything in the pool—except for Lance.

Lance held out his right hand and caught the tornado of water, manipulating it so that his palm was now the center of the Risima's source but also where it would be attracted to. Then Lance manipulated the tornado to become bigger in circumference, spanning nearly the entire width of the pool.

"This is incredible...I can *really* control water however I want to!"

Then after Lance got used to the force of the tornado, he released his Energy, letting the right feeling in his chest and hands disperse to the rest of his body and then back out into the rest of the pool with no further intention to control any of it.

Just as Lance expected, the tornado instantly disappeared. The pool remained kinetic, massive waves crashing into the ceramic tiles of the pool, proving that Water Risima, even if it was a weaker element when it came to raw power, could still produce monstrous effects when used by a proficient wielder.

But to hell with that. Lance could make Water Risima powerful as a weapon anyway. And he knew exactly how to do it. Energy consolidated within Lance's body, turning his light blue eyes a dark navy blue. With great emphasis on power, speed, and force, Lance amassed as much Water Risima as he possibly could and focused it in his hands, preparing to release it all while continuing to manipulate its trajectory well after he released it all. This was one of the advanced techniques he had been studying in his book for years. As soon as Lance gathered as much energy as he could and settled on where he would release it all, he trained his eyes on that location and fired. Exactly on cue, Lance's entire body strained under immense pressure as a loud powerful beam of Water Risima was fired from Lance's hands. The Water was almost scorching hot as it torpedoed across the pool at a ridiculously high speed before completely penetrating the concrete wall of the pool, leaving a nasty hole in the wall the size of a pickup truck.

Lance nearly laughed out.

*****

Miss E noticed that in the center of the pool there had been a spot where water had refused to travel to, as if there had been a sinkhole in the pool.

She had been confused at first.

But then a smile appeared on her face, one that she didn't even realize had been there.

"You are truly unbelievable, Lance…," Miss E whispered to herself, making sure Chase didn't hear. "How on Earth did you…"

*****

Lance felt free. He felt energized, like he could explode with Risima Energy. He felt no weaknesses. For water to be considered the weakest elemental prowess out of the nine, Lance felt *power* coursing through his body no less.

He could already imagine hundreds of ways to use his water abilities. He imagined using Water Risima to surf or deep-sea diving.

Lance knew that with such a vivid and powerful imagination, Water Risima would become his greatest strength. Water Risima required innovation to compete with other Rasrims who simply needed power and stamina to become strong. Water wasn't as strong as Fire or as fast as Electric or Wind Risima. That meant that Lance needed to focus a large part of his training on becoming as versatile as he could.

He knew he needed to learn how to defend himself as if he didn't have powers to begin with.

But there was one glaring issue: Lance *couldn't* imagine how he planned on using his powers to fight.

Osamos was a dangerous place. From the short stories that Miss E told him, he knew that the incredibly large environment on Osamos and abundance of radioactive Energy had produced massive creatures the size of skyscrapers and with the power to wreck entire cities. He knew that Rasrims themselves, having to defend themselves from these creatures, were also incredibly powerful and could use their abilities to destroy virtually anything they pleased.

But Lance also knew how most Water Rasrims fought. They concentrated their Energy into dense streams of high-pressure water to slice through their enemies. They also used water as a tool for distancing themselves from threats or as a way to contain creatures who couldn't fight in or near water.

Lance's attention turned back into the pool once he realized he had hit the bottom of the pool once more.

He found his balance and placed his feet square on the tile once more. There was still one thing he was unsure about. Now that Lance had complete control over the entire pool, did that mean he could…?

Miss E barely spoke a word. In fact, it was Chase who spoke. wondering just what Lance was up to. First, water had come up, and one massive wave had crashed into the barrier. If it hadn't been up, he was sure it would have reached the center console.

Chase looked down at his feet and took a step away from the pool, realizing that a puddle had been forming by his feet.

"He's gotta clean all that up!" Chase pouted. "I mean, look, now the pool's not even moving! Is he just messing around in there?"

"I believe he's testing his control of the pool."

"The *entire* pool?"

"I think so."

"Nah. No way."

"It's possible. Maybe he's just having fun."

Chase snickered.

"Yeah, I guess. What, is he gonna try the ocean next?" Chase joked, rolling his eyes. But then he looked down as if he had been hit with a sledgehammer. "Wait…would he really…?"

But Miss E just kept quiet, watching the gauges on her displays.

But then both Miss E and Chase suddenly felt an intense presence. The room in the air got stiff. They could feel a massive Energy approaching. Chase felt and understood it first.

But then Chase's head shot back to the pool as he felt an *intense* energy approaching. It felt like the Fire Energy he had now been able to produce, but this time, it *stung*.

Chase noticed that the floor underneath his feet was shaking. "What the—!"

Suddenly, the pool changed before their very eyes as massive amounts of water spouted upward out of the pool!

Chase watched in disbelief; it had looked like a bomb had gone off in the pool!

The sound was like being on the beach, but in a confined room, it had been an ear-shattering sound.

Chase stood up quickly, but Miss E didn't move. Again, she only watched cautiously.

"Woah! What just happened in there? *L-Lance?*"

Chase and Miss E stared forward as, a silhouette appeared from behind the water, rising up with the motion of the water.

But it was only Lance emerged from the water, bringing his body out of the water and stepping onto the pool deck, slightly hunched over and breathing normally.

All the water that had spouted from out of the pool sloshed back into the pool in one, synchronized motion.

Chase watched in bitter awe.

Lance stood up tall as he saw Chase and Miss E.

Lance took a breath as if he were refreshed.

"What's up?" Lance simply said. He had seemed as if he were a new person, his body radiating Risima Energy. Chase scrunched his nose and turned his head. "Showoff...," he mumbled.

Miss E stood up and applauded Lance.

"That was incredible, Lance!" She gestured to the pool. "You can now stream Water Risima...and with such precision on your *first* attempt!"

Lance turned back and looked at the pool once more. The water was calm, unmoving. The deck had been dry. Lance even somehow ensured that no dirt had remained in the pool. Where it had gone was a question he didn't have, but he also didn't care.

"I guess you could say I cleaned up nicely," Lance said.

Chase's face had been heating up. "Yeah, because you drained all the water off the deck. So cool. We would've made you do that, anyway!"

"Or," Lance said, holding up a finger while walking over to him, "*you* could've just blasted some Fire at all of the water and dried it that way, *right?*"

Chase scoffed. "Yeah. I could've. So what?"

Lance laughed.

Miss E answered for Lance. "I think he's asking how your training went, Chase."

"Nope. I ain't tellin'." Chase turned his nose up.

But Chase couldn't help to brag, determined to undermine how much of a jerk Lance had been acting like he was cool or something. "It went *great*, actually. Thanks for asking."

"No way! You're telling me that you actually began using your abilities too?"

Lance leaned in closer to Chase—who had moved back in bitter disgust—and observed the pattern in Chase's eyes more thoroughly.

Chase turned his face up. "The heck're you staring at, fish boy?"

Lance was enthralled with something on Chase's face, causing Chase to cringe.

"So *that's* what Risima looks like! I can see it all in your eyes!" Lance exclaimed.

Miss E felt confident that both Chase and Lance were beginning to have a solid idea of how Risima worked.

From what she had observed from her years on Osamos, young Rasrims were able to begin using their abilities shortly after *birth*. She had witnessed countless Rasrims from early stages in their lives walk into bodies of water and effortlessly stream entire reservoirs of water into new locations—or even depleting water sources all together to suit different ecological purposes.

Of course, some of these observations involved a lot of risk from her part. She learned the hard way, for example, that young Electric Rasrims spent most of their time playing during thunderstorms, using their powers to manipulate the position of ions in the air—effectively controlling the position of lightning strikes. The young Rasrims were never harmed, but they were frequently harassed by other Rasrims of the same age such as Earth Rasrims, who were never fond of all the destruction brought to the surface thanks to the carefree Electric Rasrims.

It was the Earth Rasrims, after all, who continuously streamed their Energy into Osamos to preserve the geographical properties of the planet. It was the Rasrim equivalent of farming and ecological preservation.

But Chase and Lance weren't on Osamos learning how to master their abilities with other Rasrims. They were isolated on Earth under nothing but the hypotheses and research that Miss Olivia Elementa, or Miss E, had prepared for this very moment. And they both passed their first trial with flying colors. From behind one of the many computers stationed at the center console, Olivia had a new task in mind for the two boys. This was still but the very beginning.

She carefully selected a series of prompts from her computer. It looked as if she were constructing something, or rather, editing a graphic of a digital layout of the training facility.

While she hadn't thoroughly explained this to the boys, the training facility was essentially one large 3D printer that used nanotechnology that could change a material known as *Phyopsiline* into *any* element on the periodic table. It was a very viscous liquid that had the ability to harden into a cubelike form when exposed to electrical currents—like water turning into ice.

Phyopsiline, however, had two more unique properties, which shocked physicists from around the world, so much so that it quickly became a government secret.

It could manipulate its own atomic structure by gaining or losing subatomic particles such as protons and electrons when near other elements on the periodic table. But it could also *use* these same subatomic particles to replicate itself indefinitely, both of which happened when exposed to large amounts of Gamma Radiation.

The blue tubes that Lance observed earlier were tubes full of Phyopsiline that also contained *trillions* of nanomachines, which constantly emitted tiny gamma-ray bursts throughout the entire network of tubes.

By doing this, the amount of Phyopsiline present within the tubes could be endlessly replicated when the correct number of protons and electrons were manipulated by the Gamma Radiation emitted by the nanomachines, allowing a continuous supply of materials to be constructed by the user.

The center console would then issue a construction order designated by the user, which would tell the nanomachines what the object was, how large it was, what it needed to be made of, and then began emitting the required amount of Gamma Radiation into the Phyopsiline within the tube system at various angles and distances to begin constructing the desired object.

In order to keep the process efficient and smooth, once a construction order was given, the center console would direct nanomachines to transport a specific amount of Phyopsiline from the tube system into "release capsules," which were 756 containers spread out all over the training facility in order to begin construction of and distribution of the desired object from the Phyopsiline within the tubes and into a selected section of the training facility.

And from there, small panels made of carbon fiber on the walls, floor, or ceiling of the facility would open and release the object into the room, either suspended from the ceiling or raised from a platform on the ground.

This was how the furnace was made and *even* the pool.

And that included the water within the pool.

The training facility that was designed to discreetly train and educate two alien superbeings was easily the most expensive facility on the face of the planet—and it was *all* constructed by Olivia herself. She only needed the help of a few trusted individuals to supply her the Phyopsiline.

The entire facility cost Olivia a grand total of *$728 million*, and this was but a tiny fraction of the amount of money she had earned from her other inventions.

Chase and Lance may have been super powered individuals—a fictitious concept worthy of a book or TV series in of itself—but Olivia's extremely grounded skill set and knowledge of science was so advanced, she had singlehandedly skyrocketed humankind into the future by at least three centuries.

Once Olivia gave her construction order to the center console, the room began to come alive once more, the intricate tube system rapidly transporting Phyopsiline around the facility as it changed atomic structures, creating several objects at once.

Within only seconds, a small panel near the middle of the wide and empty facility opened, and an elevated platform gently rose from the floor, holding what appeared to be a black box on it, smoke slightly rising from its faces as if it had recently been on fire.

Olivia cleared her throat, "Chase, I want you to focus on this box. This is your next test in mastering Risima."

Happily turning his attention away from the fish boy, Chase took notice of the box. It was a medium-sized box. It didn't look special or anything. The faces of the box just smoldered.

"What do you see when you look at this box, Chase? Is there anything you see *in* the box that you wouldn't normally see in another object?" Chase seemed surprised. It was such a simple request.

"Yeah. Uh, lemme look for a sec."

Olivia paid close attention to Chase's reaction and his evaluation of the box.

Chase examined the smoldering faces of the box. It was beginning to warp and lose its shape as if it were melting. But he couldn't see anything *inside* or through the box.

Chase assumed this had to do with his ability to sense Fire Risima. It made sense. Perhaps he would be able to distinguish what happened to the box or even absorb the heat from the box itself to save it from being destroyed.

But when Chase looked really hard, he could almost see what he believed were tiny particles dancing and twirling in and around the box, carried by the smoke.

And when Chase focused even harder on these particles, he could begin to notice red flashes of light coming from within the box as if he could visually distinguish the invisible forces of heat being used to burn the box.

"Huh. I think I see—"

But Chase squinted harder, partially thrilled that he was seeing *something*, but he couldn't exactly describe it yet.

"I can see particles of Risima surrounding the box. But I can't tell if the Risima is causing the box to melt or if the presence of the particles I'm seeing are an aftereffect of the box being burned."

Oliva nodded to herself, allowing a smile to form on her face. That was a great start, and a very good scientific observation.

Lance took notice of Olivia's expression. He had been reading the room the entire time, unsure of if he would be able to relate to whatever test Olivia had planned for Chase or not.

When Lance observed the box, he could easily see red and yellow particles swirling in and around the box—almost tiny embers of lights loitering around the hottest areas of the box—but to him, they seemed almost stationary, which was unlike the kinetic flowing particles of Water Risima he saw within the pool.

Lance figured out quickly that he could not see the *flow* of its Energy like Chase could because he could not use Fire Risima. When Rasrims could see Risima Energy transitioning from one area to another, it always meant that they could *interact* with the Energy in transit and disrupt its path. Otherwise, stationary particles were unable to be interacted with by another Rasrim.

Lance began to understand the relationship between Rasrims of different elements and why combat between Rasrims ended up being so destructive.

He could visualize, for example, an Earth Rasrim reinforcing a structure with Earth Risima that an Electric Rasrim would not be able to destroy with their own Energy. This was simply because they were unable to manipulate the particles of the Earth Risima that was reinforcing said structure.

The only way, therefore, to damage or disrupt the Earth Risima was to overcome it by directing an even *greater* output of Risima Energy and penetrate through the streamed collection of Earth Risima, causing the Earth Rasrim to discharge the Energy and produce a large explosion of Energy that may or may not harm the Earth Rasrim alongside the force that penetrated through.

But there was something odd about the inept ability Lance had to understand and visualize different elements without having ever *used* them.

Not to mention…how could Lance even *see* the Fire Risima? Not being able to infuse or stream it made sense, but why was a Rasrim who could not use an Element be able to *see* it anyways?

Lance sat up, partially unsure of himself. "I can see the Fire Risima too. It's similar to how Chase described it, but I can see the collection of particles in the center."

Chase sighed. "No way! You're just imagining it!"

Lance was lost for words. He knew he was interrupting, but this was an important matter. "I…I swear! I can see it!"

Olivia placed her elbows on the table, resting her chin on her knuckles.

"It's possible. I don't doubt you, Lance."

Chase groaned. "He's a fish boy! Not a Fire man!"

Olivia didn't know enough to make a definitive conclusion. Sure, there were a variety of tests she could use to determine whether Lance truly could see Fire Risima, but that wasn't important.

Some Rasrims *could* use more than one element, but Olivia needed to give Chase and Lance the tools to find out what they could do on their *own*.

So she decided to give some scientific insight.

"Your eyes act as a map," she began.

"Rasrims have an additional gland in their bodies called the *Nucerebrium*. It's located in the brain and connects to the Rasrim eye. This is one of the reasons Rasrims have the ability to locate Risima *visually*. In fact, without eyes, a Rasrim loses his ability to use and sense Risima by about 75 percent."

"Yeah, Chapter 6 in my book explains a little bit of that. It said that blindness was almost a certain death and that a Rasrim who has no color in his eye is a lost cause," Lance acknowledged.

"Which is certainly true. It explains why the iris of a Rasrim eye changes color when using or sensing different elements—it literally begins to draw in Energy from that source using the eye."

"But wait"—Chase's sudden voice snagged Olivia's attention—"if we're the ones to create, sense, and direct Risima Energy, how do inanimate objects also have it in them?!"

"Inanimate objects are a byproduct of living things. Planets are living creatures, Chase. The *universe* is a living creature. Rasrims create *usable* Risima Energy from the universe, which are simply tamed fluxes of Energy that the universe allows them to take control of."

Chase had his mouth hanging open, staring into space, confused.

Miss E held up a finger. "Allow me to elaborate. So an outpost of Risima Energy, like in the pool, is simply a site where Risima Energy exists by default. When it is left unbothered, you wouldn't even notice it. Risima Energy is just a series of particles, just like other naturally occurring elements and compounds. However, by connecting site and navigator, or Energy and Rasrim, you actually *manipulate* the flow of Energy away from its site and outside of its naturally occurring properties to use however you please."

She noticed that Lance had been catching on.

"So it could be like taking a wild animal from the wild and teaching it new tricks."

"Right. That's a very broad way of explaining it, but the concepts are there. Let me ask you this: A fire will burn on its own, but how can a fire leave its own source without assistance and without other flammable materials around?"

"It can't!"

"You see? That's one example of a Risima *site*. It will exist as it is in nature and perish in nature on its own. Of course, this is an *extreme* example where it comes down to the individual ability of a Rasrim, but in some cases, you could hypothetically manipulate fire even when underwater."

Olivia shifted her attention back to Chase, crossing her legs and moving away from the screen in front of her.

"But once you infuse enough Risima Energy, *you* can create the site yourself. When you stream Risima Energy, you take control of its essences away from wherever the site may be."

A lightbulb went off in Chase's mind. "So I have to be the site... When I was in the blast chamber, I infused Energy from the chamber and *became* the new site. Only then can I stream it back out!" Chase sat up. "You said that was one of the 'few' ways to use Risima, though. What're the others?"

Miss E sighed. "Unfortunately, not even I am advanced enough to explain the extent of Risima's usages to you. You'd have to meet another Rasrim for that."

Miss E rolled back up to her computer and entered a new construction command.

This time, Olivia would be constructing a new box with carbon alloys and other materials, but instead of manipulating the construction of the box to superheat the materials, she would be fusing *water* into the box itself.

That is to say, that the box would still remain dense on the inside. The water would become a structural component of the box, showcasing the tremendous power Phyopsiline had when it came to chemistry.

Sure enough, after the command was given, a panel opened up from the perfectly smooth and uniform-looking floor before another black box rose from the ground on a solid-gray platform.

"Now, Lance, observe the blue box now."

Lance turned and faced the box resting on a gray platform twenty feet away from him. It was just a plain blue box. The blue was a dull color on a dull box. It didn't look painted but rather stained, the color meshing to the box and its metaphysical structure. It didn't have any other characteristics or designs on it.

Suddenly, when Lance heard the clicking of computer keys from the center console, he saw that the same cannon blasted a thin Energy of white, frosty substances at the box. Once it hit the box, the substance reacted quickly, turning the box into a block of ice.

"Lance. Try to focus your Energy on the box now."

Lance didn't understand the objective at first. What was the reason behind all this? He was looking at ice. He understood it was virtually the same as water, but its bonds became crystallized and formed a new matrix of molecules and a pattern that turned water into ice.

Crystals, Lance thought. "Huh. That's new," was all Lance could think at the moment.

Lance tried to focus on the ice once again, this time, understanding that the Risima he would see would not be as open and vibrant as the Risima particles in fire.

Lance could begin to see it. By connecting his Energy to the ice, he could feel the Energy. His eyes turned a light blue, specks of white light sparkling within them.

Lance was able to outline the crystalline structure of the box. He could see Water Risima within the block of ice. At first, Lance thought the particles seemed stagnant and unmoving. Instead, he watched as various particles of Risima flowed into one another to create larger specs of Energy, which ultimately stopped moving and rested in place. Once this happened, the particle split, and the process started over again.

Water Risima maintained itself by streaming itself over and over to form ice. That was an interesting concept. If Lance manipulated the stream of Water Risima and prevented these fusions, he would interrupt its structure, turning ice back into water.

Lance tried it. He focused on two particles that slowly began falling into each other and stopped it by streaming his own Energy into the ice.

Lance watched as a small "river" of Water Risima flowed into the ice, interrupting the particles of ice from meeting. Instead, Lance's Energy pulled the particles into his stream. Overtime, the ice began to melt and turn into visible water which Lance was controlling.

In only a matter of seconds, the entire block of ice had disappeared, and Lance had about two gallons of water flowing around the box, following the same pattern it was when he had started.

Now Lance could see the particles of Water Risima entirely. He could see clusters of particles everywhere within the water, which only moved when the flow of the water was altered. In this case, they followed a synchronized pattern upward in a counterclockwise spiral.

"I can see it," Lance said. "I saw how Water Risima remains stagnant in ice but begins to move more freely in open water. In Ice Risima, the particles join together and form larger particles, but in water, I see they're clustered around each other."

"Excellent observation!" Olivia beamed.

Her expressions were as professional as they were straightforward. Lance expected more enthusiasm, but he had to remind himself that for some reason, Oliva Elementa was a woman who knew Risima better than anyone else.

Chase watched closely. Now he was in Lance's shoes. He could see the clusters of Energy but could not interpret the Energy when it moved from one position to another. Instead, he could only see and "feel" its movements. His eyes were not equipped to trace the idea of Water Risima in *movement*, only while it remained still and when he was connected to it at rest.

Chase shook his head. "Unreal," he mumbled to himself. In only a few hours, Chase and Lance had gone from thinking they knew all about Risima to learning that its basics were anything but simple. They still had some work to do.

Miss E stood up and stretched, but she was far from tired. Even so, she felt as if she had wrangled the boys' minds enough for one day.

"Water Rasrims can influence the flow of water. They can see Water Risima in action even if the site is at rest. Fire Rasrims can manipulate fire. They'll be able to see Fire Risima throughout any source of fire or heat even while it changes its properties such as temperature, surface area, color, and the like. This could technically mean Chase could begin to manipulate *extremely* hot water if he was advanced enough to manipulate the Fire Risima in the water away from the Water Risima."

She yawned. "It's not too hard to understand."

Neither Chase nor Lance said anything at first. They shook their heads in unanimous agreement.

"No. It's not that complicated," one of them replied.

Miss E stretched, rolling her words out. "Good. Because now you can practice manipulating your elements on your own. You should observe each and every occurrence and interaction you can that could influence the properties of Risima. This is how Rasrims learn how to defend themselves in battle."

Chase and Lance looked at each other.

"When it rains, Water Risima becomes more accessible in new sites. When it's sunny, Fire Risima takes its place. As Rasrims, you can control where these sites are, how rich they are with Energy, and from there control your ability to stream it back into the world."

She stood up and gently pushed her seat under the desk. "You should also practice using your energies on one another to observe what happens when two elements clash against one another. Pay close attention to these situations…and don't kill each other."

Miss E hunched over the desk and quickly pressed a few buttons. Suddenly, some of the overhead lights in the room and at the center console dimmed and went into "standby mode."

Then she began toward the elevator, turning and facing the boys as she walked.

"I'll be back at seven o'clock tonight for dinner, 'kay? Don't break anything!"

And then she boarded the elevator and disappeared behind the large metal doors, leaving Chase and Lance sitting still with blank expressions on their faces.

Chase and Lance sat still, looking at each other for what felt like hours.

"So...she just leaves like that?"

"I still have a billion questions!"

"Yeah, like, how am I supposed to study the flow of water if I *am* the cause of the flow of water? Do I study myself?"

They both sat back in disbelief.

And these were the times they remembered that they were brothers, not rivals, and not just students.

Chase nudged Lance a little forcefully, clearly trying to get on his nerves or something.

"Those were some cool moves in that pool there, *fish boy*."

"Is that what you're calling me now, hothead? What are you getting at?"

Chase rolled his eyes, hiding a smile underneath his façade.

Chase walked over to the center console, eyeing over the various controls to assemble the actual "training grounds," which included a number of preset environments designed to simulate various conditions one could expect in a real emergency.

Chase pressed a few buttons, remembering the sequence Olivia had done so.

"I think you know what I'm about to ask you."

Lance didn't even bother to hide his excitement. A wide grin stretched on Lance's face from ear-to-ear. As Lance walked over to the training grounds, he called out to Chase from behind his back.

Lance waved his brother over.

"You don't have to say another word. Bring it on, Chase! Don't hold back!"

CHAPTER 4

Sink or Stream

Three hours later

Lance crashed on his backside onto a matted floor and rolled backward as fast as he could, dodging an explosive ball of Fire as it landed next to his head. Lance had nearly been caught in a flame, hearing the proofing sound of Fire toss embers across the floor.

Lance shot up, noticing his next instinct was to create a wall of Water Risima to protect himself from another attack. Although it had only been a few hours since Lance took control over Water Risima, it was only getting easier for him to use. His agile body, incredible level of intelligence, and vivid imagination showed him that Risima was like a tool of art: the only thing holding him back was his belief in his abilities.

Wasting no time, Lance brought his hands up as he streamed Water Risima to the palms of his hands and shrouded his body with his Energy. Drawing power from his core site of Risima, Lance manipulated as much Water Risima as he could into manifesting a shield made of water, which protected his entire body before another ball of Fire crashed into it.

He had barely made the shield in time as he was barraged with attacks. Lance tensed himself, the force from the Fire attacks produced by Chase pushing him back along the floor of the large training area. It was obvious that Chase was unnatural using Fire Risima. He constantly fumed with energy and excitement. Using a physically demanding element like fire came easily for someone like Chase.

Quickly, seven more balls of Fire the size of bowling balls flew at Lance from two different angles, forcing Lance to pivot and move his shield of water from left to right. Lance watched as his wall of water sizzled, the blue Water particles clashing with the intensely red Fire particles, causing both of them to explode in bright, beautiful orbs of light as they collided against each other. Lance had to make sure he streamed more Water Risima into his water wall, or Chase's Fire particles would still hit Lance after the explosions. *This is fine,* Lance thought, *I still have plenty left. Maybe I should step it up if he keeps this up.*

But before Lance could find an opening, rushed in from out of nowhere, using the smoke that had covered the room to his advantage. Chase held his fists out, thrusting it out to strike Lance.

Chase's entire body was glowing.

A reddish aura created a misty presence around him, which sizzled as he moved. The sizzling sounded like grease popping on a hot stovetop but only with a much hotter temperature and a crazy amount of grease. His eyes had also become brighter, showcasing the amount of Risima Energy he had generated. He had to ensure that he was maintaining his output of Fire Energy; otherwise, his attacks would be dull and weak, especially in a situation like this. Lance's Water would easily counter Chase's Fire. And so he had to mix it up.

But Lance was quick. He used Water Risima well and was very agile in his movement. Chase's palm thrust missed Lance, who streamed Water Risima into his leg and threw a solid kick into Chase's stomach, causing him to fall and roll back in pain.

But Chase was tougher than that. During the fight, he realized that he could use Fire to propel his movements. It had been a split-second decision that reaped huge benefits, but it took a tremendous amount of Fire Energy to sustain.

As Lance tried to trap Chase by submerging him in water—effectively securing a victory—Chase thrust his arms against the ground and released a massive amount of Fire Energy, blasting him off the ground and away from Lance's attack.

Lance looked up at Chase, who managed to propel himself into the air by about fifteen feet in less than a second.

Chase laughed at him, waving his hand, Fire Risima and smoke igniting the air around him. "Nice try!" he yelled down to Lance.

Lance scoffed. If Chase stayed in the air, Lance was limited on the number of attacks he could use.

But then he had an idea.

Right before Chase landed, Lance concentrated a large amount of Energy in his hands, focusing on the site of the Risima he felt all around his body and gathering it with his hands. At once, he flung his right hand outward horizontally, twisting it so that his fingertips had been facing Chase at the last second.

Water Risima accumulated in the palm of Lance's hands and flew out like a saucer at the speed of sound, taking up a much greater portion of the energy Lance infused thus far.

Chase gasped, his body falling back in the air as he nearly stumbled out of shock. *Damn! He's using the same technique I came up with! And he's accurate with it too!* Chase yelled in his head, watching as the saucer came slicing through the air toward his body.

He released his Energy and began plummeting toward the ground, hoping that the disc would miss him.

But Lance had guessed this. He had thrown the disc at Chase's body in such a way that it was impossible to dodge in midair. It was just the right size and right speed. This would put Chase out of commission but not severely hurt him.

Chase gritted his teeth once he realized he was bound to be hit. At the last second, he yelled out as he spun his body 360 degrees in the air, focusing Fire Risima in his legs.

At the right time, Chase engulfed his leg in Fire and kicked the disc, causing it to explode in a sizzling firework and evaporate into steam.

Chase hit the ground hard, clearly out of breath. Chase lowered his head and punched the ground, trying to recover as quickly as he could.

Lance sat back for a moment, trying to gauge his options.

But he knew something was wrong.

Lance stood up, noticing that Chase had still been kneeling on the ground, breathing heavily. After a brief moment, he got furious with Lance.

"Why'd you stop?" he asked, panting.

Lance stood up straight, realizing that he could feel Chase's Energy levels. Before now, he had thought the intense heat he had felt was from Chase's attacks, but as the room suddenly felt cooler, he realized this was Chase's Energy levels depleting.

"You're tired. We should call it here."

"No way! I'm fine!" Chase pushed himself to his feet and stretched his arms out, locking eyes with Lance, who seemed to be in pristine condition. They were both determined to win. "Let's keep going. I want to keep fighting."

Lance huffed. "All right. Just do yourself a favor and go easy on the Fire."

But Chase's response, of course, was even more Fire.

Before Lance could think of anything else, Chase managed to create an explosion of Fire Risima in a wide area around Lance, a ring of Fire engulfing the perimeter and igniting everything in its way. It was able to prohibit Lance from moving in any direction, confining him to one area. That was payback. And it was genius. Lance scanned the ring of fire around him with careful eyes, deducing hundreds of strategies that Chase could utilize with this style of attack, and did his hardest to find counterattacks for them all. Lance's mind played countless scenarios in microseconds like he was waiting for his opponent's move in a game of Chess.

Lance jumped into the air, trying his best to move back as the entire floor had been engulfed in powerful flames.

Lance noticed a searing pain shoot up through his leg. He had been hit in the leg, but he continued moving backward after his feet hit the ground to evade the follow-up explosions. Chase's explosive power was already witnessable. It would be hard to defeat Chase if he had more stamina.

Lance recovered quickly, but he realized that Chase had moved about twenty feet in less than a second, Fire quite literally in his eyes. For a moment, Lance was startled. But then he took a deep breath, found his site of Water Risima, and made a play.

Chase went in for a rush-tackle preparing to infuse Fire Risima to fuel his next attack, but Lance had seen it coming. Lance could use Water Risima to sense movement around his body, including his blind spots. If he honed in on the general flow of Risima Energy around Chase's body, he could use his abilities to predict what would happen next. Chase had been watching Lance, making sure to look around himself for anything that could have been a sneak attack. If there was a puddle of water lying around, Lance could theoretically use it as a weapon and create virtually anything he wanted from it. He found himself growing nervous when he noticed Lance had just been standing still, waiting for Chase.

Chase raised his hands, preparing to conjure more Fire Energy— but Lance's next move knocked Chase off guard. With an incredibly quick wrist flick, Lance blasted Chase with water making sure to soak the area around Chase with puddles of energized water, causing him to stumble backward and step into one of the foot-deep puddles from the blast.

This time, Lance was on the offensive. He burst off into a sprint, moving toward Chase as he began taking into account where each section of water was compared to Chase, using this information to calculate a plan.

As he moved, Lance's eyes scanned the room, mapping five specific sections of the room around Chase, all within five feet of Chase's body. At the same time, he focused energy on each of the spots, streaming his Risima Energy to make those sections of the room the new "sites" of Water Risima.

Chase didn't know what Lance was planning. Although he quickly recovered from Lance's strike and fired back at him, he had no idea that this was exactly what Lance was counting on.

Of course, as Chase had been moving, Lance used his excellent sense of perception and mathematical mind to keep his placement of his water sites equal to Chase's position in the room, making sure to build up energy the more Chase moved out of range from the puddles.

Then with one burst of Energy, Lance manipulated five large waves of water to rise from the sites and attack Chase at every angle, torrents of water crashing into him relentlessly. Chase instantly put the brakes on, sliding to slow himself down and at the same time dodging the first two waves of water surging from where the puddles were. He was amazed at the speed and force they had to them Lance flicked his hands left and right, manipulating the Water Risima to strike Chase's body with an equal and overwhelming force of Risima, competing with the Fire Risima surrounding Chase's body. Although Chase's energy alone was strong enough to destroy some of the waves approaching him before they struck, Chase found himself unable to defend his entire body while preserving the Risima he infused to retaliate.

Chase had gotten frustrated, unable to decide what to do. He brought his hands up and shielded his face, noticing that every time he took a step, a torrent of water would crash into him, forcing him to move in the opposite direction. If he continued streaming Fire Risima around his body in this state, he would likely discharge it all.

Chase tried to yell out but had gotten water in his mouth. He became furious. The water had been preventing Chase from concentrating on streaming his Energy properly.

The waves of water continued attacking, but Chase didn't falter. It only caused his body to erupt with more uncontrolled Fire Energy.

Chase had enough. Angrily, he placed his hand together and unleashed a beam of Fire at a random spot in the room.

Lance winced and stopped in his tracks as the beam of Fire charged straight for him. "D-damn!" he yelled out.

Lance had to act quickly; otherwise, the blast would likely leave a hole straight through his body.

Lance put his hands together and infused a large amount of Energy in them, accumulating as much Risima as he possibly could.

Lance flicked his head up, his eyes burning bright blue. He gritted his teeth hard, Energy coursing through his body.

Once the time was right, he unleashed the Energy he had stored into a jet stream of water, colliding it into the beam of Fire headed for him. The blast had only been a few feet in front of Lance, but as the two energies collided, a massive explosion in the center caused both to stumble as ripples of now untamed Risima Energy surged throughout the room in a flash, electrifying the battlefield.

Chase continued pouring energy into his attack once he noticed that Lance dug his foot into the ground and resisted the powerful explosion. In fact, Lance managed to manipulate the stray Risima Energy and took it as his own, amplifying the power of his Water Risima blast that was beginning to overpower Chase's blast.

Chase smirked.

Neither one of the boys stopped. Both flooded their bodies with as much Risima Energy as they could.

Lance spread his feet and gripped harder, straining as he focused more Water Risima into the blast.

He had a sly smile on his face. His heart was pounding and his muscles felt as if they were on fire. The intensity of this fight added another level of excitement to everything that happened today.

The entire room began to shake, wailing with massive amounts of Energy, but Chase and Lance only poured more Energy into their attacks, hoping the other would submit.

After a few seconds, their attacks had become so large and destructive that the center of the collision began discharging streams of untamable Energy as the two elements began to mix in a frenzy.

A stray ball of Energy crackling with untamed Risima Energy crashed into the training room, setting some of the room on fire and drenching other parts in scalding-hot water.

Lance grunted. Water Risima did not stand up to Fire Risima in terms of raw power. Lance had to be smarter than that. He tried shifting his feet, getting a feel for if he was able to move out of the way. But Chase's power was increasing at an alarming rate, and Lance's grip on his Energy slipped. He realized that streaming Energy this massive required utmost focus. He couldn't afford to break his concentration.

Moving out of the way now was impossible. Chase's beam of Fire had become so large that it would catch Lance no matter how fast he rolled out the way. Chase knew he had the advantage.

Lance struggled. His left eye was pulsating and his head was spinning. He couldn't even breathe due to the immense pressure on his body. He focused hard, trying to come up with a plan. If this kept up, he'd simply have to yell to Chase to stop and accept defeat.

But he wouldn't let that happen. Not today.

Suddenly, Lance's eyes flashed to a spot on the floor a few feet away from him. Water Risima had been guiding him somewhere, reminding him it was his ally. Even if Lance was struggling to continue streaming Water Risima, he was always able to sense new sites around him.

Lance tensed up when he noticed he was looking at a large puddle of water lying on the floor.

Lance smiled. This would work.

Lance turned his attention back to the destructive beam of Energy in front of him. Once he felt comfortable with it once more, he focused a smaller portion of his control on the puddle of water, manipulating it to rise from the floor.

Suddenly, Lance's body jolted, aching in pain. His eyes throbbed. He felt fatigued. It was too much to handle.

But Lance decided to risk it anyway.

In one move, he surged all the Energy he could into the puddle, creating what Lance manipulated to look like a large, intimidating beast with the face and body like a dragon made of water to emerge from the puddle and crash into Chase. At the same time and with hardly enough strength to continue standing, Lance threw himself out the way, using his core and leg muscle to lunge several feet to the left and onto the ground.

The Water dragon crashed into Chase's arm, causing his control of the Fire to slip. But the large collection of Risima Energy caused massive amounts of Risima Energy to erupt across the entire room, crashing into the walls and the ceiling and left a crater the size of a bus on the floor.

Lance gasped out. He was lightheaded, hanging on to his consciousness. His entire body shook and for some reason, he couldn't even infuse any more energy. He was completely drained. He had only learned to use Risima today, so it was easy to say he far exceeded his limits.

Lance examined the room, still ready to fight even though his Energy reserves had been depleted, leaving the center of his body sore and like it had been dried out. Trying to infuse more Risima only caused Lance's body to tense up in excruciating pain.

Still, he pushed himself up to his knees. He couldn't move, his body aching in every area.

He nearly called out to Chase but reduced himself to a syllable of the first word he was about to say as he saw Chase sit up, completely unscathed from the massive explosion. He had been bleeding from the mouth, but had been smiling, laughing out loud.

"That was insane…this dude made a *dragon!* On day one?! Maybe Rasrims *are* gods!" Chase laughed to himself, brushing his shoulders off.

Chase, overcome with determination, rose to his feet, but his eyes had been shifting from a bold red to a weak orange. Somehow, he still had enough stamina to heat his body up once more.

Lance put his guard up, ready for more.

Chase twisted his neck, a sly smile on his face.

They both remembered their positions and gathered more Risima Energy, infusing as much as they could for the next volley of attacks.

Without a moment's warning, Chase and Lance suddenly rushed forward, letting out battle cries, Chase's hands glowing red and exploding with Energy, and Lance's body emitting a dark-blue color, water swirling around him.

Ding!

Chase and Lance stopped, screeching to a halt, nearly bumping into each other as they both turned to face the far side of the underground bunker. The doors to the elevator slid open, a figure stepping out into the light of the room.

"Oh sh——!"

"She's back already?"

On cue, Miss E immediately took notice of Chase and Lance standing in the center of the room, almost like they were greeting her!

"It's 5:30! I'm here ahead of schedule! How are you two holding u—" Miss E stopped as she got further into the training facility, looking at the two boys, bloody and bruised, Water and Fire pouring out of their bodies as an energized stream, almost as if they were about to explode with power.

"Up." Her voice faded as she took a slow stride into the room.

"Uhhh," Lance began, looking at Chase, worried they were in for an earful and a night full of intense lectures, but before they could say anything more, Miss E Put her hands on her hip.

Chase gulped.

"Three hours, three hours, and this is what I find myself walking into?" But as Miss E stood still with an expression that caused the boys to brace themselves for an attack that was sure to kill them, she suddenly burst out into a wild, almost-joyful fit of laughter. It had been a pleasant laugh, one that caused Chase and Lance to feel even worse about it all. "Should I have honestly expected anything else?" Miss E's voice echoed throughout the large facility.

Chase was the one to speak. "I started it!" He raised his right hand high.

Lance nudged him. "You really think you'll get brownie points *now?*"

Miss E walked over to the center console. She wiped specs of dust and ash off the various machines.

"Thank goodness you didn't touch any of this!"

"We had the barrier up. I figured out how to disable it from the outside," Lance said.

Chase nodded. "Yeah, we thought ahead. For once!"

"There must've been a storm inside there then! You got dust all the way over here!"

Chase coughed, soot falling out his hair. "Did we? I didn't notice," he said sarcastically, covering his remark with another poorly timed cough.

"Well, tell me about it already! What're you waiting for?"

Lance rubbed his shoulder. "It wasn't all that much, to be honest. We had already been practicing streaming our energies before Chase *suggested* we spar to learn how to stream Energy on the fly."

Chase giggled to himself. "I mean...we did it." He shrugged as he stretched his legs out. It was miraculous that Chase had already recovered. His wounds had already closed, and Lance swore that he noticed Chase's eyes begin to glow a darker red.

Chase rubbed his eyes. "Using Fire Risima is tough. I managed to learn how to turn my Risima into projectiles quickly, but it didn't help me much since my Energy kept depleting."

"So how did you compensate? Or did Lance take it easy on you?"

Chase shook his head. "Not at all. I stayed on the move. Whenever I couldn't stream Risima, I was building it up inside while dodging Lance's attacks."

"Excellent. We can use that as a reference point in your next lesson. You don't have to *constantly* be supplying yourself with Risima Energy in order to use it. If for example, Lance wanted to move and attack at the same time without overexerting himself, he could simply use the water from the pool as the site of his concentration and attack from there *without* infusing unnecessary amounts of Energy—"

Lance perked up, truly impressed that Miss E herself had thought of such a thing. "Yeah! That's kinda what I did!"

"*But,*" Miss E exclaimed, holding her finger up, "it's absolutely *crucial* for you both to remember to keep your Energy reserves balanced! That way—"

But she stopped once she got to the center of the room, inspecting the crater in the middle of the floor, stooping down to her knees before she rubbed her finger in it.

"You don't accidentally stream *too* much Energy and begin discharging it all..."

Chase and Lance groaned.

Chase leaned over and whispered to Lance, "Dude! I told you we should've covered it."

Lance's expressions flared up. "*Huh?* When?"

"Just now! I was doing all sorts of things to signal to you! You could have filled it with water or something!"

Lance shook his head in disbelief. "This guy...!"

Miss E. spoke to them, still hunched over with her legs bent. "Your lessons will change from this point on." She made an effort to look at both Chase and Lance before speaking again.

"I won't make either of you read or study science anymore. I trust that you two will keep up on your own studies as you see fit. You two learn too fast!"

Olivia pointed to the crater in the ground.

"It's been a little over six hours and we're *here*. I mean..." She rubbed the back of her head, clearly in awe.

Lance felt a little guilty. It was true they had progressed unreasonably fast having *just* learnt how to use their abilities, but they had wanted this for a long time! Was it really that hard to believe? And they were *boys*—rough, hard-headed boys at that!

Olivia sighed.

"What else can I say?" She laughed to herself.

"You two wonder why I waited this long to teach you how to use your abilities? Imagine what could have happened had you not matured a little first."

Chase and Lance looked at each other oddly. Where was this coming from suddenly? They had been doing stupid things *forever*!

"And no, I don't think there are other ten-year-olds who are playing with bombs and million-dollar gadgets in their underground bunker..."

Olivia brushed her hair behind her ear, keeping her appearance as sharp and intelligent as it had always been. But the boys noticed she suddenly had this look of relief on her face—as if a suspicion of hers had cleared up or something.

"I suppose what I'm trying to say is—I anticipated this."

Chase tilted his head. "No way! You really *expected* us to do this? It all happened on a whim!"

"Most Rasrims begin using their abilities from *birth*, remember? All you two needed was the key to the engine and a little...room to

drive, no?" Olivia turned and gestured to the sheer size of the training facility.

"And it made it better knowing there was no mean old lady
breathing down your neck the whole time, yeah?"

Lance nearly gagged. She wasn't joking—she *did* anticipate all
of this! She had full confidence knowing that she had left the boys
without enough material to test their abilities out on each other. It
was…bold! What if they had killed each other?

Chase whistled. "You know, being a scientist and all, wasn't it
dangerous to allow us to progress as fast as we did?"

Miss E rubbed her index finger and thumb together, soot falling
off of them.

"Not in the slightest. You now understand what your strengths
and weaknesses are. You two also have developed hobbies that involve
many things that I've taught you. We've accomplished a *lot* over the
years. I would not limit your progression to purely the events that
comprised today. This was more of a *final test* than just one of my
stupid lectures."

That struck Lance in an odd way. He never considered what
he had done up until this point in his life "progression." There was
always *something* missing from his life, and today finally showed him
what that was.

"From now on, I want you to use everything you've ever learned
and combine all of skills and talents and *master* your powers. And
you'll do it all down here together."

Lance tapped the toe of his shoe on the ground, holding back a
smile he felt he didn't deserve now.

Lance knew that he had a lot of work to do—no, they *both* did.
But Lance felt that as the older twin, he would have to step up even
more to ensure that he and Chase became strong.

When Lance looked back up, he noticed that the bruises on
each other had healed already. Chase's scar on his shoulder had been
gone.

Lance rubbed the side of his face where he had scraped it rolling across the ground and realized that the cut that had been on his

cheek had closed and disappeared. And his Risima felt just about replenished.

Miss E cleared her throat, taking control of the environment once more. "I can see here that you generated quite a bit of Energy within the facility," she said, typing buttons and pulling up various displays.

She pressed a button, and a holographic display of the two boys appeared in front of them, floating in midair. It was an image from just moments ago, when the two had fired beams of Energy at one another.

Miss E cleared her throat, the two boys oblivious of what was to come.

"*This* was impressive, but also *extremely dangerous!*" Her sudden outburst, that of a wild beast or even a demon, carried itself across the entire room, sending chills down Chase and Lance's spins.

Miss E suddenly had a frown on her face. "This here?" Miss E began, pointing to the blast that had developed in the center of the collision. "That's the equivalent of fifty *kilotons* of TNT!" she exclaimed starkly.

"Oh, sick!" Chase grinned. "Is that a lot?"

Lance blinked.

He had sat back, tried to visualize some numbers in his head, and with a cold chill taking control of his body, Lance slowly realized that *fifty kilotons of TNT would destroy an entire city.*

Miss E sat down in her chair, folding his hands together, thinking hard.

"I'll need stronger materials…," she began.

"No…we'll help." Lance said sternly, walking over to the center console.

Miss E denied Lance. She shook her head. "No. You'll focus on training. You need to learn how to be less reckless and more productive with your powers. Your Water Risima can be *much* more lethal and powerful with much, much less the destructive force behind it! I feel bittersweet about this, that's all. I mean, in only one day, you learned how to stream Risima. That's great. Seriously."

"But," she said, raising a finger, "continue to practice sensing Energy and knowing how to put down your opponents with minimal collateral damage. You should be able to visualize the effects of the power you conjure. You don't want to kill each other, right?"

Chase shrugged. "I dunno. Maybe?"

Lance kicked him.

Then they started chuckling, prompting a death glare from Miss E, which struck them to remain still.

"Tomorrow, I'll teach you how to *infuse* Risima on a large scale. That way, you'll emphasize durability and stamina more so than offense and firepower."

She swiped her finger on her display skipping through sections of a playback of the two boys using their elements in hand-to-hand combat.

"We'll also have to make sure your martial arts skills are up to par. Lance, you've gotten sloppy!" Miss E said playfully.

Even though she had been joking, her words struck Lance hard. Chase laughed, mocking him.

"Chase, you did well, but your stamina needs improvement. Lance outlasted you in both stamina and technique. Had he been sharper and more offensive, he would have had you when you were in the air here. That was a good idea, Lance, streaming your Energy out in thin slices to create a water disc. Dangerous but practical. And, Chase, for a Fire Rasrim, you compensated well by switching between offense and defense." Lance snorted. Chase let out a long groan.

Miss E swiped to the end of the playback and spread her fingers out on the display before quickly bringing them together in the center, shutting off the playback and ending the holographic screen in front of the boys.

"Just...lay off the angry counterattacks *when you are training with your brother,*" she said.

Miss E sat up with a renewed energy.

"That's enough for today! Let's go have dinner!"

*****

A man whimpered in excruciating pain as he lay against the side of an armored vehicle, trying his best to stay quiet and remain hidden.

He sobbed uncontrollably when he heard other people scream out in terror before what could only be described as the gut-wrenching sound of a sharp object moving through the air at high speed caused the man to close his eyes and began praying.

"Forgive me, Lord! Forgive my transgressions and my outlandish sins! Forgive my disobedience and ignorance!"

The man balled up, wrapping his arms around his knees as tears streamed down his face, blood spilling down from his arms and shoulder.

But at this point, he knew he was dead. He didn't even bother running.

The man continued sobbing before he felt a cold chill fill the air, causing his teeth to begin chattering.

"*He* was nearby."

The man nearly screamed out, on the verge of begging for mercy. But he knew that would only bring him to his execution even sooner.

And besides, there was no point begging a demon for mercy.

The man slowly opened his eyes, wondering if perhaps he was spared. He heard the faint sound of sirens and a helicopter in the background, but then he realized that the police and ARF were a lost cause. Not even the Division could prevent what was bound to happen. This demon could not be stopped.

Foolishly, he fumbled around with his arm, twitching uncontrollably as he dug around for something in his right pants pocket.

He stopped when he felt what he was looking for: a radio.

The man checked his surroundings, his face trembling as his heart rate increased dramatically. He could hardly see or think straight—the adrenaline in his body made it impossible to focus. Nothing he had witnessed throughout his thirty year career at the Division and CIA could prepare him for this.

The man swallowed hard. He didn't see anything.

The awful sound metal and flesh being torn apart also ceased. For a moment, the man believed he had been hidden.

But he had been mistaken.

The man lifted the radio up to his face and squeezed a button on the side. There was static on the other end, but the man spoke anyway.

"M-mayday! This is Control One calling in from point One-Zero-Nine-Delta! My team was ambushed by the target and suffered heavy casualties! No visuals! Send immediate backup from HQ ASAP! Again, requesting immediate b—"

The man froze, stricken with fear when he heard a heavy object crash into the ground just a few feet from where he was.

The man trembled, clutching the radio near his mouth as tight as he could, not daring to make a single sound.

After ten or so more seconds, the man slowly shifted his body and lifted himself up to the window of the armored vehicle he was against—trying to get a view of the other side.

The man looked through the window.

The sight was devastating. There were at least fifteen or so bodies scattered around in the street, completely mutilated. Some were missing limbs; others had their heads severed.

But the worst sights were those of the *supernatural* occurrences he had seen.

There were several large pikes made of ice sticking up from the ground, almost as if they had formed underneath the crust of the Earth and penetrated through the crust like a stalagmite.

And at the tip of these spikes of ice were *bodies* pierced like a kebab, blood dripping down on the streets below.

The man could hardly look.

He started to turn away from the sight and was about to continue speaking into the radio.

But when he finally turned back around and leaned against the armored vehicle, his eyes immediately noticed a person standing in front of him.

The man screamed at the top of his lungs and squeezed the trigger on his rifle as hard as he could, firing several rounds at the demon standing in front of him. But it was pointless as the man ran out of the ARF bullets and was now firing standard 7.62 × 51 mm ammunition. He watched in bewilderment as every single bullet he fired bounced right off the body of the demon, who was watching the man with intense, cold-blooded eyes. Blood was dripping from the demon's hands.

The man scrambled, using all his energy to get up.

As soon as he was on his feet, a hand seized him from his shoulder and dragged him to the ground with so much force his shoulder had been dislocated and nearly removed from the socket entirely.

His body hit the ground hard, the wind knocked out his chest.

The man wheezed, trying his best to stay conscious.

He fumbled around for a weapon before he saw the monster that had attacked him standing right on top of him.

The man cried out like a baby.

"P-please! I beg you! Don't kill me! Just let me go! Please!" But the being standing on top of him said nothing. It just stood there and watched the man grimacingly.

It took two steps around the man's body, getting a look at the man on the floor from a better angle.

The man held his hands up, shielding himself from the demon in front of him.

"T-they had no right! They shouldn't have imprisoned you like that! It wasn't right! I-I would never do such a thing, believe me! I didn't even know you existed until they told me! I had nothing to do with it at all!"

The being twisted its head, analyzing the words the man had just said.

But when the being suddenly raised its right hand and a misty white aura began appearing in the palm of its hand, the man screamed out once more.

"P-please! Don't do this! P—!"

Another horrible crashing sound was heard as a giant spear of ice was lodged into the man's skull, piercing straight through the man's mouth.

He died instantly.

The being sat there for a moment, staring at the lifeless corpse on the ground in front of it.

"In-pris-on-ment?" A low, raspy voice tried to replicate what it had heard the man say.

The being watched the man, curious to understand what he had meant.

He was never imprisoned. He had always been free.

But now he would simply show the world what *he* had been exposed to. All the pain, misery, and suffering he endured, he would make sure each and every single Human on Earth understood just as well as he had.

The being turned away from the dead man and began walking through the streets once more.

But as the being walked and hunted down the Humans who had ironically been hunting *him* down, he never once noticed two more beings watching him from way off in the distance.

*****

These new individuals watched carefully, studying what he had been seeing closely.

"Is that him?" one of the voices asked.

"Yeah. He escaped from an experimentation facility only an hour ago."

"And you're sure that he has both? Risima but also *the Mark?*"

"I'm positive. Otherwise, I wouldn't have picked up the reading in the first place."

"And you think that…what was his name again?"

"He goes by 'Chile.' He's an Ice Rasrim."

The first man nodded. "Ah, yes. I see. What a magnificent prowess to be able to call upon."

"Indeed. He's the first one I've ever seen who can use ice."

"Daxxon," the first man began, "why did you bring this Rasrim to my attention?"

But this was merely a test. The man *already knew*. In fact, unbeknownst to his ally Daxxon, *he had staged* Chile's escape in the first place.

"Because it could go along with our plan, Master Melterai," Daxxon replied as if he were confused.

The first man, commonly referred to as Melterai, continued watching Chile.

Even now, he had been using his Ice Risima abilities to ruthlessly maul and massacre several of the individuals sent to capture him. He had been able to manipulate the environment around him with such fearsome displays of power: turning entire streets and buildings in thick ice and was even able to create weapons in thin air made of near impenetrable ice.

But what stuck out to Melterai the most was Chile's cold, lifeless eyes. He had the eyes of a killer, a ruthless monster that was set out on a path of revenge and destruction.

Melterai understood that feeling all too well.

"Yes, of course, Daxxon. It will aid our case well, actually."

Melterai turned his head toward Daxxon but kept his focus on Chile. "Have you located the *twins* yet?"

Daxxon shook his head. "Negative. It's possible they haven't gotten advanced enough in Risima to begin using their abilities. Otherwise, I'd be able to sense and track them down."

Melterai chuckled. "Or"—his deep, menacing voice rose—"they're masking their energies."

Daxxon looked offended.

"But they're mere children! How could they already know how to mask themselves?"

Melterai continued to chuckle, turning his attention away from Daxxon.

"Go on, Daxxon. Recruit the boy. Convince him that we're the 'good guys.'"

Melterai stopped once he reached the edge of the building he was standing on.

"And once you do, bring him to the location I tell you."

Daxxon squinted.

"Yes, sir, but how will you tell me if you're about to—"

Melterai held up a hand, silencing Daxxon.

"*You will know* where to find me, understood?"

Melterai turned and faced Daxxon, his sinister appearance striking Daxxon as hard as it always did.

"Perhaps you'll hear a *whisper* in the depths of your mind. Start there."

And then right in front of Daxxon's eyes, Melterai disappeared, leaving no trace behind whatsoever.

Daxxon stood there, looking in the direction he had last seen Melterai before he bitterly turned away and directed his attention back to Chile, who had slain another eight people and destroyed several armored military vehicles in mere seconds.

"Melterai...," Daxxon mumbled to himself. "Just what the hell are you *really* planning?"

*****

When Chase and Lance finished their day and decided to call it after a long, eventful experience of sorts, Miss E left the two boys for something she said had to do with her "work" promptly. She made the boys some dinner and made sure they had what they needed, but she left as if she were in a hurry for something and didn't call back for the rest of the night.

She didn't usually leave the boys alone at night, but today was different.

Lance thought nothing of it. But while he made a comment on it as soon as her car pulled out of the driveway and left, Chase lingered behind, suspicious of her sudden departure.

Lance left the kitchen, citing his need for some sleep, but Chase stopped him before Lance could leave the foyer and up the steps, stopping at a table with plants on it that needed to be watered soon.

"What's up?" Lance asked, as if he were in a hurry too.

Chase scratched the back of his head. "We just figured out how to use our powers today, and Miss E's leaving us *again*. You don't

139

find that odd? She's done this twice now! Wouldn't she expect us to literally burn down the house or something?"

Lance brushed some dust off the table as he turned to view Chase's concerned face. Both of their eyes had faded into dimly lit reds and blues, but they still felt as energized as before. Perhaps once a Rasrim unlocked the ability to use Risima, it was a skill that never faded but one that only got better overtime.

"Like I said, she's probably meeting someone again."

"You don't think she'll tell someone about us, do you?"

Lance was puzzled. He couldn't believe his brother would ask such a question. "Seriously?" he replied. "You really think she would?"

"I just don't find it convenient that we have a million-dollar basement with million-dollar equipment in it to train two *aliens* when we're in the middle of a space war!"

"Chase, I don't know! Yeah, it's strange, but aren't you thankful? Where would we be without her? We don't have a choice! Could you imagine what would've happened if we were forced to learn how to control our powers *out there* instead of here? Imagine the chaos we would've created! Don't you remember that one young Electric Rasrim? He killed *three hundred* people in seconds after accidentally finding out he was a Rasrim!"

Chase shut his eyes. "Yeah. I remember that," Chase said bitterly. "I just want to make sure we can keep doing what we did today but for *good*. I just hope that people will understand that."

Lance didn't have an answer for that, but he suspected that Chase knew the reason. It was simple. The answer was that nobody would understand. They couldn't. The attack on Osamos just days ago made it all even more complicated. But Chase and Lance didn't know any better. They had been thrown on this path since the first day they could speak. Some of the first words they learned were *Rasrim* and *Energy*. It was supposed to remind them of who they were; what they wanted to do, however, was entirely up to them. But that freedom came with some obvious do's and don'ts.

Lance looked at Chase, and Chase rubbed his shoulder. He knew he shouldn't have brought it up but couldn't help himself.

"What if…," Chase began thinking hard, "what if we started going out and helping people with our powers?"

Lance shook his head. "We can't do that. We were explicitly told that."

"I know that!" Chase replied. He didn't want to hear another lecture, not from Miss E and certainly not from his older brother. "But what if we *could*? What if people needed our help, and we did that, and they began to see that Rasrims weren't all that bad? We'd be the first ones anyways! Who knows what would happen?"

But Lance wouldn't have it. He turned to go up the stairs.

"The idea is stupid, Chase. Forget it. We'd be captured as soon as anyone saw either of us use them."

"Haven't you thought about it? I know you have! C'mon, Lance!"

Chase grunted but followed along, determined to change Lance's mind.

The stairs creaked as Chase took a step. "Lance, seriously!"

Lance stopped, holding onto the railing at the last step. He took a deep breath.

"Yeah. I thought about it," Lance said before taking another breath. "I thought about a time someone would have been under the water like me a couple years ago, except this time, actually in danger."

Chase stopped.

Lance continued, "'If I used my powers to help save a drowning person, wouldn't I be seen as a hero?' Yeah. I've thought about that a thousand times."

But then Lance turned and faced Chase. His face hadn't changed.

"But I also imagined among the crowd of people who thanked me, a group of people who watched. A group of people who have weapons. I thought about defending myself and getting someone *hurt* instead of saved. And then I *can't* imagine anything beyond that point."

Lance kept up the stairs and toward the room. He was tired.

Chase knew Lance had a point, but he was being oddly dismissive. Normally, Lance would lay down facts or evidence in order to stop an argument for good. But today, Lance was just as curious as Chase was. Today, Chase would win.

"No, Lance, you're wrong," Chase said. "It might be like that now, but it doesn't have to be if we don't fight!" He hurried up the steps behind Lance.

"So what? You'd just let the military gun us or Miss E down? What happens to her if we get discovered?"

Chase grunted. "But that's my point! Wherever Miss E is, she trusts us! Why else would she allow us to break crap in the basement with literal superpowers and then leave us by ourselves?! What if this is just a test? She's a scientist after all!" Chase began to break down, laughing hysterically. "Wouldn't she benefit from whatever the hell we do out there?"

Lance didn't answer. He simply went into the room and began to change his clothes.

Chase was right behind him. He sat down on his bed as Lance pulled off his shirt and slipped his slides off before he lay out in his bed on his back, staring straight up at the ceiling, lost in thought.

Chase had an idea. He knew how to change Lance's mind.

"If someone broke into our house right now, would you fight them off?" Chase sat on his bed, facing Lance. "You would, right?"

"Dude. Of course I would!"

"If you heard an attack going on down the street, would you help?"

Lance swatted the air. "Whatever, Chase."

"Answer the question! Would you?"

Lance paused for a moment. He didn't return Chase's intrusive look. "It depends."

"Sure. It depends. But if you *knew* the only way to save someone's life was to use Risima, would you?"

Lance began to get irritated. He didn't want to think about this anymore, but he wouldn't lie to Chase no matter what.

Lance sighed. "Yes, Chase. I would." Lance closed his eyes and tossed in his bed. "But I wouldn't make a scene about it. I'd be just as likely to call the police as I would use my powers."

Chase crossed his arms. "Well, what if it were Miss E in danger? Would you wait for the police then? What if it were *me* in danger? What then?"

Lance opened one eye and glared at Chase. Then he closed it and rolled over.

"Are you done, Chase? I don't feel like wasting an opportunity I know hardly anything about. Do you want me to say that I'd have no problem using my powers if I knew it would simply *help* someone? So what? We save one life and then create a snowball effect which gets an *entire planet* destroyed. Then what?"

Lance rested his head on his arms and shut his eyes tight.

"Shouldn't we then," Chase said in a light tone, "discover the *limits* of our opportunities? Shouldn't we figure out how far we can *truly* go?"

Lance shook his head. "Don't go there," he murmured.

"When you find out that because you decided not to take an action that something preventable turns into a disaster, you'll do whatever it takes to correct it next time, *including* exposing yourself. I know that!"

"This is different."

"Is it though?"

"We have powers! People aren't ready to know that yet! 'Oh, hey, Chase! My oven isn't working, could you use your Fire powers to help me cook dinner? I like my steak *burnt*, by the way, so don't worry about overdoing it!'" Lance mocked.

Chase nearly burst out in laughter but quickly solidified himself.

"It doesn't even have to be using our powers directly!" Chase scratched his chin, scrambling for words. "I mean, shoot, what if you could use Earth Risima instead and saw that, like, a building needed to be repaired and you knew that it never would be. If you sat by and witnessed, I dunno, crazy accidents happen on this same road because it needed to be fixed, what would you do?"

Lance didn't say anything.

Chase kept going. "Well, I'd fix it. I'd make sure no one saw me and then—"

"But if someone *did* see you, what then? 'I was just doing my job as a Rasrim, sir'—is that what you would say?"

Chase was irritated. He had pushed this far; he might as well go until they couldn't. But then Chase started to laugh. "The first thing we were ever taught was that it didn't hurt to help. We learned that it hurts more to sit back and watch someone get hurt than to help. You remember that, right?"

"Yeah," Lance replied with little concern, "but I don't see your point."

"Why is this different? Because we'd be the ones in danger by helping someone out? That's their loss, not ours."

"I have no interest in dying a martyr anytime soon."

"Who said you'd be a martyr? What about a harmless Rasrim boy looking to save the world?"

"That definitely sounds like a martyr to me. Maybe a prophet instead."

"But...we are prophets."

"*Illegal* prophets."

"That just means no one has realized the good we can actually do yet. Let's start now!"

Finally, Lance gave in. As much as it pained him to admit it, he had ideas on how he wanted to help people out, although he was sure it wouldn't last long before they'd get caught.

"Okay," Lance said, sitting up in his bed, "what's your idea of help?"

Chase was surprised he'd get this far. He mumbled for a bit, looking through his thoughts. "Well, let's go back to the road example! We could volunteer or start somewhere where we could use our powers to help the community."

"Why not just do regular volunteer work then?"

"The whole point is to use our powers so people can see that we aren't dangerous."

"No, the whole point is to not get caught, which we do by *not* using our powers," Lance began before he turned his head and scratched underneath his eye. "And we're *still* dangerous, powers or not. You could punch through concrete with no effort before you mastered Fire Risima. You were fast enough to run down speeding cars. Don't you remember all we did and how close we got to being exposed before either of us even knew who we were?"

Chase brushed his hair back and beamed. "Oh, yeah. That's true!"

Lance shook his head in disbelief. "Okay. I *do* believe that we could do it, but I'm emphasizing the fact that if we get caught, we're in danger. It doesn't matter who sees us or what we just did. As long as someone knows we're Rasrims, we're targets. Do you think they wouldn't recognize us out in public again? And don't you like to go out shopping?"

Chase shrugged. "We can make disguises."

Lance actually snorted, trying not to laugh but did so anyway. "*Disguises*? Really? You want us to wear masks and capes?"

"Maybe not capes. That's too showboaty! But a mask? That's perfect. We can even use our powers to create our masks! Look!"

Chase concentrated. Lance watched carefully. Instantly, Chase's face turned red before his entire face was engulfed in a flame. Lance was almost impressed. It was indeed difficult to tell it was Chase and not just a boy on fire.

"All right. You got me there. But are you sure that's the image you want to give people you're tryna help?"

"You try, then."

Lance shook his head.

But once he stopped to think about what he was about to do, he realized that it wasn't a "terrible" idea. It just needed a little more creativity. It needed to be "Human-friendly" too.

"Well...," Lance said to himself, thinking.

He focused Energy in his face before the skin in his face became swishy, a light-blue color, his face almost turning entirely into water. Unlike Chase's demonstration, Lance still looked like himself, yet his facial features were impossible to determine due to the waves of the water crossing his face. It would be impossible to scan it or compare it to his original face without knowing prior who he was and that he was indeed a Rasrim.

Then Lance had another idea.

By imagining a new set of facial expressions, Lance could nearly morph his face to resemble that of another person. His nose became smaller, his eyes became wider, and his mouth became thinner.

"Dude! That's exactly what I mean! That's perfect!" Chase said, pointing at Lance crazily. "That's the disguise!"

Lance stopped it. He thought to himself, the water in his face moving to different areas of his face before they remained still and faded, creating Lance's face again, as perfect as it was before without any modifications.

"It takes too much Energy and thought to do," Lance said. "If we were ever in a stressful situation, it could fade on us. Plus I couldn't imagine what would happen if we got hurt when using it. Who knows? Maybe it could get stuck on us like that."

"Still! You did it," Chase said. "If we ever needed to use them, now we know we can!"

Lance looked at Chase. "You gotta work on yours first. I guess Fire isn't great for molding things, huh?"

Chase shrugged. "It shouldn't be that hard." Chase lay back on his bed. He turned over to his lamp before he stopped, looking at the bulb in the lamp, staring at the light from the lamp.

"Hey, do you think there are other Rasrims out there on Earth who feel like us?" he asked.

Lance rubbed his tongue over his teeth before he lay back in bed too.

"Not sure. I mean, it's possible."

"I wonder where they are and…if they could teach us anything."

"Like what?"

"About Osamos. About other Rasrims and other powers."

"Like their elements?"

"Yeah. Wouldn't it be cool to train with a Rasrim who could use every element?"

Lance chuckled. "That would be cool. I imagine we'd have a hell of a time trying to beat him, though."

Chase and Lance both laughed at the idea.

"Some dude beats me with my own element, burns through even my Fire. Ha!"

Lance laughed. "I couldn't imagine! I mean I would be *pissed* if someone blasted me with Water Risima."

Chase shook his head, laughing at the thought. But then he got an idea.

"Hey. If you *could* use another element, what would it be?"

"What made you think of that just now?"

Chase shrugged. "I dunno. I just really like the idea of being able to use Earth Risima too. I feel like it would really make my Fire powers better."

Lance shook his head. "Yeah. Fire and Earth Risima seem like a crazy-good combo, doesn't it? Maybe I'd choose earth too."

"No way! You can't pick the one I just said!"

Lance scoffed. "Well…I guess I'd choose electric."

"Really? You wouldn't be afraid of using an element like that?"

Lance didn't answer right away. He imagined himself summoning lightning or moving around at light speeds, powering up a city or creating large charges of electricity to fight monsters.

"No. I don't think so."

"But your element is water! That would probably kill you!"

"Hmph. It kinda makes me wanna learn it more now. I could use water to maneuver in and out of attacks and electric as an offensive weapon when I get in close, combining it with my martial arts. Yeah, you're right. That *would* probably kill someone."

Chase cringed. "Man, you're crazy!"

Lance smiled at that. He turned and faced Chase. He settled on an idea. He knew it would make Chase happy too.

"If we can use more than one element, then let's do it," Lance said.

Chase looked back at Lance. "Do what?"

"Help people. If we can master our own elements and learn more, let's swear to use them to help as many people as possible."

Chase didn't need to hear anything else.

"All right!" he exclaimed, balling up his fists in the air. "You've got a deal!"

Lance sat back and nodded to himself.

"I hope we can master 'em all someday."

"Yeah! Let's start early tomorrow and do the same thing again! I can't even stop thinking about being able to finally use Fire Risima!"

Lance agreed with Chase silently.

But in truth, Lance felt the exact opposite. For quite some time, Lance had moments when images and voices flash into his mind at random. Sometimes they were dreams, but other times they were during the day. Lance never knew what the images were or whose voice he was hearing, but while he was in the pool today, one particular image finally made sense to him. It was a body lying in the middle of an ocean. It was Lance's body. He could feel nothing but dread every time that image flashed into his head. He at some point knew that his powers would make that image come true—that he would be stranded, lying at bay in the middle of the ocean as a result. As for the other images, he could tell that someone was going to die because of him. Someone he cared about.

Each of the images Lance saw was of him from another person's perspective. Whose? Was he being watched? And it seemed as if all these images came from the future as if some divine being or perhaps God was watching Lance's life unfold on a grand timeline of events.

But then whose voice did he keep hearing? He swore that it was a girl's voice, one that sounded relatively young but also very bubbly and friendly, so it wasn't Miss E's. What did this girl have to do with it all? Was Lance going to somehow end up...

"Hey, good night, Lance!"

"Yeah, good night, Chase."

Chase flicked off his light. Despite being so enthused, he'd be knocked out asleep in no time.

Lance, on the other hand, only stayed awake a while longer, staring up at his ceiling, thinking about water and the other elements.

"Electric Risima, huh? I wonder if I'll have *that* dream again... no matter."

Lance closed his eyes, feeling the unnatural surge of Risima quake within and around his body. How was it that Lance never noticed this feeling before? Or was it that he was literally unable to detect Risima all this time?

Lance's resolve became solid, his mind fixated on one thing only.

"After years of patience and senseless theorizing, I finally got what I wanted."

Lance lifted his left hand, a small, tamed orb of Risima adhering to Lance's willpower and Energy.

With minimal effort, the orb of Risima began manifesting, changing into pure water in an instant, obeying Lance's commands.

Lance studied the energy in his hand, feeling how his body responded to the sensation, allowing his muscles and brain to tense up as his body fueled the supernatural Energy known as Risima.

"From here on, I swear on my own life that I *will* master everything Risima has to offer. I can't allow patience to interfere with progress. I need to learn the *truth* behind who I really am."

CHAPTER 5

Storm Calling

August 28, 2052
Three months later

Lance wasted no time as he leapt into the swimming pool, eager to jumpstart his training for the day.

It was currently 4:03 a.m. Lance caught a glimpse of his clock as he leapt out of bed and silently sprinted down the steps, not stopping until he had reached the secret elevator leading into the basement.

Lance had trouble falling asleep last night. In fact, the past couple of months had been like that for him. He knew this was because he had wanted to train with his powers as much as physically possible.

Once Lance had a solid grip on his ability to use Water Risima, he began experimenting ways to actually *use* his powers like Miss E suggested. And this made sense to Lance once he had enough of playing around with Water Risima like he was performing party tricks. When it came to *fighting*, blindly throwing Energy around to attack simply wouldn't cut it.

Lance spent the last few months figuring this out. Although he was sure he had accomplished this just weeks after he initially learned how to stream his Energy, he knew that experienced fighters would be able to put Lance down regardless of how cool he thought his attacks were. They needed structure. They needed to have *meanings* behind them. And most importantly, they had to suit Lance's fighting style and imagination in order to be effective.

When Lance got up, Chase was still sound asleep. He was comfortable with where he was with his powers. In only a few weeks, he had learned how to fly to an extent, using Fire to propel himself upward like a rocket and could move incredibly fast *on his own*. He had taken his training seriously.

Lance had long since finished his book, but he frequently recalled various lessons from it. For instance, he remembered that the book said that once a Rasrim had begun using an element, they would develop something called *physical prowess* or, in other words, a physiology that reflected their element.

Chase's physical prowess was largely based around speed, including his ability to stream and infuse Risima attacks without fatigue, which was nothing short of incredible. He was faster than a bullet, proving that much when he asked Miss E to test it in the training facility one afternoon. Miss E had chosen a weapon that fired rounds at three hundred meters per second, and sure enough, Chase was more than twice the speed of it, able to hit the wall the weapon was fired at and then able to retrace his steps halfway to Miss E before the bullet hit the wall. And he hadn't gotten slower—only much faster since.

She never once overstated how incredible of a feat that was for him to reach in such a short amount of time and with only small exposure to her training regimen. But to Chase, it was nothing out of the ordinary. It, to say the least, surprised her, reminding everyone how crucial it was to remain disciplined and to stick to their training. If Chase used this speed anywhere in public, he'd gain attention instantly and not just from potential fans or curious scientists.

Lance was only slightly slower than Chase on foot, but Lance's physical prowess was even better than Chase's. Although he was a Water Rasrim, Lance had immense physical strength, able to flip trucks with minimal effort. He had always been strong, but since he had been able to sense Energy, his strength multiplied several times over. It was a good counter to Chase. Chase could hit hard and was fast on his feet, but Lance was strong and could use water in many situations, making their rivalry a spectacle for sure.

Lance touched the bottom of the pool and got to work.

He closed his eyes, and the pool erupted with Energy, skyrocketing water upward before it spiraled around in a circle. This was a drill that Lance taught himself. It was a good warm-up, not just streaming Energy but actively manipulating it too.

Lance pushed his arms outward, and the remaining water in the pool spread out, touching the sides of the wall, leaving Lance on solid ceramic tile on the bottom of the pool.

Lance estimated that if he were to weigh the water he was manipulating with his powers, it would equal about thirteen tons! And this number was *far* from his physical limits. With that in mind, Lance had developed "techniques" involving the application of Water Risima, using them to attack in different ways.

Just a few days ago, Chase proved to Lance that he was fast enough to blast Lance with ferocious beams of Fire. His fireballs were big and potent. He was fast enough to predict Lance's movement, and his firepower had become strong enough to evaporate more water than he could before.

Lance released his grip on the water, and at once, all of the water plummeted back into the pool, Lance underneath it, watching it drop. He imagined it just like Chase's fireballs.

Lance closed his eyes, sensing the water as it came closer and closer to his head.

Right before the first drop even touched Lance's head, he acted, streaming all the Energy he could straight upward before a beam of energy erupted from his body straight into the air, creating a ravine between the two sections of water on both sides of his body.

Then he tensed his leg hard and jumped straight up into the air as hard as he could, straight through the ravine he had created.

Lance had managed to jump completely out of the pool, a miraculous thirty-two feet into the air. Lance flipped in the air, holding his hand out toward the surface of the pool and flicked his hand out, feeling for Water Risima Energy present in the pool and streaming it in the direction his hand moved.

A long stream of Water swirled out of the pool.

Lance's feet touched the stream of the Water, and Lance held his hands out, stiffening them, using all of his Energy to hold the stream of Water still.

At that point, Lance had been floating in the air, standing on a platform of stiff Water Risima.

Lance smiled. *Good warm-up*, he told himself.

Lance front-flipped off the platform of water and landed on the edge of the pool deck, balancing himself, trying to land as smoothly as possible.

He stood up tall, noticing the water had retracted back into the pool and didn't just simply fall out of the air. Lance nodded. He had imagined it all in his head, but it worked out exactly the way he wanted it to.

Then Lance had a new idea.

Lance knew that water was often used to cut through rock and even metal. It was similar to the idea behind hydraulics. Centuries ago, water had first been used to power old-age machines, like mills and farms, using the power of the water to turn wheels for all sorts of purposes. In the later years, water had been used in hydroelectric power plants. Water pressure had been used to spin large turbines which generated electricity, powering entire cities and factories. And nowadays, a large amount of the world's Energy relied on nuclear power, which instead of relying on water pressure to turn turbines used steam.

The way in which water had been used to power several things, turning and firing pistons or being used to cut into solid materials inspired two of Lance's new "moves," which were called *Hydraulic Beam* and *Tsunami Flash*, two attacks with completely different usages depending on the situation. These names allowed Lance to create preset visual representations of how to stream his Water Risima; that way, he could begin building muscle memory and *even* begin to condition his usage with his powers.

At least that was the overly "scientific" way of thinking about it. But the truth was Lance simply liked the idea of having moves like he was the star in an anime or something.

Lance jogged over to the center console, hopping over the desk and into a seat in front of the control panel.

Lance pressed a series of buttons on the panel with intent, now a pro with managing the entire facility. The training section, marked off with red paint, flooded with the light-blue light created from the hidden compartments containing the Matter-Phaser, which ran through the entire floor and the walls, sectioned off with tiny black patterns etched into them, which had been the storing units for the nanomachines.

Lance commanded the NPMs to create tall platforms and wide blocks of large, solid boxes made of carbon fiber using the Matter-Phaser.

The training section had transformed from nothing but a floor to a jungle gym full of structures all of different shapes and sizes. Lance noticed that around the perimeter of the training room, the barrier had reminded the Matter-Phaser what its limits were, forbidding any material from crossing the line that separated the training room from the walkway between the underground pool and blast chamber, about thirty feet away from the perimeter.

Lance pulled up an overhead view of the training room, examining it from above to gauge how much space he had created between the structures. He was impressed with himself. He left only about seven feet between each one, which was exactly what he had hoped to do.

Lance essentially simulated what he referred to as a "town" or "village," which he would soon simulate to be full of dangerous enemies.

Then Lance wheeled over to another section of the console and ripped away at the buttons, programming a few robots he wanted to create using more of the Matter-Phaser, designating the NPMs to materialize in the town of the training sections.

Lance had grown proficient enough to tweak some of the NPMs himself to his liking, allowing him to become more creative with his training.

Lance decided he wanted the Matter-Phaser to create tougher robots, which required a lot more Energy—something it was more than capable of doing.

He wanted to design NPMs with a durability of Titanium with output forces equal to a bulldozer, one of the hundreds of preset settings that Miss E had cleverly built into the NPMs for Chase and Lance's convenience, although Lance preferred sticking to the raw numbers instead. Lance figured out by training with these machines that the bulldozer setting gave the NPMs enough force to punch large holes into solid concrete, or exert a force equal to *40,000 Newtons* of force.

At first, these numbers intrigued Lance; 5,000 Newtons of force was enough to kill a Human!

But once Lance realized that the Risima Energy in Lance's body was tougher than titanium and accounted for most of a Rasrim's defensive abilities, Lance had no problem sparring with and even outputting *more* power than a robot that could hit with the "bulldozer" preset. He had rigged the console to begin monitoring power indexes instead of vital signs, changing the User Interface on the computers to gauge velocities of attacks and movement speed, acceleration of projectiles, the weight and pressure exerting on the environment, and of course, Lance's destructive Energy outputs either from physical attacks or from using Risima Attacks instead.

What Lance found was that he was much, *much* more powerful than a bomb or even missiles. Water Risima, despite its low destructive power, was still able to output large amounts of Energy such as creating small hurricanes or tornadoes of water. Of course, by manipulating Water Risima to create large waves of water, Water Rasrims could achieve similar levels of power compared to other Rasrims.

Once Lance finalized his design, he quickly pressed the "Done" button on one of the console screens, which created five NPMs of various shapes and sizes within the training section. Lance smiled, looking at the study build of the machines. This would do nicely.

Lance had three of the NPMs programmed to be especially aggressive once he activated them. These specific NPMs had been equipped with weapons that could produce weak jolts of electricity, shoot rubber bullets, but throw insanely powerful punches.

Lance jumped off from the chair and vaulted over the console, running straight into the training section. He tightened a bracelet he had been wearing, which he had stripped parts of the receiver from and made into an accessory he could wear at all times that was similar but more technologically advanced than his old watch. It was also more discreet.

Lance pressed a button on a bracelet and flicked his wrist upward, which signaled to the console to enable the barrier.

Lance then pressed the button again, as he didn't want to accidentally activate the receiver again when he was training. Then the barrier disappeared, becoming transparent as if it was never there.

At the moment, the simulation began and the humanoid NPMs powered on. All of their eyes glowed blue, indicating that they were on. Then they turned red and fired up, moving their joints to rush at Lance.

Lance put his hands up. He moved cautiously but with swift agility through the city made of nanomachines, only moving to evade long-range attacks or to set up his next attack. The robots had been programmed to operate efficiently but were purposefully flawed to a degree. They started off using basic awareness and progressively became more keen and observant as time went on.

The first two robots had been too close together, only a few inches apart. Lance focused an immense amount of Energy before he streamed it outward, emphasizing a great deal of pressure and speed into his own long-ranged attack.

A thin, pressurized jetstream of water erupted from Lance's palms, tearing straight through the robots, causing them to explode before they dematerialized completely. The beam of water stopped as soon as Lance willed it. Lance was very precise and accurate with his timing of using his Energy and trusted himself to use moves like this in open environments. Otherwise…what would be the point?

This was the *Hydraulic Beam*, Lance thought. It was a highly pressurized beam of water that could tear through seemingly anything, and had destructive capability. He had to make sure not to use it in buildings or in large crowds. The best place to use it was in an open field or near a large body of water.

It was "ambitious," Miss E told him, but still not quite what she had in mind. Lance looked to his right then quickly to his left as he saw quick blurs moving toward him.

The other three bots had surrounded Lance. They were intelligent. They were not ignorant to how the first two robots had been destroyed and knew to avoid Lance when he had his hands up.

One of the robots baited Lance, weaving in and out, firing bullets at him.

Lance lifted his right hand and created a barrier of water in front of him. The bullets sunk into the wall of water and lost all their velocities inside it. It was a perfect defensive maneuver.

The other robot fired a grenade at Lance, which released an electromagnetic pulse from its canister that had a small diameter.

Lance rushed out of the way, using his speed to dodge the blast radius of the explosion altogether.

One of the robots saw an opening and rushed into Lance, throwing a punch at Lance.

Lance was quick. He stayed sharp on his martial arts too. He ducked, slipping the punch by inches before he weaved in and unleashed an uppercut at the robot. Lance's body had become tougher. The first time Lance did this, he had hurt his hand, almost fracturing his wrist, but today, he cleaved the robot's head off completely.

Lance followed up by throwing a kick at the robot's torso—not expecting to take it out with one punch. The robot dematerialized. That left two more.

The other two robots analyzed Lance's movements and became confident in their ability to fight Lance head on.

They rushed him at the same time, making sure to leap and vault over the various platforms at high speed, nearly catching Lance off guard.

Stay calm, Lance told himself. *There's no need to panic*. He knew what he was doing.

But the way the robots moved…they moved like natural-born hunters, their AI programmed to work with lethal efficiency if commanded.

When Lance investigated the code used to work the robots, he initially couldn't crack the coding behind how the works operated, but once he could, he could tell a great deal of work was especially put into being able to accurately predict the pattern that Rasrims used to attack. Plus, the modules they could use had been sophisticated, designed to replicate scenarios observed in battlefields but also in space.

They were deadly machines to say the least, and Lance had essentially ticked them off.

Lance began moving. His training was lively; he was to stay on the move or, at the very least, know *how* to.

He vaulted up a small platform, bouncing off his foot to get more height before his hands caught the top of a larger platform about five feet away.

A robot's fist crashed into the platform, causing blue Matter Phase to shift out of position as if on a digital grid before materializing back into form. The platform, however, didn't move.

Lance started running. The platform he was on was about 50 feet long. To his left were several more platforms, all various heights and lengths, and to his right were stacked blocks simulating buildings.

He quickly glanced behind himself to see one of the robots preparing to fire more bullets at him.

Lance quickly jumped and spun in a 360-degree rotation, firing a disc of Water Risima at the robot preparing to shoot bullets. The water hit the robot and pushed it off the platform, leaving the other which was now in full pursuit toward Lance.

Lance hit the ground and didn't lose any speed as he kept forward. He'd cleared the fifty yards in just a few seconds, so before he was over the platform, he turned to his right and lunged off, swinging his arms to get more air, but he had miscalculated the distance to the next platform. He was only a few feet off the ground but still didn't want to give the last robot anymore advantages.

Lance created Energy in his chest before streaming it to his feet. He had created floating platforms of Water Risima durable enough to stand on, using his own manipulation of water to keep it and himself in the air. At the last second, he jumped off and rolled on top of the building, taking a knee before he turned back to the robot, which, too, had decided to take the jump.

Lance brought his hands up, preparing another attack, before he realized that the second robot had climbed the building and was closing in on Lance's left.

Lance grunted. It was time for his second move.

As the two robots inched closer to Lance, he infused Risima Energy, compacting as much as he could in his body before he made a cupping motion with his hands, water appearing in the center of them.

Just like the pool, Lance thought.

One of the robots was an arm's length away from Lance, preparing a punch. The other was in the air and approaching fast, preparing another EMP blast directed toward Lance. It was time.

Lance tensed himself and then released a surge of Energy out. At once, a circumference of approximately twenty-five feet around Lance surged with water, creating a massive, powerful wave that spiraled around Lance like a torrent of water experiencing a tsunami. Then Lance flicked his left hand out, fighting with the pressure to control the wave of Water Risima, and forced it to surge away with tremendous speed and power, sending both the robots flying in two different directions, totally drenched.

But that wasn't all *Tsunami Flash* could do. *This*, Lance told himself, was what Miss E expected from him.

Lance knew that he had a solid connection to Water at this point. He could sense it, he could stream it, and he could call upon it however he wanted to.

But what if Water could call upon Lance *himself* instead? Could Lance stream himself through water?

Lance focused on a puddle of water suspended in the air next to the more aggressive robot. By focusing nearly all the Energy Lance could possibly produce, he could morph his body into Water for a period. Lance had done this before.

But today, he would take it a step further. Now he would see if he could stream his physical body when morphed entirely into Water Risima into to *another* body of water. If he could pull this off, he would be able to follow up on his attack and catch the robots completely off guard. All he needed to make sure of was that he was properly focused on the location he wished to move to and that he had enough energy to sustain him while he moved.

At once, Lance was on the building, but suddenly, materializing from the puddle of water from off the robot's body, Lance's own physical body reemerged, each and every atom realigning and replacing itself exactly how it had been before. In other words, Lance had created a way to teleport using Water Risima!

Lance brought his right hand up, and with the same Energy he had stored in his hand blasted the robot, a sphere of water spiraling out of Lance's hands into the robot.

But somehow, the robot had been expecting it. It had calculated the possibility that the water on his body could be used by Lance's attack, and although it never expected an attack like this, it was more than prepared to counter.

The robot shifted its body, dodging the second phase of Tsunami Flash, and rocked Lance hard, landing a solid punch on Lance's chin that slammed him into the ground and through a platform, dematerializing it completely.

Lance was dazed, confused. Was his move too slow? How did the robot see it coming? He raised his hands, creating a shield of water as the robot plummeted on it, attempting to slam its fist and end the fight for good.

Lance grunted. Perhaps he overdid it today.

Lance whisked his hands up, sending the barrier of water outward, crashing into the robot before he ended it with another Tsunami Flash, this time, with enough force to destroy it while it was caught in the torrent.

Lance coughed out. His face hurt, and he was exhausted now.

But all three of his moves had worked. They had proved effective in real-time scenarios. He had no reason to complain, although he felt like he had failed the day.

He sat down, lying against another platform to catch his breath, holding his head back to take in as much air as he could.

"Damn...," Lance muttered to himself. He couldn't stop replaying the moment he had initially teleported in his mind. Did it even happen, or did Lance imagine it?

Lance sat up, pushing himself to his feet.

He flicked his hand; a large orb of water flew out of his hands and crashed into a building about ten feet in front of Lance.

Lance slightly bent his knees and focused on the puddle again.

His eyes throbbed, the room becoming dark for a moment, but it didn't even disrupt his concentration. He forced himself to power through, feeling the Energy in his body, and externalized it. He looked at his hand. It turned mushy before turning into water completely, remaining suspended in the air as if it were still attached to his wrist.

Then Lance turned his attention to the puddle of water.

Lance took in a deep breath and then streamed his body to the Water Risima in the puddle, using all the power he had once again to both *infuse* and *stream* the Energy at the same time before, again, he had moved spaces, emerging from the puddle across the room, and materialized back into his body again.

Lance crashed onto the ground and laughed. It felt so surreal! It was quite the trippy experience, but Lance had thought nothing of it. It felt like all the bones in Lance's body just disappeared, but the move itself presented no distinguishable feeling. Lance saw nothing, and he honestly didn't feel anything either as there was already such a strong emphasis on feeling the puddle of water he had emerged from anyway.

Lance brushed his hair back, letting his hand flow through it.
Am I the first to do this? There's no way!

The thought trailed off in his mind. He was trying to imagine other Water Rasrims doing it, but for some reason, the idea just didn't make sense to him. It was something he felt Humans would utilize more than Rasrims.

But he had never heard of such a thing happening ever, not in physics, not even in *theory*, and certainly not in the realm of Risima.

When Lance thought about it, the concept made sense. He had thought of the idea a long time ago, in fact, the first time he had been in the pool. It was one of those silly ideas you would have when first learning about something, only to later discover the laws behind it were too complicated to delve into. But in Risima, the more sophisticated the lessons became, the more sense the idea made—it was just a matter of endurance. He had played the same exact scenario in his head. It was a matter of attraction. If he could attract something to him, why shouldn't he be able to reverse the flow? All he had to do was "activate" the Risima in the area he wished to manipulate, just like any other time, right?

But it was the fact that Lance executed such a thing on his first try that made him ponder what other things with Risima he truly did not know yet.

Risima was a power to manipulate nature's Energy, and yet, the more Lance learned about it, the more he realized just how destructive and unpredictable it all was.

Lance shook his head. "I did it. Why am I still thinking about it like I *didn't* do it?"

But like any significant thing that happened in Lance's life, it quickly became a moot memory—a mere tool stored away in Lance's mind until it was needed.

A timer went off somewhere in the distance. It was Lance's phone. Lance hopped up, at first not remembering where he had left it.

He scanned the area. The buildings were in the way.

He climbed up the platform he was on before he frowned, shaking his head to himself.

Of course, it was on the Center Console. Lance scratched his head. His memory seemed out of order. Was he losing his mind?

Lance maneuvered over the buildings and through the training center, hopping off one building to catch onto the roof of the next. He had enjoyed this. He only wished he had more space to do it all.

Lance jumped off the last building, landing hard on his feet. He forgot to use Water Risima to stop his fall this time, but his muscle memory remained. He wasn't subconsciously streaming Risima, or maybe he was just too tired.

Lance took a moment to catch his breath. It was only then he noticed that his eye had been bleeding. A drop of blood trickled down Lance's face and onto his shirt.

Lance grunted. He did overdo it today. He hadn't bled in months.

Suddenly, Lance got lightheaded. He took a knee, breathing hard. Lance's headache. He felt dizzy.

And then, an image flashed into his mind. It was Lance, again, but this time, standing in front of a strange, almost mystical-like being who seemed to be observing Lance with studious, cautious eyes. The being then looked away and peered directly into the direction that Lance's perspective of the vision took place from, almost as if the being was looking at the *real* Lance himself.

"*You are moving too fast. The storm is now coming. Za'laoul is watching you,*" the being suddenly said before the vision promptly ended."

Lance recoiled fast, his heart pounding. His eyes were bleeding badly and his mind was fried, everything around him spinning fast.

"What the hell...was that?" Lance tried to stand up but doing that his entire body was shut down, an unknown feeling paralyzing him from head to toe. He looked down at his hands and saw that there was a strong yellow glow of energy crackling in them. Before he tried to move them, a flash of blinding yellow light whipped across the training facility from out of Lance's hands. The lights in the facility flickered.

Lance's sight darkened before he fell. He collapsed to the ground with a thud and passed out.

*****

Two figures stood atop a mountain peak, somewhere in rural southeast Asia. It was cold and barren. Because the altitude had been so high, the air had been thicker and was dry, but thankfully, the two individuals had no trouble breathing. One of them was a natural-born assassin, trained in many martial arts and had access to several powers across the universe, outside of his proficiency in Risima.

The other figure had been a genetically modified Human, who now had the privilege of wielding Risima thanks to his new Risima blood. It had been an operation that only recently was discovered and tried immediately with, fair to say, unexpected results. However, thanks to this newfound success in blood transfusion, the Humans who had operated on him had been sloppy and all too eager to experiment on him, resulting in his rebellion. He had clawed and fought his way out of captivity before an unknown being would come to his rescue. This being had extended his gratitude and commitment to looking over the boy—swearing to keep him safe from his captors.

This being's name was Melterai.

At first, the boy feared his new master would be as barbaric and heinous as the ones who created him. But he was wrong. He had been freed and ascended to a plane of higher purpose…divine purpose…if you would. He was here in Asia to meet the man who had planned his rescue and who had more than enough power to fulfill every wish he ever had and then some just for fun.

A man in a dark cloak with a hood over his hand glanced at the boy and spoke to him in a low, almost anxious voice.

"He should be here soon. I'll let you know that Melterai is a busy man." The words drifted out in the cold, windy night, trickling off the snow flurries that carried over the mountain peak and rolled off the side into the sky. They had been above the clouds. They had a view over a village they believed held Rasrims in secrecy too. But that wasn't their concern.

At least not yet.

The man turned to the boy. He hadn't spoken a word since he had left his confinement. And that was three weeks ago.

"Hey, keeping your tongue stowed away from me is fine. I couldn't care less." Daxxon stiffened up. "But when Master Melterai speaks to you, you *best* respond, understand?"

Still, the boy didn't say a word. He simply turned and glared at Daxxon who felt cold, icy blue eyes peering into his soul. That had been a threat in the world of Rasrims. This boy was not ignorant but still extremely foolish.

Daxxon snickered, snatching his head away from the boy. *Pathetic*, Daxxon thought.

Daxxon had come across only a few Rasrims who had a degree of power like this boy—but none like the element he had possessed. He could control an element that was near impossible to obtain without immense training and a godlike physical prowess that had been stronger and more durable than even the toughest Earth Rasrims on Osamos.

But what made this boy even stronger than the countless Rasrims that Daxxon fought were the dark patterns and marks embedded on the boy's body. They had come from another universe, one that possessed immensely powerful energies and even more frightening creatures that harbored powers that could destroy Rasrims and perhaps even both Osamos and Earth at once. These marks were gateways to power that only led to suffering and despair, which is why hardly anyone in this universe had them.

Had this not been true, Daxxon may have killed the boy himself by now.

He chuckled to himself. *Let Melterai teach him a lesson*, he thought. Probably wouldn't even last a second.

Daxxon turned to look out into the sky. It had been long since he had felt the chilling atmosphere of Earth from an altitude this high. Other places in the universe had been much harsher and severe. Instead of mountains with frosty tips, you had mountains quaking with electricity and sulfur pits at the top, reaching several thousand degrees. Some places like this even had ferocious beasts lying dormant within them, awaiting for the day they could unleash their power, having their planets remember how violent the universe truly was.

Daxxon turned to face the boy. He noticed the boy had tensed himself. He was scanning the sky, looking as if he were tracing quick movements, his eyes and head jolting back and forth. His head turned quickly before he turned around to look behind himself.

Daxxon was confused.

"The hell're you up to, boy?"

Then Daxxon himself felt it. Daxxon's feet started to sway before he realized the entire mountain had been shaking. He felt a surge of Energy above him, dark clouds circling above him. Was there an earthquake? What was causing this massive surge of power?

Suddenly, a massive bolt of lightning erupted, crashing across the sky in a blur before it struck the mountain peak, only feet away from where the boy and Daxxon stood.

Daxxon nearly lost his footing. He realized the boy had assumed a stance, bending his knees, his body ready to burst with power.

But Daxxon sat up quickly and straightened himself as he realized a third figure had been on the mountain peak. He stood still, trying to decide if he needed to be concerned or not.

This new figure was wearing a set of heavy golden armor, completely cladded from head to toe. His armor had been designed with black and purple lines that reminded Daxxon of ancient murals found somewhere on Earth, but on the man, it looked nothing short of godly. His helmet had been designed specifically for the man, with curved edges around the chin and a place on his face to mark where his eyes and mouth had been, although he couldn't see into them.

"Master Melterai!" Daxxon exclaimed, half-shook. "It's good to see you!"

Melterai nodded, acknowledging Daxxon. "Yes. It's good to see you too, Daxxon." Melterai then turned to observe the boy accompanying Daxxon. He was average size and looked like he was in shape. He had worn nothing but the jumpsuit he had taken from the lab he had been kept in but had a scarf around his neck.

Melterai took a step closer to the boy.

"Melterai, the kid doesn't speak! I tried getting him to talk, but—" Melterai held up a hand, which silenced Daxxon. Neither said anything else.

Melterai leaned forward, observing the eyes the boy had.

"Fascinating. You *do* have a Prowess that few Rasrims have ever had," he said.

"Daxxon, do you not know where you are?"

Daxxon did. "The country known as China." He said too plainly, almost as if he didn't want to be there.

Melterai put a hand on his chin as he nodded slowly. "This mountain is known as the Meili Snow Mountain. I learned about it in my youth. It's beautiful and is known for its snow-covered tops. Quite the tourist attraction from what I've learned. Looks amazing in pictures."

He turned to the boy.

"What's your name?"

The boy didn't move.

"Sir, like I said, he refuses to speak. He'll hardly eat too. I mean, what's up with that?" Daxxon said. "If I don't practically shove food down his throat, he'd starve!"

Melterai sighed. "Have you taken even *one* moment to acknowledge the conditions this boy has been forced to live under?"

Daxxon stuttered, "W-well, I…well, no, sir."

Melterai took a step back, and suddenly, the top of the mountain became alive. Snow erupted from the mountain, tons of it at once. It swirled around the trio like a hurricane, spiraling in unpredictable rhythms, dancing about every which way.

Daxxon raised his hand. It had become hard to see, and the wind was incredible.

The snow in the air suddenly converged in one area above Melterai before it condensed tightly, Energy pouring from the ball as it became tighter and tighter. Daxxon watched, on edge, preparing for it to explode.

Then in one fluent motion, the ball of snow became solid ice, crystalizing, producing a magnificent, cut stone of ice that shined like a diamond.

The sphere of ice fell slowly, drifting calmly into Melterai's open hand.

Daxxon looked bewildered. How could he use such an element without any modifications or help?

Melterai controlled the sphere in his hand gently, allowing it to float near the middle of his palm.

He raised his hand up and faced the boy, bringing the sphere into the boy's view. The crystal ball slowly left Melterai's hand and floated over to the boy.

The boy hesitated, fringing at the sphere that was coming toward him, as if it were hostile.

But Melterai nodded toward the boy.

For some reason, the boy could *hear* what he believed to be Melterai's voice, reassuring him. *It's okay. This won't hurt you,* the voice told him.

The boy slowly reached out with his hands and caught the sphere, cradling it in both hands. He looked to be in awe, admiring the shape and design of the ice.

He looked up at Melterai, before backing down at the sight of the sphere.

"Go on," Melterai gestured. "Stream your Energy into that crystal there."

The boy hesitated at first. He looked down at the crystal like it was some sort of alien device, half-wondering if it was a trap. He'd been tricked into using devices like this before, ones that ended up stripping him of his power or causing him to overexert himself.

The boy rolled the crystal ball over in his hands. This seemed like no trick; it was just a crystal ball, a perfectly shining one at that. He wanted to just keep looking at it.

Daxxon watched with caution. What the hell was Melterai doing? This boy was crazed, clearly delusional! Could he even use his powers, or were they just for show?

But the boy understood the request. In fact, he knew exactly what Melterai had asked him to do.

The crystal ball of ice resonated, glowing up alongside the boy's eyes. They shined the same color, a light, frosty blue color.

The ball then exploded in a magnificent way: shards of ice shimmering, flying out into the air, producing a low-pitched ringing sound as it did so. The ice floated around the three figures, creating an area of sparkling light and shining crystals that remained in the air, flowing in the sky. They persisted, moving around in a circular movement.

Daxxon looked around, impressed.

Melterai turned to see the display as well.

"Beautiful," Melterai said. "Like I thought, you have the ability to call upon *Ice Risima* as an Elemental Prowess." He looked around and opened his hands. A thin white Energy appeared in his hand before a shard of Ice formed in his hand. Chile watched eagerly.

Daxxon, on the other hand, stared at him in disbelief. How was this possible? Rasrims should not be able to explicitly use Ice as an Elemental Prowess! It made sense if you combined the Elements of *Water* and *Wind*, two of the nine Elements of Risima, but even if you combined these two Elements, you still wouldn't be able to manipulate pure Ice like *this*!

Daxxon watched Melterai turn his hand, his fist turning into a frosty display, ice forming all around his hand. "How can you use Ice Risima? It's...a fallacy!"

"Quite a sight to behold, is it not?" Melterai chimed. "I can use Elements even the Kings' Guards are unaware of. So that technically includes you too, Daxxon."

Daxxon muttered. Well, duh! Of course Melterai could! He was a god in his own right! Daxxon laughed to himself. If Melterai had suddenly decided that the oceans on Earth should be full of acid instead of water, he had the power to do it with a literal snap of his fingers!

Melterai continued, delighting the boy with his own Ice powers. "Watch as the ice shimmers on the crystals, reflecting small freckles of light. Ah, it's so refreshing, like seeing mists of water on a hot summer day!"

The boy smiled, although it was obvious it was his first time doing so. It had been awkward, yet Melterai knew it was genuine. It had been the first time in the boy's entire life that he had felt joy.

Melterai turned to the boy.

"Forgive me for the small talk, but I *do* know who you are already."

But then, Melterai stopped as he saw the attempt to speak. He opened his mouth to produce words and struggled at first, his voice harsh, producing a foul sound that resulted in a cough.

Melterai stopped the boy, gesturing to his own chest.

"Air," Melterai simply began. "You must stream your Risima into the air, starting in your body, and then exhale it out in a calm manner."

He demonstrated, showcasing how the pitch of his voice suddenly became richer and smoother as he inhaled, and took a slow exhale right before he began speaking, using Air Risima to purify the molecules in his diaphragm. It was a technique that Rasrims could use in high altitudes, underwater, and even in the vacuum of space.

The boy watched Melterai curiously. He had an amazing ability to reproduce movements from observing it once and tried it himself. At first, his voice cracked, but then, the sound mellowed, producing a low, soothing sound. Melterai raised his hands, signaling that Chile had done it right. The boy stopped to laugh, flattered. Then he tried again.

"M-my name is Chile." The boy spoke, his voice raspy and cracked as if it were dry.

Melterai applauded. "Excellent, Chile!"

Daxxon looked confused. So the boy *was* mute after all? He hadn't even learned how to talk until just now. "Huh. Well, I'll be damned…," he muttered to himself.

Melterai paid Daxxon no mind, instead focusing on Chile, who wasn't sure what to think. He looked at Melterai with eyes of admiration.

Melterai knelt in front of Chile. "I know who you are and where you came from, Chile. I'll save you time and spare you the tale I'm sure you were bound to hear. While you are a unique boy, you are in an equally unique situation that does not have your interests at heart."

Chile looked upset, remembering the time he spent in the lab. He only remembered being confined to a cell, locked away behind thick glass, where he had been injected with various chemicals, exposed to different chemicals and gasses, had to survive being submerged in water at sub-zero temperatures, and even had to fight strange creatures, all the while actively streaming and infusing his Ice Risima. He had no friends and knew nothing other than the assignments he had been given. He had, fortunately, been taught what his powers were and how to use them, so Chile understood very well what the Rasrims were and even how he was different. He didn't know the history of the Rasrims or the Humans. He hadn't been taught about himself, either. He only knew he was a boy with a tough body and even tougher emotions. He didn't know empathy and joy, only pain and rage.

Chile looked down at his left arm. Melterai saw it too.

And the mark...

A large portion of the pain Chile endured was aimed at figuring out how to harness the power of the marks located all over Chile's body, including his arms, chest, and neck. His captors frequently argued, yelling at one another and several individuals who had come to inspect Chile.

Once, they had come close to activating the marks, but for some reason, the man who came close to doing so suffered a heart attack and died just moments after. Chile was angry and in pain, but he knew he didn't have anything to do behind it. He had no way to even access the man, although the other scientists blamed it on Chile and amped the experiments on him tenfold.

It was only two weeks after that day that he had killed his captors and escaped from the facility, burying the entire place in ice that would forever be impossible to breach. *Perma-Ice* had been one of the things he had been forced to produce for his captors. In the end, they got exactly what they wanted.

After traveling out in what Chile thought was nothing but dry lands, he was rescued by Daxxon. And now, he was facing the man he could thank for putting an end to his suffering.

"So. Your mark travels from your torso, ends at your neck, but reappears on your left forearm?" Melterai observed.

Chile nodded. "Yes," he simply replied.

Melterai rubbed his chin. "Here, let me have a look at it. Please remove your shirt."

Chile hesitated at first. His captors had told him to do the same thing.

Melterai shook his head. "I won't hurt you. I promise you, I know what these marks are and how to properly handle them."

Chile obeyed. He trusted Melterai. After all, Chile could sense power in Melterai he knew he had in himself. He was more similar to Melterai than anyone he'd ever met before.

Melterai observed the mark on Chile's chest and neck. Daxxon watched too.

"He's never used 'em," Daxxon suggested. "I can tell already."

Melterai suspected the same. "That's quite all right. I doubt he will ever want to. It isn't exactly a 'friendly' Energy, now is it?"

Melterai turned his attention to Chile before he placed his hand on Chile's chest, focusing Energy into the marks which covered Chile's chest and trailed up his shoulders to both his arms.

Chile wasn't sure what to expect.

Suddenly, Chile's body lit up, turning a dark-red color. His marks glowed with an intense red Energy that produced heat.

Daxxon gasped. "The Crimson Marks? Impossible! He's part Human!"

Melterai shook his head. "A Human with Rasrim blood *can* have the Crimson Marks, Daxxon. I would know better than anyone."

"But how? The Realm of Sacora—!"

Melterai held up a hand and silenced him again.

"Forget it, Daxxon. Chile is a product of science. I have no doubts that under normal circumstances, I'd be concerned too. But today is not that day."

"Hmph," Daxxon grunted, "if you say so."

Melterai sighed. He stood up, and Chile's body cooled off. The marks on his body faded to almost scars once more.

"I know what you meant," Chile suddenly said, facing Melterai. "Memories…I have some that I don't understand."

Melterai looked at Chile. He does? That must mean that…

Melterai was quiet for a moment before he changed the subject, although Chile wouldn't have known this. It didn't seem Daxxon did either.

"Chile, do you feel comfortable streaming Risima in battle?"

"Yes." He shifted a little. "I did it every day."

Melterai nodded. "Would you mind showcasing to me some of your skills? There's a few things I might need you to do for me."

Chile nodded. Although he didn't have the words nor did he understand the feeling, Chile was long since ready to die. But he knew that the day he met Daxxon, he had a new purpose.

He stood and face Melterai, acknowledging the calm, bold, and confident demeanor that Melterai exhibited, contrary to both his captors and even Daxxon. Melterai instilled a feeling in Chile he never knew he had before: hope. He was prepared to do anything for Melterai.

"I will do whatever you ask."

Melterai nodded, not surprised to hear Chile's loyalty. He was expecting it. Melterai turned and began speaking.

"Good. Because as a Rasrim on Earth, you know that there are several individuals, groups, and even other Rasrims tasked with eliminating you. Since you come from a place where these groups meet and decide agendas, I'll be asking you to go back once you feel ready."

Chile's face drowned color, turning pale briefly. He swallowed hard and stood straight, not festering to the idea. He was prepared to go back, especially if Melterai had been guiding him.

"You want me to destroy them?"

Melterai turned back to face Chile. "Not quite." He cleared his throat, before walking over to the edge of the mountain that he had been looking out into for quite some time. Chile followed behind.

Melterai pointed straight down the cliff side, his finger aimed at a small area with a few buildings huddled together. Melterai knew this place had only recently been built. He had known every person who lived in it and what they were doing there too.

"This is an outpost for Rasrims. Although they are like us, they've sworn allegiance to a cause that I am fighting against. My team and I are in the midst of several battles and conquests for infor-

173

mation and the power to create change." He turned to quickly see Chile staring down at the mountain, deep in thought.

"They hold a key to a piece of a puzzle I'm uncovering. It's crucial that I get it, *today*."

Daxxon chimed in. "The fate of the universe. What they have can completely change it," he simply said.

Chile looked at Daxxon. "Uni-verse?"

Melterai spread his arms out wide, as if he were trying to simulate the size of the universe. "Yes, Chile. You see, we are just an ant compared to the size and scale of what's truly out there. For the past ten years, I've been traveling the universe to figure out what's been causing all this chaos and nonsense that's riddled our planets and torn our people apart."

Suddenly, Melterai's tone became a lot darker.

"And what I've learned is that many see the universe as we view ourselves within it: that as mere *ants*, we only exist to be crushed. I won't tolerate that any longer."

Chile suddenly felt what he knew was fear. He didn't like that. But he understood that Melterai had been angry. Chile understood that.

But Chile had felt fearful because of how humble Melterai had been. He had only known strong individuals to be loathsome and drunk on power, tearing down anyone beneath them.

Compared to the strongest individuals Chile had ever met, he knew with certainty that Melterai was no ant but perhaps a universe in his own right.

Chile paid attention to Melterai when he began moving to the edge of the mountain, overlooking everything below.

Melterai pointed to a small village out in the distance.

"There are beings that do not belong on this planet hiding out in that village there who can get us information that we desire."

"You mean information on *the Gods*!" Daxxon pointed out. "But, Melterai, If I may try to understand, you recently said your travels pointed you back to Planet Axcour, not Earth!"

Melterai remained silent, staring over the hilltop into the snowy distance, watching the snow fall through the clouds below.

"Well, things change. Priorities adjust themselves, and new tools emerge as our old ones begin to wear. After all, the alien refugees hiding in that village are savage scum," Melterai spat. "What they're doing here on Earth and the fact that they infiltrated the planet and bypassed my surveillance so easily disturbs me. They must be eliminated immediately."

"Then they are—"

"Axcourians, yes. They got here using the Power of Drakour."

Melterai turned to Daxxon. "And that means they're likely working for that nasty bastard known as Mo'Yur. The information they could give us will prove most vital."

Melterai gestured to Chile. "And Chile here has the perfect tool for eliminating them with no traces left behind.

Daxxon looked troubled. Was he seriously going to allow an amateur to take on Axcourians? Was he mad?

"What makes you so sure of that, Melterai?"

Melterai lifted his chin. "Let's just say that the forecast here calls for an *avalanche*."

Daxxon suddenly gulped, fear instinctively overcoming his emotions when Melterai flicked his right hand up in the air before a massive sword suddenly appeared in it, reflecting radiant light that shone like a beacon.

"And I have yet to use *Exeridon* on an Axcourian. With this, I'll be able to take *everything* I so please from them."

Chills ran down Daxxon's spine, his eyes finding it difficult to turn away from the magnificent sword that Melterai possessed.

The double-edged sword known as Exeridon was almost as long and tall as Melterai himself was. It had a gold, almost transparent blade that had a strange, reddish Energy pulsating throughout the blade, swirling from the tip down to the handle. The sword was over five feet long, whereas the blade itself was about eleven inches wide. The sword even "hummed" with a low frequency that told Chile it was a powerful weapon. He had no idea what material the colossal weapon had been made of.

Melterai suddenly shifted his body and aimed Exeridon at the village in the distance.

"Chile, your Ice Risima is more than capable of striking that village from here, right?"

Chile leaned over the edge of the mountain, gauging the distance between the mountain and the village. It would be easier to reach the village, Chile thought, but unless they had a way to trek down the mountain from this angle, they would have to hike down to it. What was Melterai planning on doing about that?

Regardless, Chile held out his hand and focused Energy in it, readying himself. "Yes, Melterai," he answered.

"Good. We'll start here," Melterai said.

Chile turned and faced Melterai, a look of surprise detailing his expression.

"Are you ready to embark on this journey with me, Chile? I'll warn you, it is a cold, dark, and dangerous journey, and our targets are powerful foes with the ability to manipulate *space* itself. You must keep your instincts and reflexes *sharp* at all times, as attacks can come from every direction."

Melterai glanced over at Chile, noticing how focused Chile had been. He never once turned his sight away from the village. He had a look of solid steel on his face.

"But something tells me you are more than capable of dealing with something such as that, am I correct?"

Chile nodded. "Yes."

Melterai then addressed Daxxon. "Your work here is done. Leave Chile to me. Continue your search for the twins."

Daxxon waited for Melterai to turn his attention away from him before he shook his head and sighed.

"Understood," he said, before with a wisp of Black Energy, Daxxon disappeared into thin air instantly, leaving no trace behind.

Melterai and Chile stood next to each other.

On cue, with a wave of his hand, Chile summoned a cold air of Ice Energy which turned slowly into a large spear of ice, perhaps the size of a small aircraft.

"Now! Strike it—hard!"

Chile's eyes widened; an intense aura overcoming his body as the Risima in his body released with extreme potency.

With a powerful thrust of his hands, Chile directed the Ice Risima he had infused in his body and streamed a gigantic spear of Ice Risima to launch through the air, moving at high speed and hurtling toward the village.

Melterai inched forward, taking note of Chile's note-worthy accuracy and reaction speed.

"Such amazing control…," Melterai mumbled to himself.

A large cloud of snow and ice was launched up into the air from where the spike of ice struck, indicating that some of the village had been destroyed from the impact alone.

Then because Chile's ability to manipulate Ice Risima had been so potent, he had caused a tactical discharge of Ice Risima to explode across the entire village, encasing *everything* into *perma-ice*.

"Now! Let's go, Chile!"

Chile was mesmerized as he watched Melterai move forward and leap off the top of the mountain at high speed, crashing into the side before he angled his body forward and slid down the slope of the mountain as if he were skiing.

Chile rushed forward and leapt off the mountain, copying Melterai's actions exactly, swinging his arms into the air to gain as much distance as he could before his feet landed into the side of the mountain.

Chile's body lurched forward, but he kept his balance and slid forward, his momentum causing him to race down the mountain upward of seventy miles an hour.

Chile's heart pounding hard, adrenaline pumping through his veins. He had a smile on his face. Although he knew this was dangerous and would probably lead to someone getting hurt, it was *way* better than killing all those harmless creatures he had grown up with in his confinement.

Chile laughed as he skied down the mountain at high speed, holding out his hands to turn his section of the mountain into solid ice, gliding down the feet as if he were skiing, gaining more speed before he caught up with Melterai in an instant. They had quickly reached well over a hundred miles an hour and were only gaining more speed.

Chile jumped into the air, hundreds of feet off the ground, practically laughing aloud, watching as Melterai instantly entered combat with Rasrims who fired blasts of Fire and Electricity at him. So he was right. But Chile told himself that he didn't care anyway. He just felt better seeing that Melterai hadn't been lying to him.

Chile watched Melterai maneuver. He was quick on his feet, dodging weapons and Energy-based attacks like it was nothing, firing his own attacks off in expert successions to counter the humanoid aliens known as Axcourians as well.

Melterai swung Exeridon around masterfully, his movements too quick for the Axcourians to react to. They too had the ability to move at high speeds, using the terrain and mist to their advantage, but Melterai had no problem cutting down his foes with ease—destroying buildings and slicing through attacks like it was paper.

"Chile!" Melterai announced, and Chile came alive. He slammed his fist into the ground before hundreds of massive pillars of ice erupted from the ground, piercing through the aliens and destroying buildings, leaving almost nothing behind.

Chile created shields of ice and defended himself when an Axcourian appeared from out of nowhere, a blackish aura allowing the alien to move through space as if they were teleporting.

But with Chile's Ice Risima, his senses were heightened to a point where even his blind spots were covered.

Chile slammed the shield into the Axcourian who tried to attack him before Chile launched his hand forward, a spear of ice forming out of thin air and piercing through the Axcourian's body, faster than the Axcourian could teleport away.

Chile couldn't hold himself back anymore. He laughed uncontrollably, sliding down the side of the mountain at high speed like a maniac and celebrated as he and Melterai began unleashed havoc on everything in sight.

"This…is…*fun!*"

*****

Lance screamed as he woke up and sat up quickly, knowing something was wrong.

He was breathing heavily, awakening from what he knew was another nightmare.

But as Lance looked around, a cold sweat began trickling down the side of his face when he realized he was not in his room or anywhere he recognized.

"What the…?"

Lance first noticed what was directly in front of him. He was looking at the edge of a cliff, overlooking a large body of water below. His breathing became heavier, forcing him to take in gulps of air he had trouble swallowing.

And then he realized that it was hard to breathe at all as if there was little oxygen in the air.

Lance pushed himself to his feet. When he stood up, he heard a crunching sound underneath himself, and when he looked down at the ground, he noticed that the ground was full of speckled stones of a variety of different colors sparkling in the moonlight.

Lance took a closer look, scooping up some of the dirt and inspecting it.

The dirt had been much smoother and richer than he remembered it, almost a liquid. But the dirt in Lance's hands also felt *different* depending on how he moved it in his hands. He noticed that the red specks on the dirt had made his hand warmer, and the yellow specks made his body tingle as if it was infused with electricity.

"What is this? Am I dreaming? I have to be!" Lance reassured himself before he turned his hand over, allowing the dirt to fall back to the ground.

And then a sharp, pulsating feeling in his eyes caused Lance to reel over in pain.

Lance groaned out, stumbling forward, clutching his left eye. He could feel an intense sensation in his body and an intense sensation near his left eye.

Lance pulled his hand away, noticing that for just a moment, a bright, crimson-red Energy glowed in his left hand before it and all the pain he felt subsided.

It was then that Lance noticed that his body now felt *electrified* as if tiny currents of *electricity* were coursing throughout his body. He noticed that his body felt as stiff as *stone*, as if his bones were made of *metal*. He could feel that the insides of his body were boiling *hot* as if a raging *fire* had been burning inside his chest. He felt as if he were as *light* as a feather in the *wind*, that there was no weight to him at all, and that his senses were in turn with *everything* around him, as if he could feel the *cycles* of life and *death* occurring everywhere around him like it was connected to all the various environments in the universe.

Lance looked down at his hands, trying to understand what he was feeling. He didn't feel bad but quite the opposite.

"This feels like…Risima."

Lance quickly turned his attention to the cliff he was on, hoping he'd find answers in his surroundings. His eyes widened as he looked down the horizon, examining the water below.

The ocean that he had seen was *gigantic*—Lance knew that oceans were big, but something about this one told Lance that it was much larger than any body of water he had ever seen before. This wasn't an ocean on Earth. This wasn't the Pacific nor the Atlantic.

Lance looked over the edge of the cliff, measuring how high up he had been from the ocean.

Lance whistled. He must've been some *thousands* of feet above the ocean surface! There wasn't any place like this on Earth, was there?

Lance heard a small rippling sound behind him. He turned around and noticed that the ground had been completely level and even once more.

"Huh?" Lance shot around, taking notice of the dirt he dug up from the ground behind him.

Lance couldn't even tell where he had dug the dirt up from. It was as if it had magically assorted itself back into its original form— as if Lance had never bothered it.

It was then Lance knew he *recognized* the area he was in.

"This entire place feels like *Risima* too, like there's Risima *everywhere*. I can't even sense the Water Risima in the ocean as well as I can everything else… What the hell is going on?"

Lance closed his eyes and took in the air around him, feeling himself as much as possible. He noticed that the air was richer than normal. He felt stronger. He felt more *alive*.

Lance looked down at his hands, his arms, his legs, and then finally took time to look at what he had been wearing. A blue jacket and athletic pants. The same thing he was wearing when...

Then Lance froze. He suddenly felt like he had been hit in the stomach hard with a sledgehammer.

That was right. Lance had passed out just moments ago in the training facility. Why was he here now then? What even was this place?

Lance looked far out into the distance. He felt as if he were looking at an endless reflection of *nothing*. There was nothing out here. The ocean stretched out seemingly forever. The sky was hazy. Lance noticed there was gray dimness in the atmosphere, but it had been clear enough for Lance to see far out in the horizon nonetheless.

Lance held out his hand and focused on the ocean.

He tried to focus Energy on the ocean, gauging its Energy levels, trying to gather Risima from it.

Lance's eyes widened with pure delight when he felt an *immense* surge of Energy come toward him, much, much more than he ever felt at once.

Lance couldn't control himself, beginning to laugh aloud. His body began to glow with Blue Water Risima Energy.

"Woah! With this much energy, I could—"

Then Lance stopped, shutting himself down as the entire cliff shook with ferocity, chunks of rock cracking off the side and tumbling down into the ocean, splashing as they fell in.

Lance noticed the Energy from felt seemed to be coming from the ocean.

Lance got closer to the ocean but fell to the ground as the much more powerful quake struck the area, causing part of the cliff to break off entirely.

Lance tumbled backward, moving back toward a wider section of the cliff and more and more pieces of dimly colored stones fell out into the ocean.

Lance had been confused. What was triggering these distur-bances all so suddenly?

Lance searched for an answer in the ocean.

He had nearly found the courage to flip over the edge and dive into the ocean below, but he stopped completely when he noticed he had felt another massive surge of Energy emerging from a spot far out in the ocean.

He could see bubbles rising and waves forming around the spot as if a tremor was occurring deep below the ocean's surface.

Lance's chest felt tight, causing the pressure on his body to increase to the point where he had been unable to infuse any more Energy, fearing his chest would explode.

Lance clenched his teeth, realizing that he was feeling more than just Risima Energy. He had felt a type of Energy he had never felt before, one that was rich and potent but so powerful it nearly wiped out all of Lance's Energy reserves within as if it was fighting with his Energy.

Then Lance noticed what it was.

Lance's breath escaped from his mouth, flowing out into the air as Lance had been stricken with fear, unable to move.

His body turned slowly, facing the ocean, staring out into the limitless horizon of water. Lance felt a certain presence within the ocean, one that had produced the *same* Energy Lance had been used to all this time.

But Lance noticed it was *billions* of times much more potent than his. It was an overwhelming feeling that told Lance to turn and run as fast as he possibly could.

A cold, icy chill slowly went down Lance's back.

Lance stepped closer to the new edge of the cliff, careful not to loosen anymore of the stones protruding from the cliff.

He scanned the ocean, looking at the sparkling shimmers of light bouncing on the surface of the water, carrying out across the horizon.

Lance continued to watch a spot in the ocean as tons more bubbles surfaced and the entire ocean began to rise and fall, causing massive waves to form as they rolled over the entire surface of the ocean, carried out in every direction for seemingly *hundreds* of miles.

Lance's mind began warning him, telling him to turn back and run, but Lance refused. Where would he even run to?

Lance inched closer, a small portion of his body hanging over the ledge. He slowly lifted his hand, trying to infuse some of the Water Risima from the ocean.

But suddenly, a massive section of water toward the middle of the ocean erupted with immense power, spouting up about fifty thousand feet up in the air, spraying Lance even from where he was standing with pounding beads of water.

Lance covered his face, listening to what sounded like a nuclear bomb strike the ocean, before a massive wave of water surged in the air, crashing into the cliff, causing Lance to stumble backward, and left the face of the cliff eradicated.

Lance coughed out, quickly regaining his balance as he fought his hardest to see what was going on.

But as something began to emerge from the ocean, Lance's heart skipped a beat.

"What is that—!"

A behemoth creature missiled from the depths of the ocean as fast as a rocket, causing Lance to fall, tripping simply to the tremendous shock wave the creature's speed produced. At first, Lance thought it had been a water spout, but the horrendous sound that came from the ocean where the massive eruption came from told Lance that this was indeed a *nightmare* from hell.

Lance couldn't believe his eyes. He watched what he saw emerge from the ocean with an expressionless gaze, trying his best to realize that he had somehow been imagining this.

But he wasn't.

Lance first noticed the creature's long, serpent-like body rise from the ocean, its movement a mesmerizing sight. Its long, slender body almost rose from out of the water like a God, its massive size and monstrous appearance striking Lance at first glance.

Then Lance noticed that the body was connected to a large, triangular like head, triple the size of a commercial airplane with a pair of red, demonic eyes resting on a large and muscular snout.

The creature's face opened up, showing a large mouth with thousands of rows of teeth.

The beast screamed at Lance, a high-pitched shrill that was so magnificent several large waves of the ocean rose, crashing straight into the cliff, pounding Lance's body with water.

Lance was carried back by the force of the beast. Lance fought back, pushing through the powerful windstorm the beast had summoned, working his way closer to the edge of the cliff.

But without a warning, the intense winds let up, and Lance unexpectedly lunged forward toward the edge of the cliff.

Lance hastily swung his arms over the ledge of the cliff as he tried to keep his balance.

Lance cautiously took a step back and quickly turned his attention back to the beast who had now taken up more than half of what Lance could see in front of him—the rest of the beast's body wrapping through different parts of the ocean as if there had been arches of blue flesh emerged from them.

The beast had summoned a thunderstorm. The ocean was suddenly alive, angry waves forming as bolts of electricity thundered in the background.

Lance couldn't control the water. He had been thrown back, pieces of rock crashing into his body as the cliff was devastated by the beast's presence alone.

Lance held out his hand and forced the water away from him, using the Energy he felt to create a barrier, fighting to take the Water Energy under his control.

Lance stood up, suddenly angry with himself, finding it hard to believe a monster from pure fiction had picked a fight with him.

He forced more Water under his control, streaming his Energy into the waves that the beast had summoned, and took control of it.

It was then Lance got a better look at the beast. The creature's body had still been hidden in the water, but Lance could see that the creature's body was a dark blue and black with several thick scales surrounding its tube-like body and several rows of spikes traveling down the length of its back. From the size of the beast's head to the portion of its body that had been above the surface of the water, Lance estimated that the beast had currently been over 2,800 feet tall—twice the size of the Empire State Building.

It didn't have arms but a set of black whiskers flowing off its face, moving as ferociously as the waves it had been controlling.

Lance stood up tall, staring directly at the beast.

The beast took notice of Lance.

With one quick breath, the beast unleashed another ear-pounding roar that summoned a frenzy of lightning strikes all around it, crashing into the ocean and parts of the cliff.

Lance leapt out of the way as a bolt of lightning struck where he was standing—noticing he had been able to dodge it.

Lance pounding the ground, forcing his nerves to solidify. He couldn't shake off the dreadful feeling of despair swelling up in his body.

Lance could hardly think straight. His adrenaline rushed so fast he thought he'd faint from the pressure. His mind and nerves begged him to run, but there was nowhere to go.

And he'd be *damned* if he dove into the water with *that* thing commanding the water below.

Lance stood up, ready to fight. He knew exactly what he was looking at. It was something out of mythology, a large, ferocious beast that terrorized the seas and had the power to decimate entire landmasses with ease.

Lance was staring at a monster known as the Leviathan, otherwise known as the God of the Ocean.

But before he could do anything else, the Leviathan summoned a grand display of electricity which annihilated the dark sky, dispersing massive bolts of electricity across the horizon. Lance's eyes glossed over with terror, and yet he couldn't help but recognize how sublime the creature was, commanding the very seas and the sky as if it were the god of everything around it.

The Leviathan shrieked with rage, amassing so much Energy it siphoned all of Lance's stamina, causing his body to writhe in fatigue.

Fearing for his life, Lance covered his face, anticipating that something was about to strike him with more force and ferocity than anything he'd ever witnessed.

It was just as Lance was about to move his hands that he yelled out in pain and sheer terror as a bolt of electricity five times the size of his body crashed into him, causing him to scream out in horrendous pain.

Lance fought against the intense force behind the lightning strike, screaming at the top of his lungs as he stood his ground, using as much Risima Energy as he possibly could to fend against the Leviathan's Electric Risima.

For just a moment, a tearing pain ripped through Lance's body, tearing his lungs and causing his heart to stop for a moment.

Lance's eyes widened, his body unable to continue breathing as the Leviathan continued to pummel Lance with enough force to obliterate an entire continent.

Lance's mind was frayed. His body was unresponsive.

Lance's eyes began to fade before at once, his body crashed into the side of the cliff, rolling off the large rock formation.

His body plunged into darkness, headed straight for the domain the God of the Ocean had undisputed control over.

Lance could hardly see or feel a thing. His body was livid and burned as millions of volts of static electricity coursed throughout Lance's body, preventing him from moving a muscle.

His eyes began to black out before right he crashed into the ocean below, and everything went pitch black.

*****

Lance shot up, panting, breathing harder than he ever had in his life, his heart aching as his body warned him something was wrong.

He looked around and double-took a look when he turned to see a familiar setting—a person lying in bed on the opposite side of the room.

It was Chase.

He rolled over in his sleep, groaning something out half-asleep. "M-morning, Lance," he yawned.

Lance forced himself to take deep breaths. He had been having a dream. He understood that much now.

Then Lance looked down at himself when he realized he had been soaking wet. He threw the covers off him and slid out of bed, realizing that he had sweat so hard he soaked the entire bed, sheets and all.

Lance put a hand on his knees and relaxed himself, streaming Water Risima into his surroundings before infusing it back into his body, replenishing his entire supply of Energy. He could better communicate not just his surroundings—the presence of water was quite literally everywhere—but also within himself too. Risima Cycling, as Lance coined it, could not only speed his recovery time much faster than simply inhaling and exhaling, but it could also allow Lance to grasp Risima Energy in the environment at a much larger rate and potency than he could during meditation. Water swirled around Lance's body, at some points reemerging into his body. He felt refreshed already.

He stood up. *Try to remember what happened,* Lance told himself. It had been years since he had a nightmare, but he had been having dreams for weeks now. They had been simple: just him meandering about in the world, sometimes interacting with people but other times working on various projects.

But this dream had been completely different.

Never before did Lance see a monster in his dreams—let alone fight one.

Lance sighed. He wiped his forehead and brushed his hair back. He turned and looked at his clock. It read 7:14 a.m. His nightstand had also been illuminated, the dark-colored wood bright and shiny. Lance didn't realize until now that it had been sunny out.

Lance paused for a moment, trying to understand what had happened.

He remembered from the short time he had been dreaming that he noticed those colored stones in the dirt. Lance also remembered *feeling* differently wherever that place was. But he *knew* that he had been feeling Risima.

Lance twisted his neck, irritated.

One thing was for sure: That *definitely* wasn't Earth. But Lance's suspicions had been doing him more harm than good.

He *knew* his dream took place on Osamos.

If Lance had to guess, he could tell he had been feeling an incredibly powerful form of Water Risima—one that had been infused with a much more potent type of Energy created by the Leviathan.

"Electricity…," Lance said, looking down at his right hand.

"When I dodged that first strike, I felt something emerge in my body. A new type of Energy. It came *from* that monster…," Lance murmured to himself.

Then Lance felt drowsy. He shook dizziness out of his eyes, trying to stay awake. It had been early in the morning when he was last awake. Had he passed out for a day, or just a few hours?

Suddenly, the idea made Lance anxious. His mind paced around, recreating images he had seen in his dream. He tried mapping out the area again but found it increasingly difficult to focus on anything. He was still sweating and breathing hard, finding it impossible to control himself. Lance stopped himself, ceasing all movements like a mannequin within a store.

He slipped on his sandals and put on a shirt, purposefully neglecting his thoughts. His heart was still racing *lightning* fast, and Lance swore his vision had been much livelier and more electric than it ever had been before.

Lance promptly left the room, slowly pulling the handle closed to not make too much noise, and practically tiptoed to the steps. He stopped when he saw lights coming from the kitchen. It seemed Miss E had been up after all.

Lance grabbed the railing and took a step down, cautioning himself not to faint again. His vision had been experiencing moments where everything would turn pitch black and then so bright he couldn't see for entire moments.

He realized he had a headache, his head throbbing with every step he took.

Lance stopped when his memory jogged. It seemed like only a second ago he was in bed, but somehow, he had put clothes on and was on the steps in what seemed to be seconds.

For some reason, it now seemed like it was taking *hours* for Lance to reach the kitchen. What the hell was going on with him? Was he still dreaming?

Once he finally got into the kitchen, Lance took one last step before placing his hand on the wall for support. He stopped to catch his breath. He was exhausted. He felt like he'd throw up.

Miss E turned. "Hey, good morning—" She suddenly stopped, suspended in space, holding a dish in her hand. Her entire body stopped before she turned her head in confusion.

Lance huffed. He nearly spat words out his mouth. "I'm not feeling right at all." Getting those words out nearly took all of Lance's Energy.

"Lance..." Miss E's voice shook, her expression swept of its color. "Your eyes. They're *yellow*! You're streaming Electric Risima!"

CHAPTER 6

Awakening

Chase opened his eyes and sat up in his bed, visibly disturbed. He instantly noticed that the air in the room had been hot and smelled as if something had been on fire. He gazed across the room, looking for anything that might hint to what Chase had been feeling. Of course, he reasonably assumed he may have been using Fire Risima in his sleep, but when Chase noticed that Lance's sheets had been thrown off the bed, he knew something was wrong.

"What the…!"

Chase tossed the sheets over himself and slid himself off his bed.

"Lance? Are you good?" he asked.

Chase took notice of the time.

He knew that Lance had spent all the previous day downstairs in the training room, but he didn't remember Lance coming back upstairs at all between last night or early this morning. That was definitely odd.

Chase scratched the back of his head but thought nothing of it. Lance wasn't one who sweated much. Maybe he was downstairs doing laundry after a long day of training. But that still didn't explain why his sheets had been soaked.

But then Chase noticed a commotion in the kitchen. Intrigued, Chase went to check it out. He also felt a little worried about Lance since it had nearly been over twenty-four hours since he last saw Lance.

Chase tiptoed to the edge of the steps and heard Miss E's voice.

She was talking to Lance, but the way she spoke to him told Chase that something was wrong.

"Calm down. Focus!"

Chase's face shriveled up. What was going on?

He paced down the steps and walked into the kitchen, holding his head up high so he could see over the counter well before he reached it.

Chase found Miss E bent over helping Lance, who had been lying on the floor in a puddle of sweat.

"What's wrong?" Chase exclaimed.

Miss E found it hard to speak. She had been too busy checking Lance's pulse. She seemed flustered. "He's—unconscious. He just collapsed!"

Chase reached out to Lance. "Hey? Are you okay? What happened?"

He shook Lance.

Then Chase yelped out in pain as his hand was shocked, a burning sensation crossing his entire body.

Chase swung his hand in the air, trying to alleviate the pain.

"W-what was that? That felt like electricity?" Chase turned to Miss E. "And he's hot as I don't know what! You don't feel that?"

Miss E looked dazed. She looked at Chase with an uncertain expression as if she were in a trance.

But before she said anything, Lance shot up, gasping for air and coughing, trying to remember how to breathe, his eyes bouncing back and forth like a maniac.

Chase jumped as the sound of a thunderstorm began pounding the house, splattering droplets of rain at the windows, water pouring from the sky and lightning blazing constantly, streaking across the sky.

"Woah! It's storming hard all of a sudden!"

Lance tried to get up as if he were in a hurry, his eyes half-open and bloodshot. He sat himself against the sink, breathing hard.

"M-my eyes!" Lance began to say, breathing so hard he barely managed to speak one word.

Chase got down in front of Lance, propping Lance's head up.

"Hey! Stay awake! What happened?"

Lance began losing consciousness again, his head slouching over, his entire body going limp.

Chase turned his face.

Lance began drifting in and out of consciousness. Chase could notice that Lance's body began emitting different colors. It was an easy detail to miss, but Chase had barely noticed it.

Lance tried speaking, finding it difficult to get his words out.

"Wh-where is it?" Lance's head dropped to the side.

"What? The what? Hey!" Chase kept Lance sitting against the sink.

Chase turned to Miss E for help.

But Chase looked confused and a little hurt. She was gone! He didn't even notice she had left!

Chase shouted out, calling for her. "Miss E! I don't know what's wrong with him! Where are you?!"

Chase placed his hand on Lance's chest, trying to find a presence of Risima Energy within Lance.

Chase gritted his teeth. He had found that there had been *too much* Energy within Lance. Chase's body was suddenly shrieking out, telling him that he was unable to take in any of this Energy he had been feeling.

But Chase had felt something else too, an Energy that *wasn't* Water Risima.

Lance opened his eyes. Chase squinted as a bright yellow flare lit Lance's eyes up, illuminating the entire room.

At the same time, the mark over Lance's eyes began to light up as well, a deep-red color purging through the birthmark that had been centered over his left eye. It was a Crimson Red Energy—one that gave Chase the chills. It didn't look or feel like Risima!

Chase sat back in fear. The sight alone had been freaky, but he had felt a monstrous energy suddenly awaken within Lance.

Lance's head sprawled over as he wrestled with the feeling inside, writhing in pain.

Lance grabbed his left eye, yelling out in pain as energy seeped from without him, an angry mix of several different energies that Chase didn't recognize.

Chase grabbed Lance's shoulders. "Fight it! Whatever it is, control it!" Chase yelled, shaking Lance's shoulders.

"Listen, Lance! You have to control it! If it's Risima, focus on it! Learn how to control it!"

Lance's body twitched, the flare of red Energy crossing his left eye slowly fading.

But Chase had just then noticed that Lance's pupils were *yellow*, a sign that his Risima Energy had changed.

"Y-yellow eyes? That's Electric Risima, but how?"

A thin yellow aura began to form around Lance's body. Lance's body began twitching—twitching so fast that Chase would see blurs of Lance's body moving from left and right.

"The lev—" Lance tried to say.

Chase leaned in, afraid he would be shocked again.

"What? Lance, *what is it?*"

"Something's here! I-I think the Leviathan was trying to…it was warning me about *this*!" Lance said, spitting the words out his mouth.

"I saw it. I saw it in my dreams and then—" Lance cringed and began to mutter in pain once more as his eyes twitched uncomfortably, the size and color of his pupils changing the entire time.

"A Leviathan, you say? But how?" Chase said.

"I took power from it." Lance coughed, holding his head back. He was slowly beginning to recover, his speech becoming smoother.

"I can feel Risima in my body…but it's different. It's not Water Risima."

Chase tried to move Lance's hands away.

"Dude, your eyes are changing colors! Yellow, green, now yellow again—what the *hell* is going on with you?"

Lance clutched his eyes again, his vision turning a golden yellow but becoming fuzzy. All he could see were fast-moving particles flashing back and forth. He noticed that whenever he looked at anything that ran on electronics, Lance could *see through* them, able to track the electricity coursing through them as if they were x-rays.

"My eyes are turning yellow, right?"

Chase gasped. "*So you know?*"

"I saw them... I feel electricity coursing through my veins... It feels like a storm is going on inside my head. The Energy is overwhelming."

Chase grabbed Lance's hand and pulled him up.

Lance leaned against the sink, recovering his breath.

He looked at Chase with a serious expression, trying to phrase his words properly.

"I can use more than one Element. I-I just did it. I had a dream where I was fighting some...*thing*, but I can't remember much of anything right now..."

Chase took a step back once Lance could stand on his own again.

"Electric Risima, huh?" Chase laughed nervously. "That must've been one helluva trip since you can use both now!"

Lance shook his head. "No, Chase. I used them *all*. The only way I could fight it was by using them *all*."

Chase's eyes widened. "H-huh? Whaddya mean? How?"

"I don't know. It had to do with a dream I had."

"You said a monster is coming!"

Lance pointed to the window.

"Look at that storm. That's not...normal. But I felt it. I felt that storm before it happened. I felt that same Energy when I was dreaming. I think me and it are linked to the storm somehow."

Miss E came into the kitchen, holding a small device in her hands.

"Lance! You're awake!" she said, rushing over to him.

Lance nodded. "I'm fine now. My head's still foggy, but...I can think clearly again."

Miss E looked into Lance's eyes.

"You were telling me something and then you passed out. What was it?"

Lance lowered his head, still feeling a tremendous pain in his neck and near his eyes.

"Something is coming. I can't say for sure what, but my dream was—it was warning me." Lance put the back of his hand over his forehead and closed his eyes, trying to relax. "I had a second vision earlier as well. Someone who I can't exactly describe told me that a storm is coming, like h-he could predict the future or something!"

Miss E suddenly froze. A straight, serious look invaded her always-calm demeanor while she analyzed Lance. He wasn't lying. He couldn't have been. But that only meant that this was not good news.

Lance shook his head, trying to reason with his thoughts.

"This sounds crazy, but I *know* that something that can use Risima is coming—now! And it's powerful! It may be here now!" Lance exclaimed with a sense of urgency, trying his best to remember what the monster in his dream looked like.

But the image in his mind was fuzzy. He couldn't remember what it was he was thinking of anymore.

He looked at Miss E, trying to show with his expression that he wasn't kidding.

"I...I think that what I saw was a warning. I don't get the impression that it's something we take lightly and let pass over us!"

Lance's breathing began speeding up again, his yellow eyes beginning to shimmer. Lance winced.

"I was telling you that I awakened to Electric Risima because something is coming...and it's coming here!"

"What did you see, Lance?"

Lance shook his head. "A mythological creature or something. It looked like a *god* to me. It was something powerful—it was *huge*, like the biggest thing I've ever seen. There's no way that thing lives on Earth!"

Olivia had an idea. But if that was the case, the entire planet—and maybe part of the solar system—was in grave danger. If *that* thing awakened—

Olivia stopped herself, trying to reassure Lance. "I see. You gained another Element as a warning. Was it a defense mechanism?"

She believed Lance anyway. Part of that proof was right in front of her. Why would Lance lie about being able to use another Element and having a strange dream? And how would these events be connected? What did seeing a monster in a nightmare and then gaining powers afterward mean?

Miss E took notice of the storm outside, hearing angry quakes of thunder and the pounding of rain against the ground.

The entire house went quiet, all listening to the storm, disturbed by what Lance had just said.

"Here," she said, handing a small tablet over to Lance.

Lance slowly and reluctantly took the object from her.

"This device is called a Neuro-atomic Inhibitor."

Lance looked at Miss E with disbelief.

"A…what? What does it do?"

Miss E didn't hesitate.

"It's a device that can inhibit the abilities of Electric Rasrims. It runs on a special type of *stone* found on Osamos."

Lance's heart dropped, his body feeling light again.

"To *inhibit* Electric Rasrims?" Chase asked. "Why would you do that?"

Miss E. sighed. She seemed distressed by the situation.

"It's not important! It *will* help Lance find his ability to use Electric Risima without discharging himself back in that state he was in."

Lance fell to the ground, holding the tablet in his hand, suddenly lightheaded.

"Lance, please trust me. It will *help* you. I promise."

Lance closed his eyes, his heart pounding in his chest. He was developing a fever as the Electric Energy in him surged uncontrollably like a storm in of itself, waiting to be tamed.

Lance tried to take another breath.

"Electric Risima is known for being an erratic and unstable Element, Lance. But if you can learn to control that Energy coursing through you…it seems to mean that there's more Electric Risima in your body now than *Water Risima*, Lance."

Olivia rubbed the top of Lance's head, trying to sway him.

"You need to trust me. Electric Risima will kill you if you do not learn how to control it."

Lance's eyes shot open, and he gasped as he felt a tremendous Energy cross his body. At the same time, a roar of thunder boomed outside, and just for a moment, Lance swore he could *hear* the sound of the beast from his dream. But the beast was not an enemy, almost as if it was trying to prevent whatever else was out there now from doing something it wished against.

Lance groaned as he sat up, holding the tablet in his hands.

"Okay." Lance clutched the tablet in his hands, looking at Miss E with a sudden resolve in his eyes, which had still been flickering between blue and yellow.

"Tell me how this thing works."

*****

A building in Washington suddenly went up in flames after a pipe in the building exploded, rupturing with scalding hot water which had found its way into a room no water should ever be in, let alone hot water. It was so hot that simply touching it would cost you a finger and even likely a hand too. But this building was vacant currently, and that had been done so on purpose.

The explosion was incredible. It initiated chain explosions across the town. Most of the town had been evacuated, but for the few stragglers who had been left behind, they had been sworn to secrecy for the amount of time they decided to remain in the city by men whose identities that were unknown.

But today, none of that mattered for both the civilians but also the men shrouded in secrecy had been killed indiscriminately by the explosions, either burned by the intense blasts or crushed by debris. The quiet city, once known for its vibrant life, had now gone completely silent, and no one would ever figure out why.

Meanwhile, a storm was brewing on the East Coast. A strange figure of light had been identified by surveillance and reconnaissance drones from orbit, but it had such an intense frequency and electromagnetic field that not even the most advanced imagery technology had been able to identify it. The storm had fried the electronics of nearly all satellite technology, throwing off what was known as Global Positioning and Inertial Navigation Systems and their abilities to track movement of objects in the Earth's atmosphere and on the ground. It would throw back Human research plans for at least a couple of years and cost billions to repair.

And from the unsuspecting people out and about who just so happened to look up into the sky, they hadn't noticed the light drift from the absolute giant ball of a planet dwarfing the night sky. It merely looked like a firefly or perhaps an aircraft with exceptionally bright lights.

But one person was more clever than the rest.

He watched this light with curious eyes, his heart rate beating at an inhuman pace.

He snagged his phone out of the pocket of his expensive three-piece business suit and held it up in the sky, waiting as a dim-blue box of light holographically formed around the phone.

The man was a very successful and accomplished tech engineer and entrepreneur. He had created one of the satellites tracking the overhead storm and the very same phone he had been using now.

The phone knew instantly what the man had wanted to do and automatically snapped a few photos of the passing light crossing the sky, storing them in a corner of the holographic display after each one had been taken.

The man brought his hand back down and swiped through the pictures. He was unsatisfied with what he saw. The pictures had been blurry. He realized his phone never once even focused on the image and held it up to try again, this time taking a video. But this time, when he pressed the record button, the light swelled and a cloud appeared, causing his phone's screen to blacken entirely, frying every electrical component in his phone. It was ruined.

The man angrily tossed the phone on the ground, destroying it. Was the light watching him?

Suddenly, the cloud burst alive, and a surge of lightning was released from the cloud, angrily awakening the city he was in, just outside of the Capitol District.

A gust of wind burst into the sky, carrying dust around the air, howling throughout the night sky.

The man watched as the ball of light ascended high into the sky and disappeared behind the clouds.

The ball of light seeped through the clouds and began to swirl in a circular motion, causing the clouds to rotate in the same direction, picking up speed every second. It looked like a tornado had been forming.

The man shook his head.

He reached into another pocket and pulled out another cellphone, ensuring he kept it low, as far away from the light as he could. He clicked it on.

He pinched the screen of his phone with his fingers and separated them quickly, bringing up another holographic display before he tapped a box which had stored his contacts list.

He used his index finger and swiped it in the air, scrolling through the screen until he found the contact he had been looking for. *Olivia.*

The line rang for an entire minute, but no one picked up on the opposite end.

The man tapped his foot, growing impatient.

"Dammit! Now of all times? She *always* answered her phone!"

The man went to press the *end* button hard but became angry when his finger went through the screen, distorting the display until it rendered the picture correctly again.

The man angrily swiped through his contacts list again, looking for a second number that wouldn't dare ignore his call.

The man didn't even bring the phone to his ear. He put it on speaker as other people in the city were now aware of the angry thundercloud.

"Hello?" the voice answered as if his nose was stuffed, as he always did.

"Hey! Do you see this cloud?"

The line went silent before the man on the other end answered.

"I'm just seeing it now. I have footage of it."

"Remember what I told you earlier this week?"

The line went silent again.

The man tapped his foot before he began walking down the street, scurrying to his car he had parked in a nearby parking garage.

"Gary, you shouldn't have brought that up in that meeting. People are asking questions now. I've already had some of them silenced."

Gary didn't seem interested. "Enough about politics! *Do you see the damn cloud?* I was right!"

The man watched as people began to walk past the man, still unaware that this was an abnormal storm. He had been gaining more attention than the storm was.

The man tried to lower his voice but settled for a whisper-yell. "I-I was right! We need to get the hell out of here now! Call your boss. Tell her I want my research funded now! This is important! I can't get a hold of her!"

The man sighed. "She's been gone for years now, Gary."

"That's what you people always say! Find her now!"

The line went quiet for a moment. "Hold on," he simply said.

But Gary simply went silent and dropped his phone as he noticed the cloud grow in exponential size, taking up the entire sky, swelling to an enormous size, and it started to glow red, crackling with powerful bursts of Energy.

A sound wave vibrated throughout the entire city, causing the entire city to shake hard as if an earthquake had ravaged the city. Buildings toppled, and signals were jammed.

All the lights in the city flicked off for a moment before the city's high-powered emergency generator kicked on, straining the electrical grid as it tried to resupply the city of its electricity.

Gary's phone shut off, a light whir that suddenly turned into an almost sad low-pitched tone as the screen turned off.

The cloud shook ferociously as a much more eerie sound wave surged across the city, causing Gary to shout out in pain. A high-pitched ringing sound thundered in Gary's head.

Suddenly, every light in the entire city shut off again, but this time, they didn't come back on.

Gary began to run to his car, and by the screams of others in the city, it seemed others were now doing the same. They had finally noticed the only light in the city had been one that had been a blood-red color, blasting the city with immense frequencies and radiated Energy that quaked the city. The heavy rain and thunderstorms that followed the light wherever it went didn't help.

As Gary shuffled through the streets of DC as fast as he possibly could, he began to notice that not a single vehicle in the large metropolitan city had been moving. In fact, the streets and even the sidewalks were riddled with cars that had not been in motion. They didn't even have their lights on. Some of these vehicles, including pedestrian cars and SUVs but more frighteningly police cars and ambulances, appeared to have crashed into each other and buildings around the city.

Gary could also see huge amounts of smoke billowing up near one corner of the city.

In a fit of rage and confusion, Gary turned the corner of the street he was on and bolted into the parking garage where his car had been parked. He had used this same garage every day, and so the route he needed to take was muscle memory for him.

Once he took a flight of stairs up to the second level of the parking garage, Gary pulled out his keys and tapped the unlock button once he was close enough to his car, but his car didn't turn on. Not even the light in his keys turned on.

Gary ran up to his car and fumbled with the keys, struggling to get a grip on the one to unlock the car, twice using the ignition key to do it instead. When he finally got it right, he nearly threw himself into his car and slammed the door shut, soaking wet.

He shook his hands off and bent over the passenger side, reaching into the glove box for a radio he had designed himself. It was geospatial weather radar, which he used to detect Risima Energy and track spikes in it around the planet. It was the same technology he had recently got fitted onto a satellite he recently learned was destroyed.

But this had to be his saving grace; otherwise, his fears were coming true. Osamos had been releasing rays of Energy, and perhaps other things, into space. Whatever this storm was, it was a storm that was alive—one that would consume life on Earth and to unknown extremes. Whether they knew or even cared was out of the question. It was Gary's job to know these things, and he was determined to figure it all out.

Gary clicked on the radio, and miraculously, it worked. But its readings were off. A needle shot to one side of a gauge and emitted a loud frequency, one that Gary recognized the storm was producing.

Gary could taste acidity in the air, and the smell of it had been overwhelming from when the cloud surged. That was *not* normal and proof enough for Gary.

But before Gary could do anything else, he watched as a huge bolt of electricity crashed into the parking garage, striking one of the cement support cylinders holding it up.

The upper levels of the parking garage swayed, causing the other support beams to crack underneath the pressure.

Gary's hand was on the door handle, ready to make a run for it. But the rest of his equipment had been here. It would take weeks to get a flight to where the rest of it had been stored.

Gary closed his eyes, praying as he tried his car again.

But he couldn't even get a click. Nothing happened.

He heard pebbles fall from above him, bouncing off his windshield.

Gary looked around, his breath still.

He pulled the door handle, opening the car door.

But then Gary heard an awful sound as the support beams in the parking garage snapped, center cracking under the pressure, and watched as the upper levels caved in.

Gary screamed out and braced himself as he was crushed and buried by debris, his car barely supporting the weight of the cement crashing in on him. He screamed as he balled up in his car, as more and more rubble cracked into his car before his muffled screams suddenly faded, hidden beneath the rubble.

*****

"I need you to hold on this tablet and keep an eye on the gauge on it," she said with a certain urgency. It had been the first time Lance heard Miss E speak almost panicked-like.

"It's a machine that's designed to communicate with Risima. I'll explain how later. For now, you need to get those eyes under control! You can already use Electric Risima, and I believe very well, at that. You're just unwillingly discharging it *all*."

Lance nodded his head, but when he took the tablet and looked down at the screen, he was confused.

There was nothing on it.

He was silent, staring unwittingly at a black screen.

He looked closer into the screen. Maybe the brightness was low.

But before Lance could say anything, the screen changed. The blackness of the screen faded, leaving another blank screen with nothing but a symbol of a battery on it.

The battery on the screen began to fill from the bottom but abruptly stopped, less than 2 percent of it filled.

The battery blinked red. "Energy level: low," a computerized voice announced.

Lance focused on the tablet as if it were alien, moving it in his hands as if that would help him.

But then Lance felt something from the tablet, almost as if it were vibrating. It tingled Lance's hands. Lance noticed that before long, his entire body had been tingling. The tablet was forcing Lance to expose his Risima Energy, his entire chest becoming tight, seeping Energy from his chest to the rest of his body. But the Energy Lance had been feeling was different from Water Risima. Instead of a cool, reassuring Energy that moved in waves and light motions, Lance could feel an intense, vibrating Energy course over his body in unorthodox rhythms as if it were in a hurry but unsure where it wished to go.

His eyes began to glow a sharper yellow color, light almost bursting from his eyes as he focused harder. Small flurries of light began swirling on the screen of the tablet, and Lance could feel heat coming from it.

Lance began to understand what he was supposed to do.

Lance was finding it easier to breathe and concentrate as he held onto the tablet, focusing this new Energy and manually directing it to the tablet in order to get a proper feel for directing the chaotic energy.

Once he got used to it, he would be able to recognize how to manipulate the Electric Risima in his own body without discharging it and overexerting himself, causing him to black out again.

He continued focusing on the tablet, breathing normally as he did so. He had nearly stopped when the tablet's display was a quarter of the way lit, full of swirling balls of particles. Lance couldn't quite understand what he was looking at. Was this what the tablet had intended to show, or was Lance quite literally manipulating the technology to reflect something else?

Lance took a deep breath as his sight became clear. His mind was no longer cloudy. He could focus much more than before, and only then, Lance recognized the feeling he had been having all along.

Miss E opened her mouth to speak but stopped herself.

Finally, she spoke. "Don't worry about me. You're nearly done. It's a quick process, see?"

Lance blinked before he looked back down at the tablet. He gasped again when he noticed small bolts of electricity shaking off Lance's hands and disappearing into the tablet. His hands had almost been completely illuminated by this yellowish glow. He could not think about anything except a frenzy of Energy crackling in his mind, a strong current of electricity without a place to go but shooting out of its source in a hurry nonetheless.

The frequency Lance began to feel had become potent. It warmed his muscles up, tensing them tightly. The muscles in his arms and legs had become taut, as if they were being pulled from opposite ends until they couldn't extend anymore. His chest was burning, but the feeling wasn't unpleasant but occupied his entire nervous system's attention anyway as if he wanted to be in pain to have a suitable response.

Lance was beginning to understand what was going on, but one question persisted in his mind.

Lance looked down once the tablet had been so bright, he couldn't look at it directly anymore. The frequency had also turned into an annoying hum in his ears, vibrating throughout his entire body.

"I think I've got it now. I can isolate the Electricity away from everything else."

And Lance didn't need another command. He handed the tablet back over to Miss E.

The feeling and sound didn't disappear. Lance could still sense it. His fingers tingled, remembering the feeling of the tablet in his hand. Lance then stopped once the world around him began to move *slower*.

His entire body became lively. He looked around and saw things move at microscopic levels, bits of energized swirls moving dust particles around, water moving in slow motion, dripping from the faucet into the sink in *microseconds*. He noticed each one of Olivia's slow, controlled movements; her breathing seemed like it had been slowed down tenfold.

She had been right: Lance could sense and feel Electric Risima more than he could Water Risima. It was as if Electric Risima had always been his natural Element!

Lance could see the muscles in her body beginning to contract, how the rhythm started in her abdomen and shoulders before it slowed down as she exhaled.

Lance's own hands, however, seemed to speed up, yellow light emitting from them and flying off into the air around him. He could see this light everywhere; it was in the center of everything, the basis of movements and reactions that took place.

The loud humming in his head turned into a static frequency as if a transmitter had just lost signal. But it mellowed out, all sound disappearing before it was nothing but a stoic white noise in his mind. He could *hear* electricity. It sounded like soft yet erratic tapping, each tap as if it had been far away but at the same time moving *behind* Lance's ears.

Lance took a deep breath and went further into this image. Suddenly, a burst of yellow Energy crashed into Lance's mind, tearing through the blackness of his thoughts as it produced a picture of brilliant light, a bolt of lightning ripping across it all.

He brought this image forward.

It was an intense pressure. It was powerful, and it moved fast. As soon as Lance felt it, it weakened immediately, creating a center of potency elsewhere which remained until Lance reached out for that one as well. Lance calmed himself down, and the feeling died down. Lance took note of that.

He returned to the yellow Energy he could sense. Lance reached out, trying once again to pull it forward to himself just like he did with Water Risima. But to his surprise, Lance again did nothing but pull a mere strand of Energy to himself before the lump of it all surged at light speed elsewhere, placing itself down but watching Lance as if it were mocking him.

Or *testing* him, he knew Miss E would suggest.

Lance had been trying to overcome this Energy ever since he had first felt it. He had tried to draw it forward and command it to state its intentions, giving Lance the ability to use its power and feel it work around his body. But it remained in his mind, unwavering. It didn't want to move.

Lance stopped to think, returning to his neutral position, and concentrated. Water Risima could be streamed when its user found a balance between the water's surface and where he intended for it to go. You needed to have the space you wanted to have it occupy in mind *before* you could call upon its Energy. But Electric Risima was different. It moved in surges at high speed. It would allow you to take pieces of its power but never draw it all at once. What if, Lance thought, instead of drawing its power to your own source, you went after *its* source instead?

Lance had an idea.

Lance exhaled and imagined the Energy in his mind as one uniform presence.

When Lance tried to infuse the Electric Risima he could sense, he noticed that the Energy became increasingly unstable as it moved *closer* to Lance's body as if he were discharging the Energy before he had even accumulated it.

So Lance had to take a different approach.

It was almost as if Lance were a magnet. He had to, first, direct the Electric Risima to a position which he had control over, *streaming* it first, allowing it to discharge the unnecessary unpurified Risima particles into the environment.

By doing this, Lance was building up his control of the Element, building his conditioning up and becoming more familiar with how to handle the Element directly.

Now this time, Lance imagined a bolt of lightning emerging from the site he had control over and attracting its Energy toward Lance's body.

But sure enough, once the Lightning came too close to Lance, it discharged out sporadically, like a firework that had gotten loose and went berserk.

Lance frowned.

What was he doing wrong?

And then it hit Lance.

This isn't Water Risima. I can't draw Energy into me. I have to fuse with Electric Risima itself. Perhaps there's a little more Physics in Risima than I thought!

Lance had another idea.

Once again, he started by streaming what little amounts of Electric Risima he could into the environment, building up a low concentration of potent Electric particles.

But *this time*, instead of drawing the Energy toward Lance's body, he tried directing all the Energy inside of him *into* the site of Electric Risima. It was as if he were infusing *himself* into the stream of Energy. It was the same thing he did with the puddle earlier in the training facility.

But then Lance realized something he didn't know how he felt about: That "teleportation" move wasn't Water Risima at all. It was all Electric Risima from the very beginning!

Sure enough, the Electricity reacted and flashed toward Lance faster than he had anticipated, lighting his entire body up, causing his muscles to jolt and his brain to tingle.

And then he understood why that had worked.

Lance hypothesized that attempting to infuse Electric Risima into one's body like, say, Water Risima, for example, *was exactly* what Lance had been doing when he had passed out.

He had been accumulating Energy that simply *discharged* inside Lance's body without a clear site to diffuse to. Electric Risima moved *fast*, and so, naturally, it discharged *just as fast*.

However, by first creating a site that a Rasrim could pinpoint and keep a continuous stream of Energy tied to, Electric Risima could freely move between the two sites, streaming, infusing, and discharging Energy and all as the user had intended.

This, in return, also made all of Lance's movements *fast* in the material world. His body would be able to move to different sites as fast as he could keep *streaming* Electric Risima into *new* sites, as if he were leaping across different platforms by imagining where the next step should be.

Lance opened his eyes.

His yellow eyes beamed with power, Lance's body surging with Electric Energy, causing bolts of electricity to surge everywhere Lance went.

Lance turned to face the dining room.

By focusing Electric Risima Energy in the direction he wanted to move, and *then* by building up Energy in his body, he could manipulate Electric Risima to change the properties of his body— enabling him to essentially become a bolt of lightning himself—or direct electric-based attacks wherever he wanted.

Once he gathered enough Electric Risima in his body, Lance *flashed* to the dining room and back in an instant, faster than a blink of the eye, releasing the energy just as fast as he accumulated it.

Miss E's hair was thrown back, and the chairs in the dining room flipped, causing a loud thud as they crashed into the wall.

Lance stopped hard, screeching his feet, using too much of his knees and ankles to stop, causing his ankle to twist.

Lance stopped, half in pain and half in awe. He had just moved as fast as lightning!

Chase threw his arms up, his face turning a bright red color. "*Holy* crap! That's unreal!" he yelled at the top of his lungs, shielding his face from the shock waves of the sheer speed Lance was moving at.

"Y-you shouldn't be doing that up here! Get outta here, man! My life's in danger!"

Lance stood still, feeling the immense power of Electric Risima speed his entire body up, draining much of his Energy.

Lance winced, his eyes throbbing in pain.

Miss E went to get Lance, afraid he'd collapse again, but Lance held up his hand, signaling he was fine.

"No, I feel fine!" Lance said.

But his body had been singing a different tune. Lance's body was quaking with Electric Energy, making it dangerous to approach him. A wave of Electric Energy rose from Lance's hands and hovered up to the ceiling, instantly exploding the overhead lights in the kitchen and temporarily frying the electronics in the kitchen, shutting the refrigerator off and causing the microwave to beep loudly, resetting the clock on it.

The room turned dark, but Lance's body lit the room somewhat, surges of yellow Energy pulsating upward slowly from his body.

Nobody moved.

But then Lance smirked as if he had an idea, "Well! Maybe I can use Electric Risima to—"

"Hey, hey! Don't start with that nonsense! I've got us covered!" Chase interrupted, exploding a flame in his hand, lighting the room up entirely.

"Thanks, Chase," Miss E said, defeated.

"*Can you be more careful?*" Chase exclaimed toward Lance.

"I was just testing it out! It's electricity for god's sake! We knew this would happen!"

"You nearly took me out! I didn't think *that* would happen!"

"I had it under control. I mean, did you even *see* how fast I moved? *No, right?* I can probably move as fast as lightning!"

"I don't care! You had me so worried just now and then you go and blow up the kitchen! The storm didn't even get to that yet!"

"Hey! Since when do you care about tidiness? Don't we get a special exception for *nearly dying* because we're trying to figure out our powers?"

"Can we just fix these lights, please?"

Thunder boomed outside, reminding the three that there was indeed a storm brewing outside.

But this time, the thunder pounded on constantly, rocking the entire house as the sound of rain banged against the window so hard it sounded like it would crack the glass.

Unsure of what to say, Chase, Lance, and Miss E watched as a large fiery ball of light appeared in the sky, massive amounts of Energy crackling from the center of the light, creating a storm cloud that took up most of the sky before the lightning ceased, leaving nothing but pitch-black clouds and pouring rain in the background.

"Chase!"

But he had already been on it, scrambling for pieces of the roof that had fallen to the ground and holding a few pieces in his arms.

Lance rushed over to the hole, standing close to Chase, staring up through the hole, straight into the sky, allowing some of the water to fall on his face.

Lance slowly held his hands up toward the hole in the roof and streamed Energy into the air. Suddenly, the rainwater bounced off a transparent shield of Energy, trickling down the sides of it.

Chase stood next to Lance, carefully measuring his throw. He swung his hands upward slowly, before at once he lobbed the pieces of rubble upward, sending all the rubble into the air.

As soon as the rubble hit Lance's shield, Chase blasted the rubble with Fire Risima.

At the same time, with only a fraction of a second to react, Lance flicked his hand at the ceiling, sending a jet of Water at the roof which cooled the rubble down significantly, solidifying it again and effectively plugging the hole.

Chase and Lance watched the ceiling, making sure it had been stable.

Lance took a breath. "We're good. That should hold for a while."

"That was good thinking. I'm glad we had the same idea." Chase gestured to Lance, still looking up at the roof.

Miss E. had been silent—impressed more than she was concerned.

Chase and Lance turned their attention to the window as more lightning streaked across the sky, the shadowy image of a figure appearing behind the storm cloud, hovering above the city.

Chase turned to face Lance, a look of seriousness in his eyes.

Lance returned the look to Chase, recognizing the look immediately.

"Is that it? What you saw in your dream?"

Lance walked closer to the windows, his hair and shirt sprayed with water, the wind suddenly a dangerous force of nature.

Lance held his hand above his face.

"No…but I-I still think—"

Lance stopped as Chase put a hand on Lance's shoulder.

Chase squeezed Lance's shoulder and shook it, trying to tell him that everything was all right.

Chase didn't even need to say a word, but he did anyway.

"It doesn't matter even if you just learned you've got it, but you have two elements, and if you're right, there are innocent people out there who—"

Lance interrupted, "I remember our deal. And I feel fine. My mind is racing faster than I can keep up with, and this energy I have feels like I've known it forever. I can and will use it. We're doing this now."

Lance promptly turned to face Miss E, his body still surging with the newly perfected Electric Risima.

"We have to go! T-this is our chance, right?" he asked.

But Miss E said nothing more. In fact, both Lance and Olivia knew that had been a rhetorical question; their minds were already made.

She only watched Lance, locking eyes with him.

They held a position for quite some time before another explosion of thunder erupted, shaking the entire house, tossing debris into it, pieces of rock and glass bouncing off Lance's back.

Miss E slowly nodded, gesturing to the storm cloud.

"That cloud is no different than anything we've worked on."

Miss E watched the cloud in the sky carefully.

"It's no different than any of the drills we've covered in the last few months. It's a part of nature, which means it can be manipulated by Rasrims. Use Risima—and destroy it."

Chase snickered. He walked over to the window, steam rising from Chase's body, the rainwater instantly evaporating as soon as it touched his body, sizzling.

"Are you nervous?" Chase asked.

Lance joined Chase. "Not in the slightest. I mean, I just learned how to use another Element."

The two boys watched as the entire sky came alive as the storm cloud released a frenzy of Energy, hundreds of bolts of electricity striking the city at different points, blasting wind much harder than before.

Miss E found a slight smile on her face as she found strength in her body, standing up straight, noticing that neither Chase nor Lance had faltered. They only looked more confident as they watched the storm—forming a game plan.

They're ready, she told herself.

That's nothing. They'll stop it. This is exactly what they were made to do.

This is exactly why he…why we were all wrong.

Miss E sat back, clutching her kitchen sink hard.

She closed her eyes tight, breathing hard.

"Be Rasrims," she whispered to herself, trying her hardest to toss bad thoughts out of her mind, focusing on her breathing.

"Protect them, Chase and Lance…!"

CHAPTER 7

Answers through Chaos

About twenty-five minutes later

A blur of yellow dashed through a metropolitan street, skipping over streets flooded with murky water, his body light and nimble as Electric Risima powered his muscles like a fuel in a machine. Lance had been moving so fast he could see nothing but screenshots of his surroundings, the various structures turning into blurs as his lightning-quick body flashed over large buildings, through narrow alleyways, and over the debris riddled in the street that was left stranded by the intensity of the storm.

Although his vision and mobility should have been impaired due to the chaos the storm generated and the sheer number of hazards the powerful winds created, Lance's agility and quick thinking, which was enchanted thanks to Risima made the traversal light work. He could use both Water and Electric Risima to trek over streams of flooded streets and through large puddles as if they weren't even there.

Lance had seen it all anyway. He and Chase took many trips to the city over the years leading up to that fateful event they experienced years ago. He knew all the routes he could take.

And now he finally had the ability to protect the city from the several disasters he and his brother witnessed.

This ability would increase the more Energy Lance could produce, and by using Risima Infusion, he could draw in an unlimited amount of Energy from the massive storm overhead.

Lance scanned the area. In every direction he looked, he fired Electric Risima out, surging weak volts of Electricity into the area and honing in on the displacements of the electrical surges into his surroundings. Using Electric Risima like this meant that Lance could essentially "feel" his surroundings by mapping out the entire area into his mind. It was like seeing an x-ray or skeletal layout outline of everything around him—even in directions he wasn't looking. Every time Electric Risima moved in ways Lance didn't expect, he noticed he was finding structures like houses, office buildings, or stores, and every time Electric Risima went through something, he had found himself survivors.

Lance turned to look behind him, noticing Chase had been very close by, using Fire Risima to speed his pace up, trying his best to keep up with Lance.

Lance turned his attention back to the shadowy outline of the city dimly illuminated by the chaotic thunderstorm overhead. Fortunately, Lance's Electric Risima had confirmed that most of the city had evacuated using whatever means they could to escape the storm.

But Lance also noticed that in the entire time he had been searching, he had found not a single car traveling past him out into the safety of the suburban neighborhoods behind him. Lance found that odd, but he simply assumed that a mass transportation system was responsible for this. If Lance could find it, he would most likely find the center of the storm as well.

Lance slowed down, screeching to a halt as he noticed a building next to him get struck by lightning. He noticed the wind speed had increased dramatically, and the intensity of the thunderstorm produced hundreds of storm clouds which blocked out the moonlit sky.

Lance held out his hand, signaling Chase to stop when he noticed a tremor developing, feeling faint vibrations rumble underneath his feet.

Chase slid across the slick ground and stopped next to Lance, still completely dry.

They quickly took notice of a nearby building in the shopping district of the city crumbling, the top caving in completely, reducing the once large building into a pile of rubble.

Chase was already on the scene, tossing cement and bricks out of the way, searching for anyone who could have been trapped.

"Was anyone in that building?" Chase yelled out against the ferocity of the storm.

Lance joined him but focused more of his attention to figuring out how the building's integrity failed, allowing him to sense patterns in other similar buildings that would suffer the same fate.

"No, this can't be real!" Lance yelled as lightning flashed overhead, briefly illuminating the area, revealing something lying out in the shadows of the night.

Lance was horrified at what he saw.

He originally thought that the city had been evacuated. The fact that he couldn't find anyone reassured him that the necessary precautions to save the innocents were met.

But as Lance found piles of bodies floating in the streets and hands and legs sticking out from underneath collapsed buildings, the horrors of reality struck Lance with unimaginable pain.

"I can't find anyone using Water or Electric Risima! It's all flooded! I-I thought everyone had—"

Lance could hardly speak, his chest suddenly tight as his eyes began to burn, unable to pry his vision away from what looked like entire families massacred by the storm, left stranded out in the ruins of a lost city.

"They're all dead, Chase! No one was evacuated! *Everyone* in this city is dead!"

*****

Two figures stood side by side, standing on top of a skyscraper, looking down at buildings crashing into one another as a storm raged on. They were silent and motionless. However, they radiated tremendous amounts of power.

One of them felt a strange sensation cross his body. He turned his head to face a direction, looking across the horizon toward a set of trees in a smaller part of the city—maybe some fifteen miles away to see the sight of a couple of figures emerging from in the distance of the stormy sky, hidden by the pouring rain and thick clouds developing in the sky.

"Hmph." The man and the person next to him turned their attention back to the storm.

They weren't even fazed by the storm going on. In fact, while they had almost nothing to do with the storm, one of them knew exactly what the storm was and what it intended to do: It wanted to submerge all of North America underneath water, using a thunderstorm to accumulate enough Energy to release everything it had been storing all at once—effectively destroying the entire continent.

The creature's reasoning was simple. It was yearning for Energy—hungry to fuel itself with Risima Energy. One of the men noted that.

But the same man also knew that the creature responsible for this storm was nothing more than a guppy on Osamos compared to the other ravenous beasts and powerful beings known as *Demiurges* that lurked on the planet. They were known as immensely powerful creatures that had enough power to change the entire climate and geography of their environment however they wanted. They were able to change a mountain range into a sea of blood, a river of fresh water into a crater of dust, or even a bustling rainforest into a tundra if they so pleased. Once even the weakest of monsters accumulated enough Energy from a celestial body, there was no telling how powerful it would become.

That couldn't have been closer to the truth as the Humans on Earth ran for safety, although they soon came to learn that nowhere was currently "safe." If you somehow escaped the storm, the frequencies the storm was producing would still leave you in shock and create earthquakes that would bury you in rubble.

The man watching the events of the storm also knew how utterly *pathetic* the response to this disaster had been. It was almost as if the innocent civilians slain by the storm were left stranded here on *purpose*, but it was nearly impossible for him to ascertain the reason.

As a result, the man was tracking several of the Humans responsible for responding to crises like this, and like most other "acceptable" responses to situations like these were, the plan was to fire explosives at the storm cloud until it died.

But they found that to be a stupid idea once their aircrafts transporting the payload found their communications system fried and then shortly afterward plummeted out of the sky and exploded only moments after leaving their bases.

The second decision was to turn to a highly secretive and extremely powerful group of genius engineers, scientists, and assassins known as *the Division* and use their resources to combat the storm cloud, which, to his surprise, had a great chance of succeeding.

But the top scientist in charge of initiating the operations to destroy extraterrestrial beings was nowhere to be found, which left the entire Division left without its most important weapon to defend the planet while disasters brewed on the surface.

It was true that the president could technically assume control of the Division under the new National Security Act, which stated that the president had the power to launch attacks against any extraterrestrial creature attacking the United States or its allies *directly*, but it was the former leader of the Division's profound intelligence and operational know-how, which allowed her to navigate even the ugliest of politics that the Division was currently facing.

It was her knowledge of how intelligence agencies worked and operated that gave her the wisdom necessary to lead the world's most powerful government agency without ever having to worry about her plans being exposed and her leadership scrutinized by the press.

But the president didn't have this same luxury.

As soon as word got out that the president would be in charge of the organization capable of reshaping the world order and directing how space policy was developed, the world's various governments would demand the president to reveal information regarding top-secret US operations and projects to the entire world—including the United States' most formidable adversaries—all thanks to a cunning United Nations Resolution. It was clearly an attempt to limit the power of the United States. The resolution, passed by the UN in 2026 with overwhelming support from over 150 countries, states, "The heads of state of each member nation is hereby bound by their sovereign duties to cooperate with other top-ranking officials of member nations during times that the Earth experiences an extra-terrestrial attack as directed by Resolution 1 of the United Nations Extraterrestrial Defense Council…" or something like that.

The man didn't care about formalities or what the world's governments had to say for that matter. But he still did his homework on the topic and quickly discovered that the last director scoffed at this resolution. She never even considered abiding by it.

He also discovered that the director of the AESD was an expert at dodging politics, journalists, and Congress—something her colleagues and underlings admired her for.

Even though Olivia Tyera went by several names and was known to have used numerous aliases when she traveled overseas, she was known in the States as "Ms. Elusive" due to her innate ability to escape situations no other person has been able to.

But her friends simply knew her as "Miss E."

Olivia's masterful control over both politics and hidden-hand operations alike secured her spot in the history books. She was an admired professional and a beacon of hope for young women and aspiring scholars worldwide.

But Olivia's many successes did not shroud others in the same warmth she received throughout her life.

It was because of Olivia's unique style and compelling ability to lead the US Intelligence Community that the Division's second director was never confirmed. The Division knew that precious secrets and top-secret information would be exposed during the confirmation hearing, something Director Tyera could always avoid with ease.

Of course, this was partly due to the fact that the information the Division currently had simply didn't exist back then. But it was proof enough that Director Olivia Tyera of the Division could never be replaced.

This was why the second highest-ranking member of the Division went missing somewhere in the American Midwest. It was because he wanted to keep his head down and prevent the government from practically forcing him to reveal his secrets to the world while strung along by the UN's rules.

With all this taken into consideration, the *only* thing that could save the people on this planet from an extraterrestrial disaster was a *Rasrim*. That much was clear.

But the man himself decided to watch the events unfold instead of getting involved himself—even though he would have absolutely *zero* problems destroying the storm cloud on his own if he wanted to.

In truth, if things went how he expected it to go, while the destruction would be devastating and several lives would be lost, this would be nothing more than an unfortunate "coincidence" that would prove favorable to his interests in the long run.

Of course, that would depend on a *certain* group of Rasrims to be successful when they intervened. And that would only be the very beginning of a much larger catastrophe. This was everything the man was counting on. It was a very calculated, very precise, and very important plan that he could not afford to fail.

The man, wearing his iconic set of golden armor, brandished by the strongest beings in the universe, which was a symbol of his power and fortitude, sat down and rested himself on the edge of the building.

The second man—rather a boy—in dark-blue tactical gear stood close by. He could feel the intensity of the storm, especially from this high up. The roars of the blasting wind and depriving screams of the thunder gave Chile insight into the storm's fury and pain. It *was* a real living creature with a soul and a mind after all. Chile wished he could soothe it, that he could give the storm the power and freedom it desperately sought, that the storm would praise Chile and recognize him as a hero or even a friend. But this was all against the wishes of his leader.

Chile turned and looked at Melterai, uncaringly dozing off into space as Earth experienced the singlehandedly worst natural disaster in its entire existence.

Chile had a feeling that his leader known as Melterai had been keeping track of the damages and tallying the deaths. But his reason for caring about *that* was unclear.

Melterai told Chile that around twelve million people would die as a result of this disaster. A third of that catastrophe had already been realized. But that number could increase dramatically if this monster decided it wanted a little bit *more* than control of the planet's environment.

The effects of the storm were ironically much more potent overseas than it was here. It seemed that the storm was merely gathering Energy in *this* location, but the effects of that intensified as its energy surged across the planet, collectively picking up more and more energy as its reach crossed the globe—returning everything it collected back to its center here.

But that was only something weak creatures on Osamos did. The much stronger ones already *had* that required energy to wreak havoc on whatever they pleased. If one of *those* had been here, Melterai would have intervened himself. But he simply saw this as an exceptional opportunity that benefited a small group of people at once.

Melterai looked overhead as a pair of high-altitude special fighter jets roared across the sky, announcing to anyone who was still around that help had finally arrived with its screeching sounds of supersonic flight.

Melterai was silent. He never assumed that the Humans had the resources necessary to thwart such a threat.

He knew that these particular fighter jets were the newest in the United States' arsenal. Dubbed the Boeing F-23 Thunderbird, these were the fastest, most powerful aircrafts that the United States currently had.

The best part was they were developed by the director of the Division and had integrated technology designed to attack Rasrim satellites in the event that Osamos decided to attack the Earth.

This was their debut.

Melterai watched as the fighter jets unleashed a series of hypersonic missiles into the storm cloud, unleashing sheer hell on the storm cloud in rapid succession as the jets maneuvered through the storm with agility and tranquility. They moved expertly in such a chaotic situation, showcasing just how proficient and high-tech the Division's equipment truly was. Melterai watched as the Thunderbirds turned with precision, frequently struck by the storm cloud's intense lightning strikes but emerging completely unscathed, firing dozens more missiles into the heart of the storm, wounding it with each strike.

Melterai was especially intrigued when he realized that each time the Thunderbirds were struck by the storm's Electric Risima, the jets managed to *absorb* and even redirect the Risima straight back into the storm as if they could somehow *manipulate* Risima! Did the Division truly have the technology capable of fighting Osamos after all?

The explosions were large and numerous. The entire sky became a showcase of firepower as balls of fire bloomed in multiple places around the storm cloud, some of them spread apart as much as eighty or so miles in mere *seconds*. The entire sky was bright and vivid with red and yellow explosions, the attacks so potent that Melterai could feel the massive shockwaves on the ground.

He watched the Thunderbirds closely, believing for just a moment they would be successful in destroying the storm.

As the Thunderbirds fired more missiles into the storm cloud, it caused the light within the cloud to swell, erupting with even more power.

The explosions, however, caused some demon-like appearance to move within the cloud, a figure beginning to emerge within the light, and the colors changed briefly, turning from a dark red to a cool orange and back to a hellish frenzy of red.

Melterai shook his head. "Fire won't work once the storm learns how to expand its control over Risima. I figured that already!" the masked menace said as if he was bored.

After all, this was *nothing* compared to a storm on Jupiter, perhaps. And you wouldn't dare try to use Fire Risima on a planet like that. You'd trap yourself in an endless inferno, cooking with not only scorching hot temperatures and insurmountable wind speeds more powerful than a Category 5 Hurricane but also while experiencing gravity two times that of Earth's.

Melterai chuckled to himself, remembering the many… unpleasant experiences he had in the past.

Chile became interested in Melterai's tone, taking notice of how lighthearted he had been even in the midst of a terrible storm.

"What would work, Melterai?" Chile asked patiently, taking his time with his speech, still learning how to talk properly.

Melterai turned and looked at him, surprised by the question. No less, he immediately had an answer.

"Water—even Earth or Death Risima, believe it or not. There are other powers, of course. But we're only talking about Risima right now."

Melterai pointed to the storm, focusing on the energized apparatuses surging out of the center of the storm, infusing Risima Energy from the atmosphere.

"A strong Rasrim would quickly figure out that his only option would be to *drain* the creature of all its Energy and not accidentally recharge it with Risima when he attacks." Melterai used the jets screaming across the sky as a point of reference as they continued to fire more missiles into the storm cloud.

"And he wouldn't dare to *challenge* the creature by trying to output more Energy than it, hoping to scare it off in the process."

Chile's expression darkened. He instantly knew what Melterai was talking about.

"Humans don't seem to understand how *not* to challenge things they shouldn't. The strategy that the Humans are experimenting on now is the very same one that this creature's life *depends* on," Melterai suggested, "so naturally, you can imagine which of the two forces competing here are more proficient when it comes to using it properly."

Chile felt strange. Never before did he have such an urge to act, using his powers to do anything but obey orders. But now it was different. Now he was being told *not* to use his powers when he knew he could. He couldn't describe the feeling. He wasn't angry. He was upset, but he was open-minded too. Melterai already described the situation to him.

"Two Rasrims boys exist on this planet, and they are nothing short of special. If they cannot rise to the occasion, they will never leave this planet. With that, if fate decides, this will be their training ground but also their graves. They'll be forced to watch the planet die a miserable death they will blame themselves for until the end of time."

Chile, despite not being the most advanced English speaker, could understand the weight and sense of dread behind Melterai's curated words. They were powerful words. He meant exactly what he said, and the implications were as serious as they were real.

Melterai turned to face the storm cloud, watching in awe as the creature within it frenzied uncontrollably as one of the fighter jets passed, catching it with a strike of Energy, causing it to fall out of the sky and plummet into a building, exploding into a fireball.

"The two boys will die, in pride even, alongside the rest of this planet should Earth decide to fall victim to this creature."

At first, Chile was confused. He was a Human just as much as he was a Rasrim, and while he definitely hated some Humans, he loved the Earth. It pained him to see something otherworldly bring about so much pain and misery about it all. He only wished that nature could thrive without technocrats bringing about the end of it all. That was the unfortunate philosophy behind Human existence.

Then Chile looked up, farther into the sky. Through the thick clouds, he could see the outline of a much larger planet.

This *was* the Humans' fault. Whoever attacked Osamos obviously awakened something much more dangerous.

But Chile conceded to the fact that the Rasrims weren't all that better. They merely sat back and watched as a dangerous creature from Osamos ravaged the Earth knowing full well that the Humans were not capable of defeating such a thing.

But Chile knew he could do it.

He could feel the intense Energy from the storm cloud and knew that if he acted, he would be able to steal every ounce of Risima

Energy from the creature and destroy it entirely in one fell swoop, using his powerful Ice Powers to pierce whatever was inside the cloud.

But Chile resigned from the thought. His head was starting to hurt.

"If those boys don't show up, will we help?"

Melterai stayed quiet. His head turned toward Chile but still faced the cloud. Melterai looked at Chile with his peripherals.

"So you want to help, huh?" Melterai asked almost rhetorically as if he were teasing Chile.

Chile nodded obediently. "Yes, Master Melterai," he said as if he was defending himself.

Melterai could sense the anticipation in Chile. He had trained several people who were bloodthirsty, power-hungry individuals. He knew too well what the feeling was and how to spot it. Chile, on the other hand, was driven by fear and pain. His lust for power stemmed from the weakness he felt within. And *that*, Melterai reminded himself, was more powerful than any force this storm could produce. It was the most powerful force in the universe.

Melterai smiled on the inside.

Only after a few months freed from captivity did Chile have the will to face such a dangerous foe. It reminded Melterai of himself. Melterai was much too powerful to care about the fate of even a large population of the Earth. He knew there was much, *much* more in the universe. He only cared about two people on this planet. The rest could rot for all he cared.

But seeing Chile's resolve moved Melterai. He remembered something important. Even if he didn't like the Earth—or rather Humans—he knew he couldn't just abandon it.

Melterai chuckled. "Fine. We'll help."

He stood up. The air around him became animated, visible streams of bluish wind spiraled around him, acknowledging him sincerely, fearful of his very presence.

Chile watched with a renewed sense of purpose. He felt even more Energy suddenly appear from out of nowhere and was determined to find that same strength in himself. Melterai carried himself honorably and without trespassing against others, but he constantly reminded the world around him he had the potential to wreck it all if he was ever crossed. His Energy was that of an unstable bomb as if it could explode when disturbed in the slightest bit.

Chile didn't even see Melterai move his body to generate the amount of Energy currently flowing around him. Perhaps some people were so advanced they could control Energy streams without even moving, needing only the thought to control Risima Energy.

That was what Chile was looking for.

Light flashed across Melterai and Chile's body, leaving Chile temporarily blinded.

The building they were on began to crack, pieces of it chipping off.

Chile tensed himself. He streamed Ice Risima to his feet and then to the rest of the building, encasing the entire building with Ice Risima, giving the civilians below it a chance to escape before pieces of rubble could break off and crush them.

That was when Melterai unleashed his attack.

The streams of wind suddenly became alive, quaking with intense amounts of Energy, causing the air in front of Melterai to stiffen with power, almost as if the air became solidified.

The Energy that formed around Melterai's body manifested into a missile of Water and Electric Risima, perfectly blended, creating an entirely new Element, which rocketed straight into the heart of the cloud so fast and with so much power, Chile barely got a chance to see it even though the blast radius of the energy had been enormous. The jet stream of Energy hit the figure inside the cloud, and it roared viciously, the cloud spiraling out of control, lightning spraying out from the cloud as if to release its anger.

Melterai didn't move. Instead, he watched the cloud reform itself, taking notice to Melterai.

Chile put his guard up.

"Master—"

"It's fine, Chile. Don't be afraid. Watch the Energy traveling between this cloud and myself. Study it thoroughly."

The cloud began to move, and the red ball that had been in the center of it moved directly above Melterai.

He looked up. Chile put his guard up again, blocking gusts of wind coming toward them.

The storm cloud began to retract, the red clouds billowing upward before at once, a tornado of Energy rocketed down toward Melterai before a massive bolt of lightning struck Melterai hard, chilling Chile to his bone. The lightning struck was vicious, decimating part of the building they were standing on down to the foundation, shattering every window and crumbling part of the roof.

But Chile watched as the lightning that struck Melterai surged through his body, traveling from head to toe, back and forth. It had zero effect on Melterai.

Melterai shifted his body, sorting through the various types of power and Energy he felt inside his body. With little effort, he isolated and focused on the Electric Energy the monster struck him with—ignoring everything else as if it were a mere tickle.

The Energy that had been coursing through Melterai's body rose up toward Melterai's chest, turning into a massive presence of power, spraying bolts of electricity into the sky before Melterai released it all at once and volleyed a lightning-fast streak of Risima Energy back toward the cloud, striking the figure inside the cloud for the second time, causing the creature inside to roar again—but this time in pain.

Chile watched in awe.

The light inside the storm cloud began to dim, causing the storm cloud to shrink in circumference.

But the creature released some of its Energy, magnifying the size of the cloud to become much larger than it had been at its peak.

Chile gagged. The wind pressure had been intense, but he was much tougher than the cloud. He held his ground and created an ice structure around his body, shielding him from the cloud's attack.

Chile's eye swelled, filling with debris, but he found it easier to breathe as the wind pressure died down. He could see Melterai standing unfeigned, staring up into the sky.

Melterai slowly raised his hand into the sky, a dark-black power swirling from his elbow and traveling up into the palm of his hand.

At once, Melterai closed his fist tight, and the entire planet seemed like it stopped moving for a fraction of a second.

Chile looked up and noticed that the storm cloud was gone—it had disappeared completely.

But then an explosion was heard far away, the same one that he had heard when he first saw the storm cloud appear.

Chile turned to see what happened, also trying to look at Melterai for an answer.

Chile gasped when he saw it, but he remained silent, staring straight ahead into the distance.

Far into the distance, far from the city—hundreds of miles away, in fact—the storm cloud reappeared. It seemed to be over an ocean now, far out of harm's way but dangerous nonetheless.

Chile turned to Melterai, who had been staring out into the distance. It was tough to say how he was feeling. He made no sounds, his helmet gave nothing away, and his body language always told Chile that Melterai was as cool as can be.

"We can say we helped now. Although, I don't believe that's a good sign," Melterai said when he gestured out into the distance. Chile ran to the opposite side of the building and froze, watching as something huge began forming on the surface of the ocean, far out in the distance.

A huge wave of water rose rolled over the ocean surface, moving toward the beachfront at an incredibly fast speed. From this distance, it seemed tiny, but neither Chile nor Melterai were fools.

"That's a tsunami, isn't it? How interesting. I haven't seen one begin brewing from such a far distance before…," Melterai noted to himself quietly.

But Melterai's fascination with the sight only proved it was a force to be reckon with. It would be a tsunami that would surely destroy the entire East Coast.

"It's acting in retaliation and all because I put it where it belonged. How ironic."

Chile struggled to produce words, having felt a wave of betrayal overcome him. How was Melterai so nonchalant, almost as if this were all a joke to him?

He looked at Melterai with intense eyes, determined to find some relief in knowing Melterai would take care of the storm for good.

"W-why?" But Chile snapped his eyes shut and turned his head, fighting with his inner thoughts. He had no right to question Melterai. He knew what the man in front of him was capable of.

But Chile found an even bigger justification for the anger he felt inside. His thoughts ran rampant: What was Melterai thinking? What was all that power he had? *Was all this strength and power nothing to Melterai?* It was as if he were only toying with the distressed creature; indifferent about whether the Earth would be destroyed or not! If he could stop this storm, why wouldn't he just do that? Instead, he simply angered it? What kind of nonsense was—

"Stop it, Chile."

The cold words caused Chile's heart to stop on command, leaving him frozen in his tracks. A cold sweat dripped down from Chile's forehead, his expression shot, completely taken off guard.

Melterai shifted his arms around uncomfortably, folding them on top of one another. He took one slow, dramatic step away from the edge of the building as if he were contemplating something. Without another sound, he began to walk alongside the perimeter of the building's flat roof until he came to another corner, where he stopped to gaze at the storm cloud in the distance once more.

Chile was still frozen, his eyes wide open, his entire body stricken with fear.

Finally, Melterai slightly turned his head to the side, his peripheral vision targeting Chile, who had been standing and staring at Melterai.

"Don't *think* such trivial things about me, please. I don't appreciate it. My goals are incomparable, I get that, but they're sensible nonetheless, Chile."

Chile's mind was blank. His mouth quivered in fear—he couldn't bring himself to continue thinking straight.

Chile shot a paranoid look at Melterai.

Did he just…? Could Melterai—?

Melterai stretched his shoulders out, turning away from Chile and toward the storm cloud once more, his mood suddenly carefree again.

"Yes, Chile. I can read thoughts. I know everything you're thinking and have ever thought. I know what you'll do tomorrow and what images flash in your mind like a record on repeat. I see it all clearly."

Chile took a step back, clearly in shock.

"I have the ability to know anything a person has ever thought throughout their entire lives, both on the conscious and subconscious level. I can even plant false memories into the minds of the unsuspecting. If I focus on an individual, I can control every aspect of their minds in an *instant*." Melterai snapped his fingers, emphasizing his point in his usual emotionless tone.

Chile eyes dropped, staring down at the floor. He was reduced to silence—especially in his mind.

Melterai took notice of Chile's desperate mind, which now appeared as if it were vulnerable and exposed.

Melterai squinted uneasily. He didn't necessarily understand Chile's fear. It had been a power he had possessed for a terribly long time. It was also the first time he disclosed this ability to anyone.

But that was because this has been one of his first abilities he *ever* had, actually. He experienced far too many instances in his life where the ability to read minds was as much a plague as it was a useful power.

Melterai gave Chile some insight on his mind-reading ability, hoping to ease his nerves.

"If you'd care to know, I mastered the ability to read thoughts here, on Earth actually. This ability made sense to me. It resonated with my personality. I was never much of a fighter but always more of a tactician."

Melterai continued pacing on the building.

"This power is also what I consider to be one of my most...'precious' tools. Its value to me, as you're imagining now, is indeed unmatched. That cannot be overstated."

Melterai looked up into the sky, right before a lightning bolt flashed across sky, crossing the horizon into the distance, thunder bombing the entire city.

But Melterai ignored the storm cloud, facing Chile entirely. He continued talking.

"The ability to read minds is but a small part of a much larger collection of powers called *Awme*. It has the potential to rival even Risima. Awme was the power I was gifted with since birth, despite it being a largely *Human-based* ability. Most Rasrims and other species will die before ever hoping to master it completely, which is especially ironic when you consider that Humans have the shortest life spans of any sentient species in the universe."

Melterai chuckled to himself, his entire body rolling as he did so.

"I guess it's actually strange when you think about it. Not that many Humans have mastered it themselves either. Less than 1 percent of Earth's population even have a basic awareness that it exists. I haven't discovered the reason behind why, however."

Melterai turned around to look at Chile and quickly noticed his distraught face. Chile's face was completely pale. He could hear Chile's fragmented mind begin spewing thoughts—primarily chunks of fragmented sentences and phrases, especially those he heard from his days in captivity.

Melterai slowly raised his head, intrigued with what he was seeing.

It seems that among the small percentage of individuals who knew about Awme included the same individuals who had captured and experimented on Chile. His mind was riddled with foggy instances of conversations where Chile *believed* he had heard the term, but his mind was still accessing and processing whether he really had.

Melterai nodded. That was a useful piece of information.

He decided to get Chile's mind to focus on something else.

"Chile, listen," Melterai began, noticing that Chile's mind was suddenly enraged, "I would never want to see Earth suffer because even I have an obligation to it all. But I also have an obligation to my duties as the Masked Menace and with that an obligation to see to the protection of certain individuals—individuals who are crucial to my plan of ridding this universe of the beings who are responsible for the suffering and chaos the universe constantly experiences. I will do that even if it costs me everything—even if it means I must destroy *everything* to achieve that end result. I have already lost much more than I can ever gain. But I will protect those individuals at all costs no matter *what*, Chile. Can you understand that? Do you understand what it means to *love* something?"

Chile eyes flickered. His heart began to beat faster.

Chile took a deep breath, trying hard not to allow any stray thoughts into his mind. But he couldn't help himself. He let every thought in his mind for Melterai could see it all anyways.

Chile had quickly realized that Melterai had been choosing his words in accordance to what he was currently thinking. It aggravated him. Melterai had the ability to read minds, and Chile had been unaware of it this entire time! Did others know? Did Daxxon? Was there even a way to know? How did one combat such an ability?

Melterai chuckled.

"Chile, Awme is not a hard ability to learn. It just takes…well, an *open mind*. I can teach you this ability of Awme that it seems you are so curious to learn more about once you are able to master your abilities."

Chile looked up at Melterai.

"What is it called? The ability?"

Melterai nodded. "It is called *Linneteq*. It's spelled with a *q* at the end but is pronounced with a *ch* sound. Does that make sense? Perhaps learning this word will help your ability to speak as well!"

Melterai took a brief pause.

"You see, *Linneteq* exists within a group of other abilities that involve senses—having the ability to sense things *beyond* the ordinary. Of course, it can be used in a variety of situations and can be strengthened depending on the personal abilities of the user."

He turned out and gestured to the storm.

"I've learned a lot, Chile. I've been to many places—I've witnessed many things." Melterai watched the swirling thunderclouds overhead, restless in its pursuit of destruction.

"But one thing I can't seem to figure out is *when* do I shift from a seat in the shadows—to an active role in the light?"

Chile saw a movement to his right—in the direction toward Melterai.

Melterai suddenly lifted his left hand. In an instant, a brilliant mixture of a burst of yellow and red Energy surrounded his hand, crackling with Energy. The Energy began attacking the creature within the storm cloud from afar—manipulating gigantic waves to rise from the ocean, which struck the creature from multiple angles without warning, causing the storm cloud to scream out in pain, releasing more thunderbolts. But the creature was too far to mess with Melterai back. And he knew that.

Chile faced the storm, watching what Melterai was doing before he noticed that Melterai had left the storm alone again, trying to absorb power from the ocean to expand the size of the large wave that it had created in the far distance.

"Like, for example, if I'm the only one who can step up to this storm, am I *obligated* to serve this planet for when it inevitably calls on me to do so again? Do I fight for this planet against the wishes of the masses? Am I suddenly recognized as a savior of Earth—or even an honorary member of Earth—a *Human*? Am I seen as one of their own? And what happens if I refuse? Am I then seen as a monster or an incompetent fool who only wishes to see the weak suffer?"

Melterai gestured far out into the distance, as a speckle of bright yellow light followed by a trail of red flashes came over the horizon.

"Or do we standby and give others a chance to make a name for themselves? To allow the ones already *here* to defend what's rightfully theirs and bear the risks of protecting the planet entirely on their own? Whose side do we take when this planet's population splits into two groups and wage war on each other over their conflicting ideologies? The side of violence or the side of peace? Do we defend ourselves and kill half the planet who seek to eliminate us, or do we risk being seen as hypocrites for killing the other half? Can we even *protect* the Humans from themselves?!"

Chile found himself thinking about that question for long and hard, quickly forgetting that Melterai had the power to know it all anyway.

"No. But we can *prevent* humanity from hurting anything ever again," Chile whispered to himself.

Melterai on the other hand, twitched his head as he pointed out to the fact that two Rasrim boys finally entered the city, noticing that the storm cloud had moved—and took off once more. Melterai chuckled to himself, but Chile didn't notice it.

As far as Melterai was concerned, another being with far more sinister goals in mind existed and was watching. And like Melterai himself, it didn't care about just one planet or one galaxy—but the entire collection. It cared about *everything*, and it was Melterai's goal to destroy this being without ever being detected as he did so.

Melterai watched as the two Rasrim boys crossed the city.

He was intrigued at how they used their Risima Abilities to masterfully navigate across the city, moving above the speed of sound, sound bursts rippling from every step as they trekked the city, using Fire and Electricity to turn a bustling city into nothing more than an obstacle course.

Melterai's goal was the ultimate game of chess, a master plan of mind games, a struggle and display of power between beings that mere mortals could only dream of.

Melterai noticed that Chile had seen the boys too, watching them with a certain look that Melterai hadn't recognized from Chile.

Chile had watched the two boys closely, almost as if he had felt threatened. That was good. That was crucial to this plan.

Melterai stood next to Chile, looking over the city of ruins, watching as the Humans banded together to do what they could to help each other. But Melterai's main focus had still been on the two boys, who at this speed would reach the storm cloud in little under fifteen minutes.

"Who are they?" Chile asked, watching the two boys.

Melterai was pleased. He turned his chin up in their direction.

"Those two are Chase and Lance Kolorio," he simply said. He turned to Chile. "They are the princes of Osamos, and they're also what I would consider *real* prophets."

Melterai rubbed his chin impatiently, deep in thought.

"At some point, I'll need you to—" But Melterai stopped himself, shaking his head.

"No, never mind that," he simply said.

But Chile insisted, "What is it, master?"

Melterai looked at Chile.

"Do you wish to seek revenge against those who wronged you?"

Chile stopped. His face gave nothing away.

"Yes."

"And if anyone got in your way, would you kill them?"

"Yes."

"Even if they were other Rasrims?"

Chile took a slightly longer time handling the question.

"Yes, Melterai. I would."

Melterai nodded, satisfied.

"In that case…there are some Rasrims who are close with a group of Humans who I know will try to destroy both Earth and Osamos—and likely the rest of this galaxy."

"Then I'll find them…I'll kill them. Whoever they are."

"So you say, Chile. But that won't be easy to accomplish."

Chile watched in silence, tracking Chase and Lance even as they disappeared into the night sky toward the ocean. Was Melterai referring to these two as the traitors?

But Chile didn't care.

For all he was concerned, a traitor was a traitor. Anyone who wished to seek harm against an innocent person should die.

Melterai stood tall. From where he was standing, his most important pieces of the puzzle were beginning to align in the correct places for the first time.

"Let's go, Chile."

Melterai closed his fist, and a dark-black Energy surrounded their bodies, spiraling around them slowly before they vanished into thin air, leaving no traces behind.

*****

Olivia was restless.

She paced back and forth tirelessly as she tried to calm her nerves, but for the time being, she could only think about Chase and Lance. More specifically, she could only think about the *people* who were already tracking Chase and Lance as they traveled throughout the city, their Risima powers a beacon for all sorts of unwanted attention.

And she knew that these same individuals were tracking *her* as well, even at this very moment.

Olivia hoped that all the information and training she gave the boys, both the lessons and the subliminal, psychological framework she worked into their minds, would prove to be enough to outsmart any of their pursuers. She had essentially turned Chase and Lance into a copy of herself when she had just been training for the field.

She knew it would be enough. Olivia had been smart. She had calculated the boys' entire childhood from how they would be raised to what they would be taught on a day-by-day basis. She had picked movies and educational shows for the boys to watch and filled their hungry minds with all sorts of knowledge and wisdom to make them as intellectually versatile as possible. She used positive reinforcement and operant conditioning to teach the boys how to locate and solve their own problems without needing assistance. They had been taught in a very discreet manner how to navigate tense situations, negotiate and barter, use technology to collect intel on points of interest, and how to stay hidden when they ventured out in public settings.

Of course, she also molded martial arts and lethal forms of combat into their minds, enhancing their skills to an entirely different level.

Olivia had turned Chase and Lance into living weapons.

But as young and outgoing boys, it was difficult to know for sure *when* the skills she had buried into their minds would emerge. Would they instead revert to and grow into their more natural personas as Rasrims as they grew?

Chase and Lance *were not* the same Rasrims today as compared to, say, their infant years. The boys were rash, bold, and compared to Human children, *violent*.

Their attitudes revolved around the idea that they needed to learn to fight in order to survive as this was the norm for young Rasrims on Osamos. It was similar to a natural instinct like that of a wild animal's except Chase and Lance were using their abilities before they even knew it. It was simply second nature to them at that point. Of course, once they were around two or three years old, their powers mysteriously vanished, never to resurface until they began training that beautiful summer day in June.

Olivia, who studied Rasrims extensively, was more than prepared to reshape Chase and Lance's attitudes and personalities. She needed them to *think and behave* like normal Humans but fight like the absolute best of them.

After all, no one would expect two bright teenagers who, if pushed into a situation, relied on wits and technical skills to solve their problems rather than blow everything to pieces using Risima.

But Olivia wasn't proud of everything she did. She made mistakes and had her regrets.

She had modeled Chase and Lance into two-faced fighters who would turn from boys into warriors on command.

If she could teach the boys to fight pain with deception and strategy instead of solely relying on destructive superpowers to, in her mind, protect Humanity, then she was doing the right thing for perhaps the first time in her entire life.

Her biggest reason for all this? Olivia knew that these were the skills that would teach Chase and Lance the most about *Humanity*. These skills mired in deception were the epiphany of what made Human beings what they truly were—and she knew *that* was a humbling revelation.

But she also knew this storm was approaching all along and this would be the first time both of those realms of behavior—those of humans and Rasrims, intelligence and power—would finally come together.

She knew that Lance would awaken to a second Element—and quite possibly more.

And she knew that the dangers facing Chase and Lance weren't just a cloud in the sky—but enemies lurking in the shadows both on Earth and elsewhere. These were demons, devils, and legends of the damned—people with extraordinary capabilities who were impossible to detect and impossible to avoid.

But in order to counter these individuals she once called her allies, Olivia had to teach Chase and Lance more than just how to use their powers—but ways to continuously *improve* their techniques and adapt for whatever the situation called for.

This was where the Rasrims were left vulnerable: They did not have the unique ability to rationalize and change beyond their natural states.

Olivia taught Chase to use his Fire Risima to magnify his strength to colossal levels and concentrate his Energy into piercing beams of Fire—able to scorch holes in virtually anything. She taught Lance how to concentrate both his Water and Electric Risima into a perfect blend and switch between the two, able to use his defensive Water abilities and keep himself energized while unleashing devastating amounts of Electricity to use as a high-power offensive tool. She had taught both Chase and Lance how to use their Risima in practical ways, combining their skills with hand-to-hand combat, turning Risima as a weapon into a technique to blend in a variety of lethal physical attacks. She knew that if she had taught Chase and Lance everything *she* had been taught, Chase and Lance wouldn't just become Rasrims with supernatural abilities—but also Humans who were nothing short of masters of death.

Olivia sat down at the kitchen table and tried to relax. She folded her hands, resting her elbows on a black dinner mat on the table.

Olivia causally turned toward the window next to her as another round of lightning lit up the night sky—pounding the Earth with magical displays of light. There was something about thunderstorms and darkness that Olivia had enjoyed, but she couldn't quite put her finger on the reason.

Olivia rested her chin on her fist, observing the outside world aimlessly, not too focused on any one thing in particular.

But it was just as Olivia started to turn away from the window that a slight sharp movement in the darkness of the stormy sky caught her attention. It was too subtle for any normal person to notice, almost as if she had been imagining it.

But Olivia's gut told her something was wrong.

She sat still for a moment, keeping her attention trained in the same spot she was looking at but using her peripherals to spy on the area she had her doubts about.

There wasn't another movement, nothing to distinguish in the large bare lawn that surrounded the house.

Rain continued to splatter on the windows, tapping the glass with a sudden urgency, almost as if the storm was warning Olivia about something lurking about, fearful of what that could possibly be.

After a few seconds, Olivia turned away from the window dramatically and closed her eyes.

She inhaled and took in a deep breath, telling herself to relax.

Then she waited for a few seconds.

Olivia listened carefully, her immediate senses ignoring the storm and listening to noises outside the ordinariness of the pouring rain and thunder outside.

Olivia exhaled, steeling her nerves and concentration completely.

And then her eyes shot open.

Without any warning, Olivia bolted up from the dining room table like a gust of wind and moved through the dining room as fast as she could.

She worked quickly, wasting no movements as she shut the blinds on the windows and flicked the lights off in the room.

In only a second, she had made her way to the next two sets of lights in the kitchen, her body as nimble as lightning.

Olivia was careful not to stay in any one place for more than a millisecond, moving the entire time and staying away from the windows.

She kept her body low and scanned every intricate detail of the house with her peripheral vision, moving as silently as a whisper, and she made sure to keep her ears tuned in as to every minuscule sound in the background as she moved, minimizing unnecessary movements down to null.

But she heard nothing in the background and especially nothing in the house—not even the sound of her own footsteps.

Olivia stopped when she reached the refrigerator in the kitchen and pulled the left-side door open, which was the freezer.

She used both her hands to move frozen bags of vegetables on the top shelf out of the way, careful not to make too much noise. Once the top shelf was empty, Olivia stuck her hand in the back of the freezer and felt around the inside of it, feeling around for a loose compartment located at the very top of the freezer.

Olivia's hand located the false panel and slid the compartment open. She reached deep into the fake compartment before she removed a modified Glock 19 and quickly inspected it, ensuring it still had all of its modified attachments on it, which included an infrared scope, armor-piercing rounds, and a suppressor.

She cocked the barrel of the gun back and chambered a round into it.

The gun didn't come with a safety.

Olivia put the gun into a set of deep pockets she always made sure she wore—making sure the gun was completely concealed. Olivia slid the false panel back into place before she quietly closed the freezer door. All of the lights in the kitchen were already off, and that left only one more set to flick off.

Olivia hustled to the foyer and shut off a set of overhead lights and then moved to a set of lights that connected to a light post outside the house.

She flicked the light switch off.

And then she froze, a chill moving down her spine.

She knew someone was watching her.

Olivia's suspicions were confirmed when she heard a light tapping sound outside the house, noticed that the lights on the porch suddenly shut off, and then heard a squish of wet grass near the kitchen window.

Olivia stayed low, keeping her senses sharp.

Olivia moved slowly, laying her back against the wall in the foyer, making sure she was out of sight from any of the windows.

She rested her hand above the pocket holding her gun, ready to draw and shoot at a moment's notice.

Olivia moved her head to the edge of the doorway. She noticed that the sound of rainfall had gotten louder and all the ambient noise from outside had been easier to hear.

Slowly, she peered her head around the corner, allowing time for her eyes to adjust to the sudden darkness.

Then Olivia stopped once more. She bit her lower lip, her heart rate increasing.

The front door had been wide open.

Suddenly, Olivia's heart dropped into her stomach when she felt cold steel against the back of her head, a hard cylinder object pressed firmly in the middle of the back of her head.

"Don't move a single muscle, Olivia."

She froze.

She tried her best to remain calm, relying on her skills to stay sharp. She replayed the voice of the intruder in her mind, trying to figure out who her intruder was.

Olivia tried to move her head around but abruptly stopped when the gun on the back of her head pushed her head forward. She slowly closed her eyes, disappointed with herself.

But then Olivia heard something crucial.

She relaxed her posture and finally broke the tense silence that had infiltrated the atmosphere.

Her voice was steady and calm.

"I'm impressed. You've gotten better. You didn't make a single sound." There was more silence for a few seconds. The intruder's movements stopped entirely, fretful of anything Olivia could have done.

But it was too late.

Olivia spoke with a sense of comfort in her tone. She knew what effect it would have.

"You don't have to act like you don't know me," she said.

"But do I?" the assassin finally responded, his dark, gritty voice matching perfectly with the tone he had set by breaking into the well-guarded mansion, somehow managing to bypass cameras, motion detectors, and even thermal sensors.

The intruder slowly moved the gun from off her head but kept it pointed straight at her head the entire time, moving, tracking even the tiniest of movements she made. But of course, Olivia knew all of this. She knew everything the man did and would do.

"You've been gone for almost eleven years now. To anyone in our line of work, you're either dead—or a traitor. I haven't decided which of those two versions of you I've stumbled across *yet*."

Olivia squinted. That was code for something, but she couldn't immediately figure out what. She needed to navigate this next part carefully.

Olivia slowly rose from the ground, keeping her limbs in plain sight to indicate she wasn't planning on attacking back.

"How did you find me?"

The man didn't answer right away.

"Well, it took me a decade. I never stopped searching."

Olivia noticed his wording. Perhaps a few things did change.

Olivia tested the intruder. "So what? No amount of time should have led you here. Perhaps it was a hunch? A lucky tip? Maybe you finished *Project Beartrap* and decided to use it on me? Is that it?"

The man said nothing.

Olivia didn't allow his silence to discredit her questioning.

"The others don't even know you're here, do they?"

"Stand up." The intruder's voice was bold and harsh. "The dining room. The same seat you were just in."

Olivia nodded. She got all the information she wanted. She was just rewiring the situation in her favor.

And it worked. She had already won. As soon as she had a chance to look the intruder in his eyes…

Olivia moved from off the wall, taking her opportunity while she could.

"Very well. I'm moving now."

She made sure to keep her movements steady as she found her way back into the kitchen. With every step she took, she listened to the light steps of the man behind her, tracking his entire body from sound alone, mapping his body and position in her mind.

Once the time was right, Olivia knew that she could easily disarm and kill the intruder. But she had a feeling that if she chose her words carefully, that didn't have to happen.

Olivia took her seat in the dining room. She always sat in the seat that faced the front door, across the table, and in the direction of the kitchen, which was to her left and the hallway leading to the basement to her backside.

From the corner of her eye, she watched as the intruder walked past her and noticed that he had always kept his pistol on her—its balance kept perfectly still and aimed at the same spot even as the two walked.

The intruder took a seat across from Olivia, leaving the lights off. But at this point, they could see each other clearly.

Olivia and the intruder sat, facing each other in silence for what felt like hours.

Finally, Olivia spoke.

"So are you here to kill me?"

The man's emotion stayed plain. His expression was like that of a robot. He gave absolutely nothing away. There was no remorse, fear, or anticipation in his eyes whatsoever.

"That doesn't have to be the outcome of this meeting."

The man cocked his head toward the window.

"We need you, Olivia. You knew this day would come. It's just a damn shame that I have to drag you in like a cat left in the rain."

Olivia's eyes glanced over to the windows, listening to the thunder in the background. "Well, I guess you would be, huh?"

The man flicked his wrist, a lightning-quick movement that Olivia had almost missed.

A bullet whistled as it pierced through the air, taking a single strand dangling down on Olivia's face near her left ear. It nearly grazed her—missing by less than an inch. The shot was completely silent. If she wasn't *staring* at the gun, Olivia wouldn't have even known it was fired.

Olivia folded her hands and leaned forward, angrier than she was intimidated. She tilted her head and questioned the man, her commandeering personality taking over.

"I suppose you still don't take well to jokes, huh? I will never miss that about the job. But excuse my lightheartedness. Please, *continue*," she demanded.

"Don't get things twisted, Olivia. Some of the other members believe that if you *are* alive, you ought to be put down, no questions asked."

Olivia sat back in her chair and crossed her arms and legs.

"Are you one of them?"

She allowed the man to sit on the question, weighing his options over an overconfident Olivia he was beginning to fear he could take. How could she always remain in control like this?

In the meantime, Olivia quickly took notice of the man's outfit: black full-body tactical gear with a minimalist styling and black utility boots suited for a variety of purposes. Olivia knew that it was what several members of the "Arms Sector" of the Division wore—or in other words, what modern-day assassins wore.

Olivia deduced that this particular outfit had been personalized to include cargo-style pouches, which held three different-sized knives and an improvised explosive in his chest pouch, a holographic transmitter on his right hip, a silencer, three extra clips on his left hip, and a multi-tool to get individuals out of a tight pinch in a smaller pouch also on his right hip.

Olivia also knew that the man had been carrying ammunition that had the ability to harm Rasrim. Ordinary bullets couldn't pierce the skin of most Rasrims. It was a type of ammunition that Olivia herself had developed.

Olivia continued observing the man, studying almost every piece of gear and equipment he had on him from the way it contorted the tight uniform on the man's body and how the man moved. She had seen some of his gear when the man walked by and gotten the rest from just now. The subtle movements he made confirmed everything to Olivia.

Oliva knew for certain that this man in particular had calculated all his moves. If he ever needed something, he was always in the right position to grab it right away—no matter where he was or what his assignment was. The assassins of the Division were not to be taken lightly. They were all perfectionists, dead-eye shooters, and knew techniques that allowed them to conquer virtually any situation you could think of. No target, whether they were a terrorist, businessman, celebrity, or even a foreign leader was safe when the Division wanted you eliminated.

But why Lloyd had come equipped with enough gear to take down a city was beyond Olivia.

After all, she *was* just one person.

Olivia made sure her examination of the man went unnoticed. She had detailed the assassin quick enough that it merely seemed that she was adjusting herself in her seat.

All that was left to uncover was whether the assassin had been wearing a wire or was transmitting any information to an outside team. But if the assassin was, Olivia could take care of that whenever she needed.

Olivia stretched her neck, rubbing the back of her head where the gun had been placed.

Lloyd didn't even notice what she had done. With sleight of hand and perfect timing, Olivia managed to arm herself with her gun, positioned perfectly on her left leg, aimed directly at Lloyd's right kidney. In her right hand, she managed to snag a kitchen knife that she left hidden under an envelope on the dining room table. In one perfectly executed maneuver, she could kill Lloyd in about two-tenths of a second.

And that was only one of the *eleven* other options she quickly prepared and had ready to go in the blink of an eye.

Olivia had her own techniques too.

Olivia noticed that the man never answered her question, and so she decided on a different approach.

"Hey, didn't you always want to be a geospatial analyst? One of those guys who picked apart Chinese satellites and all that? Why are you here now? And who taught you how to operate like this?"

Her voice had a sense of sardonic curiosity in it as if Olivia was mocking the man.

The man turned his head up; he looked concerned.

"So you don't remember?"

Olivia's face lightened up. She scoffed.

"Of course I do." She leaned over the table, her eyes fixated on the man's emotionless posture, her eyes suddenly cold and mean.

"That's because it was *me* who trained you for the field! I taught you how to hold a gun and how to talk to girls for Christ's sake!" Olivia laughed obnoxiously, trying to unsettle the assassin. "I'm just making sure that *you* remember that, Lloyd."

The man shifted his expression, the faintest bit of discomfort on his face. To anyone else, even a trained psychologist, it was nearly impossible to notice.

But Olivia could imagine and outplay the impossible in every situation.

She changed her playbook and cross-examined the assassin. "Of course you were still a teenager then—fresh out of basic training. Don't you understand that I allowed you to put me in this situation? That almost everything that ever happened in your life was because of me?"

The man ignored her. "You're getting sloppy, Olivia. You didn't even hear me come in. If I wanted to kill you, I would have."

Olivia laughed. When it came to reverse psychology, Olivia was a magician.

She wagged her finger, taunting the assassin. "Nu-uh! Nice try, but I *saw* you, Lloyd!"

Lloyd shifted in his seat, keeping his gun training on Olivia.

Olivia continued mocking the man.

"All these years as an operative, and even an old lady who hasn't seen action in years could spot you, Lloyd! You think *I'm* getting sloppy? If I had a gun, you would have been shot dead before you even reached my *driveway*."

Lloyd straightened his back, keeping his composure cool.

Perhaps she had a point. But Lloyd was unnerved, nonetheless.

"That's a shame," he said, "but you *do* have a gun. Or at least you left it in your car. That's *sloppy*, Olivia, even for a retired agent but especially for the one who trained us *all*."

Lloyd reached into a pocket on the inside of his jacket and placed another nine-millimeter Glock on the dining room table.

Olivia shrugged, bewildered with the audacity of her former student.

Olivia sat back in her chair, looking Lloyd directly in his eyes. "And what makes you think that I don't have another one?"

"That wouldn't change the fact that I've got you at gunpoint now."

"You could be in the middle of a cross-hair yourself."

Lloyd chuckled. "How fast is your quick-draw nowadays, Olivia?"

Olivia chuckled back. "Blink and you're dead—the same it's always been. I shoot every once in a while."

Olivia raised an eyebrow. "And I don't miss *any* of the headshots."

Lloyd lifted his chin. "Some would consider that amateurish these days. We're up against creatures who can cross the planet in *seconds* and change the entire physiology of their bodies. And there's not just Rasrims anymore but actual monsters with *terrifying* powers. If they're awakened, they could destroy Earth without even leaving Osamos." Lloyd leaned forward, making sure Olivia could see him clearly.

"But you already knew that didn't you? Did you really think you could keep all your Operations and plans a secret even when you left the Division?"

Olivia looked irritated. It was one of the few things she regretted. But it didn't matter now.

"So what? Will you kill me, or will you bring me back in? But that doesn't matter, does it? After I handle that storm—since that's what it seems you're asking of me—you'll kill me anyway, right?"

Lloyd shook his head. "That's not my call."

Olivia sat back, clearly in disbelief. "What? What do you mean?"

"I'm not one of *the Five*. But doing this—"

"Bullshit! Why else would you be here?"

Lloyd shook his head again. "My assignment's been changed. I'm not even eligible to become one of the Five anymore. I've been given the honorable title of '*deceased*,' which extends across every government file, medical record, and every federal database. That includes Interpol. I'm a ghost now, Olivia, and that's why I have so much free time on my hands now."

Olivia's eyes narrowed, her mouth nearly hanging open. She knew *exactly* what this meant, but the poor fool didn't even have a clue.

Bringing Olivia in was Lloyd's only chance at preventing an untimely fate. Being undercover in the AESD and written off as "deceased" meant that you had a significant chance of being sent into space or on a trip you had a very low chance of ever returning from. It was the perfect example of predestination.

This was the only way to directly engage with extraterrestrial beings without risking public backlash or the exposure of an operation when operatives ended up dead in space—it protected no one but the AESD itself. If you were dead before you were sent to space, how could anyone prove you were there to begin with?

But this was an operation Olivia never agreed with. She launched several satellites and rockets that secretly housed drones and small teams of operatives to spy on Osamos and even foreign countries, but she never faked an agent's death for the sole purpose of sending them into space just to be slain anyways.

The tide of the conversation had changed with this information, and it was unlikely that the old friends even realized it.

Olivia's body tensed up, her fists firmly pressed against the table. "Who gave you those orders?" She raised her voice. "Which asshole intentionally went behind my back to authorize those programs? I need an answer, and I need it *now*."

Lloyd gripped his gun tightly, solidifying his composure as he kept the weapon pointed at Olivia.

Olivia's body slowly tensed up. She recognized the look in Lloyd's face. It was the face of regret—one that attempted to resurrect itself with determination. It was a reckless, barbaric expression. A regretful man in this line of work was a dangerous man. It diluted his perception of reality.

And only one person came to mind when she saw it. There was only one man capable of permitting such atrocities and ingraining such torment into cold-blooded killers.

"Troy. It was him, wasn't it? Who else?"

Lloyd dismissed the question entirely. "That's enough. You'll find out once you come in."

Olivia crossed her arms arrogantly.

"Where is he now? Headquarters? Sweet-talking the president? If Troy is in Washington meddling with agency affairs without me knowing about it, *you're all screwed*, don't you get that?"

Lloyd gestured to the front door with his pistol.

"Get up. Let's go."

"I'm not leaving, Lloyd," she said sternly, "so get lost! Tell Troy and the rest of the Five to clean their own messes up now."

She gestured to the window next to her.

"If they want to launch another attack then they need to be prepared for the consequences that follow. I know that a fleet of Thunderbirds were launched to go fight the storm cloud. If our enemies figure out we have technology that can fight Osamos this early on, what do you think the Chinese and the Iranians will do next?"

Lloyd studied Olivia closely. "So you are a traitor then." He knew something wasn't right about her. Her last sentence revealed it. She *wanted* the Division to suffer without her being there.

"You went to Osamos to handle Operation Stormkill by yourself knowing it would result in a disaster. You brought our enemies closer to us and *never* returned afterward. You knew the Division was doomed without you."

Olivia tried keeping her cool but found she was beginning to lose patience. "Get lost, Lloyd! You *do not* want your current 'status' to become reality, do you?"

Lloyd licked the top row of his teeth, trying to decide how to continue his approach.

"You should know that Chile escaped a month ago." Lloyd stopped, giving Olivia time to process the information before continuing.

"He killed six scientists and even a handful of agents. His whereabouts are currently unknown. You know anything about that?"

Olivia returned Lloyd's serpent-like stare, careful not to show any emotion. That was *big* news! Even with all the tabs she kept, she never knew that Chile managed to escape from the Division! Chile had the potential to be the biggest threat to humanity! If left unchecked for too long, Chile could grow so powerful he would gain the ability to annihilate the *entire* Earth!

But so did two *other* individuals, Olivia reminded herself, and judging from Lloyd's lack of insight, it appeared as if he didn't know about Chase or Lance.

Olivia looked to the side, looking away from Lloyd, making sure she maintained the persona she wanted Lloyd to see.

Olivia played it off.

"No. This is my first time hearing that." Olivia adjusted her glasses, pushing them up to her eyes.

"They never knew how to control his abilities. I bet I'm *still* the only one who can."

"Really? Your value to the Division continues to undermine your trifling arrogance, Olivia."

Lloyd sat back in his seat but still held the gun in position. "You can rest easy knowing we could never manage to replace you."

Olivia squinted. "But you all still think that raising a Rasrim to become the Director will work? That he would willingly cull his own people for the benefit of a single country that he doesn't belong to? Are you *serious*?"

Lloyd smirked. "We got close, didn't we? If you came back, the others would gladly reinstate you."

Olivia scoffed. "That's called desperation, Lloyd."

"No. It's called loyalty."

"It's more like a 'mutual reassurance.'"

Lloyd perked up.

Olivia continued going. "I'm the only Human who truly understands Rasrims and their abilities. In exchange, I'm not placed in a cell and experimented on but in an observatory and tasked with conducting the experiments *myself*. Where could you possibly find loyalty in a situation like that, especially when I know what the alternative would be?"

Olivia's eyes bounced toward the window as lightning streaked across the sky, briefly illuminating the dining room.

She gestured to something behind Lloyd. "Would you mind shutting the front door? The floor's getting wet, and I don't feel like cleaning up two messes today."

Lloyd didn't notice Olivia's obnoxious wordplay. "Close it on your way out. Get up," he said bitterly.

"The only way I'll ever return is if we end the trials! Otherwise—"

Olivia shut her mouth, biting her lower lip. She rubbed her forehead with her hand, realizing she had made a mistake.

Lloyd's face lit up, marking the first time he had visibly shown real emotion.

"The trials? So that's the reason why you hid for this long?"

Olivia exhaled. She looked down at the dining room table and rubbed her forehead. "Christ...," Olivia whispered to herself.

Lloyd turned to look around at the house, suddenly suspicious. "This is an awfully big house, Olivia. Much too big for one person, isn't it? Tell me, are there *others* living here?"

Olivia's face gave nothing away. But she made a mistake. She said too much.

Lloyd suddenly stood up. "I'm not wasting another minute on this. The Five will hear your case and decide your fate. I'll count down from ten. If I reach one and you're not out that door, I'll put a bullet in you and drag you there myself."

Olivia lowered her head, clearly frustrated with herself. "Oh... Lloyd. What did I just do?"

Lloyd lowered the gun, aiming directly at her heart. "*Ten.*"

Olivia turned and looked at Lloyd, giving him a mean glare. "Don't do this. Come on."

"*Nine.*"

"If you pull that trigger—"

"*Eight.*"

"Lloyd! Don't do it! I'm warning you!"

"*Seven.*"

Olivia turned to look out the window. Of course, even at a time like this, all she could think about was Chase and Lance. Her boys. If they were safe, she didn't care about anything else.

"*Six.*"

But they still needed her. At least for the time being. Chase and Lance were not strong enough to take down the Division alone, even if Olivia herself was. But that was utter nonsense to hope for anyway.

"*Five.*"

Olivia looked at Lloyd from the corner of her eyes, but she didn't move. She only faced the window and watched rain splatter against the window and the grass. The ferocity of the storm, for just a moment, seemed to disappear entirely. The *real* storm was in the house now.

"The others have no idea you're here. How foolish can you be to come alone?"

"*Four.*"

Olivia chuckled to herself, her patience all but gone. "You destroyed *every* chance you ever had to be anything, Lloyd! The Division will lose their chance at pulling themselves out of a grave they dug for themselves years ago, and you're here to start burying the bodies, can't you see? Go and listen to them sweet-talk the UN Security Council into creating a 'Ground States' Union Military.'"

Lloyd squinted. He didn't want to drag this out any longer but found it hard to resist listening…if only for a moment.

Olivia scoffed. "Oh yeah, that's right. You were in Analysis when the idea first surfaced. You would have never heard of the term. But now? As an operative, *you* will be the scapegoat the Division throws under the bus if the war doesn't escalate! And once it's revealed that GSUM only existed to take control over the entire world, the Division will crumble!" Olivia became restless, furious with the situation she found herself in.

"Then God *forbid* Osamos or even *another* group attacks… What will the world do then? Who will the defenseless turn to?"

Lloyd stood stiffly, almost as if he were considering Olivia's words. But his mind had been made long ago.

"*Three.*"

Olivia's head shot around from the window and aimed at Lloyd. "D-dammit, Lloyd! Don't you get it by now? Even if you pull that trigger, only *you* will be the one to suffer!"

"I'm prepared for that. That's what we both signed up for."

Lloyd gripped his pistol and aimed at Olivia's right knee, aiming *through* the mahogany table in front of him. He knew his bullet would hit his target spot on.

"*Two.*" Lloyd's voice was just as restless and irritated as Olivia's attitude.

Olivia's hardy glance suddenly became a frightening leer.

Olivia's voice turned into a low, ruthless growl.

"*You will die here if you pull that trigger. Do you understand me?*"

Olivia and Lloyd locked eyes, fire in their pupils. Olivia's calm, intelligent demeanor was now that of a demon's. She had become unrecognizable. It was as if she had mutated and changed entirely— as if *she* were the monster now.

Olivia closed her eyes and sighed, an emotion she hadn't felt in years surging inside of her.

There was nothing left to be done here now.

"*One.*"

"Goodbye, L—"

A single gunshot went off.

The storm raged on, rain banging against the windows. One last lightning bolt streaked across the sky, lighting up the sky once more.

A body thudded and hit the floor.

There was not another sound—not so much as a whisper.

The only sound that anyone heard was the storm outside.

CHAPTER 8

Stormkill

Lance froze when he felt a chill cross his spine. He felt as if he had been watched. But he noticed that he had yet to find even a single survivor.

"Hey, Lance! Take a look at this, quickly!"

Lance turned his head and looked up at the sky, finding Chase standing on top of a large apartment complex, maybe ten stories up.

But Chase didn't need to say another word. Lance could see what the issue was right away.

"The storm, how did it get all the way over there?"

"I dunno! But you needa get your ass up here, quick! We need to make a new plan!"

Lance obliged with no hesitation and hustled over to the apartment complex, slowing down to pinpoint a place on the building where he could scale it easily.

He settled for a drainage pipe that looked sturdy enough and muscled himself up.

Lance climbed expertly, using his strength and agility to his advantage. He had found this to be no different than the hundreds of exercises he did back in the training facility underneath the basement in his house. It was *easy* with or without Risima.

In under six seconds flat, Lance flipped over the roof of the building and found Chase standing at the corner of the apartment complex, staring into the distance.

Lance saw it too.

Somehow, the large storm cloud had moved maybe a hundred or so miles to the east. It was currently looming over the Atlantic Ocean, off the coast of Maryland.

"How did it move so fast?"

"I dunno, but we need to get going! Are we still running with your plan? You hit it with Electric, and I pummel it with Fire!"

Chase turned and faced Lance. Chase's heart rate increased as he saw a look on his brother's face he had never seen before.

Lance's eyes had a strong resolve in them. His entire face had been intense. Chase could feel the overwhelming power building up in Lance's body.

Lance faced Chase. "Yeah. We'll hit this thing exactly how we worked it out. We were supposed to do it here but not much will change!" Lance pointed to the storm cloud. "How fast can you make it over there?"

"Ten minutes. And you?"

Lance looked down at his hands, crackling with Electric Risima. "I *could* flash over to it right now." Lance closed his fist.

"But when I do get there, you'll have to build up the momentum of Fire Risima—increasing the intensity of the heat you're producing before you strike it alongside my *Tsunami Flash*. You remember that drill we did last week, right?"

"Oh, *that* one? You mean, the *Quickfire Flash* I've been working on?"

Lance seemed motivated. "Yeah! By now, we both should have enough power to destroy that damned thing! Remember, siphon off all the Risima you can from it when you're hitting it!"

Chase nodded. But there was another thing on his mind.

"And I hate to say it Lance, but haven't you felt the Energy in the air to be...darker somehow? Aside from that one family you saved on the way here—"

Lance grunted. So Chase had noticed it too. Lance scanned the city. Even though it had been close to midnight and the entire city's electrical grid had been damaged, he could see the entire city in its gridlike layout.

"The people in this city—!"

"Are dead. They're all dead, Lance!"

Chase and Lance exchanged looks with each other, both of their looks uncertain and full of anguish.

"B-but unless we want those across the world to feel the pain of this storm, we need to move now!"

Fire Risima seeped out of Chase's body, creating the same bright-red aura that Chase produced every time he began streaming his Energy.

"Alright! Phase One, starting now!"

Without warning, a bright red aura surrounded Chase's body, swirling around his body as fast as a tornado. At once, the roof underneath Chase's body exploded as Chase propelled himself into the air.

Chase's voice became an echo in only seconds as Lance watched him blast through the sky. "Ten minutes!"

Lance stood back, keeping clear of the opening in the roof.

Lance turned his attention away from Chase. His mind had been full of dark images. He began to remember the awful event that he and Chase nearly died in. He remembered his promise to protect his younger brother and the Earth from *anything* that threatened it—even if that included Osamos.

The Earth was Lance's home, and Chase was his only family. He couldn't let harm come over to either of them again.

"Dammit!" Lance suddenly yelled into the air, Water and Electric Risima escaping his body.

"There's *no one*! Not even a police officer or a soldier! No cars, no helicopters, nothing!"

The storm in the city dissipated, fearful of Lance's Energy. It had retracted, relocating toward the main body. But Lance didn't even notice.

Lance's body began surging with Energy—his eyes fixated on the storm cloud over the ocean.

"I...I was afraid of doing this. If I head straight through that thing, I could end up destroying much more than it. But I can't stop now! It's gone too far!"

A bomb of yellow Energy spiraled around Lance's body, filling him with Energy, so much that he felt he would burst.

Lance closed his fist and gritted his teeth.

He angrily scoured at the storm cloud, his entire body as tense as it could possibly be.

The rooftop began to crumble, the entire building suddenly shaking.

"As fast as lightning..."

Lance cracked his neck, streaming out eye into the environment, lightning flashing across the sky—this time, because of Lance's overwhelming surge of Electric Risima infiltrating the atmosphere.

Now he had become the storm.

Lance shifted his feet back, straightening his body, allowing Electric Risima to surge throughout his entire body, traveling from his foot up to his head and then back down.

Lance noticed that bolts of electricity were shooting from out of Lance, surging from the building across the block. He had become a center of massive amounts of Energy.

Lance's eyes aimed at the center of the storm cloud, looming over the ocean. "If only we had been prepared for this sooner! I could have saved all of those lives! Not a single more—you won't kill another person!"

Lance quickly closed his eyes and focused intensely, accumulating both Water and Electric Energy in his body, allowing it to surge throughout his body painfully as he fought with controlling the overwhelming pressure the Risima exerted on his organs. Lance surged Risima through every muscle in his body as his body quaked with Electric Energy, crashing out into the area around him. He began to open his mouth to yell, as right before the pressure became too much, he shot open his eyes—looking directly at the storm cloud a hundred miles away.

At once, Lance shifted his body forward and exploded with Electric Risima. A flash of lightning crossed the sky, moving at high speed—much faster than anything on the planet.

But it was too fast and far too destructive. It was an uncontrollable force of nature that had been designed to be reckless, a warning of coming destruction.

Lance held out his hand and released a massive amount of Electric Energy into the storm cloud, yelling as his body clashed against the internal Energy accumulated by the storm cloud.

In an instant, everything had turned black. Lance had moved so fast he had hit the storm cloud head on, colliding with what felt like solid material.

But this was an Infusion of Risima Energy—and it was as tough as diamond in this state.

Lance's body crashed into the storm cloud's Energy—at first leaving him to believe he'd pierced it.

But Lance screamed out in agony as his body was brutally attacked by a massive force, crushing his windpipe, stealing his oxygen, and almost destroying his entire body.

The storm cloud erupted with Energy, and thunder boomed within the storm cloud, the entire sky roaring chaotically.

Out came Lance's body, falling from the storm cloud, over ten thousand feet up in the air.

Lance had still miraculously been awake.

Lance clung on to his consciousness and chuckled to himself.

"Yes…it was exactly as I thought!"

Lance laughed to himself—giving no regard to the monster looming above him.

In the back of his mind, this plan began pushing its way to the center of his head.

"How do we even attack that thing?"

"It's simple. It relies on the weather to attack. It uses the ions in the sky to build up its Electric Risima and the nearby water surface to infuse Water Risima. Then it dishes out attacks in order to gain more control over the environment. When two storms collide, they destroy each other, mixing their destruction energies into one another until only one much larger storm emerges. We'll do the same thing."

Chase slid through a puddle, stopping next to Lance.

"We need to find a large place to safely stream our attacks then."

"Yeah. If we use too much Risima from the ground, we'll risk destroying the city."

"Damn! If only we had a wider space!"

"It doesn't matter! We're prepared to do this. This is our first and only test, do you realize that? We always wanted a real-life example to test our powers out. This is our time!"

Chase and Lance ran forward once more, reaching the entrance of the city known as Rockdale.

"We'll attack in three phases. The first phase is simply gathering our Energy by stealing what we can from the storm, turning its site into our site."

Lance flipped his body, regaining his posture.

Lance crashed into the ocean, the speed of his body hitting the ocean causing the water to rise with a loud splash, creating a huge wave to ripple hundreds of feet in every direction, but his body didn't break the surface.

"In Phase Two, we'll send large amounts of Energy into the storm. It likes to convert Risima Energy into Water, Wind, and Electric Risima to simulate the storm we're seeing now. It relies on it. I had enough time to study everything about this thing. That's how it destroyed the Electric Grid in this city. But if we overwhelm it—"

"We can cause it to discharge its own Energy, leaving it vulnerable!"

"Right! Then we initiate Phase Three and destroy it for good!"

Lance began streaming massive amounts of Water Risima into his feet.

His head had been pounded by Risima Energy, clogging his mind. He could barely feel his body as adrenaline rushed through his veins and Risima fed his every intuition and instinct.

Lance rose, standing on the surface of the water, staring up at the storm cloud.

He watched as the storm cloud opened, a huge gaping hole in the black clouds swirling around the center of the creature within the cloud at high speeds.

A bright red light had become visible in the center of the opened section, showing Lance what was inside.

But before Lance could do anything else, the storm cloud attacked again.

Lance flashed to the right, switching back to Electric Risima as he dodged a lightning strike from the storm cloud that hit the surface of the ocean with terrifying power, leaving a sinkhole where it struck.

From the corner of his eye, a bomb of fire emerged through the black clouds. *Ten minutes on the dot. How 'bout that!*

The creature began infusing more Energy, causing the storm cloud to swell in size once more before a frenzy of attacks came rocketing toward Lance.

Lance flashed again, dodging several more electric attacks. He ran across the surface of the water at high speed, infusing Water Risima into his body while he streamed as much Electric Risima as he could—stealing Energy from the storm cloud the entire time.

Lance smiled to himself. With this much open space, he could dodge any of the storm cloud's attacks.

But Lance stumbled as the wind speed picked up, and a circular formation of wind spiraled down from the storm cloud, hovering above the ocean.

As soon as it hit the water, it surged Water Risima into the wind formation, rotating the Water Risima at high speed before shooting off toward Lance, skiing across the surface of the water.

Lance tried to flash again, but as soon as he took off, he was carried upward by the high-speed winds into the sky, left fending for himself, unable to move.

He watched as the Water Cyclone the storm manifested hurtle toward him, whipping up the ocean as if the ocean were nothing more than a toy.

Lance skied backward, gliding against the surface of the water, using his Risima Energy as the guiding force to keep his body above the water.

Once Lance could feel the intensity of the cyclone, Lance fought against the wind pressure, lifting his right hand to oppose the storm by streaming his own Risima against the storm's Energy. He knew what would happen next.

Lance focused on his Energy, calculating all his moves as if he had been directing the pieces on a chessboard.

When the Water Cyclone reached Lance's body, he released Risima Energy into the area, turning the entire Cyclone into his own site of Risima.

At once, the Cyclone's Energy died down, the speed of its rotation slowing down dramatically as the pulsating Energy swirling within it was sucked into Lance's body.

Lance aimed his hands back at the gaping mouth of the storm cloud.

With strong resolve, Lance fired the Water Cyclone into the storm cloud's center and released its Energy—creating a large discharge within the storm cloud to occur.

The effect was excellent. Lance watched as the Risima Energy he released into the cloud lit up the entire sky, blue and yellow Energy searing out from every inch of the dark storm cloud, instantly evaporating all the clouds in the sky.

The storm roared in agony as it took the force of Lance's attack, moving across the sky as if it were trying to escape the attack.

But Lance wasn't finished.

Lance's eyes turned yellow once more, Electricity pouring out of his body.

Feeling deep within himself—his body felt like a battery, a place where currents of electricity roamed around, waiting to be released.

When Lance focused on this sit in his body, he found it increasingly difficult to control it the more he wished to stream it out. It was as if he was squeezing a rubber tube that was releasing a stream of water at high speeds—trying to amplify its already hectic path.

But Lance had spent the last three months familiarizing himself with how to use Risima Energy at various pressures. He knew that while Electric Risima was new to him, if he could demonstrate an ability to control even a tiny amount of its Energy, all he would need to do was condition himself to use larger amounts of Electricity on the fly—when he was most worked up.

And that time was now.

Lance charged his body up with Electric Energy, sending massive currents of power to his entire body. He could hear the Electricity surge throughout and around his body—showcasing tremendous power.

Once Lance had enough Electric Risima within his body, he released a beam of Electric Energy with a circumference the size of a quarter—it was so much Energy in such a small area moving at such a high speed that it would surely destroy *anything* it crashed into.

Lance's body screamed out in pain as he released the beam of Electricity, feeling a tearing pain in his shoulders but also a scorching hot one in his hands and forearm.

But Lance followed through, watching as the beam tore into the center of the storm cloud and penetrated straight through, electricity surging across the storm cloud, pounding at it from every angle with a monstrous force.

The sky lit up with flashing white Energy, Lance at the center of it all. It was as if a flash bomb had gone off. He was sure the entire East Coast could see what was happening.

Lance yelled as he pushed more Energy into the storm cloud, moving his hands slightly to direct the Electric Risima to continue hitting the center of the cloud—before he achieved his goal.

The storm cloud ruptured in half, splitting at the center before a burst of Risima Energy rocked the entire ocean.

Lance's body was knocked backward, his body skidding across the surface of the ocean before he crashed into a wave of water that rose from the ocean.

Lance tried to regain control of his body but found himself constantly bombarded with more Risima Energy even when submerged underneath the water.

His ears and lungs felt as if they would pop as the pressure on his body increased tenfold.

Lance forced himself to remain calm. He had the power to beat the storm cloud. It was nowhere near as powerful as it made itself seem; despite the thousands of lives the storm cloud claimed—it was nothing compared to a Rasrim.

Lance would have it destroyed in only a matter of minutes.

Lance surfaced from the water.

He flipped his hair out his eyes.

And then he released another surge of Risima Energy.

From even in the water, Lance could attack the storm cloud as efficiently as he could on land.

"Alright, Phase Two! Chase, hit it now!" Lance yelled into the air.

Lance quickly closed his eyes.

"Tsunami Flash!" Lance yelled, signaling to his mind and body what his intention was.

A large cyclone of water—one that was much larger than the storm cloud—rose from the water, swirling around the perimeter of the weakened creature.

And then Lance saw it: a series of bright red lights populating the sky in a straight line—heading straight for the storm cloud.

And then he heard the explosions as the red lights turned into fiery explosions like a barrage of missiles had been dropped from orbit. The attack had created a sonic boom of red Energy and ferocious Energy, firepower in each of the explosions that must've been the size of several buses put together.

Lance watched the explosions ripple across the sky, each one occurring one after another, seconds apart from each other, moving toward the storm cloud at high speed.

The storm cloud had no time to react as hundreds of bombs were dropped on it—the red lights were so large and so frequent it was like the sun had found its way in the sky once more.

At once, a firestorm of Energy blasted into the creature, exposing it from dark clouds it had been in all along.

But Lance had no time to see what it had looked like.

"And in Phase Three…remember the first day we learned how to use our powers?"

Chase laughed. "You mean when we were sparring? Fifty kilotons of TNT?'"

Lance laughed with his brother.

"Yes. If we increase that output, we should be able to destroy it!"

"How are you so sure? We've never done anything like this before! We've only been training for a few months."

"But we're ready, Chase. We were destined for this. We aren't like others. We move much faster and hit much harder than anything in the Universe. We *will* destroy it."

Chase sighed, a hopeful smile on his face.

"You already did the math, didn't you? All right, how hard should I hit it on my end?"

Swimming against the current of the ocean at over forty meters per second and using Water Risima to flip underneath waves and projectiles as he dodged several bolts of lightning underwater, Lance forced himself to stay attentive and aggressive against the forcing of the storm's powers. He used a breaststroke kick and maneuvered through attacks by diving far below the surface. It seemed that Lance's hypothesis was correct: The storm was a purely aerial attacker. It could not directly attack its enemies who sought refuge underneath the ocean's surface. That made Water Risima one of the best natural counters to the storm's powerful wind- and electric-based attacks. Lance stayed agile even though he was about one hundred feet below the surface in pitch-black water. He kept tabs on where the center of the storm was at all times, using every opening he could get to suddenly roll over to his backside and fire large streams of water into Hydraulic Beams and Tsunami Flashes.

Lance was surprised to see how well the storm defended itself. It created hurricanes consisting of Category 5-plus wind speeds to negate much of the Water Risima Lance threw at it. But by doing that, Lance's Risima eventually began to overwhelm the storm and continued to cause its size to shrink dramatically. It was only then that Lance finally propelled himself upwards and leaped out of the ocean, using all his core muscles to power through the surface of the water. Wasting no time, he streamed Water Risima to his feet, allowing him to stand on the surface of the water once more.

Lance looked straight up into the air, straight through the center of the storm cloud, which looked like it was all on fire.

He yelled at the top of his lungs.

"Now! Phase Three!"

Lance didn't wait for an answer. Instead, he brought his hands upward and felt tremendous pressure surrounding his shoulders as he built up a torrent of Risima Energy, Water rising from the ocean slowly, surrounding Lance's body, quaking with the power of Risima.

Lance clasped his hands together, igniting the Water Risima, and created large beasts of Water to rip into the storm cloud from the southern end of the storm.

The storm fought back ferociously, sending cluster bombs of Electric Risima out in retaliation, knocking away Lance's Water Risima.

"Chase!"

But Lance got his answer.

The firestorm of Risima Chase created turned into a sun of potent Energy—a missile of power that rocketed into the storm cloud from the north, fusing with Lance's Water Risima as if they were meant to be placed together.

Fire and Water fused into one another. Because they were wielded by different users with different Energy types, the result created a violent reaction that ripped across the entire sky—the force of the collision so great that the entire ocean felt its power. The uneven blend of power was one that the universe could not sustain, causing the entire area to explode in an angry frenzy of magnificent power, unleashing a large, immensely powerful discharge of Risima Energy. But it was already over as soon as it started. Just like that, the world witnessed the godlike powers that Chase and Lance possessed.

"But not all was well yet."

Lance yelled as a wave that size of a skyscraper crashed into his body, crushing his entire body underneath the pressure of the ocean.

Chase, who had been in the air, had been clipped by the explosion, hurtling down into the ocean, smoke pouring out of his body.

Chase's body crashed into the ocean before a large cone of fire erupted from where his body hit the ocean.

The explosion had created a massive sinkhole in the ocean, creating a tsunami that stormed underneath the surface of the ocean—a second gigantic wave of water following directly behind it.

Chase and Lance had been knocked unconscious, leaving the largest tsunami ever created to find its way toward the entire East Coast of the United States, parts of South America, and even the western coast of Africa.

*****

Melterai laughed aloud and clapped his hands in the air, a loud, booming laughter, which for some odd reason warmed Chile's heart.

"*Yes!*" Melterai roared hands in the air, fists balled up. He watched as the storm cloud exploded, creating a large fireball to surge over the ocean, leaving nothing but specks of multicolored ash to trickle down from the sky into the ocean.

"They *are* strong enough! What was I so worried about? The gods be damned! Hahaha!" Melterai celebrated, leaving Chile to watch him in an awkward trance, confused.

The man wearing the armor was bad enough, but what was this emotion he was exhibiting? Was he upset?

Chile inched closer to Melterai, holding his hand out, thinking his master needed help.

Melterai turned and acknowledged Chile. Suddenly, his overjoyous celebration mellowed and disappeared.

"Yes"—Melterai's voice suddenly relaxed, bringing his normal attitude back—"what's wrong, Chile?"

Melterai pointed to the ocean, far out in the distance.

"Chase and Lance were victorious. And it was terribly simple too! Their plans worked beautifully—two brilliant tacticians with nothing but the sky above them!"

Melterai burst out into laughter again. "But talk about anticlimactic, right?"

Curiously, Chile turned in the direction Melterai had been pointing at.

It was true that he, like many other survivors in the city, had seen the storm cloud explode across the entirety of the Atlantic Ocean, leaving nothing but a pitiful cloud of dust falling to its doom in the middle of the Atlantic.

But Chile had noticed something else over the horizon. Something far worse than the storm cloud was coming. It was the result of unchecked power wielded by amateurs.

Chile knew that the storm cloud was nothing more than a child crying for attention. It was obvious in its torment as well as its method of attacking. It was powerful—that was undeniable. But the storm cloud attacked with no goal in mind, and it relied on elementary tactics to defend itself. Any Rasrim could have done what that storm cloud did. The only reason the damage was so catastrophic was because the response was poor. That was why two Rasrim amateurs had no problem destroying it.

But Chile knew that wasn't the end of it. He saw that through the thick darkness of the night that a large, powerful wave was

STORMKILL

approaching the eastern shore. It was about the size of the storm cloud itself—maybe a few miles in length.

Chile lifted his right hand, hesitating at first. Even from here, he could simply stop the incoming wave. He had long since surpassed his limit to stream Risima Energy. He suspected that his ability to use Ice Risima was among the best in the world.

"Master…," Chile said in a low tone, afraid to upset Melterai, "the storm is dead. But something else approaches."

Chile outstretched his arm, reaching out toward the horizon, and pointed to what he saw in the looming darkness.

Melterai looked in the direction Chile gestured to. At first, he was silent as if he were caught in between making two important decisions. He moved his head back and forth as he tried to get a better look.

"Hmm. It looks like another tsunami," Melterai said in his same uninterested voice. "What about it, Chile?"

Chile clenched his teeth.

"Those boys. I can't sense their energies. They can't stop it."

"And how do you know that?"

Chile shook his head.

Like he thought, Melterai took a dangerous back seat on a road to destruction. Like a wealthy king or arrogant politician, Melterai's power trumped his likelihood to help those beneath him.

Chile tensed himself. "I'm going to help. I'll stop the… su-na-me?" Chile looked toward Melterai for reassurance. "Please let me help! I'm worthy!"

But Melterai gave no immediate response. He only watched Chile.

Chile turned back toward the tsunami. And without another warning, he leapt off the building, releasing his reserve of Ice Risima.

Chile crashed on the floor below, ice streaming through the sidewalks, cracking into the part of the building he was on, turning everything into solid ice.

Chile set his sights forward. He knew he had about half an hour before the wave reached the shore.

267

Chile began walking in the direction of the beach, his eyes cold and laser-focused on the massive wave approaching the shore.

Once Chile had proof that he had the power to control even nature's most ferocious monsters, he would turn his attention to what he *really* had in mind.

Chile never believed that he had been a hero.

Chile was a demon. And this was nothing more than a little test for what was soon to come.

CHAPTER 9

Echoed Peril

When Lance regained consciousness, he instinctively gasped hard, sucking air into his lungs as hard as he could. Lance coughed out, gagging on his own breath before spitting water out of his mouth.

Lance quickly remembered where he was, trying to remain calm, his eyes automatically scanning the sky. Was that really it?

Lance's feet began to touch something gritty and mushy while he tread the water.

He was back on the beach.

At that exact moment, Lance noticed that the temperature had dropped dramatically. It felt as if he were inside a freezer. At first, he only thought it was because of how long he had been in the water and how dark it had been. Perhaps he was simply imagining it.

And then Lance finally turned around to begin walking on the beach, deciding that the storm and the ocean were now safe.

Lance's heart dropped. He threw his hands up quickly, his eyes rapidly bouncing back and forth. Something was terribly wrong.

"What the h—!"

Lance was looking at a massive wall of ice that stood at least sixty feet tall, spanning the entire perimeter of the eastern shore, blocking off the beach from the rest of the city!

Lance began to stumble, his head and body unable to turn away from the enormous wall of ice in front of him.

It must've spanned some fifty miles in length *at least*. It was so tall that Lance could hardly see the sky over top of the ice wall, and it looked so thick that Lance could have mistaken it as a glacier or even figured he had been transported somewhere out in the arctic.

Words couldn't even describe what Lance was seeing as he tried to produce words, but all he could let out were confused mumbles as he tried to reason with himself.

What the hell happened here?

Lance turned his head when he heard a commotion down the shoreline. Lance was in a dissociative state, trying to convince himself that this wasn't another of his bizarre dreams or hellish nightmares. Lance squinted as he saw what he thought was a guy waving his hands over his head like a maniac.

"Heyyo! Lance! What's going on?"

A reassured grin flashed on Lance's face as his body turned around in the direction of the familiar voice.

He saw Chase running down the small area of what was left of the beach toward Lance. Other than a tattered shirt and the fact that Chase had been holding his shoes in his arms, he looked fine.

But Lance asked anyway, "Chase! Are you okay?"

Chase turned his jog into a walk as he closed the distance to Lance. "Y—well, yeah! I'm fine!"

But the awkward silence that infiltrated their reunion answered at least one of their questions.

"So this wasn't you?"

Lance looked up at the enormous ice wall that was likely better described as a fortress or mountain.

"No. It wasn't. I've tried making ice using Water Risima, but I can't do anything like this…," Lance trailed off.

Chase looked just as confused as Lance.

Then a lightbulb went off in his mind.

"The storm! What about the storm?" Chase exclaimed.

Lance looked at Chase's face for a moment, trying to remember something. "Huh…? Oh! Right!" Lance put his right hand on his chin. "After our attacks combined, I think we ended up destroying the storm, right?"

Chase nodded. "Yeah, man, we totally did!"

Lance did as well. "But then there was that wave of water, and then…"

"Yeah! That big-ass wave that we created, wasn't it as big as that wall of ice right there?"

Chase turned and faced the wall of ice.

Lance did the same.

The two studied the wall of ice for a moment, allowing their worst suspicions to become fruition.

"No way…!"

"No, it couldn't be, right? *How?*"

Lance took a slow stride up to the ice wall. He reached out his hand to touch the ice but prevented himself from doing it, his instincts telling him not to touch it.

"Someone turned that wave of water into this. But that would require Risima! Who could have done such a thing?"

Chase and Lance froze in their tracks as another round of fighter jets roared overhead, heading out in the direction of the ocean.

Chase watched them pass overhead. "They just came from the opposite direction. Why go back out across the ocean?" He turned to face Lance, suddenly worried. "Do you think they're on to us?"

Lance stopped, letting out a breath he had been holding in. He quickly closed his eyes to think.

"No. They haven't found us yet. They probably don't even have a clue we're here, let alone know we're the ones who destroyed the storm."

"Then maybe whoever created the ice wall?"

"But that still leaves an important question."

The two stopped as they noticed the pair of fighter jets conduct a U-turn in midair and rocket their way back toward the wall of ice—faster than before. Lance noticed that the pair of jets took a formation, the large aircrafts creating space from each other in the openness of the sky.

Lance's eyes widened. "They're about to attack the wall! Let's move!"

But right before he and Chase took off, Lance reached out and grabbed Chase's arm. "No Risima, though! They'll see our auras even from up there!"

"Y-yeah! Right!"

Chase and Lance took off into a sprint, running down the length of the beach as they heard the payload release from the jets, before dozens of large explosions lit up the night sky, the sound of each explosion deafening as it rocked the entire beach.

Chase and Lance stopped, crouching down to avoid any debris from hitting them.

The jets roared overhead, passing over the ice wall, leaving the smoke from the attacks to settle.

But as the smoke cleared, the two noticed that the missile barrage hadn't even so much as *dented* the ice wall. There had been no damage to the mountain of ice whatsoever!

Chase sat up. He started laughing. "Damn! That was no good!" His lighthearted tone revealed no sense of urgency whatsoever.

Lance nudged him. "You're laughing? Are you happy they didn't destroy it?"

Chase threw his arms up in defeat. "*Dude?* Of course I am!" He began walking closer to the ice wall, examining it from its base to the flattened top. "Whoever made this thing clearly saved millions of people! Who knows what would've happened—we were knocked out cold!"

Chase gestured to the fighter jets and a crew of helicopters putting a searchlight on the mountain of ice from high in the sky. It seemed like quite an angry crowd of Humans had come for revenge they would never get.

"And look at 'em! They didn't do a single thing the whole time all this was happening! Whoever made this wall thingy has got to be strong as hell!"

Lance stood up and brushed dust and sand off his legs.

He could feel the Risima within the massive mountain of ice only a few feet away from him.

Lance knew that like Water Risima, Ice Risima seemed to array its particles in whatever pattern it needed to erect the creation the user wished to create. Ice Risima, however, was not malleable or as fluid as Water Risima, and so there were only so many patterns and ways to array the particles that the user *had* to be an expert in streaming and infusing Energy, otherwise, even the slightest deviation in alignment would either discharge the Energy or produce a wonky and impotent effect.

"No…you're absolutely right," Lance said weakly, beginning to walk forward.

The Rasrim who made this mountain was not just strong but was also *dangerous*.

If he had missed or discharged Energy this large…

This time, Lance put his hand on the ice wall, determined to discover the origins of it.

Instantly, he felt something: *Energy*. But he could also feel what he swore was the site of the Energy as well. For some odd reason, this mountain of ice was not the site of its projection. It wasn't borrowed energy from the Earth nor was it manipulated to rise from the ocean itself or even manipulated by using the wave of water approaching the city.

That meant that the entire thing *came* from the Rasrim who made it! It was all his own Energy!

Chase yelled out to Lance, "What do you see? You know I couldn't do anything with—wait! What is *that*?"

Lance snapped around, looking to what Chase was gesturing to. He took notice of Chase looking up toward the top of the ice wall.

And then Lance saw it too.

A figure stood above the ice mountain, peering down at the two boys below.

"Yo! Are you the one who made this thing?" Chase yelled.

Lance gritted his teeth and whispered to Chase, "No! Don't give up anything to suggest we're a part of this! It could be a Human!"

Chase looked back at Lance. "But what if this is the guy? We have to thank him for what he did!" He replied in a whisper-yell.

The figure at the top of the ice wall started to move. The boys watched.

The figure shifted his feet, and then without warning, leapt off the ice wall and crashed into the beach below, landing perfectly on his feet. The ground shook as his body landed, kicking up a truck-load of dusty sand into the dark sky.

Chase and Lance felt a bone-chilling energy from this guy; even the way he moved seemed to produce an energy on its own.

But the dude's movements were stiff and slow as if his entire body had been made of ice.

The only part of his body that seemed to be lively and awake were his *eyes*, and like Lance's, they were a cold deep-blue color that reminded Chase and Lance of ice or the ocean itself.

Lance studied him closer. He seemed young. He couldn't have been much older than he or Chase was, and he was a little shorter than they were as well. He was wearing a black jacket and black jeans but a white-collared T-shirt underneath his jacket, the collar on top of the jacket. His blond hair had been cut short but was curly.

Then once more, Lance looked at the eyes of the Rasrim: hungry, quiet, even deadly. They were eyes that belonged to a killer, not a hero.

Was this a Water Rasrim who specialized in Ice projection? Was such a thing even possible?

Chase grinned from ear to ear. "Okay, dude, that was actually amazing!" He walked up to the boy, holding his hand out. "What's your name?"

The boy looked at Chase's outstretched hand. He didn't move. He didn't let out even a sound. He just looked at Chase's hand like he had no idea what it was.

Lance's heart began to race. He could feel pressure building up in the boy's body—he had been infusing *extremely large* amounts of Risima, perhaps more than Lance could use without straining and discharging himself. The energy was just like Water Risima, but it was much thicker and less viscous than the Energy that Lance had been able to manipulate in his own body!

Lance's head slowly rose up. He began to reach out to Chase before the boy's eyes snatched over toward Lance's.

Lance stopped.

The boy watched Lance closely. His entire attitude changed as if he felt threatened by Lance.

"Who are you?" Lance asked without any intention to be polite.

Lance stopped, planting his foot and standing straight, locking eyes with the mystery Rasrim. Lance could read the Rasrim's body language like an open book. But that never once gave Lance any sense of comfort.

It only told Lance one thing: someone was about to die.

Chase chuckled awkwardly as he took his hand back and brushed the back of his head.

"Maybe he's just shy! I mean, it must be hard bein' a Rasrim around here, ya know?" Chase noticed that the boy and Lance had been staring at each other, their eyes interlocked as if they had gotten bad vibes from one another.

Chase tried to signal something to Lance, but when he realized that Lance was immobilized by this mystery Rasrim, he laughed nervously.

"Well, look. My name is Chase, and that's my, uh, brother."

Chase noticed that the two were still eyeing each other up, not saying a word to each other.

Chase nervously rubbed the back of his head, unsure of what to do.

"Yeah, that's...that's uh Lance there. The one you're staring at," Chase said, pointing to Lance.

Finally, the boy began to talk.

"Chase. Lance...," he said in a low voice, as if he had been learning how to say the names for the first time.

Lance shifted his back foot, putting pressure on his heels, infusing Risima.

He knew that Chase was unable to sense what *he* had been feeling.

But the feeling was undeniable—this boy *was* dangerous. And he was preparing to do something even now.

Lance had to try something.

He gestured up to the ice mountain. "So you know about Risima, I take it? Are you a Water Rasrim?"

The boy cocked his head to the side as if he were confused. "Not Water. I'm *Ice*."

Chase whistled. He put his hands on top of his head and began pacing around. "Hey, guys, we should probably get out of here soon. We can, uh, talk more tomorrow? Are you close by, mister ice guy? Am I the only one who's seeing more and more choppers by the minute?"

Chase stopped. His back had been facing the boy, but he turned his head around to face him. "Yeah, wait a second. Didn't we already ask what your name was?"

The boy looked at Chase. His face seemed devoid of any humanity; instead, it looked like that of a twisted zombie who didn't have the ability to feel emotion of any sort. It was creepy, and perhaps that's what made what was about to happen ten times worse than it was.

"Chile," he spoke.

Chase chuckled. He started pacing again. "'Chile?' Like the place? Really? That's your name?"

Chile looked insulted, the look in his eye one of an evil demeanor. Lance noticed this.

Lance reached an arm out toward Chase. "Hey! That's enough, we don't know anything about this g—about Chile."

Chase shrugged. "I already tried thanking him."

Lance looked back at Chile, who noticed that his eyes never once left Chase's body, his eyes and head tracking Chase as he walked around in a circle.

Lance had a very bad feeling about this guy. He seemed barbaric almost. Even the way he spoke was just off.

"Chile. Your powers. Was it you who made that ice wall?"

"Didn't we already figure that out, genius?" Chase yelled.

"Shut it, Chase!" Lance turned back to Chile.

Lance looked confused as he watched the expressions on Chile's face change.

Chile faced Lance with an angry look—the same one he had when he landed on the beach. But for just a second, Chile seemed *afraid*...as if he remembered something. Was it because Lance yelled?

276

Lance inched closer to Chile, still extremely cautious of him.

"Can you tell me how you did that? It was to stop the wave of water, right?"

Chile, again, looked as if he was insulted. He looked into Lance's eyes.

"You failed," Chile simply said.

Chase stopped, his hands still folded on his head.

Chile started talking. "The storm was destroyed. That was good. But you left another disaster, one worse than the storm."

Lance grunted. So Chile knew about everything all along. That was not a good sign.

"We've already thanked you for what you did. We're just surprised to meet another Rasrim, that's all."

Chile watched Lance curiously. "You were…'surprised'? Why?"

"You're the only other Rasrim we ever met."

"But you wish to protect the Humans. Why care about other Rasrims?"

Lance's heart dropped down into his stomach.

"And h-how do you even know that?"

Chile took a step closer to Lance, intent on his movement.

"Master Melterai does not lie. And he told me to eliminate anyone who gets in my way."

"Master who? And yo! Back down!" Chase stepped in between Chile and Lance.

Chase put his hand on Chile to push him away from Lance.

And that was when Lance felt the Energy release.

Without another warning, Lance grabbed Chase and flashed Electric Risima into his body, throwing himself and Chase out of the way as the ground erupted with power.

Spears of Ice came from out of Chile's body, forming out of an icy aura he produced from his hands that jutted outward like a lightning-fast piston, flying out into the air.

The entire ground reacted with Chile's attack, where the same number of stalagmites made of ice rose from the ground, traveling in the same direction and same speed as the spears of Ice that Chile created.

Lance rolled out of the way, jagged in his left shoulder by one of the ice spears from the ground, fortunately recovered quickly, bouncing back on his feet, sliding into the water of the ocean.

Lance continued watching the attack, focusing Risima into his shoulder. A second too late and the ice spear may have gone through his neck instead.

It seemed that the spears that Chile threw directed the ground attack of stalagmites underneath. After traveling about one hundred feet, the spears disappeared into the air, and the stalagmites stopped growing but persisted.

Even now, Lance noticed that the Ice protruding from the ground looked exactly like the ice wall surrounding the city. The cold ice seethed out in the openness of the summer air, the cold ice released a small breath of misty ice that surrounded the entire structure. But the ice itself never melted nor did it change.

Chase sat up, angry. "What the heck was that for? Why did you attack us just now?"

Chase looked between Chile and the floor, trying to make sense of what he had witnessed.

"And was that a spear *made of ice*?"

Chile angrily flicked his hand, creating another round of stalagmites to shoot up from the ground at high speed.

Chase threw his hands forward and scorched the ice, blasting powerful Fire Risima toward Chile, determined to get a little payback.

"Hey! Don't kill him!" Lance said before he stopped in his tracks watching the Fire and Ice clash.

Chase kept his attack directed toward Chile, feeling that something was off.

Chase quickly began to grow nervous when he noticed a thick ice structure started to form in front of Chile's body and expanded outward, as if it were simply ignoring Chase's Fire Risima.

Chase released his hand and dropped them to his side, a little worn out at the sight of the ice.

"*He can stop my Fire?*"

The shield of ice exploded.

Shrapnel made of ice dug into Chile's body when he realized it was Lance who had struck Electric Risima into the exposed corners of the ice wall and directed his concentration of Risima from the shield of ice through it entirely, overloading Chile's ice wall and producing a discharge.

But Chile didn't show a single sign of weakness. He put his hands up, streaming his Ice Risima into the air around him. The remaining bolts of Electricity that Lance directed toward Chile faded away into what appeared to be icy mist surrounding Chile's entire body.

Lance took a more direct approach, sending Electric Risima into his body before he flashed at Chile and struck him hard in his face, whipping Chile's head backward.

Lance followed up with another attack, but before he did anything else, he noticed Chile's aura increased dramatically, his body taking in Risima Energy, the entire beach rumbling as Lance held his left fist out for another punch. Lance's eyes opened wide, his instincts telling him to move.

Lance yelled out as he flashed backward, his feet gliding on the surface of the ocean.

Chile's entire body released hundreds of sharp, spiked pillars of ice in every direction.

Lance put his left hand into the water and pushed, slowing himself down, his feet still on top of the water, allowing his eyes to change from yellow to blue.

Chase released another concentrated beam of Fire Risima into Chile's shield of ice pillars. As Lance watched from afar, he noticed that the inside of Chile's ice structure began to melt where Chile's body was, giving him mobility inside his structures.

Lance watched carefully. He streamed Electric Risima into his left hand, and with a swoop of his arm, he sent a strike of Lightning to crash into the left side of Chile's shield, cracking it.

Lance rushed forward.

"His shield is weakened. Attack from the—"

But Lance stopped as he noticed the water underneath his feet began swaying.

Lance flipped into the air as a huge pillar of ice rose from the ocean where Lance had been. He kicked backward, awkwardly rolling in midair as the pillar of ice continued growing, ascending past Lance's body. It would've pierced Lance's body and killed him if he had stayed still!

Lance allowed his body to fall in the air, using his momentum to place his feet on part of the ice pillar and kicked off hard, launching his body backward.

Lance extended his arms out and focused but this time intent on using Water Risima.

Several of Lance's own pillars of Water rose from the ocean, and Lance directed them to crash into Chile's shield at high speed and precise pressure. The *Hydropressure Cannon* was an attack that accumulated large amounts of Water Energy and streamed fractions of them at high speed to resemble a pressure washer which was much more powerful than Hydraulic Beam.

The Water pillars struck Chile's shield but, like Lance guessed, was unable to pierce it.

Chase, on the other hand, had barely broken through Chile's shield from another angle and rushed in, his body exploding with Fire Risima as he streamed Fire to his hands and feet, ready to pummel Chile with a barrage of attacks.

Chase's first punch hit Chile head on, his left hand catching Chile just below his chin, exploding on contact.

But Chase's second attack missed entirely, his right hand swinging over air, and before Chase could even continue attacking, he realized that Chile had been *gone*, leaving only the backside of the ice shield in front of Chase's fists as the ash of Chase's Fire Risima slowly disappeared into the air.

Chase quickly shot around when he sensed a buildup of Risima and gasped, bringing his hands up to defend himself as Chile reappeared and, this time, struck Chase with his own immensely powerful right-hand straight.

Chile punched Chase so hard that the force of the attack discharged Chase's Fire Energy, instantly destroying the ice shield.

Unfazed, Chile followed through with his punch, his hand scorched by Fire Risima but his power noticeable, nonetheless.

Chase's body was sent flying into the Ice Wall. His body crashed into the wall and cracked it, a thick line tearing upward toward the top of the ice wall, releasing several large boulders of ice to fall from the wall and crash onto the beach below.

Chase spat out blood, his mouth covered in it. His head was spinning, and he was almost certain his nose was broken. He wiped his mouth and angrily exploded Fire Risima outward, destroying the boulders of Ice, his eyes flaring with Risima Energy.

"Lance! You shock him, and I'll put him down with Fire!"

Chase pounded his chest with his fist and threw them back up, finding Chile staring him down, his eyes moving back and forth as Lance flashed around his blindside.

Chase feinted Chile, lunging forward.

But Chile snapped around and flicked his hands, summoning more Ice structures, which attacked even Lance as he came in for another move.

The ice dug into Lance's chest, piercing him a few inches.

Lance coughed out in pain, but he was quick to evade further attacks, using his Water Risima to watch any changes in the environment—turning the entire beach into his own site. If he and Chase were fast enough, they could possibly negate Chile's ability to manipulate more Ice Risima.

But Chase had different ideas. With such ferocity, Chase streamed a bomb's worth of Fire Risima into the beach and ignited the ground underneath Chile's feet, causing even the sand to bubble. In only a few seconds, the cool, moist beach turned into a molten red floor of lava.

Chile stopped in his tracks—turning his sprint toward Chase into a dead stop. Chile fell to his knees and slammed his fists into the molten lava effortlessly turning it into a floor of ice. The beach sizzled as it dramatically changed temperatures before the thin layer of ice covering the beach began to settle and crack—only allowing Chile to walk on it with no problem.

Chase was livid with shock, clearly confused as to how he was constantly being outmatched with no difficulty like it was child's play. He took a few steps back as he realized the ice was slowly spreading to the entire beach, perhaps covering some three feet every other second.

This was a battle Chase and Lance would quickly learn they were unable to win.

Even when Chase tried to keep Chile's attention occupied and his blind spots vulnerable to Lance's long-range Electric attacks, Chile's ability to keep his rear covered was incredible.

But Chase and Lance pressed on, utilizing what skills they could to prevent Chile from producing another massive Ice attack. When Lance flanked Chile from behind, streaming Electric Risima to cover his movements, Chile could easily keep Lance away by creating diamond-tough crystals of ice, which protected his entire body up to the back of his head.

Chase was relentless in discharging fireballs at Chile, creating balls of Risima in his hands before igniting and hurling them at Chile.

But Chile was as quick as he was powerful. Even with awkward movements, Chile could duck and dodge every fireball thrown at him—trade with Lance's quick hand-to-hand martial arts—and then retaliate against them both with his own skill set of abilities.

Chase blitzed in for another attack, covering Lance in the corner of his eyes, as he tried his best to keep his focus on Chile.

Chase threw an uppercut at Chile, engulfing his entire arm in heavy flames as he rocked Chile's torso. Chase had a sly smile on his face. Not even Lance could withstand a punch like this.

But to his surprise, Chase hesitated as Chile moved with the punch, blowing out air as he dodged a roundhouse kick aimed at his head.

Chase had no time to react as Chile swiped an object at Chase's face. He gashed Chase's cheek with a spear made of ice and then followed through with a powerful front-leg kick, sending Chase's body tumbling across the beach.

And he couldn't find the strength to get up after that. His body ached in pain with every movement he made. He was on the verge of blacking out. Chile had far too much stamina.

Chile crossed his arms in front of his face and tucked his head into his forearms as several monster waves of Water rushed Chile at high pressure, knocking his body around.

Lance watched as Chile defended—analyzing his attack patterns, using Electric Risima to pinpoint the tiny movements Chile made right before he figured out how Chile moved when he shifted into attack-mode.

And then he saw what he was looking for.

Right when Lance moved in for an attack, Chile shifted his left foot back and dropped his right arm, preparing to summon more ice spears.

But Lance saw it coming.

Chile turned to his right and gasped as another wave of Water rushed him, disorienting his body entirely, causing him to lose balance.

Lance crashed into the ground hard and emphasized a massive amount of Energy into his hands, causing the entire beach to awaken with power, brilliant blue lights rising from the ocean and accumulating around Lance's hands.

Lance gripped his left hand tight, imagining what it was he wanted to create.

Chile stumbled, roughly shaking his head to stay focused.

But when he looked up, Chile couldn't hold back his amusement as he watched Lance's Energy condense itself into a large, sturdy-looking sword entirely made of Risima.

Lance clenched his teeth and held his left hand up, gripping the sword at the bottom with his right as it finished materializing. Lance swung the sword around in his hand like an expert swordsman, not taking his eye off his target for even a moment.

Chile lifted his hand, angrily blasting Ice Risima at Lance.

Lance rushed forward, sweat pounding off his head as his eyes began to throb and bleed.

With one eye closed, Lance ripped his sword as hard as he could at the ice spears Chile created and sliced clean through them, moving forward toward Chile, this time knowing he would put Chile down for the count.

Chile sat back, dumbfounded. But determined not to lose any momentum, Chile slammed his hands into the ground, creating an avalanche of ice and snow erupting toward Lance.

Lance charged forward, clenching his sword tight.

At once, Lance's mind went blank. He briefly closed his eyes and focused intensely.

Once he saw the image of a lightning bolt in his mind, he aimed toward it, telling his entire body to put all its Energy into his arms and his sword.

Lance's eyes shot open. He slashed his sword at the avalanche as hard as he could, unleashing a loud thunderclap as Electric Risima ripped the avalanche in half, sending currents of Electric Energy toward Chile.

Chile couldn't prevent himself from flinching as the Energy rocked his body, electrocuting him and causing him to stumble, but just as Chase and Lance went in for another attack, Chile's left eye throbbed. In sync with his eye's movement, the entire beach shook ferociously as the Risima Energy located in the beach responded to Chile's own Energy.

Chase's face turned into a dark frown as he slowly trudged his way to the fight, while his nose continued to bleed.

Lance swung his sword. "Stay on your toes. Chase! He could turn the beach into Ice at any time! If he catches us in his Ice, we're as good as dead!"

Using agility to their advantage, Chase and Lance pivoted around Chile, waiting for anything he could do, cautious not to make any sudden moves. One wrong move, and they would be pierced in half by Chile's ice spears or stuck and bludgeoned by another avalanche of solid ice.

Chile stared as his eyes switched from Chase to Lance, his cold vision forcing the two to keep their guards up.

The sound of jets beaming overhead temporarily caught Chile's attention, watching as they fired more missiles into the wall of ice bordering the eastern shoreline.

Chase and Lance were hesitant to continue fighting. They watched as Chile diverted more and more of his attention to the jets flying overhead before Chile finally raised a hand, his eyes glowing with Energy.

As one of the jets swooped in from over the ocean, Chile focused Energy into his hand, and with a swift motion, a large spear of ice formed from out of the ice wall and struck the jet, piercing it by the tip, causing a massive explosion in the sky.

Chile stood still, his hand in front of his body, an icy aura surrounding his fist as if he had been holding a pose, admiring what he had accomplished.

Chase and Lance were pissed.

Just seconds ago, they had been hesitant to act out of fear of the unknown. But now, they rushed back into action, anger fueling their movements. Chile was no hero. He was a murderer.

Chase brought his hands together, breathing heavily as he infused a large amount of Risima in his body and unleashed a rocket of fire power at Chile, anchoring himself in place with his back leg.

Chile covered his face and blocked himself, taking the full force of the attack. Walls of ice closed in from both sides of Chile, providing cover from the blast.

When Chile let his guard down, he turned around and noticed that Lance was in the air behind him, bouncing off the curved ice wall and sending his ankle into Chile's face, streaming Electric Risima into the kick as it connected.

Chile crashed into the ice shield he created, sucking hard as the wind was knocked out of him. He ducked as Lance's sword ripped across where Chile's head was, nearly severing it completely.

Chile lifted his hand, focusing Energy toward Lance's direction, determined to turn him into a frozen corpse.

But an explosion from behind him yanked Chile's attention away, who yelled out as Chase's rocket burned a hole through the weakened shield and blasted Chile with full force; all of the blast's power focused into the openings in the shield that Lance created.

The force of the attack launched Chile into the ground, falling to his hands and knees, and Chile yelled out in excruciating pain, a yell that was full of pure hatred.

His howl of pain and fury erupted with massive amounts of power. In moments, he managed to turn the entire beach—down to even some of the ocean—into solid ice, pillars of ice and thick fog covering everything as far as Chase and Lance could see.

Chase continued blasting Fire Risima into the air but found it was now so cold that his body seized up. Chase balled up and fell to his knees; his entire face and body began to turn blue, snow covering his body.

Lance, right before he was able to land a finishing blow on Chile with his sword, was caught in the gust of icy wind that Chile had produced when he howled. With such tremendous force, Lance's body was flung into the ice wall before he was struck hard by something, a sharp, jabbing pain near his abdomen.

Chile's body hung over in pain; his teeth clenched as the sheer coldness of the air did its best to appease his aching body.

The burning sensation in his back and the crackling pain on his face angered Chile, but he found himself calming down as the horrific ice storm raged on the beachfront. Snow and hail covered the entire sky. The entire beach was slick and icy, and part of the ocean had been frozen. The temperature had dropped from 68 degrees Fahrenheit down to a bone-chilling –55 degrees in mere seconds.

Chile huffed, breathing hard as his body recovered.

And then he noticed a wet liquid on his face.

Chile slowly raised his stiff right hand and wiped his eye. The liquid was warm and red.

"B-blood?" The words came out as chilling as the ice on the beach. Chile looked at his finger with a disturbed expression.

Chile's eyes widened. His mouth slowly opened as the horrors of his past swelled up in his mind.

Bleeding is bad, he was once told. *It means you are weak.*

Chile growled, making a sound like a beast. His head swung over to Lance, who had been slouched over against the ice wall.

Chile took a heavy step forward, his foot crunching in the layer of snow that now covered the beachfront.

Chile rolled his head, cracking his neck and back as his face pulsated with Energy, healing the scar that Lance had left on his face.

Chile clenched his right hand and raised it as he was only a few feet in front of Lance, a sharp spear of ice forming in his hand.

Chile stood still, a crazed, manic look on his face as he held death itself in front of Lance's unconscious body, Ice Risima surging from Chile's body as if it were uncontrollable.

"That's enough, Chile!"

Chile growled, looking around for the voice that called out to him.

What? Who said that?

"We're finished here!" the voice called out from afar. "You've done your job excellently."

Chile kept looking around. Even for an Ice Rasrim, Chile had trouble seeing through the thick layer of snow and hail raining from the sky.

"Let's *go*, Chile!"

The booming, commanding voice seemed to be coming from above.

Chile raised his head and looked up, allowing snow to fall on his face. He had seemed irritated, as if he intended to defy the voice's orders.

"Melterai," Chile said with a dissatisfied tone, "I am *not* finished yet. My job is to kill these Rasrims."

Melterai watched Chile from on top of the ice wall, unbothered by the storm. He crossed his arms and held a tough position, challenging the boy.

"And yet you will learn and accomplish more by keeping them alive then you'll gain from killing them now!"

Chile growled, his hand twitching with Ice Risima. His energy seeped into the air around his body, fueled by the persistent rage in his mind. But to Chile's amusement, his energy was unable to reach

Melterai's body. It suddenly dissipated when it came anywhere near the mysterious man's aura. Knowing he had no chance at survive a fight with the Masked Menace, Chile continued to listen to Melterai.

"This power, Chile, you were always searching for a way to awaken it, weren't you?"

Chile stopped. He slowly dropped his hands and stood straight, looking directly at Melterai.

"Power is all that I need!"

"And you finally found it!" Melterai shouted back. "It took a lot of pain. I get that, Chile. You let go of the emotions that kept you from realizing your true power, yeah? That's what I observed. And I wish to commend your efforts, just not *here*. Understand?"

Chile's eyes dropped from Melterai and down to Lance.

He gazed upon Lance's body.

For some reason, he knew that Melterai was right. He could feel several emotions that he never had or processed before. Right now, he believed he was beginning to feel remorse.

Chile squinted, as his eyes began trickling more blood.

Reluctantly, Chile raised his bloody face and answered Melterai. "You're right, Melterai. Let's go."

Melterai watched Chile carefully. "Good. We have more work to do. What happened here is only the beginning, Chile. You will have your chance to unleash what's hidden beneath when the time comes."

Melterai raised his hand and engulfed Chile inside a void-like black Energy before Chile's body disappeared entirely, leaving no traces behind.

And then, the same black energy that Chile observed the Axcourians used suddenly surrounded Melterai before he too disappeared, leaving a beaten, half-dead Chase and Lance Kolorio unconscious on the frozen beachfront.

CHAPTER 10

The Welcomed Reckoning

A man in a very expensive three-piece suit walked with an entourage of individuals in a large corridor in a congested section of Washington, DC. They were all wearing black suits and sunglasses, monitoring everyone and everything they walked past. Although no one outside this entourage was aware of it, there were even swarms of pin-drop-sized drones following the man leading the group, all ready to attack any hostile force—especially extraterrestrial ones—at a moment's notice. As if this wasn't enough, the five Secret Service agents and two other agents of the government accompanying the man were also carrying modified handguns in case any Human or Rasrim threatened the man they were following. It was their sworn duty to protect him at all costs.

The man passed individuals who were either surprised or suddenly intimidated, their entire demeanors shifting as they ditched whatever job they were doing to turn and watch as he walked by. Some pulled out smartphones or other devices to snap pictures. But they found that for some reason, their devices were unable to function properly when aimed in the direction of the man and his entourage.

The man walked cautiously but with a tempered disposition. He knew where he was going, and personally, he felt like he was late. But that didn't matter. What mattered was still being decided in a facility far underneath the ground—the same building he just left from hours ago.

The man finally turned and walked into a press room, onto a stage where thousands of people waited for them. These were reporters, service members, doctors, lawyers. However, in this room, pictures could be taken. They were actually encouraged.

The man stopped in front of a podium. Before he even opened his mouth, he was bombarded with flashes of cameras and questions from the audience.

"Mr. President, Mr. President! What are your thoughts about the recent attack near the beach? Is it true that *both* the storm that wreaked havoc on the DMV area and the new attack on the Eastern shore were linked?"

"Mr. President, sir! Is this the work of Osamos? Were any Rasrims or Humans involved?"

"Mr. President, please! Tell us what you know about the beach attack? Were any American citizens involved?"

President Thomas Grayson was undoubtedly one of the busiest men on the planet. Not only was he the first president to break news of an alien presence in space and on Earth, but he was also the first president tasked with responding to them in terms of using the military.

Despite that, President Grayson only had a very limited authority when it came to *how* to deal with the Rasrims. That was left up to another individual in the government. His job, at least as of now, was damage control.

As pitiful and ironic as that sounded, it was a crucial job that not many had the ability to do well. But Grayson had the charm, the wit, and the mannerisms to win over any crowd he stood in front of. A graduate from Harvard University who worked his way through law school and through both Chambers of Congress, he was on track for a successful career no matter where life took him. But once he was advised by a very powerful man who worked for a powerful three-letter agency to run for president, he did without a second thought and won in a landslide victory. Now as the fifty-first president of the

United States, Thomas Grayson was one of the most admired men on Earth and among the most successful presidents in US history.

President Grayson cleared his throat. "The point of this press conference is to address the public directly at a time of uncertainty and to be frank, a time where we all need clarity and reassurance."

He paused, allowing the shutter of cameras to briefly take over.

He continued, "Eight hours ago, the United States witnessed what we believe to be the biggest attack on US soil since the 9/11 attacks. The attack was believed to be carried out by a creature from the Planet Osamos who infiltrated our society and is currently living among us."

He scanned the room, full of confidence.

"But clearly, by my being here in person addressing this conference today, neither I nor other members of the government believe this creature to be a grave threat to our society or the integrity of our country. Without diverting the prosperity of our nation and allowing it to wither into chaos and paranoia, we will unite and remain unwavering citizens as we work to negotiate reasonable terms of coexistence with the alien presence known as the Rasrims."

There were murmurs in the room, but the overall reaction seemed to be positive. Although much of the DMV area was still being evacuated, he knew with absolute certainty that the attacks were over. He was told this by a Rasrim, whom he trusted with his life.

That was all President Grayson needed to do. His job was done.

Yet he continued speaking. "I have worked tirelessly with respectable members of our military and Congress to take action against the presence of Rasrims not just within our borders but elsewhere on Planet Earth. We have created very capable task forces and worked closely with allied nations on matters concerning the existence of threats from alien species on Earth, and the general consensus has remained unchanged: We will work toward peace but treat every threat on *any* Human life as the basis for extermination of said alien species living on Earth. No, this does not ignore the recent catastrophes that the United States, Europe, and Asia have faced. The world is cooperating and has worked to unveil relief packages to rebuild infrastructure and provide healthcare services to *anyone* involved in these attacks—at record speeds!"

There was applause from the room and even more camera clicks and flashes. The president stood tall, his face emotionless as he allowed the room to take pictures and applaud him.

After another moment, he spoke again. "Currently, the United States government is working toward a new agreement with Osamos. It underlines the necessity to protect and preserve *all* life but places an emphasis on improving the security measures involved with protecting Human life on Earth before any alien presence. With that said, the United States military is now working together with the militaries of other nations around the globe and will create a new military. It is called the Ground States Union Military, and its primary objective is to capture and eliminate any threats from alien or related targets that wish to inflict harm on the United States or its allies."

The president continued speaking over an uproar of applause and cheers.

"These attacks will *not* continue! You have my personal reassurance that if the Rasrims continue to allow their kind to stray from their sovereign location and wage attacks on our homeland, we *will* respond to them directly and with certain retaliatory force to ensure that Osamos understands and respects the presence of Human beings in the United States and other allied nations completely!"

The president stood in front of the audience for a moment before he waved to his audience. It was his signature: a brief, overhead wave that was similar to a salute.

And then, leaving no time for comments or questions, the president turned and left the conference room.

Millions of individuals from around the world saw the brief speech from the president. It received mixed reviews from the international community, as some countries welcomed the Rasrims with open arms and even encouraged them to seek refuge within their borders.

But among the crowd of people who saw the speech, the only ones with enough power to challenge it remained at home, in the United States itself.

No words were said. No comments were made. No remarks delivered online or social media. Not even physical reactions were given. But a certain group of individuals watched the president speak, and in a unanimous fashion came an agreement that would never be spoken. No satellite, cellphone, government, or Human being outside this group even had a clue what was about to happen. The response would only be manifested and carried out as the Human-Rasrim war raged on and continued. It was one that would change Earth and likely the universe—forever. And it would be done so entirely in secret.

*****

When Lance opened his eyes, he noticed that he was freezing cold and barely clinging on to life.

His body ached in several places. His head was spinning.

Lance knew that he was still on the frozen beach. It had looked the same since the encounter with Chile. There were sirens and lights everywhere, but it appeared that he had been hidden in a layer of ice and snow that hung over the massive ice wall.

It was even then that Lance noticed that the ice wall itself had gotten smaller in size and width. That was a great sign for humanity but an awful one for Lance and Chase.

Then Lance's face lit up.

"C-Chase?" His voice was hoarse. It was so cold he could barely speak.

Lance tried to sit up but reeled in pain when he did.

He looked down at his stomach and realized he was covered in blood and that there was a huge gash in the side of his stomach.

Lance groaned out as he forced himself to roll forward, clutching the side of his stomach, and he crawled on the beach with his other hand, desperately searching for his brother in the midst of the chaos of lights, sirens, and screaming engines of jets and helicopters.

"Chase! Chase, where are you?"

Lance looked frantically, sifting through the bitter cold snow.

He slipped and tumbled down the beach, rolling in pain before he finally stopped when he reached the shoreline, his feet only inches away from where the waves used to crash onto the beach.

Lance's head fell back. He sucked in air, breathing hard.

His entire body ached, burning sensations all over his body. It was hard for him to even think straight, but he tried his hardest to sift through his memories and remember where he last saw Chase.

"D-dammit!" Lance yelled in the air.

His arms flared out, lying out on the beach. Lance looked into the sky.

Should he find help? He knew that he was the only person on the beach and that the only way he'd find help was if he were spotted by an aircraft or crossed over the massive ice wall.

Lance struggled to sit up, trying to gather his thoughts. Chase was nowhere in sight. What was he supposed to do?

Lance turned around and faced the ice wall once more.

He struggled to remember something before he lost consciousness, but he wasn't entirely sure what it was he was thinking about. His memory was too foggy, and he was also tired and hungry. But he had gotten lucky. If the fight had gone on any longer, Lance would have been dead. Perhaps he would have never regained consciousness. It was a miracle he was alive now.

The sound of helicopters flying overhead made Lance freeze. He looked up in the sky and saw several flying over the beach, maybe a few miles down the shoreline. Lance got low. If he got caught out here with all these injuries, there would be no telling what would happen to him.

"Chase!" Lance yelled, staying low to the ground as he moved in the last direction he saw his brother.

"We've gotta go! Where are you?"

Lance's head was still spinning, but his vision was starting to become clear.

The sound of the helicopters closed in, the whir of their motors becoming louder as they suddenly adjusted their course.

But Lance didn't care. He scanned the entire beach, straining to look through snow and ice as he continued to call out for Chase.

As Lance turned and scanned another direction of the beach, he saw what he thought was an uneven section of snow piled up on the beach, maybe just a hundred or so feet from where Lance was now.

Lance set off, skipping through the ankle-high snow as he trekked toward the section of the beach.

Once he got closer, he saw a body, one that looked like it was almost frozen.

Lance's heart rate sped up dramatically, his mind thinking the worst as he started running through the snow, but he slipped and rolled down the beach again, fighting against everything to regain his balance to get to his brother.

Lance crawled his way over to Chase, lying motionlessly in the snow. Lance's face was horrific. Chase was not in good condition. His entire body had been ice cold, his skin a blue color.

"Chase! Wake up!" Lance's voice began to break, but he forced himself not to sob.

Lance looked around quickly. There was no one or nothing in sight.

Lance turned back to Chase. He grabbed Chase's arms and hoisted him up over his shoulder, carrying him gently but with haste.

Lance's face was trembling, tears streaming down his face, but he bit down on his tongue and began walking through the snow.

Lance needed to think of something. Could he use Risima to warm Chase up? It was possible, but Lance barely had enough energy to walk, let alone carry his brother. His movement was growing sloppy, but Lance pressed on. He would not let his brother die out here like this.

Lance noticed that the sound of the helicopters was much louder now than it had been before, and when he stopped to look up, he noticed that they were heading in the direction toward Lance, making a path down the length of the shoreline.

Lance gritted his teeth. If they were caught...!

No, Lance couldn't allow that to happen.

Lance strained himself as he cleared as much snow out of the way before he laid Chase on the ground and huddled on top of him.

He needed to think of a way to hide using Risima. But how could he do that?

The helicopters were nearly on top of them, using a search light to examine the snow and the ice wall. Lance had maybe ten seconds to figure out what to do before being spotted.

He had no time to think.

Lance tensed his body, feeling for all the Energy he could within himself, and buried his head into the ground, imagining creating an ice shield—one just like Chile had—to cover himself and Chase.

Lance's body screamed out in pain as his entire body tensed, pumping much more Energy out to do a task he had never done before. He felt pain in his chest, legs, and arms. It felt like the Risima in his body would rip in him two, but Lance bit down hard, shut his eyes tightly, and fought with the Energy, forcing it to obey. The helicopters seemed to continue moving down the shoreline, but Lance left nothing to chance. It was possible that they had already been found.

Lance held the position for what felt like entire minutes before it became too much for him to handle.

Right before Lance's head exploded, he released the tension in his body and sat up, taking in large gulps of air. But something strange happened.

Around Chase and Lance was a sturdy-looking sphere of solid rock. It covered them on all sides and hung low, preventing Lance from standing up. At the same time, he noticed that he could hear massive amounts of water rushing from outside the rock, crashing into it and sloshing behind him in the direction where the beach was.

Lance placed his hands on the rock that surrounded himself. Without doing anything else, Lance could *feel* the rock in a way that transcended plain touch. He could sense the subatomic particles within the rock, all the various components and atoms it was composed of.

And when Lance began to sense the Risima Energy within the rock, he understood what had just happened.

He had used Earth Risima to create the sphere! How was that possible?

Lance, before even trying to figure out how or why he had been able to create the rock, set his attention to dismantling it. Placing his hands on the rock and concentrating hard, Lance could sense the buildup of Risima Energy that constructed and since resided within the rocky structure. When he attempted to draw the Risima Energy back into his body or even dispersing it into the environment, the sphere of rock shook for a brief second before shattering completely, turning into ash and dust as if it had never been there.

But then Lance instantly noticed there was another problem.

He nearly yelled out as he grabbed Chase and fought against the torrent of water that came crashing down into him. Had he not been looking after Chase, this would have been no problem for Lance. But Chase couldn't deal with Water like Lance could.

Lance held Chase close to his body, allowing the water to engulf them entirely.

Concentrating once more, Lance dispersed the Water Energy away from his body, creating a ravine in the waves that retreated into the ocean.

Lance stood up, holding Chase over his shoulder. He couldn't believe what he was seeing in front of him. "The iceberg. And the snow. It's all melted. But how?"

A sound of Chase coughing made Lance stop and stand still.

Lance gently placed Chase on the ground, continuing to direct the water from the melted ice berg away from him as Chase regained consciousness.

Lance leaned in. "Yo! Chase?"

Chase coughed out again and slowly opened his eyes.

Lance nearly laughed aloud, falling backward as he took a sigh of relief.

Chase groaned as he sat up and looked at Lance, a very weak but noticeable trail of steam beginning to rise from Chase's limbs.

"Hey, what hap—" Chase stopped as he noticed the rushing water on both sides of himself. "Uh, why is there like a crap ton of water around us? Are we in the middle of the ocean again?"

Lance burst out into laughter. "The iceberg's gone! I-I don't know how or why, but it's all gone!"

Chase squinted. "And Chile? Where is he?"

Lance reached out and pulled Chase up to his feet.

"He's gone. I don't remember much. My head's still spinning."

Chase looked at Lance with a concerned face. "Yeah, and you're bleeding too!" But seeing that Lance was in high spirits, Chase could understand how was feeling.

"Guess we got our asses kicked, huh?" he said.

Lance sighed. "And *that's* how you try and lighten the mood?"

Chase shrugged. "Seeing that we're alive and that ice wall thingy is gone, I wouldn't say we need much of a mood lightener to begin with. We destroyed the storm too, didn't we?"

Lance began walking, groaning out when he did, limping forward.

"Nah, dude, you *are* hurt! Should we get help?" Chase asked.

"No. I'm all right. We just need to get out of here before we get spotted. Our luck won't last forever."

Chase, who was still recovering from his injuries, agreed.

"Hey, uh, if you didn't destroy that iceberg, how did you manage to keep me warm? I…remember passing out, freezing cold."

Lance turned to Chase but shook his head.

"I didn't have anything to do with that. Maybe you warmed yourself up using Fire?"

Chase nervously shook his head. "Right. But about that, I didn't have any more Energy. There's no way I could have produced enough to counter that bastard's insanely strong Ice Risima. And I could've sworn I saw, what, a rock covering us too, didn't I? That wasn't you either?"

Lance didn't say anything. The two trekked forward, making their way off of the beach and back into a residential area.

Before he could say anything else, they noticed a swarm of armored trucks and other vehicles swarming the area, piling onto the beach and driving down the residential area.

Lance pulled Chase to the side and got low.

Then Lance pointed to something and whispered, "Let's hide in there!"

They quickly made their way through a narrow road surrounded by gates and bushes and toward a truck that had crashed into a light pole.

Lance opened one of the back doors on the truck and climbed in. Chase was right behind him. He climbed in carefully and shut the door behind him, the old metal doors creaking as they closed.

The two got low, each one of them sitting against one the doors across from each other, hugging their knees.

Lance saw police cars and SUVs drive past, waiting a moment before speaking. He tried his best to peer out of the window as they sped by.

And then something came to Lance's mind. "I totally forgot!" he whispered. "They had no access to the beach the entire time we were out there!"

Chase and Lance tucked their heads as several police cars passed them, turning onto the beach from almost every available road.

"So what?" Chase exclaimed in a whisper-yell. "There's nothing there now! What are they doing there now? The storm and Chile are both gone! And we dealt with the ice wall, right?"

But then a loud, commanding voice caused both of them to stay quiet.

"Search the entire area! Rasrims were here. Even though they've evacuated the area, they could still be looming around! I want the Coast Guard on the water and eyes in the sky now!"

Chase and Lance looked at each other, frightened looks on their faces.

Chase mouthed the words "What do we do?" to Lance.

Lance responded by gesturing with his hands something before mouthing "We run!"

Chase slightly turned and looked out of one of the windows in the truck. He didn't see anyone on foot but just cars driving to and from the beach.

Chase turned back to Lance and leaned in and whispered, "How much Energy do you have?"

Lance looked confused. "Why?"

"You can move at the speed of light, genius! How would they catch us if we flashed back home with Risima? I wouldn't be too far behind!"

"That's too risky! They know they're dealing with Rasrims! What if they have a way to track Electric and Fire users?"

"It's either that or we play the innocent kids caught in disaster when we get caught!"

Lance laid his head against the door of the truck.

Chase persisted. "C'mon, Lance! We need to get back and figure out where Chile went! What if something else happens while we're stuck out here playing hide 'n' seek?"

Lance sighed.

"You're right. But it's still too risky to use Risima this close to so many officers. We need to gain enough distance before we pull something like that. And besides, moving at that speed is risky! We couldn't even do it on our way down here! There's bound to be way more people outside now that the storm's gone!"

Several more vehicles blaring their sirens passed the truck, causing Chase and Lance's heart to skip a beat.

Chase gave Lance a look of urgency.

"It's now or never!"

Lance looked back at Chase for a brief second.

He trusted Chase. He always did.

"All right. Let's go. But you follow my lead!"

"Whatever! Go!"

Lance turned and pulled the handle on the truck slowly, peering his head out to look for anyone.

"Clear?"

"Yeah, let's go!"

Lance climbed out of the truck. Chase was right behind.

The two stayed low as they made their way west, heading through the residential area and away from the shoreline.

They stayed close to the few buildings that were still standing and used the cover of vehicles left in the road to navigate, making sure to evade posts of officers and barricades with armored cars. However, like the one officer from the beach said, it appeared as if the threat had suddenly disappeared. There was no reason to converge in one place or continue barricading, and so the vast majority of police officers diverted their attention to the beach where they searched for clues. Although the storm was dead, the sky was still dark and misty, giving Chase and Lance the cover of darkness to move. They didn't even notice how well they had evaded the troves of officers and soldiers on foot, moving as silently as ninjas through the night.

It took Chase and Lance half an hour to escape the residential area and into a more congested area of people, who were together trying to clear debris from the road and move stationary vehicles out of the way for others. The two boys stayed low the entire time, but whenever they were spotted by people, they resorted to staying close to each other and keeping their heads low, trying their best to hide their eyes and their injuries from the civilians.

Some of course, being good Samaritans, called out to them and asked if they needed help, but the two boys simply ignored them and continued walking.

But in all that misery, they so desperately wanted to say "yes."

Chase and Lance had left when it had been dark out, but now that it was lighter out, the destruction was visible everywhere: roads flooded, trees blocking roads or falling into houses. It reminded the two of *that* day, and while they didn't speak about it, at one point, Chase tugged Lance's arm and gave him a look of despair that Lance completely understood.

It was safe to say that any time people encountered a disaster, it left a painful scar on those afflicted and in their communities. Even when all the debris was cleared, were things ever the same afterward?

Just before the sun began to set again, Chase and Lance managed to make their way back to the gate in front of their house and were exhausted, close to fainting again. In the end, they decided not to use their powers much at all due to how much civilians were out. Of course, there were plenty of trees and hills to use as cover—and while this is what the two settled on, they learned the hard way that using Electric and Fire Risima to move through trees and rocky elevations was not as easy as it seemed. It was definitely *not* like in the movies.

Chase and Lance leaned on each other, helping one another get up the driveway and to the front door of the house, noticing that for some reason, something seemed…different.

But they ignored it, practically falling through the front door, which was unlocked. They stepped inside, sure they would find their caretaker inside with a plate of food or even lessons to give them about their experience.

But she wasn't in the dining room or the kitchen.

"Hello? Miss E?"

Chase slouched into a chair at the dining room and rested his head on the table.

"She's probably asleep, dude. How long have we been gone?"

But Lance was worried. He almost called out for her again before he heard a sound from the steps.

He hesitated ready for anything, before a person came into the living room.

"There you two are! I had no doubt you'd return unharmed!"

Lance's face lit up, and Chase gave a thumbs-up, not even bothering to lift his head.

Miss E. hugged Lance, not even taking time to mention his injuries. She pivoted, holding Lance in one arm before he reached and rubbed Chase's head.

"It was…fun. We definitely did a lot out there, but we sure as heck ain't 'unharmed,'" Chase's mumbled voice said.

"Oh, I'm sure! C'mon. We'll have this conversation in the basement. A serious one at that."

Chase groaned. "But can't I just sleep here? We just saved the world for crying out loud."

But Lance, seeing as he had done it once, decided to grab Chase's arms and hoist him over his shoulder again.

"Yeah. This works too…," Chase's voice trailed off as Lance carried him down to the basement, still processing what had happened at the beach only a two-hour drive away.

*****

"Now, Chile, watch and learn."

Without a moment's notice, a man in a cloak moved at high speed around Melterai. His movements were so fast and smooth that Chile's eyes bounced around from every angle in the room, chasing afterimages and displacements of light.

Melterai stood in the center of a large area, in a location that existed between space itself, an alternate dimension that powerful beings could only gain access to after encountering and surpassing *death.*

Daxxon moved at high speed, blindsiding Melterai using his highspeed to mask every potential opening in his form.

At once, he struck Melterai, catching him in the side of the face with a punch infused with Electric Risima—moving two times faster than the speed of light.

Daxxon was pleased with himself. It seemed his skills had been improving! Maybe after this sparing exhibition, he would receive more respect—and *money*—from Melterai.

But then Daxxon's eyes slowly widened when he realized that just as soon as his punch connected, his target disappeared in front of his eyes.

Daxxon looked to his left and then to his right before a blindingly quick Melterai appeared in the air before him, unleashing a powerful blow into Daxxon's chest.

Daxxon was launched some fifty yards backwards, tumbling over his own body. He coughed out, winded.

"Allow your enemies to think they've struck you," Melterai announced to Chile, using Daxxon as nothing more than an example.

"And *then* unleash your attack. All your power must be utilized in the precious moments you've caught your foe off guard!"

Without another warning, Melterai's body lit up and emitted a bright white aura, covering the entire battlefield.

Daxxon knew what was coming.

Daxxon rushed into Melterai, getting too close to him to allow an Energy attack to be fired off.

Daxxon infused his body with a new type of Energy, the same one Melterai had been using. This was called *Stellar Riora*, or Risima in its most purified and potent form.

Using this power, Daxxon threw blow after blow at Melterai, each punch with killing intent behind it.

But Melterai laughingly dodged each attack, using slow, dragged-out movements to dodge attacks that would have likely destroyed anyone else.

"Stellar Riora when used *correctly* is meant to become a multiplier of force, not just a simple means to advance one's position in battle," again he announced to Chile while disregarding Daxxon.

And then Melterai turned all his attention to Daxxon. Even in the midst of dodging all his attacks, Melterai assumed a new stance and brought his hands up, infusing Stellar Riora into his body.

Melterai slipped one of Daxxon's punches and with blinding speed unleashed an overhand left, which rocked Daxxon, a combination of Elements discharging over Daxxon's body.

Daxxon, in a fit of rage, fired a beam made of Fire *and* Death Risima at Melterai, fusing the two Elements together in what was now called *Hell Risima*.

Melterai laughed, blocking the Risima Energy, and sucked it into his body, causing the radiant aura around him to glow even brighter and much larger.

Melterai decided he had shown enough.

Melterai streamed together the White Energy from around his body and fired back with his own beam of Energy, Stellar Riora fired off with a roar of magnificent power, distorting even space as it nearly ripped Daxxon into two. Daxxon had no time to yell out as the blast launched him off far down into the battlefield before he crashed into a mountain some eighty *miles* away in mere seconds.

Melterai stood back, noticing that Chile had watched everything with a loud expression, his mouth practically hanging open.

But his eyes told Melterai he had been doing more than watching. He had been *studying* what he was seeing.

Melterai approached Chile, paying no attention to the mountain that was exploding and crumbling out in the distance.

"The next step in your journey as a Rasrim is to unleash the *true* power within you. Ice Risima is only the beginning for you, Chile. When you were on Earth at that beach, you inched ever so slightly closer to Stellar Riora."

Chile looked up at Melterai, giving him his full attention, ignoring the loud rumbling sounds in the background.

Melterai continued talking.

"Your anger back then allowed you to fuse a multitude of Elements together in an instant. This is no easy feat even for Rasrims on Osamos who have trained for centuries, mind you."

Melterai gestured to the mountain.

"Some say it requires even more than Risima itself to do, that Risima is only a small piece of a larger puzzle us mortals have been a part of since the dawn of time but have no awareness of whatsoever."

Melterai turned back to Chile.

"Whatever the case may be, your journey is just beginning. While you had your first glimpse of Stellar Riora, your adversaries known as Chase and Lance did too."

Chile suddenly looked offended.

However, instead of talking, he just shot Melterai that same look he gave when he wanted more insight.

"Yes, Chile. When we left, Lance was somehow able to conjure Earth Risima and used it to destroy that Ice Wall of yours."

Melterai turned away from Chile.

"Stellar Riora remains a mystery to most Rasrims, but it seems there's a pattern that most Rasrims agree with. We now believe that Stellar Riora is a combination of *every* Element put together, a purified mixture of nature that allows a Rasrim to manipulate almost every aspect of his environment no matter his natural Elemental Prowess."

Chile looked rather enthralled.

"Every Element? How is that possible?" Chile asked.

Melterai remained quiet for a moment.

"It doesn't appear that every Rasrim can do it. Like I mentioned, it seems that it requires more than meets the eye to accomplish. Using Stellar Riora is like becoming a vacuum. You would suck in every Element from your environment until you had a uniform blend of every Element available to release back into the environment. Water, Fire, Earth, Wind, Electric, Death. These are the most common Elements. Of course, there are others like Ice and *Ultima*, but these all blend in together to comprise Stellar Riora. Once you use Stellar Riora, you aren't controlling any one Element but all of them at the same time."

Chile looked uninterested.

"Of course, you could simply revert to just using one Element or *try* infusing more of a specific Element into Stellar Riora, but this is incredibly hard to do."

Chile looked at Melterai.

"Is there more to know about other Elements?"

"Sure. I originally suspected that you, as an Ice Rasrim, were just using a combination of two different Elements. But I was wrong. However, it *is* possible to do that. The strange thing is, Rasrims can *only* blend a maximum of two Elements together and receive a uniquely different set of abilities and attacks to use. If you try blending three or more together, you'll find yourself discharging all of that Energy as soon as you accumulate it or end up acquiring Stellar Riora anyways. So if you find two that you like, including Ice, try mixing them together."

"How do you know all of this, Melterai?"

Melterai chuckled, crossing his arms.

"Experience, Chile! I'll give you a piece of insight into the extent of my travels."

Melterai turned to Chile and held up his hand.

"There are *five divine planets* in the universe. Each one has its own corresponding *Divine Prowess*, or ability, if you will. Each one, on top of that, has an array of secrets aimed at keeping your ordinary tourist from simply 'learning' how to use its abilities—no, it demands 'permission' of some sort to be able to do so. With that said, considering I myself know all Five Divine Prowesses and have been to countless universes with their own abilities, I have yet to discover why this all is."

Chile studied Melterai with a curious look on his face. "How did you—"

But Chile had been cut off.

The entire mountain in the background exploded, a fireball of raw energy turning the entire sky orange, red particles of ash falling from the sky.

Melterai turned toward the mountain slowly.

He scoffed, "I suppose I left something rather important out, an Energy you possess that we're witnessing now."

Melterai held up his hand and blocked a projectile as it blazed across the battlefield, a bright orange orb of light that pushed Melterai back a few feet.

Behind him, Daxxon materialized with no warning, yelling out with anger and rage as he attacked Melterai, his entire body glowing scorching red as strange marks on his body coursed with red Energy, causing the air around him to steam.

Melterai had been far too quick but had nearly been caught in a devastating attack.

Worrying more about Chile's safety, however, now Melterai was pissed. Had Daxxon had his way, both Chile and Melterai would be dead out of sheer spite and rage.

Melterai called out to Daxxon, raising his voice to a level that startled Chile.

"Daxxon! Have you *lost* your mind?"

Daxxon's destructive Energy blasted the entire arena. Chile blocked his face and tried covering himself in a thick layer of Ice, fearing for his life.

But Chile stopped when he realized that Melterai's body had been covered in the same Red Energy, absorbing Risima Energy from every source around him, sucking up Chile's Ice Risima before he had a chance to stream it.

But Chile had no time to react, let alone see the next thing that happened.

Before his eyes, Melterai had moved swiftly and with so much finesse that Daxxon had been pummeled to the ground in an instance, blood splattered across the floor and soaking the ground beneath him.

Powerful gusts of wind pushed Chile back, the shock wave of Melterai's movement so intense that the ground ruptured beneath him and the air dispersed above him, separating even the clouds in the sky from his magnificent power.

And then Chile gasped out when he realized Melterai had been holding something against Daxxon's neck.

"I warned you *specifically* not to use Forbidden Arts when I'm around Chile. Did you forget that?" Melterai's voice boomed throughout the area, shaking even the hills in the distance.

Daxxon groaned out, spitting out blood. His body had still been covered in strange crimson-red marks that swirled and spiraled throughout his body. They began to flicker, but its vibrant glow dimmed with each passing second as Daxxon began to lose Energy, breathing heavily, blood pouring out of his mouth.

But it was only then that Chile understood why.

Chile looked at Daxxon's arm, covered in blood.

Daxxon's left hand had been severed at the wrist, the Energy he had been focusing just moments ago completely vanished.

Daxxon's body steamed as it slowly began to regenerate the bones in his wrist, his body slowly reconstructing the hand, and it seemed as if this same red Energy that was about to lay waste to both Chile and Melterai was now the Energy reconstructing Daxxon's lost hand.

Melterai seemed uninterested either way.

"Forgive me, Melterai," Daxxon pleaded weakly.

"*For what?*" Melterai jammed his sword against Daxxon's neck.

Chile examined the sword that Melterai had been holding, his eyes rolling over every inch, admiring its quality. It was a massive broadsword that looked like it must've weighed several hundred pounds! But its most striking quality was that the majority of it had been made of crystals—its texture reminding Chile of ice—both edges and the face of the sword were masterfully grooved sections of ruby-red crystallized material that was obviously strong enough to sever limbs with minimal effort. The pattern that grooved the sword had stretched from the tip of the sword down to the handle, which was wrapped in black and golden material, sturdy enough to swing the massive sword around comfortably for the user.

Of course, its wielder needed to be competent enough to use such a weapon.

Chile examined the crystallized sword. The same crimson-red Energy that had blown up the mountain and covered Daxxon's body was swirling and gleaming throughout the sword, its magnificent light shining in the glimmer of the sunshine above, making the sword look as if it were glowing.

Chile inched up to Melterai, cautious of the massive weapon he had been holding.

Daxxon groaned out again.

"I stepped out of line. Forgive me, Melterai. I'm still learning how to control my Sacora Marks... I didn't think I would turn into such a frenzy, I swear..."

Melterai held his position for a moment before he stepped off Daxxon's chest and swung his sword to the ground.

Melterai's head slowly gestured toward Chile but didn't face him entirely.

"Forgive me, Chile. I do believe that this situation can be transformed into a point of growth for you too."

Daxxon sat up, holding his wrist as it had now been fully regenerated. He squeezed and rotated it, clearly still in shock. The red marks glowing on his body faded, leaving nothing but ugly scars they had been temporarily illuminating.

"What you just witnessed is something you are not ready to deal with as of yet, Chile. But it exists like a demon deep within you. It is called Sacora."

Melterai looked at Daxxon again, clearly disappointed with him.

"Like I suggested earlier, it is a Forbidden Energy that comes only to individuals who have experienced *death*. Therefore, it is much too dangerous and too serious a topic to discuss with mere children at this stage."

Melterai turned his back to Daxxon and to Chile, facing off in a direction out in space.

Suddenly, the area around the three of them morphed, the sky, ground, and even the structures in the background fading, their colors and shapes swirling and swishing together before they faded entirely.

The three now suddenly found themself back on Earth, in the Midwestern deserts and plains somewhere near New Mexico.

From out of nowhere, Melterai began laughing to himself, chuckling.

"Let this be a lesson for you, Chile. No matter what you plan on doing, you must always think and understand what it is you're trying to accomplish before setting out to do so."

He lifted his sword and aimed it back at Daxxon, who nearly gasped out and tripped himself up.

"We used Forbidden Energy to protect this planet from our skirmish, where I then berate you for then using its monstrous power to destroy what it was we set out to protect in the first place. Ironic, isn't it, Daxxon?"

Melterai released his grip on his sword. Before it even fell out of his hands, it disappeared from everyone's sight entirely, leaving nothing behind.

After a moment of silence, allowing the calm, hot sands to breeze over their bodies, Melterai gave a new order.

"Daxxon, I'm taking Chile back to the east. As of now, your help is no longer needed on Earth."

Daxxon suddenly looked intimidated.

"Y-yes, sir!"

Melterai held up a hand.

"I want you to return to the base to assist however you see fit. Mainly, get those Sacora Marks *under control*, understand me?"

Daxxon shook his head nervously, clearly fearful of being attacked again. Melterai could be attacking him now and he wouldn't even realize until the next day!

"I'll do my best, sir!"

"Good! And play nice with the new recruits. *Especially* Toro. I wouldn't want to see him lay waste to your usefulness in only his first couple of days of training. I understand you and his family have... issues."

Daxxon turned away from Melterai and grunted, cursing him under his breath.

The audacity of that fool! Of course Melterai wouldn't leave Daxxon hurt with a physical wound, but Melterai was more than glad to damage his pride! He knew how to push the buttons well! That damned menace!

Melterai chuckled to himself, clearly thrilled with something.

"Get to it, Daxxon."

Daxxon froze. His heart sank. He had responded too quickly. Did he...?

Melterai turned away from Daxxon. "I *do* know how to push buttons, and I'm always glad to, but only when it's *absolutely* necessary. I believe this was one of those times, was it not?"

Melterai waved him off, making his way east with Chile following close behind. Melterai had left Daxxon with a blank expression, covered in sweat and blood, stranded in the desert with no clear objective and all without a care in the world.

It was a necessary time to push buttons indeed.

*****

Chase, Lance, and Miss E all gathered together, facing one another as they took seats at the Center Console in the basement. Lance had been patched up, a bandage wrapped tightly around his chest, and Chase had been in a large blanket covering his body entirely.

Miss E, before saying a word to Chase and Lance, first pinpointed her attention to a large screen that hung above them in the

311

Center Console. She typed something on a screen in front of her and projected the news to display on the screen above their heads.

Chase and Lance didn't need an explanation. They saw first-hand why she had put the news on.

A reporter stood on a beach, waves crashing just a few feet behind her as several dangerous-looking men wearing hazmat suits scoured the entire beach with tools and equipment, studying everything from the ocean water to taking samples of sand on the beach.

"As you can see here, several hours ago a massive attack carried out by what officials believe to be the aliens known as Rasrims right here on this beach, including a gigantic wall of ice that blocked off the entire beach that was right where I'm standing now. Of course, with no evidence of the suspect as of yet confirmed, officials are still discussing the events of what truly took place on this beach last night." She turned and pointed into the sky.

"We still are not sure what the origins of that massive storm cloud that ravaged the East Coast were, but officials are claiming that it was a Category 5 Hurricane that Rasrims were somehow able to—"

Miss E shut the television off.

She crossed her arms and sighed, unsure of what to say.

Chase and Lance looked at each other. What should they say when so much of the ordeal was something they still knew little of themselves?

"You were attacked," Miss E finally said, claiming both of their attention at the same time.

"Yeah! It was so weird. We were—"

Miss E. held up a hand and spoke over Chase.

"More *specifically*, you were attacked by another Rasrim. Not a Human, not a man in uniform, correct?"

"Correct," Lance answered. "He had Ice Powers. I-I didn't even know Ice Risima was a thing!"

Miss E's watched Lance, her attitude and entire demeanor serious.

"'He'?" she asked. "What did he look like?"

"Well, to start"—Chase sat up in his chair—"his name was something weird, I think it was—"

"Chile," Lance interrupted. "He wore light clothing that was clearly meant for him to blend in. Black jacket, black jeans, curly blond hair. He looked like he was the same age as us. Maybe fourteen or fifteen. He didn't say much either."

Miss E crossed her legs, her hand on her chin as she listened to Lance.

"Are you absolutely certain that his name was 'Chile'?"

"Yeah! He said so himself!" Chase responded. "He was a douchebag! He attacked us after we tried thanking him for saving our lives and the entire country!"

Miss E turned in Chase's direction.

"Why would he do something like that, Miss E? Why would another Rasrim attack us? I thought...maybe I just thought—"

"Chile is not a real Rasrim. But he's very dangerous anyway! He's likely suffered from tremendous trauma and brain damage as a result of psychological operations and experiments in his youth. You should never have encountered him to begin with. He would have killed you two!"

Lance was astonished. Why in the world would their caretaker know *this* of all things?

Desperate for answers, Lance blurted out, "*What?* What do you mean by that?"

Miss E shook her head. "He's a government experiment, cloned using DNA from another Rasrim. That's what gave him his mutated abilities. He isn't from Osamos. He was born here, on Earth."

Lance seemed even more confused, but Chase seemed furious.

"That doesn't explain a damn thing! He tried to *kill* us! He attacked us with all these weapons made of ice! He's as strong as a tank and as durable as titanium! Not to mention how damn *cold* it was literally everywhere he was! I mean, I nearly froze to death just by getting near the dude!"

Miss E was frustrated with herself. She clearly seemed more patient than she was letting on. She knew everything the boys told her already. Their recounts of Chile didn't make the situation any better. They didn't even know the worst part about him.

"I know, Chase. He was a very violent boy. He never knew how to control his powers."

But a dark secret whelped Olivia's mind like a demon feasting on her soul. She knew the ugly truth behind Chile. She continued to hide the fact that Chile had the potential to acquire the power necessary to obliterate not just the Earth but also be able to stream so much Ice Risima that he'd be able to destroy the moon *and* Mars as well—in a *single attempt.*

And that would be at *75 percent* maximum output.

Regardless, Olivia continued to reassure Chase by engaging with him directly, using eye contact and speaking softly. It wouldn't help to rile the boys up now.

"Chile *hated* his powers, and he hated us even more for giving them to him."

"'Us?'" Lance chimed in. "Who's 'us'? You work for the government?"

Miss E didn't respond right away.

Instead, she rolled up to her monitor and typed a series of keys on her computer, Chase and Lance watching closely. But she had worked fast, pulling up command prompts and typing sophisticated strings of text faster than the two could read them.

Before too long, Miss E had clicked a browser open and revealed a page of pictures, videos, and text files on the screen.

Right at the type of the screen was a seal Lance swore he recognized. It was a black and red triangle with a small triquetra in the center of it. The three tips of the mesmerizing triquetra perfectly aligned with the bold perimeter of the triangle. It was a seal that symbolized precise, meticulous calculation and mastery over science. It was impossible to miss.

PROPERTY OF THE ADVANCED EXPERIMENTAL SCIENCES DIVISION—TOP-SECRET MATERIAL ENCLOSED

Lance immediately had a bad feeling about what he was seeing. "Wait, this isn't stuff that regular people can see, is it?"

"Hey what is all of this?" Chase asked, reading some of the text. But Olivia remained silent, looking at the page herself, her attention immediately put toward one specific part of the entire page.

Lance listened as Chase began to read off the headlines.

> March 7, 2022, Codename "Black Eyes" captured in Alaska. March 9, 2022, "Black Eyes" subjected to series of experimental tests. March 21, "Black Eyes" found unresponsive…confirmed dead…

Chase's voice trailed off, his eyes wearily shifting from different text files to pictures.

His eyes wandered to another section of the page.

But then Lance noticed something. "Hey, wait a minute, this scientist right here. That looks like you, Miss E!" Lance pointed to a video file where a scientist was sitting in a room facing an individual.

Miss E's eyes suddenly turned dark when Lance asked her something.

"You…experimented on Rasrims, didn't you? You worked for this…Advanced Experimental Sciences Division?"

Miss E's eyes were glued to the screen, focused on an entirely different section of the forum, one that the boys didn't notice.

> January 2040, Director Tyera confirmed dead on Osamos. AESD Land, Space, and Intelligence Operations temporarily postponed.

Miss E's eyes trembled. She couldn't believe what she was seeing. That same year? That unfortunate yet inevitable year? Why had they chosen *that* year of all years to conclude that she was dead?

Finally, Olivia began to speak again. "Yes, Lance. I worked for the Division," she replied in an almost automatic calm voice that startled Lance more than it reassured him.

At once, a multitude of ideas popped into Lance's mind, ranging from her skills and hobbies, to her background and mannerisms. Everything now made total sense!

She took control of the screen and scrolled down, looking for something.

"Hey, stop there!" Chase said, pointing to another headline.

And so Miss E did.

He read, speaking a mile a minute, clearly engaged by the content he was seeing. "Right here it says that in April 2043 that Codename 'Chile' is captured in California and then experimented on from 2043 until—hold on. Woah, wait a second."

Olivia's eyes widened. She had seen it too.

"Until just five months ago! It says that in June 2051, 'Codename Chile escapes from Experimentation Site!'" Chase slowly looked up and directly at Lance, who returned the same serious expression.

"Holy crap! This means—!"

Olivia felt tense, but she knew that there was little that could be done at the moment.

"So it's true," she finally said, "Chile really has escaped. The horrors that poor kid could unleash on this planet..."

"But this is insane, Miss E! How long have you been doing this?"

"I *don't* do it anymore," she replied in a stern voice. "I was always opposed to it."

Lance pushed back. "And that one Rasrim, Black Eyes! What happened to him? We deserve to know the truth!"

Olivia didn't say anything immediately.

But Chase spoke up. "All this time, you kept all of these secrets from us! We almost died because of this guy you've been experimenting on! Lance is right—you gotta tell us the truth!"

Miss E seemed as if she was caught between frustration and desperation. She breathed in, relieving her tension.

She breathed out. "I was *not* experimenting on Chile. That was not my decision and not something you need to be concerned about."

Lance was just as upset as Miss E was, but he was determined to find out the truth.

"But *this* is you," Lance said, pointing to the video file he noticed above on the forum, "and this looks like a Rasrim. He fits the description. The tag underneath says March 2022. This was 'Black Eyes.' You say it doesn't concern us, but this is *you*, Miss E! You're our caretaker…you're all we've got! We should know what you have done! What happened to *him*?"

"He was pushed too hard! H-he discharged too much Elemental Energy and died from exhaustion. It was before we knew the truth about Risima and all of its limitations," she answered immediately, hoping it was enough to satisfy them.

Lance sat back in his chair, unsure of how to feel about what he just discovered.

And then Chase began to laugh.

"I mean, look. We always knew she was hiding something."

And then Chase's attitude changed, his eyes glowing red.

"But I'm not worried about what Miss E did or *ever* did. She's our caretaker, Lance. I'm worried about the bastard that nearly killed the two of us, and likely her too, for that matter!"

Lance grunted, about to respond, but he refrained himself from doing so. Chase was right.

"Thank you, Chase," Miss E said. Her tone had pain and regret in it. She had been holding it back all this time. It seemed it was becoming tough for her to mask her true feelings.

She rested her hands on the table. "All right," she simply said. And then the air got stuffy as the mood changed dramatically. The boys could feel the tension as Miss E prepared herself.

"I'll tell you from the beginning. Look, I worked for the Division for a *long* time. I never had a normal life, barely had a normal childhood. You must understand that before anything else."

Chase and Lance nodded, looking at each other.

"I think we can understand that."

Miss E smiled. She loved the boys' sense of ironic humor.

"Yeah. I guess you could." She breathed in and out through her nostrils.

"I was only a teenager when I was 'chosen' for a special program that was deemed unprecedented at the time. 'Aliens were real!' 'The aliens were *here*,' they told me. Psssh! I had already known by then."

Chase and Lance looked at Miss E, a somber tone in their face.

"This was no longer about politics, money, or status. I had to stop worrying about school, my friends, sex, my entire life stopped. But I saw it coming. *All* of it. I'm the reason why we're in this mess. I had to ditch my entire life to deal with *aliens* because I was the only one who knew anything about them."

Miss E chuckled, bringing up old memories.

"I was so young and naïve. No one could have predicted what was about to happen. I mean, I even tried to cover it all up. Little did I know…" She laughed to herself.

Lance leaned in. "What happened?"

Olivia looked off into space. "I was in a lab at MIT, doing a project for a class I really enjoyed. I remember I was there with a friend and asked to borrow some of his research equipment to do an experiment of my own. I had most of what I needed, but he was studying nanotechnology and had one last thing I really needed to do my experiment. See, I wanted to jumpstart my career in molecular biology, and I was writing a thesis that revolved around universal atomic structure, researching whether planets and stars had genetic sequences, and if they did, their resemblances to life on Earth or influence on other species out in the Universe. Of course, I had to prove there *were* aliens out there for it all to really matter."

"*Woah…,*" Chase said, clearly impressed. "That's cool stuff, I didn't understand a word of it, but keep going!"

Miss E continued.

"I must've been, I don't know, a week or two into my thesis when I discovered something in the lab that day, *way* past time for me to be allowed in there. It was past midnight, and I remember having maybe four or five different computers hooked up to a telescope, all evaluating the universe for different signs of life. And then one of them picked up an electromagnetic frequency that fried my computer's sensors. Of course, I didn't panic or react. I quickly replaced the module that ran the program for that computer with a new sensor that fired a series of high-powered lasers into the targeted area. This was *my* personal invention, and I had been *waiting* for something like this to happen. Along with my friend's nanotechnology I incorporated into the lasers, I had better equipment than NASA did when it came to researching the universe."

"But wait a minute, you knew that something would go wrong staring out in space like that? So all that was just setup until you had a good place to actually use the lasers then?"

Miss E nodded, continuing to tell her story.

"Right. Up until that point, it all was textbook experimentation and stuff that had been done already. Like I said, I wanted to *jump-start* my career, not piggyback off other experiments. So I launched my own. I fired those lasers and captured an area that thoroughly examined life, rendering its molecular composition into a 3D model my lasers were equipped with diagramming. If I missed my opportunity, I would've wasted millions of dollars of research equipment and experimental tech on nothing. So I timed it correctly, and then...I broke the law," Miss E said.

"You broke the law? By using a telescope? No way!" Chase said sarcastically.

Miss E wagged her finger.

"Oh, you see, I had been *borrowing all* that technology and money. Not all of it was courteous of MIT's distinguished laboratories and student club activities, mind you."

And then Lance began to catch on.

"They were the government's."

Miss E smiled. "Yup. I knew that the government was working with MIT and other institutions on new projects that were initially meant for space and cyber warfare. But I had different aspirations. I just *knew* something was up above."

"What did you steal?"

Miss E looked at the two boys carefully.

"An electromagnetic radio transmitter that can 'teleport' matter—it was considered top-secret at the time. A professor at MIT was helping the government modify and experiment on it—the same one I was writing my thesis for."

Lance rubbed his chin. Chase, on the other hand, had his mouth hanging open.

"So let me get this straight, after firing the laser, mapping out your diagram, you emitted a frequency that exposed whatever it was you were seeing?"

"Not quite. I was *attacking* it. I used the transmitter to fire radio waves into space that released a surge of energy into space. After it was received by satellite or anything else that could pick up radio waves, it would burst into wave electromagnetic pulses of kinetic energy that exploded anything that tapped into them. Alongside my lasers and nanotech, I was able to map out and diagram whatever it was that was intercepting my signals. I thought I would find, you know, Hollywood stuff like a UFO or something." She chuckled.

Lance began to laugh with her, but he was catching on rather quickly.

"So you essentially threw a bomb into space and baited aliens into catching it, sending a high-powered x-ray of electromagnetic signals and radio waves throughout their receivers in order to diagram the molecular composition of whatever it was 'the aliens' were using to intercept the signal? Genius!" Lance exclaimed.

Chase looked at Lance like he had been speaking a foreign language.

Miss E sat back in her chair and scoffed.

"Yeah, I know, right? But it wasn't a machine or satellite I began mapping out. It was a *planet,* one that was masking its identity and place in the universe using technology of their own."

Chase and Lance sat up. "Wait, are you saying that—!"

"Yes, boys. It was Osamos that I discovered. And it was an Electric Rasrim that intercepted my transmitted radio waves and took the force of the EMP blast. Astonishingly, the Rasrim began infusing the energy from the blast into his own but was nearly killed in the process. It fried his senses and jammed all of my equipment. I was left with a detailed sketch of the Rasrim's mind and body— his entire anatomical structure and had even transmitted the DNA sequencing machines from the nanotech incorporated into the laser into his body. It gave me access to a full sequence of Rasrim DNA by chance alone. But I quickly realized that my telescope was no longer able to continue firing the EMP or the laser into space. With all that space between us, the data I received could have been faulty or corrupted, providing me with only a glimpse of the full picture. It had never been pulled off by anyone before me, and I had learned 75 percent about an alien species due to an accident."

Chase looked confused.

"So you really discovered Rasrims?"

Lance ignored him. "That was no accident, Miss E. All of that must've been the result of his Risima, including how you managed to collect all of the data, and even how it remained intact as it crossed space back to you—the data was being preserved and transferred by Risima Energy! Had you not had some sort of electrical source connected to that telescope and…woah, wait a second!" Lance's eyes lit up.

"A brain *and* a computer were communicating with each other in real time, exchanging information, that means that the data was quite literally *alive* when you received it!"

Olivia whistled. "That's one interesting theory, Lance."

Lance rubbed the back of his head, an astonished look on his face, his own theories and ideas flashing through his mind at light speed.

"While I can't answer that directly, I can say that when my computer was collecting the Rasrim's information, he was collecting the same information about *my* computer, stripping its electrical energy away from my laboratory, millions of light-years away. He didn't even know what hit him, but he kept trying to absorb energy from it."

Miss E took a deep breath.

"I didn't even say a word about it to anyone. *They* already knew. They had been watching me the entire time. They knew everything about me."

A cold chill went down the boys' backs.

"The next thing that I know, I'm stopped on my way to my first class at seven in the morning by four or five guys in all-black suits. They escorted me off campus and to Washington, DC, without telling me a word of why. 'You need to come with us,' was all they said. Being the frail and nerdy girl that I was, I listened. They didn't bag me though. They didn't so much as touch any of my hairs. We stopped somewhere in Washington, and I found myself facing a man by the name of Raymond Tyera who, at the time, was the Director of the Central Intelligence Agency. The CIA was the predecessor to the AESD, although at the time it was only known as Operation Starburst, a joint task force led by the CIA, NSA, Department of Defense, and NASA to collect information and build countermeasures in response to extraterrestrial activity. You could guess what the CIA wanted with *me*, right?"

Olivia took a breath.

"The CIA and NASA handed me the helm of Operation Starburst due to my expertise on the matter. From there, that single operation ended up influencing the creation of an entirely new Intelligence Agency known as the Advanced Experimental Sciences Division, also known as 'the Division.' As you know, the AESD secured a tremendous amount of respect from the government and later became autonomous due to the massive successes we had when I took over. Although, it wouldn't be a while until I was appointed to be the director. At that point, I was only the 'Chief Liaison' between the CIA and the AESD until Raymond could decide if the Division would become a permanent thing or not. But I wouldn't have had it any other way. There were too many secrets that needed to be kept and too much work that needed to be done. But it wasn't always easy getting there. Raymond knew that we needed to create a new organization which only one person headed to optimize the efficiency of operations and all but ensure internal secrecy. The United States has so many adversaries and far too many leaks in the most sensitive of areas. Raymond had opposition from the Defense Department at first—they wanted me to go work with Military Intelligence exclusively—but I obviously sided with the CIA on that one."

Then she took another brief breath.

"A few months later, I was successfully able to crack the genetic code of the Rasrim I had discovered on that day and hypothesized almost everything about him *correctly*. Yes, I even discovered and theorized that Rasrims had special abilities which differed from each one in the earliest days of my research. Coupled with my technical skills and growing proficiency with CIA tradecraft, I rose through the ranks of the Division quickly after that. My knowledge and skills became vital to a field I never knew existed."

Olivia pushed her glasses up to her face, taking her time saying this next bit.

"I gained a huge amount of trust from Raymond. He pulled me aside one day and told me he was sick—that he wanted me to be the first director of the AESD and formally lead the organization." Olivia's glassy eyes were out in space, wandering about.

"He died only a week after we had that conversation. I never figured out what the true cause of death was. His death remains a mystery to me and several others."

Chase and Lance were wide-eyed, jumbling over their own words.

"I just want to say one last thing, and then I'll answer all of your questions. I promise."

She nodded slowly, biting her lowly lip.

"'Black Eyes,' the Rasrim you saw me interrogating, was the Rasrim I initially discovered back at MIT. I poured tremendous amounts of money and research into devising a way to capture him. Turns out we didn't even need to. He came here, crash-landed in Alaska. Of course, I was the first and only person on the planet to know an alien had landed on Earth. In just fifteen minutes, I devised a plan to capture the most dangerous thing to ever exist within the borders of the planet. I had to act fast but be smart about it, leaving nothing to chance. I assembled a team, briefed them in what was likely the most intense conversation held between Human beings, and dispatched them with enough gear to take down an entire country. By the end of the day, he was captured near the border of Canada. He never even used his abilities."

Miss E sat up in her chair. "We kept him contained in a cell for seven days. We just watched him 24/7. He had no access to food, water, or even sunlight. It was raw analysis—how he would react, what he would reveal he needed or wanted. But he was kept in a bare cell with nothing in it whatsoever. Not even any cameras and definitely no electrical signals or frequencies passing through the room." She took a breath before continuing.

"The room was set up so we could watch him from behind a one-way mirror."

Olivia sat up in her seat.

"The mirror was bulletproof, but if for some reason the screen was ever broken, if so much as a crack had been put into it from the other side, the *entire* room would instantly plummet into the depths of the planet's core before being blasted with a force a hundred times the power of the largest nuclear blast in history and all of its contents completely annihilated with no trace left behind whatsoever. That weapon only exists to eliminate threats of extraterrestrial beings. No one even knows it exists. And that bunker was *my* invention, couldn't you believe…?"

Lance's face had been sweating. He couldn't have imagined a weapon like that.

But to think that the calm, gentle woman in front of him had been capable of such a thing?

"Of course, this was all before the Division had the resources to begin investing into weapons that could harm Rasrims. Who knows if it would have even worked?"

"Were you responsible for researching other weapons to use against Rasrims? Is there anything that could harm us now?"

Olivia nodded, brushing her hair behind her ears.

"The military and most police forces have access to guns that fire special bullets coated with a material known as 'Myoplicide.' It's a special nerve agent that was developed in 2026. It completely wrecks Rasrims' abilities and can penetrate their skin, temporarily giving their bodies the same durability as a Human. It's actually made from a mineral found in space. We were never sure if there was a connection between it and Osamos, though."

Chase slowly sat back in his chair. His eyes had said it all and gasped and gestured to Lance when he realized something.

"That's what they used on that one Rasrim, when we were still little! Remember how his entire body seemed to spaz out?"

Lance only shook his head, agreeing with Chase but trying his best to block the memory out. "I remember. I never understood the events of that day, but now, it's all clear."

Lance turned to address Miss E with a serious question in mind.

"About the other Rasrim, what ever happened to him after you captured him?"

Olivia crossed her legs and closed her eyes. She had the memory in mind as if it were yesterday.

"While he was in his cell, nothing happened."

Her voice had been calm, but she spoke seriously at the same time, her words crisp and full of emotion.

"He never spoke. He never moved. He cooperated with everything we wanted him to do. And so, on day eleven, we freed him from his restraints, and I decided to have a look at him face to face. Of course, the *same* protocol was unenabled. I was risking everything for one precious moment."

Olivia began twirling her hair, biting her lip again.

"I quickly realized that my suspicions were confirmed: he was brain dead."

Olivia took a deep breath before continuing, trying to keep herself calm.

But then, Olivia began smiling before she let out a brief chuckle, startling Chase and Lance.

"But get this: Rasrims were aware of Human existence for *centuries*. Apparently, Osamos had known about Earth before Humans even began speaking, let alone develop their own civilizations. Black Eyes, whom we never gave a proper name to, was *infatuated* that one of us Humans managed to send such a powerful signal out into the universe like that."

"So what? He became curious and came snooping?"

"That's exactly what he did. But how Black Eyes managed to get here, and *why* he did so on his own remained a complete mystery to us all. I asked him, not thinking about language barriers or anything, 'Were any others coming?'"

Miss E laughed to herself, nervous on the inside. Her voice began to tremble, as fear and shock swelled up in her eyes.

"And the Rasrim spoke English too! I mean, I just couldn't believe it! The very *first* question I asked him…and he responds to me in perfect English!"

She was clearly livid, and it didn't take a genius to understand why.

"How did an alien species from way out in the universe understand our language? How did he *know* how to speak it? I-I mean I could understand if he was familiar with Latin, Greek, or maybe Hebrew but English? How was that possible?"

Miss E sat back, clearly still having a hard time processing the ordeal.

This was huge news. They had never had a glimpse into the challenging life that their caretaker had in her youth. Chase and Lance couldn't find themself to understand how she had been feeling, but they understand the severity of it all coming from a Human who had just discovered the existence of an alien species. It must have been haunting to say the least.

But she had played her part marvelously. And considering that almost everything the Division—all their wins and discoveries—were due to Olivia's vast intelligence and brave charisma? It was eye-opening and humbling to say the least.

But even that protocol had been *her* idea… The Division had used such wicked and gruesome tactics in order to ensure their safety and secrecy of their programs. Of course, this was why Miss E had always been able to remain calm in tense situations.

"So what did he say? When you asked him if there were others, what did he say to you?" Chase asked hesitantly, his voice cracked and hoarse.

"'No. Just me here.' Those were his words *exactly*. Everything was being recorded."

"But the others never believed him…"

Realization struck Lance hard as the numbers began adding up in his mind. He understood *everything* now. Perhaps he even understood why Miss E had taken up the role of raising Chase and Lance. She only wanted to help Rasrims, to learn more alongside them.

"I'm so sorry, Miss E," Lance apologized, "I shouldn't have questioned you like that. It was wrong of me. I—" Lance fumbled his words, trying to find the best way to apologize.

Olivia tried to cheer him up, offering him a warm smile. "No, it's completely okay, Lance," she said. "I'm actually grateful that you questioned me like you did. It seems it's been too long for me. I've grown numb and indifferent to the whole experience. I needed to remember how I felt back then."

Lance could believe that. He supposed having that amount of power and being sworn into secrecy for that long would change anyone.

"Is that why you refused to experiment on Chile? Was it out of fear that something like *that* would happen again?" he curiously asked, hoping not to draw any negative energy or remorse out of Miss E.

Fortunately, it didn't, and she answered openly.

"Yes. That's part of the reason. It was also because the Division was growing too large and too powerful. And they were becoming crafty too."

Olivia took her glasses off her face and wiped the lens clean.

"I kept my own secrets as the director, but my underlings were clever. They were out in the field on an operation dissecting and applying my research in unspeakable ways. But I was always one step ahead of everyone, both my adversaries and my allies. I discovered one of the meticulous bastards figured out a resemblance between 'qualified Humans' and the average Rasrim. He liked to refer to it as those who were simply 'susceptible to external stimuli and psychological operations.' It was just an ugly way of calling someone a test subject."

Lance looked at Miss E as if he realized something, but it was Chase who questioned her.

"But hold on, what exactly does that mean? How fast you adapt to a new environment or something?" Chase asked.

Olivia put her glasses back on and pushed them up to her eyes.

"Well, yes. Very much so. But to be more specific, he was looking at the undetectable changes in the Human body when it's exposed to *extreme* conditions such as radioactive materials, ultraviolet radiation, sound-directed energy waves, or electricity…to name a few."

Chase looked horrified. "*The government was doing all this?* Did people know? What, did they want to see if there was a way to mutate a Human into being able to conjure Risima, to replicate what was lost from Black Eyes? Even so, how could anyone ever believe all of that?"

Miss E nodded. "You can't expect anyone to. That's why the entire organization and its employees are shrouded in strict secrecy. I would be executed for what I know in a foreign country, let alone for raising two Rasrims in my home. Can't expect anyone to believe that either."

Chase and Lance looked at Miss E with unsureness, as if they were trying to reason for her recklessness.

"As far as Black Eyes goes, they were never able to replicate his DNA. But that's because I never helped them. But much has changed since then. And with Chile on the loose, the Division certainly has backup plans."

Chase turned his head sideways. "What, you left or something? I mean, I'm not judging!"

Miss E chuckled. "No. I decided I wanted to take a stab at the whole space-traveling thing myself. So I ventured to Osamos with research equipment. Of course, I was risking my life, but I was the only one suited to being able to handle such a job."

"Hold up! You actually went to Osamos? What was it like?" Chase exclaimed.

Miss E quickly raised an eyebrow. "It's beautiful, Chase. I couldn't say much more if I wanted to. There's species of plants and wildlife that are absolutely mind-boggling. But you see, I was so focused on my mission, I remained unbiased and unfocused on the complexities of the planet."

"What *was* your mission then?" Lance asked promptly.

Olivia shut her computer down and stood up from her chair… and stretched. She began walking in the direction of the machine that enabled the Matter-Phasing properties of the training grounds.

"It was to meet the King of Osamos and inevitably begin raising you two!"

Chase and Lance turned toward each other, whispering.

"What in the actual—"

"Yeah, I know right! This is all just insane!"

"She *was* working for the government! Dude, that explains everything in this room!"

Olivia, after pressing a series of buttons on the Matter-Phaser, called over to the boys.

"With all of that out of the way, we need to discuss something of even more importance!"

Chase looked worried, looking at Lance directly. He lowered his face before taking his time, deciding seriously how to phrase himself before he spat it out.

"Do you still trust her?" he asked Lance.

The question hit Lance like a bus, catching him off guard.

Lance stuttered.

Olivia glanced over at the two boys huddled over. Cleverly, they had hidden themselves behind the computer monitors, out of view from her.

But Miss E turned away and chuckled to herself. They would figure it all out soon enough. This was just part of the process. She had done the same thing, after all.

The only difference between her and the twin boys was that Olivia was all alone when it came to figuring out how to use all her abilities. As a genius prodigy, she believed she was always being tested as a child. She discovered what her differences were from an early age and was conscious and smart enough to keep it from *everyone*, not so much as speaking a word about it to anyone her entire life. No one, not in the government, nor did any of her school friends ever find out the truth about *her*.

No one except a man by the name of Raymond Tyera, that was.

Lance looked around, trying to think of every situation he could.

"Y-yes! I do trust her," Lance finally answered, closing his eyes and clenching his teeth. "We don't have a reason to stop, do we?"

Chase smiled. "No. I'm just making sure we're still on the same page. I wouldn't continue trusting her if you didn't, Lance."

Lance looked at Chase mischievously. "Are you kidding me right now?"

"Nah. Not in the slightest."

Chase stood up from his chair and stretched, clearly relieved to finally know the truth.

Lance on the other hand slowly rose from his chair, unsure of what he was feeling on the inside.

Of course, he loved Miss E, and he loved Chase too. That meant he trusted them, right?

Would Miss E ever turn her back on them? Turn them into the Division? Would she restore her position there in exchange for giving up two aliens she most likely didn't want to raise in the first place? Even with all the answers the two boys got from her, Olivia Elementa was still hiding a bunch of secrets.

Chase, with his hands behind his head, walked over to Miss E. "So what's in store for us now?"

Lance hunched over the Center Command, joining in on the conversation, but his eyes were elsewhere, keeping his mind deep in thought.

Olivia glanced over at Chase and then Lance before turning her attention back to the machine.

After about thirty or so seconds, she finally stepped away from the machine and faced the two boys.

"You two have grown tremendously this year. You began using your powers. You encountered and overcame pain. You learned the truth about me and your origins. You're stepping up, and I want to acknowledge that."

Chase beamed with confidence. "That's right, isn't it, Lance?"

"Yeah. We have," he reluctantly responded from the desk of the Console.

Miss E continued, "How did you two feel using your abilities for *real?*"

Lance down at his hands. "Natural. I felt like we handled the storm pretty well."

Chase sighed. "But when we fought Chile, we were sloppy. He tore us apart."

Miss E rubbed her chin.

"Why? Was he stronger, faster?"

"He controlled his Element like it was nothing—and *so much* of it at that. He could've turned the entire Atlantic into a skating rink if he wanted to," Lance said.

Chase shook his head, but he wasn't disagreeing with Lance. "Not only that," he said, raising his finger, "but he *was* faster and stronger too. His punches were terrifyingly strong, not to mention that thing with the frickin' jet!" Chase exclaimed.

Miss E widened her eyes. If Chase was referring to the Thunderbirds…!

"Jet? What happened involving a jet?"

Lance answered her, "He struck a jet using a spear of ice! He caught it in midair! Even if I was using Electric Risima, I'm not sure I could've actually hit it while it was flying overhead. Chile just got pissed off and did it!"

"Dude," Chase said, turning to Lance, "tell her about the other thing you did, though."

Olivia raised an eyebrow, turning to Lance.

Lance seemed unbothered. "Oh, that was nothing. I guessed I somehow managed to use Water Risima and hardened it into mud or something."

"No way! That was Earth Risima! You used Earth out there! And I swear you took down that Ice Wall too!"

Miss E was practically ecstatic, but she kept her composure solid as she addressed Lance.

"Is this true? Be honest with me, Lance."

Lance looked confused. "I mean, maybe? But there's gotta be an explanation. There's no way I can just use Earth and Ice Risima too! I'm still learning Electric Risima!"

Miss E's expression lightened up a bit. It seems her suspicions weren't confirmed yet. The boys weren't being targeted by the Thunderbirds back there. Lance would have confirmed that. That was a huge relief. The Thunderbirds relay information to the

Division that most definitely would have allowed its spies to track the boys with unrealistic accuracy.

Olivia relaxed herself, turning her attention to the next important thing.

"You're wrong, Lance. You *can* use Earth and Ice Risima. It's possible for a Rasrim to learn every Element, remember? Haven't I told you this before? It's very possible you already can use *every* Element, Lance."

"Fine, but *me*? Why would I be able to use every Element? And wouldn't I know if I could?"

Chase began sucking his teeth. "Yeah, that does seem kinda random, doesn't it? This dude gets every Element and all I get is Fire? Nah. I'm with you there, brotha."

"Lance. What you experienced is an ability Rasrims call 'Stellar Riora.' It's the penultimate ability for a Rasrim to manipulate the environment around them, able to change every aspect of anything they so choose."

Lance's eyes lit up. "Wait, that sounds familiar!"

Miss E nodded.

"While it's very uncommon, some Rasrims have the ability to use more than one or two Elements. In fact, as soon as we learned you had the ability to use Electric, I suspected you could use them all. And I'm sure you did too, didn't you?"

Lance was lost for words.

Chase raised his arms. "Hey, what about me? Seriously?"

"It's possible for you *too*, Chase," Miss E rubbed Chase's head, "but if I had to guess, I would say you have an entirely different ability even if you can use more than just one Element."

Miss E looked over at Lance.

"But this news changes a lot of things. When a Rasrim begins to use more than one Element, it's a sign that he can already then use Stellar Riora, otherwise known as just 'Stell Risima.'"

"So you're saying I can use all of the Elements *now*?"

"I'm saying that you, from here on out, will spend a much greater deal of your time and training to focus putting your Risima where you haven't already: the earth, the sky, trees, fire. In order to master all of the Elements, you'll have to start from scratch with them all, just as you did with Water and Electric Risima."

"I see…," Lance said.

And then an image flashed into his mind.

"But would it be possible for me to just use Stellar Riora right now? What if, for example, I worked backward and used Stellar Riora to better help me locate and hone in on other Elements instead?"

Miss E pointed her finger toward Lance.

"That's called thinking like a scientist, my boy! I can't answer that question, but I can say for certainty: Experiment with it. I'm giving you two a great deal of time and freedom to discover for yourself who you truly are and what you can really do."

"We'll have to start training again, then," Chase said. "We made mistakes. Some of our weaknesses were exposed. But if we start with that, I'm sure we'll both begin to discover even more of our abilities."

Lance agreed with Chase, impressed with his sudden initiative. Lance knew that Chase was finally starting to emerge into the person he had always wanted to be. That was great. Lance loved to see it.

"I'm with Chase on that. But I also think we'll need more… material to work with. We can't exactly replicate a storm here, can we? Nor can we just ask another Rasrim to teach us more about Risima."

Lance's eyes began trailing off. "There's someone…teaching him, though," Lance whispered.

Olivia looked at Lance, confused. "What was that, Lance?"

Lance shook his head, looking at the ground. "I remember something else now. Someone was *with* Chile. I heard a voice right before he put me down for good. He told Chile to stop. He said there were more opportunities to learn and grow. More 'power,'" Lance said, visibly disturbed with the memory.

Olivia looked astounded. "Another Rasrim? Maybe even…?" She shook her head. "Never mind. That couldn't be possible."

"You don't think it's the Division?" Chase asked.

Olivia shook her head. "Very unlikely. They wouldn't be coaching Chile. That's something I would do, evidently, and I was disliked for that tremendously."

"He sounded strong," Lance said, recounting his thoughts. "He spoke with purpose. He wasn't afraid of Chile and wasn't speaking to satisfy him. Chile even stood up to the man but *backed* down after the man told Chile enough was enough. I don't think he would have done that to anyone who could tame his power."

"Jesus," Chase said. "I mean, that sounds right but, who could that guy have been to command Chile like that? And you're saying that the reason why we're alive is because he told Chile to stop? He wasn't sparing us then?"

Lance agreed. "Yeah. That's exactly what I'm saying. Whoever this guy is, he saved our lives. But he's also the reason why Chile's free and able to do all this damage."

Chase and Miss E were paying full attention to Lance.

"If I had to guess, I'd say that Chile was being tested that day by this man. Why else would he conveniently show up after Chile is able to stop the tidal wave, number one"—Lance took a breath, speaking straight from his thoughts—"but number two, allowing Chile to fight with us but not to kill us? That was a test to gauge his abilities, especially if the Division wasn't involved."

Olivia processed everything she was hearing.

While she remained silent, she had her own theories.

Was it *him*? That strange man that could predict the future? Or was this something else? Did she know this man? Did they have anything against her or the Division? Even so, there was too much risk involved. Something needed to be done about Chile.

Olivia tuned back in, hearing Chase and Lance bouncing ideas off one another.

"Did you hear a name?" she asked Lance, interrupting their discourse.

"Uh, no, I don't think so." Lance scratched his head, his eyes moving back and forth.

"Wait, yeah! I remember now! Chile called him 'Melterai.'"

Olivia squinted. That name sounded familiar, but it didn't ring a bell. It most definitely wasn't anyone in the Division or a rival intelligence agency either. She knew that much.

"Melterai…"

"Do you know that name, Miss E?"

Olivia shook her head after a moment of uncertainty. "No. I don't," she simply replied. "It could be an alias. It could be a Rasrim. Whoever it is, he's just as dangerous as Chile."

And then her tone changed again.

"Are you two certain that this isn't too much for you to deal with? Can you continue going on, knowing that you will have to live a life of secrecy with access to a great deal of power just as I was? That you may find yourself in situations where your decisions could change the planet forever but you could never speak about it to anyone?"

Chase and Lance looked at each other. Of course, they always did this when faced with serious situations. They needed to know how the other felt first. There was no one any one of them would just ride solo—no, they had to be in it together or not at all.

But that was their strength. They *had* each other and even Miss E. Did they need anyone else? As far as the responsibility goes, they more than proved their ability to risk their lives for the bigger picture and keep themselves hidden. Wasn't that enough indication of their maturity?

Now sure of how each other felt, having a moment to speak to each other without saying a word, Chase and Lance turned away from each other and answered Miss E.

"Yes. We're sure."

"One hundred percent!"

A great deal of stress was taken off Olivia's chest. It wasn't because of their answer—she knew they would say yes.

It was because they answered together after taking a moment to feel for each other first. That was important. They would act as each other's moral compass and guide each other.

That meant they were already able to make even more serious decisions than she could. And this was about to come in handy.

"Good," Olivia said, causing Chase and Lance to stand tall, "because now that we all trust each other and know enough to make serious decisions, I'm going to ask you two of something of dire importance."

This caught Lance's attention. He looked up, looking at Miss E. "What is it?"

Miss E looked at Chase and then Lance—and then back at Chase.

She continued doing this, using her eyes to study the two boys before closing her eyes and taking a breath, pausing before continuing.

"Well, for one, I'm going to emphasize on training you two in environments that *counter* your prime Element every day. Starting tomorrow, Chase, you'll be in the pool, learning how to keep your internal stimuli constant and controlled even when you're unable to use Fire Risima."

Chase had a gaze of bewilderment on his face.

"The pool? R-right..."

Miss E pointed to the Fire Chamber when she made eye contact with Lance. "And you, Lance, will learn to manage your Elements in the Fire Chamber. But in order to give both of you the maximum benefits or this training exercise, you won't pass this assignment until you *both* can use your Elements as comfortably as you can in your *natural* environments."

Lance looked amused.

"And what does that accomplish?"

Olivia looked rather surprised.

"Oh, you don't know? It's simple, really: conditioning."

Lance tilted his head back.

"Conditioning...in the event that we suddenly find ourselves in an extreme environment that nullifies our abilities. Such as—"

Chase caught on too. "Ice!"

"Yes, exactly," Miss E affirmed.

Olivia opened her eyes, her expression straightening out before she spoke serious, unexpected words. It was a single command that would change their entire lives forever.

"I'm going to emphasize that you two are comfortable both in environments that do not agree with your Risima Prowesses but also in simulated environments that involve sub-zero temperatures."

Lance squinted, intrigued with the prospect.

Olivia continued vocalizing her plan. "I want you two to be able to think, fight, and remain calm even in the harshest of situations."

Chase seemed upset, like the idea didn't make sense to him and he couldn't figure out why.

"But why go this far?" Chase sat up in his seat, irritated about something he knew Miss E was keeping from them.

"Why shouldn't we just train with our Elements more and learn better fighting techniques? Why do you want us to prepare for Chile specifically?"

Olivia closed her eyes and prepared her next statement carefully. It seemed Chase could sense the animosity radiating in Olivia.

But she had no choice but to deliver her statement nonetheless—and see it through till the end.

It was a statement that would alter Chase and Lance's lives forever, the first step to achieving power at the expense of humanity.

"That's because I want you two to find Chile. And when you do find him, I want you to kill him."

CHAPTER 11

Stellar Riora

November 2054
Two years later

Chase and Lance knew the routine.

A loud buzzing sound, and an emergency program was initiated, turning a safehouse into a barricade, heavy metal doors sealing the walls and covering the windows.

An overhead red light flashed while its alarm blared, illuminating the room each time the alarm rang.

Chase and Lance weren't anywhere near each other.

In fact, they had no clue where each other were. But that didn't diminish the importance of their job. They knew what they needed to do and trusted each other to keep their side of things clean and orderly. Only then would they meet up at the end.

Lance kept his movements low, running across a hallway before taking cover by a wall, peering into a room, watching for every movement.

He had been using Electric Risima to monitor every step, every heartbeat in the room.

He counted four individuals inside the room. That was easy.

Lance placed his hand on the ground and closed his eyes, focusing his Energy through the solid marble floor he was standing on.

He could feel the vibrations of the men's steps—even their breathing—through the ground. Lance's ability to sense Risima grew exponentially. He now had the ability to identify individuals he didn't even have a visual on—down to being able to tell what type of clothing they wore and even if they were nervous or not.

After focusing Energy and tensing his body, Lance released the Energy he built up into the ground.

The four men cried out before going silent, their bodies thudding to the ground as what sounded like a fissure swept through the room.

Lance moved quickly.

He turned into the room and paid little attention to the four men lying unconscious on the ground. He was more concerned about the server room contained in a section deep within the building. All he needed to do was reach that room.

Lance stayed low but hustled as he moved through the hallway, passing closed doors, office suites, and an occasional guard patrolling the building.

Lance stopped at an edge of one of the hallways, hearing a set of footsteps approaching him.

He waited patiently, tracking the guard using Electric and even now Earth Risima, using its power to monitor the vibrations of the ground.

But right before the guard turned the corner, he stopped.

Lance was a little confused.

Out of nowhere, the guard shot from around the corner and began firing a weapon into the hallway, a hail of bullets slicing through the air toward Lance.

Lance's eyes widened, but he remained calm. He was much faster than bullets even from a submachine gun.

With calculated moves, Lance weaved between the bullets while inching toward the man, charging Electric Risima in his right hand.

The man swung the gun onto his hip, thankful he had been wearing a harness to carry it. The man quickly pulled a knife out of his left-hand side pocket and swung it at Lance in an expert fashion, his movements crisp and efficient.

Lance dodged the first swing and evaded a thrusting motion, the tip of the knife missing his head by inches.

The man was quick though. He tossed the knife into the air and kicked at Lance, hitting him in his knees, tripping him before he caught the knife in his other hand and swiped again.

Lance rolled on the ground, the knife missing him only by a centimeter, taking off a slice of his hair.

Lance recovered, getting back on his feet before he rushed the man, closing the distance between him and his attacker.

The man seemed surprised as Lance grabbed the hand holding the knife and wrestled him. Clearly, Lance was much stronger as he twisted the attacker's left arm before Lance spun around, pivoting his right foot between the attacker's legs and lifted up with his hips while bringing the attacker's arm down, effectively lifting him into the air.

Lance, in one fell swoop, used all his leg's momentum and slammed the attacker into the ground, knocking him out cold.

Lance smirked to himself as the man groaned out. "No Risima necessary," he told himself.

Lance ran on.

He had made quick work of the building, surprised to see the cameras located at every angle of the building had still been disabled. He had maybe less than a minute to find the server room.

Lance reached the end of the hallways and kicked a set of doors open, which revealed a stairwell behind it. He grabbed the handrail and flipped his body over it entirely, letting his body hang down from the handrail, calculating his fall to the bottom.

Lance took a deep breath, and let go, falling to the bottom.

Once Lance's feet hit the bottom, he rolled fast, breaking the impact of the fall as best as he could. Again, he tried his best to conserve his Risima. Not that he *needed* to, anyways.

Lance looked around. There had been another hallway leading to more office suits and eventually a garage to his left, but he needed to travel in the opposite direction first.

Lance jogged in the direction he needed to until swung around another corner, coming face to face to a large metal door with an electronic keypad at the end of the last corridor.

"Bingo," Lance whispered to himself.

Now he had a variety of ways to crack this thing open.

Lance laughed to himself. He stood back, and tensed his body, infused Risima into his body.

Lance lunged forward and swung his fist into the door as hard as it could. The door was blasted off its hinges and crashed on the floor.

Lance stood tall and entered the room, looking at everything he was seeing.

But Lance quickly found what he was looking for. Right in front of him was a computer with its screen on, displaying an image of something.

Lance walked up to the screen and analyzed the image, memorizing the words on it.

As Lance read, he began to feel a strange aura behind him.

Lance squinted, listening.

And then, Lance's instincts told him to move *fast* as something dangerous was approaching.

Lance didn't waste a single second as he sidestepped to the left, a machete swinging into the computer screen in front of him, cutting the screen in two.

Then another round of bullets lit up the server room. Lance hit the ground fast and blasted Risima Energy into the ground.

On command, a huge wall of solid rock rose from the ground, shielding him from the bullets.

Lance held his hands up and manipulated the wall of rock to slide back, crashing into the gunmen who had been waiting at the door.

The first attacker had been reckless. He swung his machete at Lance but was confused when another wall of rock blocked his machete entirely, causing it to snap in half.

Frustrated, the man pulled a gun off his waist and fired at the wall of rock in front of him. But as the bullets simply bounced off the wall, the man began to grow even more frustrated.

"Coward! Fight me, Rasrim scum!" he yelled.

The walls of rock retreated into the ground.

The man raised his gun but made a sound of confusion.

There was no one there.

"H-huh? But he was right there a second ago!" the thug said weakly.

From above him, hanging onto an intricate system of pipes, Lance dropped from the ceiling and landed silently behind the man, wrapping his arms around the thug's neck and taking him to the ground, against the wall.

The thug tried to yell, but his airflow was blocked off by Lance, who could have strangled the man right then and there.

Water dripped from the pipes above, splashing onto the man's face.

Lance had the thug in what was called a Rear-Naked Choke, using his left arm to squeeze man's throat and his right hand to support his left arm but clearly so much stronger against the thug, Lance let his right hand go, moving it away from his neck.

Another droplet of water splashed onto the ground, and in one swift motion, an object materialized in Lance's right hand—completely made of Water.

Lance brought his right hand back to the man's neck ever so slightly, holding a Water Dagger against his throat.

"I'll need the rest of the data from that computer," Lance said.

The thug groaned, resisting.

Lance tightened his grip, bringing the dagger to the thug's skin, breaking the outer layer.

"I don't want to hurt you, but I'll make this quick: the data… or else."

The man groaned out again. "F-fine! I'll give you the data! It's the drive in my breast pocket!"

The dagger in Lance's right hand disappeared, turning into steam before Lance choked the man and put him to sleep temporarily.

Lance rummaged through the man's pockets and found what he was looking for.

Lance held the drive up to his eye.

"Mission accomplished."

But before Lance could celebrate, an alarm in the building went off.

"*Warning: building lockdown initiated*," an automated voice announced through the speakers overhead.

Lance held onto the drive and made a dash forward, flipping over the wall of Earth he had created before he noticed the gunmen was against the wall speaking into a radio. He was most likely the one to call for backup.

"Shoot!" Lance told himself. He should have dealt with the gunmen better!

In only seconds, Lance closed the gap between him and the gunmen. After swinging his arms and jumping into the air in order not to lose any more time, Lance placed his foot into the gunman's face and kicked off, knocking his body to the floor as Lance used the momentum to launch forward, making a dash for the garage.

He had approximately *thirty* seconds to escape before the entire building would be locked down, trapping him inside.

He began counting the seconds in his head.

Lance ran through the corridor, pouring Risima Energy into his body, speeding himself up tremendously.

He turned the corner of the hallway and bounced off the wall, wasting no movement speed even as he changed directions.

Ahead of him, three armed gunmen stepped out into the corridor, holding their guns up in front of them.

Lance swiped his left hand, and a pillar of Earth Risima jutted out from each wall and struck the gunmen in the face, knocking them out cold.

But one of them had managed to dodge the attack and unleashed hell at Lance with his submachine gun.

Lance's entire body focused, his eyes trained on the gunmen. His body and all his senses had been in tune with one another, operating in perfect sync.

Time slowed down dramatically as Lance shifted from Earth to Electric Risima.

Lance was no stranger when it came to weapons—having spent the last two years studying all types of combat, including learning how to wield various types of firearms.

Lance could see and point out in less than a second that the sole gunmen had been using a Heckler and Koch MP7, a German variation of a popular submachine gun. It had a high fire rate and decent recoil compared to other choices in its category.

But this gun had come with some extra tools and tricks designed to protect against Rasrims, including bullets coated with Myoplicide. If even one of those bullets hit Lance, he was as good as dead.

The gun squeezed the trigger.

Lance ran lightspeed calculations in his head. *The hallway is twelve feet wide. I'm about twenty-two feet away from the gunmen.*

Lance's eyes studied the gun in front of him, watching as the barrel exploded, firing the first round of bullets.

This submachine gun fires about 1,500 rounds per minute, or 25 rounds per second.

In less than a microsecond, Lance had found a path to navigate.

These are moving at 2,800 feet per second. With perfect timing and movement, I can move eight feet to the right and—

The first round of bullets appeared in Lance's face.

Lance dodged the twenty-two bullets from the gun, counting each one as they missed his body, flashing to the right side of the room.

Lance's eyes bounced back and forth, continuing to track the trajectory of the bullets, and the gunmen adjusted their aim.

Lance smiled to himself.

That's it then. I've found the path. I know exactly what he'll do next.

Lance ran straight ahead, weaving in and out and bullets sprayed down the hallway and slammed into the walls and floor. As Lance dodged some thirty more bullets, Lance moved expertly, dodging the tiny projectiles by only fractions of an inch, wasting no movement to energy as Lance closed the gap to the gunmen.

Only 5.2 seconds have passed since the alarm sounded.

The gunman adjusted his aim, going for Lance's legs, firing some twenty more rounds in less than a second. Lance studied the trajectory of the bullets carefully.

He moved quickly and expertly, dodging the spray of bullets aimed at his legs by running across the wall, using his speed to keep himself against the wall. As the gunman adjusted his aim one last time, Lance pushed off from the wall as hard as he could flipped over the gunmen, dodging the last spray of bullets from the gunmen by a dangerously close margin, feeling every sensation and movement as if it were a playback in slow motion.

At the last second, Lance flicked an item from out his left hand toward the man as he continued to spin in midair as he flipped right over the gunmen, who wasn't even able to keep up with the blindingly fast Rasrim that flashed straight over and past him.

Lance crashed to the ground and rolled forward, huffing hard.

He took no time to look backward as he bounced back to his feet and continued running forward, hearing the man grab his throat and gag before crashing on the floor, choking on blood.

That had only taken Lance 3 seconds total. He now had 22.8 seconds left to escape. Easy.

He had been keeping track of everything.

Lance continued moving, running through the twists and turns of the building as the alarm continued flaring overhead.

As he neared the garage, he heard a series of explosions above him, followed by several people screaming as they fell from a high height, crashing into the floor just outside the garage.

Lance slowed down, giving no time to think about what was going on.

He busted a hard left and entered the garage, happy to see the large doors of the garage had only just started moving down. But he was four floors up on a platform—with more armed men on it.

Lance ran down the platform, evading more gunfire as he moved. Lance leapt over one of the gunmen, using him as a stepstool and evaded them all entirely, crashing into the solid floor of the garage before just before the garage door closed, Lance managed to slide underneath it and escape into the outside air of the building.

Lance slowed down, opening his right hand.

The drive was perfectly fine.

Lance heard another explosion from above, and from out of nowhere, the entire first floor of the building burst into flames before a being emerged, jumping out of the explosion and into the night sky.

Lance watched with a smile on his face as the being descended smoothly, using the high pressure of fire to control their movement as they inched closer to the ground.

"Why so dramatic?" Lance asked.

"*Someone* set off an alarm. For once, I don't think it was me," Chase said.

Lance rubbed the back of his head.

"Well, did you get yours?"

Chase opened his hand, revealing a flash drive. "Sure did. After all that, I hope you got *yours*."

Lance revealed a black flash drive to Chase. "Got mine too. I guess we didn't do so bad after all, huh?"

Chase looked around, peering through the sky. "Hey! Can we get a time check now? I'm hungry!"

Suddenly, the entire area became distorted. The building, the men, and the sky transformed from a real area, into a large sectioned-off area in the huge underground basement that Chase and Lance spent most of their time in.

Of course, these were all fabrications using the high-powered Matter Phaser, using nanotechnology to create real models of people and structures with striking accuracy, able to replicate movement, emotion, and functionality and even simulate real-world combat.

"Thirteen minutes, thirty-three seconds," Miss E said from behind a huge protective display within the Center Console.

"Those are your best times. It seems triggering the alarm sped your decision-making times up a bit, even in combat. I'm impressed!"

Lance gestured to Chase, smirking.

Chase scoffed. "Puh—lease! You got lucky! That's all!"

"Not according to the statistics. We just performed well."

"I will say," Olivia said, "Lance, your interaction with those guards was smooth and flawless. True marks of a professional. You've blended your abilities with your physical skills and environment extremely well. That was most impressive."

Chase scoured toward Lance. "He's a showoff! I'm telling you!"

"*But*, Chase!" Miss E said, raising her finger.

"Oh, God..." Chase dropped his arms and expression, ready for an earful.

"The way you took out the gunmen at the top and recovered the flash drive, blasting a hole into the safe and snagging it without being seen? I mean...*incredible!*"

Chase frowned. "Oh? *Me?*"

Miss E continued speaking. "Even a trained professional would have had trouble getting through that safe, but you cleared the entire floor and recovered the data like it was a walk in the park. I...words can't describe how incredible of a performance that was!"

"Even though I blew up the entire floor?"

Olivia grinned at Chase, telling him she was no fool.

"Chase, I *know* what you were thinking. You thought you'd be able to divert attention from Lance by putting a larger target on yourself. And yes, it was brilliant. You both have shown such improvements in everything you do. I couldn't be more satisfied."

Olivia stood from the Center Console and pressed a few buttons.

The sectioned room of the training facility began to change, releasing armored barricades and platforms from the sides of the facility and returning the training facility to its normal state. Lance could hear gears and anchors moved underneath the floor, suggesting that everything could be moved and interchanged to turn the room into anything they wanted.

Of course, one section of the platform opened up to reveal a pool in the far-left side of the facility, and another section of the facility opened up, allowing a large metal structure to rise from the ground before sealing the floor underneath it.

Olivia began speaking again, Chase and Lance noticed that her voice was no longer being transmitted through a speaker overhead since the Console's defenses were deactivated.

"I think that will conclude training for today. Lance, you clearly have gotten more proficient using now *Five* Elements, and Chase, your attributes using Fire Risima have grown so much that you can now compete with Lance on every arena, correct? You can keep up with the speed of his Electric Risima and hit as hard as his Earth Risima, agreed?"

Chase rubbed the back of his head, clearly in the blues.

"Yeah, I can, but..."

Lance wrapped his arm around Chase.

"It's no big deal. I'm sure you'll be able to use another one soon."

Lance tugged on Chase. "Even so. Yeah man, you *are* fast now! You're faster than me and don't even have to go all out anymore!"

Olivia nodded. "I'm just very happy you're as strong with Fire Risima as you are! I mean, there are Rasrims who can't even use their given Element. There's something out there, Chase, some hidden secret, I know it! Perhaps it lies in your other abilities or maybe even someplace out in the Universe we have yet to discover?"

Chase chuckled nervously.

It was all true. In two years' time, Chase did train *hard*.

But Chase devoted *all* his time to becoming a master of Fire Risima and hardly anything else that *he* could truly be proud of—something he could really call his own. He had enough power to melt tungsten in his hand with *minimal* application of Energy, was fast enough to beat Lance in a race—who could now seriously contest for being able to move at light speed—and was also strong enough to lift several hundred tons without much effort.

Chase had also become *much* stronger using Fire Risima. He could create jets of high-powered Energy and explosions that could likely level an entire city. He could even control Fire by just *thinking* about it, and Chase could also fly, something Lance was still learning how to do.

But oh, wait. That's right. Lance could *also* use Fire Risima now. And he could use Earth. And Wind Risima too!

"So how does using Stellar Riora feel, Lance? Are you able to control it steadily yet?"

Lance looked at Miss E, a little distraught.

"Well, to be honest, I haven't tried using Stellar Riora yet. I know the drills we go over and try infusing it when I have free time, but I feel like if I started using Stellar Riora now, I wouldn't be able to control it. I just think it would get out of control and something bad would happen. That's what it feels like. That's what my mind is telling me now when I think about it."

Miss E looked a little concerned, remembering the effects using Stellar Riora could have on a Rasrim. She had seen countless examples of Rasrims, not discharging their but instead losing their ability to sense Risima *at all*. Stellar Riora consumed and destroyed Rasrims from inside out, especially when they tried to perform a technique which was known as Risima "Purification" in order to achieve a state of even more power.

But that was a concept far too advanced for the twins now.

Lance waved his hand, changing the subject. "I have another question."

Lance paused, thinking about the time he fought with the Storm on the beach and then the time he was running the simulation, switching his infusion Energy from Earth to Electric Risima. Could he somehow combine them together and receive the perks of both Elements at the same time *without* straining himself by using the combined form of Stellar Riora? Sure, it was true that Lance could use every element at once with Stellar Riora. He would be as quick as lightning and as durable as Earth, provided he had the energy to sustain the power for that long. But was there a more manageable middle ground of Elemental abilities he could use?

"So Miss E, what do you think would happen if I tried using just two Elements without trying to use Stellar Riora? Is that possible?"

Miss E thought for a moment.

"On Osamos, there's rumors of a sage that understands the components and mixtures of Risima better than anyone else. All I know is that Risima is a very easy Energy to use incorrectly, especially when individuals who are not of the right state of mind attempt using it. That being said, even the strongest minds have difficulty using more than one Element together at the same time without discharging it all. So to answer your question, it *may* be possible, but there's people who know better than I do."

Olivia took a brief pause, typing something on her computer.

"But just as I told you last week, you need to try and experiment with your Elements on your own and discover new ways to use your powers. I'm sure before long, you'll master even Stellar Riora in its entirety."

"Huh," Lance said before holding out both of his hands. In his left hand, a swirling blue orb of Water Risima materialized, floating in the center of his palm. In his left him, a bright, crackling Energy of Electric Risima sparked, swirling around in a spherical shape in his hand.

Between his hands, three more orbs of Energy began forming, Lance's eyes twitching as he struggled to maintain the Energy.

Chase watched in disbelief as an orb of chunked Earth Risima orbited in the air, a blast of scorching hot Fire pulsated next to it, and a hazy, fast-moving tornado of Wind Risima, all levitating in front of Lance's body as he began to emit a strange, vibrant white aura. It was potent, one that Chase could feel but couldn't draw Energy from.

He couldn't even direct his Fire Risima into it. Lance's aura produced from Stellar Riora had completely dispelled Chase's own Energy entirely.

Sure enough, as soon as Lance tried manipulating all the Elements on its own. Lance's entire body tensed as each Element began glowing, drawing in more power. Chase watched with his mouth hanging open. Could he actually control Stellar Riora now?

Lance strained, gritting his teeth. He found it tough to concentrate hard enough to infuse Energy for *each* Element while having enough fortitude to combine them together in one unanimous Energy. It required a tremendous amount of Energy. Nothing on Earth had the ability to produce the Energy necessary to sustain this level of power!

The Electric Risima responded, discharging bolts of electricity across the training ground, causing the lights in the basement and on the computers to flicker.

Chase took a step back, covering his face.

He watched as the Earth Risima began absorbing stray materials from the basement, picking up screws, metal fillings, and even dirt, absorbing all of it into its spherical orbit.

The Wind Risima began producing massive bursts of air, nearly knocking Chase to the ground.

Lance's eyes began to throbbing, turning a bright red color, before he yelled out, releasing all the Energy into the air, various vibrant colors and lights dispersing into the room before fading away.

Chase watched in horror. "Dude!"

But Lance laughed as if he were defeated.

"Well, I see your point now. It *is* tough to do! I'll keep working on it."

Chase shook his head. How was this fair? He was completely dismayed from *anything* that involved being able to use more than one Element! It was never "You too, Chase!" or "Try *your* own combos out too, Chase!"

It didn't matter that he was becoming as strong as Lance or as fast as him. Why was Chase still stuck on Level 1? What was he not doing that Lance was?

Or was he just not as special as Lance? Was Lance just destined to be that much better than him?

Chase shook his head. "Hey, you guys wanna eat now?" he asked.

Lance let go of him. "Oh yeah. I'm starving right about now. What time is it?"

The two stopped in front of the counter surrounding the Center Console, looking over at Miss E.

"It's a little after eleven. I think we're all due for breakfast at this point. Let's head up now."

Lance slapped the back of his hand on Chase's chest.

"We can run another one in the evening after we cool off. How's that sound?"

Chase beamed, putting his hands behind his head. "Yeah, I'm down! I'll race ya up there!"

Olivia watched the two boys take off toward the concealed elevator that would take them back up to ground level.

She watched the two passionately. She was happy; she felt content.

From the point of view of both a caretaker and teacher, the boys gave her more fulfillment than anything in the world. And they made her so proud.

They weren't just splitting images of her—her opposite personalities on polar opposite sides of the spectrum—but they also completed the parts of her that were missing.

Olivia looked down at the screen in front of her wearily.

"What would I do if I lost them…?"

And then, with no warning, a haunting memory forced its way into Olivia's mind. An image flashed in her head—the picture of a sweet, innocent boy she had once known and loved dearly.

She had done everything to protect him, taught him everything she knew.

But she failed miserably.

And now that innocent, happy little boy who had tried to do everything to please Olivia was dead.

A tear welled up in Olivia's eye.

She whispered to herself quietly, making sure no one could hear her, not even the microphones on her cellphone or her laptop, allowing a single tear to stream down her face.

"I failed you, Sonrio. I cannot fail them too. But I love you. And I'll always show them that same love too."

CHAPTER 12

Operation Polar Vortex

Chase, Lance, and Olivia tried to enjoy what seemed to be their first family breakfast in ages.

They had spent the last two years preparing for the inevitable time when Chase and Lance would come face-to-face with the Pseudo Rasrim once more.

Chase and Lance, to begin with, spent most of their time conditioning their bodies against stress, fatigue, and Elemental discharges. It was a long, painful, and grueling process that took the full duration of the two years to accomplish.

Some days seemed more intense than others. Chase and Lance would spend hours at a time concentrating on sensing Risima under extreme pressure or when subjected to climates, including anything from sub-zero temperatures to molten hot ones.

Other days were much more productive. In two years' time, Lance managed to hone in on what Stellar Riora was at its core and studied it closely. He learned that Stellar Riora was like a planet, a massive collection of energies that affected the gravity of much smaller or less massive items in its vicinity. Stellar Riora essentially influenced the world as a whole. When left as a small, unmanaged particle, the Risima particle interacted with the atoms and molecules of other Elements as a coordinator. It ensured that Water flowed freely and that Fire burned passionately. When the two Elements of Water and Fire collided naturally, Stellar Risima was merely an observer, watching the circumstantial occurrence play out naturally; the outcome solely dependent on the potency of the present energies to decide which of the two would emerge stronger than the others.

And this was how the world was meant to behave. When two forces collide, it was the stronger of the two that survived and flourished, while the other simply perished. And it was Stellar Riora, the full, unlocked potential of Risima, that governed over this reality, ensuring the continuation of the natural world.

However, just like a massive star being introduced to a new solar system or collection of planets, when a Rasrim began to manipulate Risima, even just fractions of the whole, *he* became the new coordinator. If the Rasrim decided that Water was to no longer flow freely and was to obey his or her wishes, then an entire ocean could be commanded to ravage the lands or consume other bodies of water. If he decided that Fire was to destroy everything and spare only the areas he considered vital or important, then the Fire would oblige and would disintegrate only what was permitted. If a massive crater prevented the Rasrim from moving between areas, Earth would be called upon to create bridges and platforms, either permanent or tentative, in order to access what was previously inaccessible. And if Electricity was needed to strike an enemy with tremendous force or transport an object at high speeds, the Rasrim could command it to lend its Energy to him however he saw fit.

This, Lance learned, was the true power of Risima: a tool to defy Mother Nature, a weapon best used by those who *understood* and respected nature to begin with. Risima could be used to instrument chaos and promote destruction en masse, but to Rasrims who respected nature, Risima was only used as a tool to reconstruct and preserve nature against the external forces that could not appreciate its beauty.

And what Lance appreciated most and what his sworn enemy, Chile, could never understand, was that Earth was among the most precious, most beautiful places in existence. It was *divine* in scope and prose. It was the sole law that governed over everything that lived upon it, acting as judge, jury, and executioner when it decided the fate of any that abused its integrity.

But to the forces lurking in the dark, Risima was but a tool to acquire the power of the *gods*, the only thing that could defy the laws of nature and thus the key to control everything that nature oversaw.

Olivia, in her own spare time, in her own effort to prepare for an altercation with Chile, revealed that she had several contacts with informants from around the world who kept her up to date with information regarding global activities. She used mailstops and PO boxes to receive information about events happening all over the world in real time.

But nothing she got revealed anything about Chile whatsoever. It didn't appear as if he was working with a foreign government or anyone within the United States after all.

But that was a good thing. This meant that the Division's activities were still unknown.

Chase bit a piece of his bacon, watching the news playing on the TV in the dining room mounted to the wall.

Lance gulped down his glass of orange juice and helped himself to a bowl of fruit.

Olivia listened to the news playing in the background, taking sips of her coffee.

While nobody had mentioned it, the day seemed...off.

It seemed quiet. It seemed peaceful.

But too peaceful.

Perhaps the trio had spent much of their time in the basement, even resorting to having meals and sleeping in there as well.

Lance was the one who found himself doing this. He recently developed a new piece of technology that even relied on Risima to make work.

Borrowing an idea from the invention Olivia used at MIT to discover Osamos, Lance was able to figure out how to develop a piece of technology that could communicate with Risima particles or mainly Electric Risima particles.

The device relied on a constant input of Electric Risima that Lance supplied to it. Based on the frequency and pattern of the

Energy Lance streamed into it, the device was programmed to translate the Energy into code that it could execute.

After downloading this software into a watch that he could wear, Lance had created a range of new ways and opportunities to use his abilities, such as having a device that could warn him when he was running low on Energy or even having a device he could use to instantly hack or destroy other electrical systems, his watch having the ability to jam frequencies and interrupt electrical signals from anywhere Lance was able to stream his Energy.

So instead of having to guess and process all that information on his own, Lance had a tool that did it for him, relaying information back into Lance's body by returning Electric Risima particles into his body by using sensors he installed into the strap.

On top of that, Lance honed his ability to conjure materials using Risima particles and even figured out a way to "store" preset structures of Risima particles into his watch. For example, say Lance had painted a picture he really liked but had no place to store. He could map out the entire picture by streaming Electric Risima particles into the picture, transfer that information into his watch, and then receive the same image and reconstruct it in an instant, essentially designing a "memory" that was even more accurate and efficient than memory itself.

Of course, the *practical* usage for this was Lance's new sword, which he didn't want to have to construct from scratch using Risima each and every time he needed it or any other weapon for that matter.

Chase had been just as busy too. While not into the sciences as much as Lance or Olivia, Chase devoted a lot of his time to mastering other skills and hobbies. He picked up archery and marksmanship and found he was a deadeye with any projectile, especially considering much of his Fire powers revolved around being accurate to land.

On top of that, Chase had trained more, learning more martial arts, and ironically, began reading more, learning as much as he could about seemingly "unimportant" or "unrelated" topics.

But Chase knew better. The things he was reading would all come in handy at some point.

Chase had grown tremendously in terms of spirit and maturity and was turning into a real team leader, knowing having some idea what it meant to stay strong in times of adversity.

Olivia, finally, other than keeping in touch with assets and contacts, was slowly beginning to travel more now that she believed that Chase and Lance could take care of themselves.

But in all her traveling, she kept visiting one place that was a lot closer than many would expect: a school.

Olivia, deep down, wanted Chase and Lance to experience what the public school system was like. The number of things they would learn and experiences they would have would undoubtedly prove to accelerate their training and personal growth tremendously.

It was true that enrolling them in school was a *huge* risk if anything went wrong, but truth be told, Olivia was confident that the risks were becoming benign the more mature the boys got. She was confident they had learned enough and grown aware of themselves enough to the point that they could have the independence to go to school without drawing attention to themselves or exposing their true identities. After all, they *looked* like Human beings. That wasn't the issue.

Olivia looked away from the news, sipping on her piping-hot coffee. A random thought popped into her mind, as if she was trying to ignore a dreadful feeling from a *warning* she had within: "Hey, how would you two feel about going to school?"

Chase and Lance paused dramatically, holding their utensils still as if they had been paused in a playback or video.

"You said 'school'?"

"What? Where did that come from?"

Olivia shrugged. "I don't know. Maybe it would be good for you two. I mean, it couldn't hurt to make some friends, right? *Human* ones at that!"

Chase almost laughed aloud.

"Who needs friends when I have *this* clown over here to keep me entertained?" Chase nudged Lance.

Lance, clearly confused, chewed his food slowly as if he were processing what Chase said.

"You're callin' *me* a clown?"

"I mean, to be fair of course, you are."

"How so?"

Olivia smiled to herself. "Well, listen—"

But the three stopped as they heard a reporter on the TV scream before everything on the screen turned black.

Immediately after, an explosion rocked the entire house, causing all the furniture in the house to shake.

"Is this an earthquake?"

"No, look there!"

The three looked outside the window, holding onto any sturdy object they could find as they noticed that way out in the distance, an object could be seen in the sky.

"What the *hell* is that?" Chase yelled, pointing at something.

Lance inched closer to the window, gasping for breath, clearly in a deep state of shock.

When Olivia looked outside the window, her eyes widened, her mouth wide open.

My god. He was right again. It's coming now!

"That's a *meteor*! Is this a joke?! Tell me I'm imagining that thing!"

Chase began to panic when neither Lance or Miss E said anything. Like him, they had watched the object in the sky, paralyzed with fear.

"That can't be real! What's going on here?!"

Chase scrambled away from the dining room and outside, stumbling on the lawn as he looked up into the sky.

"No way! This is—!"

Lance and Olivia followed behind.

A siren went off in the city of Rockdale. From where their house was on top of a hill, the three could see sirens flashing and droves of people rushing out of the city and to safety.

"That isn't going to hit *us*, right?" Chase chuckled nervously.

"Look at the path it's taking! It'll hit the same exact place the storm appeared! That can't be a coincidence!"

Chase turned to Lance.

"Jesus! You're right! Do you think it's from Osamos?"

"No," Olivia replied. "That's *not* from Osamos. Look." She pointed in the sky.

"Osamos is over *there*. You can see it with the naked eye now that it's this close. That meteor came from a totally different direction, and I don't know many Rasrims that can manipulate something this big from that far a distance away."

Olivia's eyes widened. "Unless...no! That isn't possible!"

Chase and Lance looked at Miss E, frightened. She had been in shock too for perhaps the first time in their entire lives.

"Woah, wait. What do you mean, Miss E?" Chase tugged at her shirt.

Olivia looked at Chase, frightening him even more when she had this look of paranoia on her face.

But Lance had seen it too.

He looked between the two of them. Neither of them had said a word.

Lance dropped his head.

"What do we do?" Chase exclaimed. "W-we could find a place to evacuate to, can't we? I mean, that thing wouldn't...would it?"

"I-I don't know, Chase!"

Lance stood up, gritting his teeth, his entire body tensed, enraged.

Chase stepped away from Lance, shocked.

Lance shot Chase a look.

Chase's face slowly returned to his normal expression, his body relaxing. But his face also had a look of uncertainty on it.

"Dude, we can't seriously... How are we supposed to stop that?"

"Are you with me or not, Chase?"

Chase pointed to the meteor, which as of now had been the size of the sun. In about ten minutes tops, it would collide with the Earth.

"That's a *meteor*! This isn't some thunderstorm or a thug with a *gun*. How do we stop that?"

Lance seemed frustrated. His face swelled up as he looked at Miss E for reassurance.

But she was gone.

Lance, in searching for Miss E, noticed that Chase took two steps closer into the lawn, staring at the meteor.

Chase sat on the ground, a nervous sweat trickling down his forehead. "Nah, dude. This is it. There's no stopping that!" Chase looked crazily toward Lance, hoping he felt the same way.

"Maybe one her friends from the—"

Lance grabbed Chase's shoulder and pulled it *hard*, yanking him to his feet, reminding Chase of the sheer strength Lance had.

Chase looked bewildered. "Crap, man! That hurt!"

"Yeah, I'm glad it did! Listen—we've gotta try something!"

Chase blinked, trying to reason with Lance.

"You *really* want to stop that meteor? You really think we can stop that meteor? Here we were just having a normal day and now—"

"And now *what*, Chase? If that thing hits the planet, there are no more normal days!"

Chase paced around, talking a mile a minute.

"This is crazy. This is *nuts*! A meteor? Now? Here? What is God trying to tell us, huh? Does he want us to blast some fire at a meteor? Maybe some Electric beams at it? Huh?"

Lance slowly looked at Chase with a look of horror.

"You don't think we could stop it? You think we should just give up?"

"We aren't giving up, Lance! We're acknowledging that we've already lost!"

Lance was beginning to lose patience. They were wasting precious time!

"We haven't tried yet. Even if we do end up chucking everything we have at it, we've gotta try something!"

Then Chase and Lance heard the supersonic boom of at least twenty fighter jets rip across the sky, flying directly over their heads.

Chase and Lance watched completely silent, their eyes and head following the jets as they headed for the meteor.

One by one, all twenty of the jets fired their rockets into the meteor.

"That's stupid! What about the debris! It'll still destroy—"

"Shut up, Chase! Let *someone* try something!"

Chase reeled back, offended. But he submitted, rubbing his shoulder as he watched.

The missile quickly found their target. The meteor, which was now maybe two hundred miles away from entering the atmosphere, was struck by hypersonic warheads fired by the best jets in the military's arsenal.

A shower of explosions rained across the meteor, the sounds of the explosions noticeable but distant, mere ants compared to the sheer size of the meteor.

"Nothing happened," Chase mumbled.

Lance was on his feet. A yellow aura surrounded his body before, with a thunderclap of Energy, he took off toward the city.

Chase was knocked off his feet, scratching the sides of his head.

He closed his eyes and tried to relax.

But he couldn't. He had been panicking.

Chase slapped the sides of his head, forcing himself to calm down. Steam began to pour from his body, sizzling as it mixed with the air around him.

Without any warning, Chase exploded.

"All right, Lance, fine!"

An earthquake shook the hills that the three-story mansion lay on top of as Chase took off after Lance, only a second or two behind him.

*****

Olivia held her phone against her ear and allowed it to ring, while she quickly typed strings into a command prompt on a computer with her other hand, her eyes moving from one computer screen to another computer, giving no time to anything else digital content was endlessly displayed in front of her.

"Yes, hello?" The other end finally answered—after *seven attempts.*

Olivia briefly shifted her attention to her phone, her eyes studying the screen in front of her carefully.

"Is this Michael Crawford?" Olivia asked.

She wasted no time. Olivia pulled up a live map of the entire planet with special emphasis on bodies of water, looking at the location of every ship in the US Navy's fleet and their current ground-to-orbit and sea-to-orbit firing capabilities.

This was top-secret stuff. If any civilian was caught looking at this, they could be sentenced to execution for espionage and treason—no questions asked.

"Yes, it is?" the man said nervously. "Ma'am, unless you have something important to say or any information, are you aware that—"

"Operation Oblivion. Call your people. Activate it *now*," Olivia demanded.

"Excuse me? H-how do you? Ma'am, that program was never intended for—"

"A Category Nine Astronomical Hazard? I'm aware. But maybe a Category Five or Six though, right?"

"Y-yes. That's correct. We haven't had the opportunity to test it as much as we would have liked."

Olivia typed furiously, her eyes bouncing from one screen to another, processing data faster than the speed of light. She was now looking at another top-secret live map of every Air Force base in the United States and abroad, a red dot above their names if they were actively responding to *any* threat, which, as of now, was only one.

"What if we paired Operation Oblivion and every destroyer, aircraft, and orbital launch cannon with ground-to-orbit firing capability in the US Military against that thing?"

The man seemed dumbfounded. He had clearly been caught off guard.

He didn't answer immediately.

"In theory, that *could*...b-but who has the authority to do all that?" Mike Crawford cleared his throat. "The president is—"

But Olivia had already known. "He's currently aboard Air Force One on his way to a secure location. I'm aware of that. Now I *do* have clearance from the vice president and a go-ahead from the secretary of defense, so it seems."

Another one of Olivia's computers was constantly pulling up news reports, live phone call conversations, and every email that had been sent on the planet in the last fifteen minutes. With high-speed efficiency, Olivia's computer was able to compile all the information it had found. Her custom-built AI then sorted, flagged, and displayed pieces of information that could prove handy in front of her eyes.

Olivia quickly scanned through the list of information, putting together something in her head as she read the information she had found. It had only taken her seconds.

"The president's too busy ensuring that a country across the planet doesn't somehow get access to vital US property and is issuing Space Command to begin preparing for a possible assault against Osamos—but neither of those things help solve the issue in front of us. He hasn't issued a single message or directorate to any US service branch as of yet. I'm sure it's safe to say that time is of the essence. I already have the support to launch this operation. I just need your cooperation."

Olivia was still restless and impatient. She had already put together everything she needed to launch a strike on the meteor, which with courtesy of NASA gave her a live-feed video of the meteor from the ISS and several other satellites in orbit.

Doing rough calculations in her head, she *strongly believed* that she had accumulated enough firepower to destroy the meteor before it would enter the lower mesosphere, hopefully minimizing its destruction output by roughly 91 percent upon impact, reducing the meteor no more than the size of a large aircraft—from the size of the entire state of Rhode Island.

At least that meant she and her boys would be safe. But she needed Mike Crawford to do his job.

"Miss, if I don't *personally* receive orders from the president, his Cabinet, or any of his secretaries, I *cannot* and *will not* authorize usage of Operation Oblivion, and especially not over an unsecured line. You need to understand that."

Olivia's train of thought had been broken when she heard this. She stopped typing and nodded, putting her full attention into the phone call.

"Yes, of course! I expected no less than that," Olivia replied sarcastically.

Suddenly, her entire tone, posture, and attitude changed. She held the phone in her hand so tightly the screen was beginning to crack. She held the phone in front of her mouth and practically yelled into it.

"This is Olivia Tyera, and as the director of the Advanced Experimental Sciences Division and therefore a member of President Grayson's Cabinet, I am *ordering* you to authorize both Operation Oblivion and Operation Pegasus for deployment *immediately*. And yes, this *is* a secure line!"

The man went silent on the other line for ten seconds.

Olivia heard chatter in the background—and even the clicking of several computers.

Of course, she had exposed herself. But it had to be done, and she was the only one capable of doing it. This was Olivia Tyera's job.

Mike Crawford came back to the line. "Y-yes, ma'am," he said in a hurry, "I am authorizing Operation Oblivion as we speak. Please standby."

Olivia huffed. She was infuriated.

In the forty years that she had been alive, Olivia had never once commanded anyone outside of the Division to do anything. She had never even so much as spoken down to anyone or in a disrespectful way.

And Mike Crawford was the Chief of Naval Operations, also known as the Commander of the United States Navy.

"Excuse me, Director Tyera, the op is a go. Current time is 0900 hours with a projected impact time of T-minus 240 seconds."

Olivia nodded, entering numbers and coordinates into her computer when she realized she now had access to new satellite feeds and electronic chatter. This would do.

Satisfied, she spoke into the phone one last time.

"Thank you, Commander Crawford. I'll take it from here."

Olivia hung up the phone and, with a second free hand to use, began typing on her keyboard so fast her mind could barely keep up with her movements.

She pulled up video feeds, sent emails, and pinged the phones of high-ranking military officers. She sent coordinates, designated sophisticated strike patterns, and included other detailed instructions to at least two thousand individuals in the United States in less than thirty seconds.

Foreign assistance was not necessary, believe it or not. The United States had more than enough in its arsenal to handle this. But she needed to work fast enough to ensure that the Division didn't get any ideas or decide to use *that* program.

In the same amount of time, Olivia had monitored the meteor's location and entry velocity, calculated its mass, and accounted for the material it was made of.

It was a material known as Bezilith, a newly-discovered natural mineral that could be found far out in the universe.

Olivia guessed that it had likely broken off from another asteroid or much larger mass somewhere near the Kuiper Belt according to a recreation of a simulation she just ran.

But Olivia was still missing a large piece of the puzzle. Assuming it *had* come from around Neptune, which she had a hard time believing, was how it had managed to end up on a flight path to Earth and had done so under the radar of every government, space agency, research institution, and even the Division itself was completely beyond Olivia.

But just as it was when she had a desk, Olivia's job was to respond to and *eliminate* any extraterrestrial threat as they arose before they had a chance to cause hysteria or wreak havoc to the United States.

And so she went to work.

Of course, while she was still *technically* the director of the Division, Olivia no longer had the ability to launch an operation from a remote location.

That meant, the only way to activate the AESD's resources from *any* remote location was from the director's computer in her office at headquarters.

Luckily for Olivia, she was no stranger when it came to hacking.

Hardly breaking a sweat and with no more time to lose, Olivia had bypassed the AESD's firewalls and stringent security protocols, taking down the toughest security system on Earth in only twenty seconds. Insider info had its perks. But ex-employees of intelligence agencies were never actually "ex-employees."

Olivia, who gained access to the Division's resources and emergency protocols, initiated a Class 9 Response Activation Force, which pinged every operative with access to Operation Oblivion and gave them the clearance to activate it immediately.

Sure enough, Olivia now had control over the *most powerful* weapons on the planet, one of them being the Energized Orbital Launch Cannon developed by the Division, which was only known as Operation Oblivion, which had the power to instantly disintegrate the atomic composition of *any* material known to man at any, regardless of its size or distance from the cannon, from any location on the planet. The second weapon was a high-powered artillery railgun that had the ability to decimate satellites using light and sound-based attacks known as Operation Pegasus. They both could hit a target the size of a penny with 100 percent accuracy from a distance as far as where Pluto currently was.

And Olivia would be taking full control of both of them. She was once more, as she had been for over twenty years, the single most powerful person in the entire world.

For record, these weapons had the combined power to completely obliterate any sovereign nation on Earth—thousands of times stronger than even the nuclear bomb known as the *Tsar Bomb*. Together, they were theorized to be able to destroy *entire planets*—even Osamos.

Olivia was *not* worried about the success rate of her most powerful creations one bit.

With everything ready, locked, and loaded, all she needed was—

Olivia's eyes shot open when a message in her peripheral vision caught her attention. It had been pulled from a news station in Washington.

THREE UNIDENTIFIED INDIVIDUALS—
PRESUMED RASRIMS—TARGET METEOR

Olivia's eyes widened as her fears became reality.

"N-no!" Olivia called out, worry splattered across her face. "I really wanted you two to—not this time—you two can't stop this thing alone!"

Olivia quickly pulled up an image from a satellite, zooming into the location given by the report.

Sure enough, she could see two boys in the city on top of a building, staring at the meteor from above.

"But who's the third?" Olivia whispered.

And then she gasped when she found the third one.

"Oh my god," Olivia said as she moved closer to her screen to get a better look. "What in the world is *he* doing there?"

*****

The sound was terrifying. It sounded like hell was quite literally falling from the sky, angry and ready to wreak havoc on all below.

Lance was standing on top of a large building, looking directly into the sky above. The roars of the meteor as it ripped through the atmosphere made it sound like a beast from another world, a screeching animal who had turned berserk.

The giant flaming rock was hurtling toward him. It was so large it covered part of the sun, casting a large shadow over the entire city—and maybe even most of the state.

Lance gulped, forcing himself to remain calm.

Lance stretched his hands out, tensing his knuckles.

"Yo! Are you ready?" a voice cried out from across another building.

"Yeah!" Lance yelled out, his head still facing up above.

Lance noticed a fleet of more fighter jets flying toward the meteor, but this time, they were traveling up the *side* of the meteor as if they intended to target the meteor from its east side or even from above rather than from the ground.

It didn't matter, though. Chase and Lance had to destroy or—at the very least—slow the meteor down dramatically enough to render its impact force to a minimum.

Chase aimed his hands into the sky and, with an explosive show of force, fired a massive beam of fire into the sky—its Energy so large and destructive it spanned the width of a football field when it finally reached the meteor, its destructive force just as potent as it was closer to Chase's body.

Lance looked over at Chase, amazed with how much power he could unleash. Maybe he'd stop the meteor on his own!

But as Lance watched, to his disbelief, the meteor continued falling even as Chase increased the pressure of his attack. Lance saw that Chase felt similarly, growing wary and nervous as the meteor slowly grew larger in size the more it descended into the atmosphere.

Lance decided to fire something as well, focusing up Electric Risima and charging it off toward the meteor. The streamed Energy of Electric Risima traveled much higher and much faster and struck the meteor with a ton more force, causing a small crack to appear in the surface of the meteor, pieces breaking away and burning up in the atmosphere.

Lance, upon seeing this, began to grow confident and focused as much Energy as he possibly could at the meteor.

After full-force fire that lasted about forty-five seconds, the two began to grow tired.

Chase dropped his arms, and Lance pulled his back, both out of breath.

They had put some work into the meteor though, a large crater visible in the surface of it.

But it wasn't enough. Even if, as Lance guessed, they were able to slow the meteor down by 10 percent, because of the sheer mass of the thing, it would most likely destroy the entire continent of North America—and quite possibly the rest of the world.

"How much was that?" Chase yelled.

"Uh...about ten percent!" Lance yelled back.

"*Dammit!*" Chase screamed in the air, Fire Risima igniting the air around his body.

Furiously, he fired an even larger blast of fire at the meteor, this time reaching it in only about five seconds.

It even caused an explosion, one that caused the entire meteor to rock and creak, the sound terrifying from the ground, as its massive size shook the entire city.

But Chase didn't let up.

Lance gritted his teeth, clenching so hard he was sure he'd crack a tooth.

Chase began straining, coughing out in pain as he fired before he collapsed to his knees, spitting out blood as he held his eye with his left hand.

Lance snapped away from the meteor, about to call out to Chase, but he stopped.

Lance slowly raised his hands, looking at each of his palms before making a tight fist.

"There's only *one* more thing that could work."

Lance slowly turned his attention back to the meteor, part of him in awe and the other part terrified and in shock.

Lance tensed his body, bending his legs and closing his eyes, focusing intensely.

The ground beneath Lance's body began to crack from pressure building up in Lance's body.

Lance concentrated, gathering as much Risima Energy he possibly could: Water, Fire, Wind, Electric, Earth—*everything* he could.

And then Lance felt a new energy source—a massive site of Risima Energy from up above.

Lance opened his eyes and focused on the new site of Risima he felt in the air.

He lifted his hands and concentrated.

Chase slowly opened his eyes, recovering his breath, controlling his breathing, and stopping the blood from his eyes from trickling down his face.

Quickly, he turned back up to the meteor but looked confused when he swore it had stopped in midair, stray pebbles and rocks falling from the sides and from underneath the meteor as it lay motionless in the sky.

Chase turned to Lance.

An uncontrollable wide smile broke out on his face.

"It's working! *Don't stop!*" he shouted at the top of his voice, straining his vocal cords.

But Lance's body was telling him exactly that. Every bone, muscle, and joint in Lance's body was on *fire*. Even his brain was beginning to stress, a massive pressure in his temple region, causing Lance to begin slipping even though he was touching anything whatsoever.

"C'mon, Lance! Keep it up!"

At first, Lance wasn't sure what had happened. He couldn't tell if the meteor had stopped or not or if he had just been straining himself for nothing.

But it didn't matter. This was the last frontier.

Lance put both his hands together, veins popping out in his arms, neck, and face.

"I can't hold this much longer! I've gotta see if…if I can stop it another way! I need *you* to do what I'm doing instead!" Lance yelled over the sound of the atmosphere burning.

But Chase did. "I can't do that! You know I can't!"

"It doesn't matter! You have to try!"

"And what are you going to do exactly?"

Lance strained.

"I'm going *up* there! You have to try and control the force of the meteor using Risima while I pummel the *shit* out of it with Earth! Understand?"

Chase nearly wanted to laugh, but when he saw that Lance was being dead serious, he reluctantly agreed.

But deep down, he had felt the same way Lance had felt.

This was it. It didn't matter what they did at this point. They were just prolonging the inevitable, allowing as many people to get to safety as they could. They had slowed the meteor down and even downright stopped it momentarily. That would buy the civilians below a great deal more time.

"Chase! Are you ready?"

Chase turned to the meteor, trusting his brother.

"Yeah. Go hit that thing!"

Chase lifted his hand and tried focusing on the meteor, thinking that he was crazy—that everything he was doing was pointless and a waste of time.

He noticed Yellow Energy surrounding Lance's body as he took off into the sky toward the meteor like an absolute maniac—or perhaps one of the bravest people on the planet.

Chase couldn't decide in the heat of the moment.

But right as Lance hit the meteor, Chase *felt* something react in his body.

Chase lifted a second hand and focused on the meteor, trying his hardest to ensure he was mentally intact and had not yet gone insane.

The building around Chase's feet began shifting, and fragments of the meteor began distorting as Chase focused more and more Energy into the meteor.

As soon as it had begun to fall, it stopped once more, but this time, Chase had been on the receiving end of the tremendous force. From seeing his older brother in utter despair, a powerful entity of energy began to manifest in Chase's body. It reacted to his emotions, Chase's entire body responding to the environment around him. But as Green Energy flowed around Chase's body and propelled onward the meteor with a hardened force strong enough to demolish skyscrapers, Chase couldn't stop to take a moment to realize what he was doing.

Chase had just awakened Earth Risima—and was using it to stop the meteor!

*****

Lance crashed into the meteor head on, immediately throwing his hands against the meteor and unleashing Electric Risima, pushing against the meteor as hard as he could.

The force, as he expected, was colossal. In an instance, Lance regretted his decision.

But it was too late to turn back. Even if he dropped back down to the air, the meteor would quickly catch up to Lance and crush him—killing him in a miserable way.

Lance realized that after only a few seconds, he felt his body begin to feel as if it were being crushed by the mass of the meteor.

Lance strained, shoving all his strength into the meteor, using Electric Risima to keep his body upright and from falling back to orbit.

This was suicide. Lance knew that he had extended all his options. He would end up being crushed by the meteor alongside everyone else in the country.

Even so, Lance shifted his Energy from Electric to Earth and hit the meteor as hard as he possibly could, swinging all his momentum in a blow.

To his surprise, he managed to put a rather large crack into the meteor.

But then he started to lose his grip and slip.

Lance tried shifting back into Electric Risima, but then he cried out his eyes throbbed in tremendous pain, causing him to curse him as he began to fall back to Earth.

"Damn!" Lance yelled out, flipping and spinning in the air as he fell.

And then the worst thing he could imagine came to reality.

The meteor's force began overpowering the force Lance's Risima pushed the mountain-sized rock with and began to move again.

Lance managed to turn his body around for just a second, and sure enough, it was only a couple hundred yards away from him, as it began to descend back into the Earth, likely only twenty-five seconds from hitting the building he was just on.

Lance's mind went blank.

With no other option, no other idea, and no other hope to call upon, Lance had finally given up hope.

He accepted his fate, allowing himself to fall back to Earth, the meteor only a few seconds behind him, his body seemingly pulled toward the gigantic space rock as if it were a magnet.

As Lance's mind quickly began to assume the worst, he couldn't help but examine the large yet empty city spread out as far as he could see below him.

Everything seemed so tiny. So helpless from a height this high. It was as if Lance were, for just a moment, a God attempting to shield his magnificent creations below him.

But Lance was no God.

God would not have failed here, today. God would have emerged victorious, unwavering in courage, mighty in prose, and triumphant in action.

As Lance's eyes began to slowly dim, he noticed a figure standing on the ground below him, something that stood out in the vast emptiness of the city. It was a familiar individual. He was standing in a certain pose that Lance swore he had seen before.

And then he noticed a strange aura fill the air around the figure, a dim bluish aura with sparkling particles dancing in the air.

It was Risima…but whose?

And then he heard a terrible rumbling sound far out in the distance—but it was more correct to say it came from directly below him.

At once, a massive structure of what appeared to be ice began to rise into the sky, seemingly flying at him at massive speed.

Lance snapped out of his depressive trance and yelled out at the top of his lungs, afraid he was about to be hit by the bizarre object building itself from the ground up.

The ice structure clipped Lance before he had an ample chance to move out of the way, although he would have been hit no matter how far he moved.

The ice structure was *massive*; a small icicle sticking out on the structure managed to catch onto Lance's shirt and carried him upward, straight toward the meteor.

Lance covered his face.

Why did it have to end like this? In what world would Lance be so unlucky to not only have a meteor fall on top of his home but some strange reason to be *thrown* into the meteor instead by some inexplicable force? What the hell even was it? Why couldn't Lance pinpoint what it was that was bothering him?

But as more thoughts crossed into Lance's mind, the more he realized that he was no longer *moving*.

Lance slowly opened his eyes.

He heard what sounded like *huge* amounts of ice cracking and breaking off as if glass had been shattered.

Lance looked up. "*W-what?*" Lance shouted, staring at a massive tree made of ice, its branches holding the meteor completely still in the air, managing to stop its descent entirely.

"What is this? This is crazy!"

The ice structure had crashed into the meteor and leveled out, covering the entire space rock from underneath, stopping its velocity entirely.

The ice was continually being reinforced, each layer of ice hardening and darkening in color.

"I-incredible! How much Energy was required to make this sort of thing?"

Lance couldn't help but be amused; this person had saved millions!

"This reminds me of the—"

And then Lance's eyes began to settle when realization hit him hard.

Suddenly in a panic, Lance pulled himself free of the icicle, falling once more.

But this time, Lance swung his fist toward the structure, and right before his hand made contact, a sword infused with Water and Earth Risima pierced into a tiny section of the massive structure, keeping the speed that Lance fell back to the floor steady—still some fifteen thousand or so feet in the air.

The entire time, Lance kept himself alert, ready for *anything*.

Finally, after maybe two or three minutes, Lance touched the ground; he placed his feet against the ice structures and ripped his right hand backward hard, pulling his sword out of the ice structure.

Lance took time to quickly glance up, noticing the sheer size and durability of the ice structure stretching up twenty-five thousand feet in the air.

"Insanity...and the bastard is around here somewhere," Lance mumbled.

Then, the ice structure began to react.

The entire ground shook, and Lance covered his face as the ice structure rose from the ground even more, penetrating the meteor in the sky before huge icicles broke free from the meteor on every side of it.

Lance watched in awe. What was going on?

He soon got his answer as the meteor began to freeze, thick layers of ice crackling, spreading across the entire surface area of the meteor, leaving not even an inch uncovered.

The icicles protruding from the meteor grow larger and larger, extending from the meteor as if it were now part of the original ice structure.

The entire meteor shook, consequentially shaking the structure as well, before the meteor and the ice structure exploded, a massive *boom* erupting across the sky.

Lance covered his face, but quickly stood up in smiles, looking into the sky and around him.

The frozen meteor had exploded into trillions of tiny pieces and twinkled as they fell like diamonds but fell as slowly as snow.

Lance investigated the sky, laughing as he was confused about the occasion, reaching out to touch the falling ash.

"Unbelievable! What power...!" Lance whispered to himself.

"Yoo! Lance! Did you see that?"

Lance spun around and looked into the air.

Chase continued talking, completely unaware.

"Look at this! The meteor's been shattered completely!"

Chase leapt off of the two-story building he was on, making his way over to Lance in an anxious jog, still out of breath.

"I mean...did you have something to do with this?! Or maybe...I-I think I might've—"

"Chase, focus! Who has the ability to make this thing? It's *Ice,* Chase!"

Lance's heart rate began to increase when he noticed the look of horror slowly appear on Chase's face.

"Wait, no! It's been years!"

"It's *him*, Chase! I saw him when I was up there!"

"But where? We have to—"

Chase slowed down, skidding on his feet and coming to a screeching halt when he noticed that Lance was staring at something in the distance.

Curiously, he turned around to see what Lance was looking at.

Chase's mouth was hanging wide open, his eyes clearly deceiving him.

He was staring at a ghost, the figure of a merciless killer who had nearly cut both him and Lance down to size two years ago. The fact he was here now told the twins that something similar was likely to happen if things turned sour.

"Oh no. This won't end well…"

Chase took a step back. He raised his hands, showing he was harmless.

"Listen, man, we don't want to fight you, all right? Can't we just thank you like last time and go on our way?"

The figure swiped a hand, and without warning, the *entire* floor turned into spiky shards of ice and rose from the floor, flying into the air.

Chase and Lance split up, dodging the attack by rolling out of the streets.

The figure wasn't done.

He extended his hands, and two giant walls of ice rose from the floor, enclosing the entire city block.

The figure strained as he ripped his hands together before the two walls of ice began moving toward each other, crushing *everything* that had been caught between them.

The ice walls retreated into the floor, and a huge mound of concrete, ash, and greenery from trees and bushes were all that remained.

But he had left the twins alone from the carnage, almost as if he was trying to taunt them.

Chile walked forward.

He huffed, wheezing almost, as his frozen body clanged with every step he took.

The ground underneath his feet froze with every step, and even the air around his body turned into an icy mist as he walked.

Chile scanned the street, looking for Chase and Lance.

Chile continued walking, looking down streets and on top of buildings before as he walked, he yelled something into the city.

"Unworthy!" The single word echoed throughout the empty city.

Chile's face was one of a demon—his eyes sharp and full of malice. His hands were clenched, ready to rip apart any and everything that stood against him.

But his soul was ice cold—that of a murderer's. And he wasn't here to change that.

Chile erupted barrages of Ice Risima, turning buildings, cars, and even trees in solid ice, before they too exploded, turning into shards of ice and snow, left trickling to the ground.

"'If the twins can't stop the meteor, they're unworthy!'"

Chile looked around, confused.

And then he looked up, into the air.

"I stopped the meteor on my own. Did you see that, Melterai? I stopped the tsunami! I stopped the meteor! I'm *not* a monster."

Chile looked ahead again, taking slow, trudging steps forward.

"Yeah. I'm a hero now, right?" Chile laughed to himself in a twisted, sadistic manner.

Chile began to walk forward. Each step that he took slowly froze the earth underneath his feet, leaving a trail of thick ice behind him.

Chile's eyes began to glow. He whipped around quickly and quickly formed a shield of ice in front of his body, allowing three fireballs to crash into him.

Chile cackled aloud, tossing the ice shield to the ground.

"Chase...," Chile said in a low, angry voice.

But Chile was confused before a much larger beam of Fire rocketed toward Chile from another direction, causing Chile to block himself, burying his body in layers of ice to protect himself from being scorched.

The ground underneath Chile's feet began to crumble.

Chile gasped out as Earth rose from the ground and ensnared Chile, wrapping tightly around his torso.

Chile strained and yelled out, banging against the Earth, but screamed out in pain as the Earth tightened around his chest, crushing his lungs.

Chase walked out from an alleyway, approaching Chile from his side.

Lance leapt from out of cover in front of Chile, keeping his guard up as he closed the distance toward Chile.

Chile growled, gritting his teeth.

"Unworthy! You two are unworthy low-lives! You can't save pathetic Humans, but you won't destroy the wicked ones either!" he yelled into the air.

Chase called out to Chile, revealing himself.

"How can you call us that? We're Rasrims! We were just trying to help, just like you were!"

Chile banged against the Earth trap, grabbing onto it, and began turning it into solid ice, huffing angrily as he did.

Lance continued pacing toward Chile, studying his face while infusing more Earth Risima into the wall.

Something seemed *wrong* with Chile. It was like he was going power hungry. His aura was sour—tainted with Energy that seemed vile.

Lance persisted, trying to persuade Chile to calm down. "Chile, we never intended to hurt you. We only ever tried to thank and help you." Lance lifted his hands. "But you're dangerous. That's why we're restraining you."

"Restrain me?" Chile said. "No. *You* should be restrained—to see how it feels!"

Chile pounded at the frozen wall of Earth and cracked it.

Lance flicked his hand, trying to manipulate another wall of Earth, but Chile grunted, throwing something at Lance at high speed.

Lance moved his head to the left, wincing as something sliced his left cheek.

Chase moved in, but Chile blasted the floor underneath Chase, turning it into solid ice before blasting Chase with a gust of Icy Wind, causing Chase to tumble and roll on the slippery floor of ice, building up tremendous momentum, before crashing into the concrete wall of an apartment building at the end of the street.

Lance flashed toward Chile, streaming Electric Risima into his body.

Lance threw several hard punches at Chile, each one targeting a different section of his body, but Chile stood still and took it all, shrouding his entire body in more Ice, essentially creating body armor.

Chile began moving after the tenth or so punch and, after he saw an opening, hit Lance back hard, throwing an overhand left punch that knocked Lance straight off his feet, pummeling him into the ground.

Chile went to follow up with another attack, hitting Lance while he was on the ground.

As his right hand was in the air, he was tackled from his left side by Chase, who blasted himself and Chile with Fire Risima, carrying them both into another building, which exploded as soon as they crashed into it.

The explosion sent bricks and pieces of glass out into the street before the entire building crumbled to the floor.

Lance stood up. He spat out blood and wiped his mouth. "This isn't good! Authorities will be here any minute. We're right in the middle of a large city!"

But Lance would soon realize the authorities would be the least of his problems.

The entire building Chase and Chile crashed into suddenly turned with ice, the concrete and bricks slowly freezing over before even icicles and spikes ripped out from each corner of the building, stretching high into the sky.

From within one of these icicles, Chile kicked out a large block of ice, which flew out into the street and busted into the side of an office building, blowing a medium-sized hole straight through it.

Lance scoffed. "New tricks, Chile?"

Lance held up his hands, ready for an absolute bloodbath.

He had tricks of his own after all.

After three steps, the ice-covered building began to melt before a pillar of plumbing hot erupted from the building and rained from the sky. Chile dodged as a fireball fell from the sky, and Chase tossed a piece of debris off his body, his eyes engulfed with Fire.

Chile stood still, shifting his attention from Chase and Lance, his eyes moving from the left to his right.

"Are you two prepared to die?" Chile suddenly taunted.

Chase growled furiously. "It's *you* who should be prepared to die, asshole!"

Chase launched from his spot, and Lance reacted immediately.

Chile turned and aimed a punch right at Chase, which missed by just a few inches. Chase managed to change his angle and catch Chile with a blast of Fire just as he passed, causing Chile to spin and stumble, falling to his knees.

Lance infused Earth Risima into his fist and rocked Chile across the face hard, causing him to spit blood out, instantly freezing the ground.

Lance hit him again and then again…and once more before moving out of the way as an icicle fifteen feet in diameter and one hundred feet in height emerged from the sky, attempting to rip Lance clean in half. Lance flashed with Electric Risima, using his quick movement speed to produce a bright flash of light that disoriented Chile. That then gave Chase the opportunity to tag in and continue with the attack.

Chase grabbed the back of Chile's head and engulfed his arm in scorching-hot Fire Risima before he slammed Chile's face into the icicle.

The icicle cracked, a large hairline crack spreading to its tip, causing the edge of the icicle to break off.

A powerful gust of wind kicked up, sending shards of razor-sharp ice swirling around Chile's body.

Chase quickly jumped back, wincing as the shards of ice cut areas across Chase's body.

Chase lifted his right arm and protected his face, using his other free hand to dish out more Fire-based attacks at Chile.

Chile barely managed to defend himself, using Risima to absorb all the oxygen in the air in front of Chase, effectively causing his Fire Risima to vaporize and disappear in midair.

Before Chase said anything, Chile lunged forward, punching Chase square in the face.

Chase was tough. He rolled with the punch and threw a kick at Chile, generating torque as he rotated his body in the opposite direction.

But Chile was even tougher, blocking Chase's kick like it was nothing.

Chase winced. Chile's durability was beyond impressive.

Then Chile gasped out as he suddenly lost balance in his left knee, turning to see Lance had kicked it in.

Chase spun and threw a back kick at the right-side of Chile's face, causing him to stumble backward.

Chile bounced back up, blocking two quick punches from Chase, his body rattling from the blows.

But Chase suddenly rolled out of the way, ditching his offensive attacks and instead defending himself.

Chile tracked Chase's movement, preparing to strike him with a timed Ice attack—putting him down for good.

But Chile yelped out as he was rushed by Lance's lightning-quick timing. With no mercy, he delivered Chile a devastating three-piece-combo: a torqued-up hook into Chile's abdomen, a nasty right uppercut right below Chile's chin, and a powerful left cross square in the side of Chile's jaw.

The force and speed of the attacks knocked Chile to the ground, dazed and nearly unconscious. It was a perfect display of Lance's martial art skills that proved handy against tougher opponents.

Chile caught himself as he hit the ground. He heaved before he coughed up blood and began breathing heavily, huffing for air.

Chase and Lance stood tall. They had won this fight. It was over. There was nothing left to prove.

"You're done, Chile," Lance announced.

"We don't want to kill you!" Chase shouted, remembering what Olivia had told them two years ago.

"Listen, if you just agree to come with us, we will spare your life. There's someone who can *help* you, Chile."

Lance turned to Chase and shot him a look.

"What? What are you doing?" Lance kept his voice low so Chile wouldn't hear him.

But it didn't matter.

Chile wiped his mouth and pushed himself to his feet, keeping himself silent. He offered no sign of surrender.

Chase and Lance watched as Chile stumbled forward, grabbing his left arm, and limped forward, clearly in pain.

"This isn't right, dude! We don't have to kill him!" Chase said.

Lance turned Chase.

"We were *told* to kill him. There's something here that we can't see! Maybe when he's done playing 'hero,' he'll be interested in seeing what the other side looks like!"

Chase didn't agree with that. "How would we know for sure? If we kill him, *we* become the villains, Lance!"

Lance lifted his head, looking at Chase with eyes of disbelief.

"If becoming a villain means we potentially save millions of lives, it's worth it *every time*."

Chase pointed up. "And yet we wouldn't be having this argument if it weren't for him. There goes your million!"

"We weren't strong enough! And you know that isn't true! Would you trust *him* to save innocent lives every time they were in danger?"

But both of them trained their attention back to Chile, watching him as he shuffled and limped away, trying to reach an alleyway that was blocked off with debris. He had gotten maybe twenty feet. He wouldn't make it anywhere at this rate.

"Hey, where are you going?" Chase called out.

Chase took a step forward, but Lance grabbed Chase's arm, pointing at him.

"You hear that?"

Chase stopped and listened.

It was then they heard what Chile was muttering under his breath.

"Kill them. Kill them all. Unworthy."

Lance looked at Chase, a worried expression in his face. They knew just how terrifying Chile's power was. Was he planning something?

But Chase wasn't having it.

"Yo, Ice freak! What're you saying?!"

Chile stopped dead in his tracks.

Lance took a step back, growing cautious of Chile.

Chile stood still, frozen. He didn't move even a muscle.

Chile's beaten, cold body slowly turned to face the two.

Chase and Lance dropped their guards, having almost felt sorry for him.

Chile's face had been bruised and bloody, tears streaming down his face. His arm had been broken, and he was breathing so hard, it looked like he would fall over at any time.

But Lance knew something was wrong when he looked into Chile's eyes.

Cold. Demonic. Blood lusted.

But they were also glowing *red*.

"Kill you. Kill you all. You all are unworthy," Chile growled, his speech slurred as he fought with an insatiable pain growing inside him.

Chile dropped his hands, his posture lowering.

Chase took a step forward.

"You wanna kill us? C'mon then! Maybe I was wrong about you!"

Lance grabbed Chase's arm.

"Stop, dude. Something's wrong with him. He's…fighting something. It's the same thing I went through when I was dealing with Stellar Riora…"

Chase pulled away from Lance and took a step forward. He didn't care. He wouldn't take threats from anyone—for any reason.

"He's the one that wants to kill you, but I don't mind beating you until you learn some respect."

Chase's eyes began glowing red.

Chile shook his head, a powerful white aura surrounding Chile's body.

Lance recognized this aura immediately.

"So it *is* Stellar Riora! I knew it!"

"I'll kill you. I'll kill them all," Chile said, tossing his head around, his hands clenching repeatedly, the ground underneath him beginning to rumble.

Chase cracked his neck.

"Chase! Wait! Don't!"

Chase lifted his hand and focused Fire Risima into his body, standing less than fifteen feet away from Chile.

"Chase—"

"I'll kill you all! Every Human on this damned planet!"

Chase grunted, his nose twitching. "Kill this first, Chile!"

The aura around his body erupted with immense force, instantly destroying every building and car around him, knocking everything else to the ground in an instant, freezing them all in a thick layer of permafrost.

Lance heard it before he felt it—An intense, demonic howling sound. It sounded like a massive snowstorm raging in the middle of Antarctica. It happened right as the police crews and ARF soldiers arrived at the scene and swarmed Chase, Lance, and Chile with rifles. But while Chase and Lance froze, having no intention of fighting the soldiers, Chile continued to walk away and past the soldiers, ignoring the commands of the shouting men.

The soldier raised his rifle at Chile, allowing the other soldiers to close in on Chase and Lance. But Lance wasn't worried about them. His attention was stuck on Chile the entire time.

"What do we do?" Chase blurted out as he counted eight men slowly lurching toward them like a pack of hungry wolves, ready to make a kill.

Lance suddenly grabbed Chase's arm, his wide eyes glued to the soldier screaming at Chile. Lance opened his mouth, "No! Don't shoot him! If you do—"

But it was too late. The foolish ARF soldier fired his weapon at Chile at point-blank range. And all the while, Chile had been completely unaware of the soldier in the first place, his mind and body compelled by the demonic energy flowing inside him. As the first rounds of ARF bullets slammed into Chile's body, penetrating his chest and legs, he suddenly broke free from his deep trance.

Lance pulled Chase closer to him as the ARF soldiers reached them, but he couldn't help but watch as Chile slowly turned toward the man who shot him, the look of hell in his eyes.

The ARF soldier pointed their guns at Chase and Lance, forcing them to stand down.

Lance turned to face his brother, but Chase had felt the colloidal energy quaking throughout the city too.

Lance tensed himself, infusing as much Electric Risima as he possibly could to escape what was coming next.

And then everything went pitch black.

Knowing something awful was afoot, Chase and Lance immediately took cover, feeling weak as their entire body began to seize and freeze all over, no time to think or discuss anything as the pressure of the storm made it impossible to hear anything, just barely dodging a shower of bullets, before the painful scream of the ARF soldiers confirmed that an absolute terror had just awakened on planet Earth.

The temperature of the East Coast had dropped from an average of 48 degrees down to an earth-shattering, record-breaking –132 degrees Fahrenheit.

And that was only the very *first* second of the storm that had only just arrived.

CHAPTER 13

Warm Blood, Cold Heart

A massive snowstorm rocked the Earth to its core. It demonstrated its destructive power by ripping buildings and houses to shreds. It decimated forests and buried the hills in snow. It froze everything in thick ice with its sub-zero temperatures not seen since the last polar Ice Age. It would prove to be a cataclysmic event racing to change the climate and survivability of the Earth forever.

Birds fell from the sky, their beaks and fur completely frozen. Airplanes malfunctioned and plummeted to their doom, erupting into fireballs that were quickly silenced by the terrible icy wind.

Railroad tracks cracked and crumbled, causing the trains that managed to survive the temperature to derail and crash into the metropolitan streets and office buildings.

Trees froze from their roots to the leaves. Forests of oaks and pines withered away and disappeared, their lineage and historical preservations wiped from history.

Dogs, foxes, bears, and bunnies perished immediately—frozen stiff in solid ice from head to toe.

Worse of all, any Human that was unlucky enough to be outside and fell within a thirty-five-mile radius of the center of the snowstorm was immediately frozen to death.

The death toll, although no one could have guessed properly this early on, was standing at 251,000 in a little under two minutes.

More than three-quarters of this number, or around 207,000 people, had perished from the first couple of seconds of the extreme cold and blistering wind speed moving upward of 170 miles per hour.

And most of these poor souls were evacuees from the meteor.

Although only a handful of people were aware of the truth, the hero that had saved the world from a doom looming over their heads had turned into a villain, presenting the very world he saved with a far deadlier and more consequential disaster they didn't even have the liberty to see coming.

He, however, was a monster of an entirely different breed. And the monster only sat back and watched. After all, he was the reason calamity had arrived.

Chile outstretched his arms, a wide smile plastered across his face.

He allowed the blistering, bone-chilling wind to pass over his face and limbs, felt the snow crunch underneath him, and the fearsome, howling gusts of the snowstorm sprinkle snow and ice on *everything* around him.

The sky was pitch black, snow and powerful gusts of wind throwing debris and shards of ice in every direction without warning, regardless of who or what was out *there* in the wasteland, Chile would call it.

He felt reborn—not a single thought other than the thought of *freedom* was on Chile's mind. The Energy he had been constantly repressing and storing up in his body ran free and rampant—bringing havoc to everything around Chile.

But that was their *own* fault, Chile told himself.

He warned them, several times, that scum.

Suddenly, the wind speed of the snowstorm began to increase much faster and howled much louder as Chile's senses began to kick back in, his eyes beginning to narrow and focus as he slowly rose from the floor.

Chile's entire body creaked, his bones and joints cracking everywhere as he stood up, adjusting his wrist and neck before he was able to stand normally even in the ferocity of the storm.

It was a *Polar Vortex,* Chile told himself, a snowstorm of an unprecedented scale.

Chile would singlehandedly revert mankind into the stone age, freezing and burying the Earth and everything with it under blankets of ice, leaving Chile in paradise.

But he had no desire for such delusions.

He only wanted to be sure that *they were dead.*

Chile hunched forward, taking a step in the snow that was now knee-high. He trudged, swinging his body through the snow, almost as if he was a cyborg or machine, his movements extremely robotic.

Chile knew that *something* was out there. He could sense that something nearby was still alive and unaffected by his disastrous Ice Risima. It was something that he needed to kill and bury underneath the ice, along with the rest of the sinners he wished to kill for years.

Everything had looked the same under the snow. There were no more abominations, no more monsters out to get them. They couldn't reach Chile in snow this deep.

Even the boogeyman had been slain by Chile.

Chile moved through the snow, his movements precise.

Even when walking on sleek ice, Chile's movements did not falter. He never stumbled or took cautious steps over anything. But he occasionally crushed the skulls and frozen limbs of the soldiers and police officers who were instantly frozen in the storm, walking over the brittle remains like they meant nothing to him.

The environment was *obeying* Chile, fearful to refute his commands. He had already fought and beaten Mother Nature by a scale of 100 to 1. Once the entire Earth witnessed Chile's power, there would be no more hypocrisy to blame humankind's problems on.

Chile stopped when he noticed something lying out in the snow, maybe ten feet away from him.

Chile squeezed his fist tight, taking control of the Risima in the environment and forcing it to submit to Chile's will. With his silent command, a large icicle rose from the ground and pierced the shadowy figure standing out in the snow, killing whatever it was for good, Chile thought.

Satisfied, Chile opened his hand and released his Energy, causing the ice spear to retreat back into the ground.

The shadowy figure plopped in the snow, falling at a slow, dramatic rate.

Chile noticed that the figure didn't make any Human moves nor did it appear to be alive to begin with. Was it possible that the figure was playing dead?

Chile trekked over to examine the figure.

As soon as he did, he stopped in his tracks. Chile bent over and picked up a wooden pike with a shirt mounted on it. It had been stuck up in the ground on purpose.

Without a warning, a whistle in the distance promptly grabbed Chile's attention and he snapped his head around in shock.

The ground around his body lit up, the entire ground suddenly turning a molten red color before a blazing ring of fire erupted from around Chile's feet, clearing all the ice and snow it touched. The blaze of the fire screamed, fighting against the monstrous howls of the ice storm.

Chile was astonished!

Fire? In the middle of all this snow?

Chile didn't know what to do or even why the ring of fire had appeared like this. Was it a trap?

Chile reacted, reaching out to submerge the fire in a layer of ice, but he stopped when he noticed a massive, angry storm cloud form right above his head, the sound of thunder and flash of lightning claiming the entire sky, countering the insanity produced by the snowstorm.

A storm cloud? It looks like the one those brothers destroyed a few years ago!

Chile paid little attention to it. He aimed a hand at the sky. A large spike of ice rose from the ground and pierced into the sky, reaching an altitude about the height as the Empire State Building in only a few seconds.

But the thunder and lightning raged on.

At once, a bolt of lightning struck the ice structure, lightning coursing through it the entire way through before a being emerged from the lightning bolt below and crashed into Chile, knocking him into the ground.

The opportunity was ripe, and Lance couldn't afford another wasted maneuver—

"Now, Chase!"

As suspected, Chile had been taken off guard, left vulnerable to the meddling the twin Rasrims had done in the dark and thickness of the ravaging snowstorm.

On a whimsical cue, almost as if a magician had performed in front of Chile's face, a ring of mad fire encircled Chile, singing his ankles, forcing his movement toward the center of the enclosure.

Chile, paralyzed by the intensity of the heat shielded his face from the scorching hot air the fire spewed even in the midst of the ongoing storm.

Chile leapt back, furthering his movement toward the center of the enclosure, readying the Ice Risima charging in his right hand.

But even Chile's masterful instincts, safeguarded by his defensive Ice Risima, was unable to respond within such an extreme environment.

Chile, his left hand still protecting his eyes from falling ash and scorching embers, quickly found it difficult to focus his Risima on the blazing ring of fire.

Tensing his right hand furiously, Chile tried amassing Risima that should have been easy for him to collect. But as the seconds went on, Chile noticed that not only his ability to conjure Risima, but even his stamina and ability to breathe was being siphoned off by the intensity of the flames' heat.

A look of terror and reminiscence swelled up in Chile's eyes, the look of an animal once again forced into captivity painted across his face.

A beast-like, guttural sound rose in the back of Chile's throat, fueling his body with a type of rage he only wished he didn't know all too well. It raged within Chile, bombarding his mind with corrupt thoughts of blood and death, compelling him to destroy everything around him.

Chile's body seized up, the intense heat causing his body to burn on the inside and out. Chile writhed in aching pain, his knee buckling to the ground, his right hand twitching uncontrollably.

But Chile's eyes and face never changed—his eyes were full of terror, his face stiffening with fury and bane.

Even when Chile's body retreated, falling silently on the melted snow and squishy, wet grass underneath him, Chile's eyes remained fixated on the site where the flame first appeared in front of him, as if he was directing all his pain and anger at it.

But Chile couldn't manage to act. His body would not obey his command; his Ice Risima refused to assemble and unleash its magnificent power, terrified of the dancing flames of the inferno that ensnared Chile from every direction.

This gave Lance a chance to finally execute Chile—and put an end to this madness *for good.*

Sparing Chile no time for solace, Lance's body leapt through the ring of fire, his entire figure engulfed by the roar of the intense flames.

Chile's attention sprang to Lance. But the force of his momentum was far too great and beyond a reasonable speed for Chile to defend against.

Chile could only watch as the twinkling blade fortified by Lance's Stellar Risima was revealed from behind Lance's body. Lance had timed it so that as soon as Lance unsheathed his sword and swiped the blade in front of his body, he would cleave Chile's head off completely.

Chile's eyes, frightened by the agonizing pain the heat battered into him, took notice of something it recognized: the look of anger and hatred in Lance's.

Chile was stunned by what he was seeing.

Such raw, determined eyes, Chile thought to himself, his eyes unable to break free from the trance it had been locked in with Lance's cold glare.

But Chile couldn't understand why his *enemy* of all people had this look in his eye. Wasn't he supposed to be protecting people? Why did the look in his eye remind Chile of—

And then Chile's eyes settled. His expression mellowed.

The pain in Chile's body disappeared as if it was simply ignored.

Lance's blade creaked in the air as it reached its target, the tip of the blade breaking the outer surface of the skin on Chile's neck.

With a swift follow-through, Lance ripped the sword through the air.

Lance's eyes were closed when his blade made contact. He found it difficult to look at as his blade sliced through Chile's neck.

Lance's feet hit the ground and slid against the wet grass.

And then Lance noticed that he had missed entirely. He was perplexed to see that Chile had managed to fall to the ground and ball up entirely, rolling on his back and managing for his head to evade most of the sword in less than a second.

And as if he wished to mock Lance, he quickly noticed that Chile had been watching him the entire time, his eyes trained on Lance's face with a new attitude that told Lance that he had made a grave mistake.

Lance gripped his feet into the slippery floor and shifted his lead foot toward Chile. Lance heaved his sword back over his shoulder, gritting his bottom teeth almost to the breaking point, cursing himself for missing the finishing blow.

If Lance didn't act now, he wouldn't get another chance.

Unleashing as much Electric Risima as he could manage, Lance took off again, racing against his own reaction time.

In less than a nanosecond, Lance's blade had found its target once more.

The sky shrieked as Electric Risima erupted from Lance's body and sword and with ferocious speed and conviction, the sharpened edge of Lance's sword traveled downward, down from Chile's face down to his torso at blinding speeds.

Unlike the first time, Lance's blade made a solid connection, but Chile still managed to evade the critical attack.

Lance's blade struck the ground, and a thick, red line gushed across Chile's body, missing his right eye by an inch. Even so, Chile reeled back in agony as Electric Risima scorched his face, entering the wound and charring his insides. He screamed like a monster.

Watching the microseconds pass in pure disbelief, Lance was astonished at how Chile managed to dodge *two* of Lance's Electric attacks at this close of a distance. It just wasn't physically possible!

Consumed with anger, Lance spun on his heel in a 180-degree motion, changing the direction of his sword at the same time, angling the blade *behind* Lance.

Chile immediately saw what Lance was going for. Feeling most of his Energy returned to him, Chile lifted his hands and focused his Energy into the small space between his hands as intensely as he could, conjuring as much Ice Risima as he possibly could.

A thick shard of ice miraculously appeared in front of Chile's body.

But Lance was far quicker and much stronger. With a yell, Lance's sword slammed into the shard of ice, the blade piercing straight through the ice and penetrating into Chile's chest, just barely missing his heart.

Lance wasted no time as he spun and pivoted on his foot once more, determined to kill Chile for good.

Chile's left knee crashed into the ground, blood pouring from the cut. His eyes were wide open, confused by the sudden jolt of pain he felt in his stomach.

Suddenly, right as Lance held the executioner's stance above Chile's neck, the ground beneath Chile's feet erupted with power—the same one that awakened when the Polar Vortex began.

Chile's eyes were tightly shut, his body quaking with unknown power once more.

The ground quaked, pummeled by Chile's Ice Risima that ripped the streets into shreds and tore into the very foundation the city lay upon.

Lance's body moved automatically, his feet nimble and light as his body leapt and skipped backward, avoiding sharp projectiles and the spears of ice shooting out from where Chile was.

Lance had managed to dodge the sudden attack, but when he heard a terrifying explosion above him and noticed that Chile managed to destroy the foundation that a large hotel stood upon, he knew that he needed to calculate his movements perfectly.

Amazed by the sheer size of the large building toppling over, directly over top of him, Lance nearly held his hand up and stopped the falling debris with Earth Risima.

But then, a wincing pain cut into Lance's hand, cutting the palm of his hand open and tearing into his left shoulder and right leg as several small sharp projectiles of ice were launched at Lance from where he last saw Chile.

Before the pain immobilized Lance, he decided to sprint, the only obvious place to escape into was the *inside* of the falling hotel, shielded his face as he crashed into the revolving glass doors that somehow managed to remain during the storm, but instantly hitting the ground and rolling to avoid hundreds more ice spears that pierced into the lobby walls of the hotel.

Lance huffed as his tumbling body came to a skidding halt and his head sprang up, slamming against one of the walls of the hotel.

Lance was pissed that he had been put on defense in only an instant, but he understood that he was in a situation that could get him killed if he wasn't careful.

Lance brought his left hand up, ignoring the jabbing pain in his shoulder as he focused Earth Risima through the outside of the hotel.

Maybe he could create a large object of some sort and use it to strike Chile from afar? Could Lance even use his Risima Transportation ability to hit Chile from multiple places at once?

But that idea went as soon as it came. Lance gasped as several large spears tore into the hotel walls and homed right in on Lance's location.

Lance scrambled to his feet, barely having the energy to move.

He was trapped by the ice spears, forced into a corner of the hotel, where he noticed there was nothing but a single door in the far corner.

As Lance evaded the spears that tore into the hotel from the outside, lodging into the walls of the hotel as if they were paper, Lance's back hit the solid, metal door behind him.

Praying that it was either a staircase or perhaps an elevator shaft, Lance kicked at the door, causing it to fly open as now even snow began to fill the hotel lobby, quickly consuming everything in it.

Not even looking, Lance tucked himself away into the door, slamming the heavy metal door shut right before another wave of icicle spears bombarded the hotel lobby.

Lance's back foot hit what felt like an elevated platform and, to his relief, found himself the stairwell he was hoping for.

Lance cautiously took one step up, keeping his body facing the heavy metal door. If Chile was foolish enough to follow Lance into the hotel, he could use the enclosed space to his advantage.

He had even laid a couple of traps back in the lobby. He just hoped Chile took the bait.

But he didn't.

Fueled by the insatiable rage and overwhelming surge of Energy the Ice Risima gave him, Chile relied on long-range, hard-hitting ice attacks to lure Lance out *instead*.

But Lance was determined to stay hidden.

The entire hotel began rumbling as the foundation was rocked by the thunderous barrages of Chile's ice-based attacks. Lance could predict that the snow piling inside the hotel was what likely caused the walls to crack and crumble, weakened by the insane pressure Ice Risima could exert on its surroundings.

Lance knew it was an awful idea to begin running to the higher levels of the hotel. Not only were the top-most floors beginning to topple over, but soon enough, the entire hotel would be consumed in ice or left as concrete and debris to add to the destruction and rubble outside.

And Lance knew the only reason that didn't happen was Chile wanted to kill Lance with his own hands.

The hotel was becoming a grave for Lance and the stairwell likely his coffin if he didn't make a move soon.

Chile's ice spears took no time at all to completely decimate the metal doors leading to the stairwell, and Lance was propelled to hop backward, taking him up two or three more stairs in order to avoid the shrapnel from the Ice spears.

But then Lance had an incredible idea.

He suddenly had the urge to yell out to the madman, which also acted as a way to grab Chase's attention if he were anywhere near the hotel.

"Hey, Chile!" Lance screamed at the top of his lungs, his attention toward the exposed hotel lobby, watching as more ice and snow filled the area.

"Those ice spears of yours look stupid! Don't tell me I actually knocked the sense out of you earlier! Don't you know how to aim?"

It was a horrible idea, Lance soon realized, because not even a second later, an avalanche of snow and ice spears pummeled into the hotel. With relentless force and destructive power, a sheer number of spears penetrated into the stairwell from even the sides and the ceiling at various directions, ice spears of different shapes and sizes missing Lance's body by inches and, in some cases, scraping Lance's back or his ankles.

But that gave Lance what he needed to know. Lance knew exactly where Chile was now.

Without wasting another moment, Lance turned and sprinted up the stairwell, keeping a mental note of which direction was north and which was *east* as he ran, counting the seconds in his head as he ran.

The ice spears slowly turned the hotel into an ice cave—the thick ice spreading throughout the floors and walls of the hotel. Chile was taking the entire building under his control, and before long, would be able to whisk his hand away and have the entire thing destroyed instantly.

But Lance knew how long that would take. He had seen too much of Chile's attacks by now.

Lance remembered something critical, his mind doing calculations faster than a lightning bolt could move.

Using the approximate size of the meteor and dividing it by the size of the hotel, I know that I have approximately twelve more seconds to make my move. Otherwise, this hotel and everything in it, will perish in what comes at nine seconds.

Lance didn't take any time away from his ascent as he calculated his next moves precisely. He used all his limbs and every structure around him to climb as quickly as possible, and it seemed that Chile had a similar idea.

He bounced off from wall to wall, skipping seven or eight steps at a time, using the railing in the middle to climb the stairwell even faster than normally.

But Chile's ice attacks were increasing as the seconds went on. It seemed that Chile was no idiot after all, he realized that his ice attacks hadn't struck anything at the lower levels and instead continued the rate of fire throughout the entire hotel.

But that meant that Chile's attacks were only focused on *one* section of the hotel: the *east* side, where, from on the ground, Chile was likely unleashing his attacks from.

After three seconds, Lance had made it to the fifteenth floor. And by this time, he had no choice but to make his move. The higher he climbed, the more he noticed that the stairwell became slanted and that cracks in the foundation of the solid cement walls and floor appeared throughout the structure of the stairwell.

The thirtieth floor and beyond had already crumbled and toppled, crashing on the floor below. And even now, at floor fifteen, Lance could see that he and the entire floor would soon be falling out of the sky, plummeting to the icy ground far below.

And Chile definitely would be waiting without an unpleasant surprise for when he caught Lance at the very bottom…

Lance forced the idea out of his mind.

Almost in a fit of terror, Lance kicked the door to the sixteenth floor open and rushed in, immediately making a run across the long corridor.

Sure enough, he could hear the sound of ice continuing to penetrate and destroy parts of the stairwell, which meant that his idea had worked.

But he only had four more seconds now.

Lance's feet began to slip as in one jolting motion, the upper floors of the hotel broke free from the foundation and began to tilt.

Lance could hear the sound of the upper floors collapsing under the pressure of the attacks, noticing debris plummet from the exposed windows. The walls on the sixteenth floor began to collapse as well, cold air pouring into the corridor.

But this was what Lance was waiting for.

Lance turned his attention to the exposed wall, watching as more and more of the hotel began to lean, before finally beginning to collapse entirely. Then Lance ran forward, bracing himself as he leapt out of the open section of the wall, hoping that he calculated the physics behind his daunting excursion properly.

But he did.

As Lance free fell in the open sky, hovering sixteen floors above ground, he noticed that the large office complex across from the hotel, or *north*, was tall enough to support the weight of the collapsing hotel Lance leapt out of.

Using light speed in his favor, Lance needed to somehow manage to escape the hotel *and* find a vantage point where he could attack Chile from without exposing himself or getting caught in the explosion Chile was about to set off in the hotel.

Lance covered his face, and with a loud crashing sound, his body crashed into the fifteenth floor of the office building, rolling across the hard floor.

The hotel building toppled over and crashed into the office building right behind Lance, causing the office complex to rock tumultuously. And for a second, Lance feared that his hypothesis had been wrong, and that he and the office building would crumble as well.

But after a few seconds of crashing sounds and a few pieces of rubble crashing into the office complex from the ceiling, the chaos subsided, and the window that Lance leapt in from was totally blocked off from the debris from the hotel.

But Lance wasn't done yet. That had been eight seconds.

Four more seconds!

Lance had memorized the structure of the buildings even from on the ground. Unfortunately, there was no way to know what the inside of each one looked like, but from what Lance could remember, he knew from the layout of the office complex that there was a large east wing with several large window panels next to computer desks.

This was a perfect place to execute his plan.

*****

"As soon as I leapt through that fire, you take cover. Then you wait until you see a large explosion occur from over there." Lance pointed to Chase.

Chase didn't understand at first.

For the last thirty seconds, Lance and Chase were huddled in a small building, temporarily protected from the windstorm outside. The entire time, Lance had been proactive, telling Chase what his plan was, and what Chile was most likely going to do next.

"So, you're sure that Chile will fall for that trap? The shirt from that…that poor guy." Chase swallowed his words.

"You're sure that Chile will think it's a person out there?"

And Lance was. "Yes. I'm absolutely sure," he began, "Chile isn't thinking straight. He never does. His strength is immense, but his mind is weak. He only cares about revenge. He'll go after anything."

Chase exchanged a look with Lance.

"That's true. He only acts on impulse and emotion. He acts like a child."

"Exactly. And that's how we finish him for good, Chase."

Lance reached over and placed his hand on Chase's head, bringing it to his own head.

"If we do this right, it'll be over, brother. We can't stop now."

Chase, overcome with fatigue and stress, closed his eyes and rested his head back on Lance's.

Chase closed his eyes.

"You're right. Let's finish this, Lance."

*****

Chase watched as a large hotel began crumbling to the ground. First, the upper floors were destroyed entirely and toppled over like a house of cards, leaving only the bottom to about half of the entire hotel left standing.

The pressure from the blast was immense. The sound of the hotel crumbling was deafening. And the dust mixed with the snow instantly, getting into Chase's face and hair but quickly blown away by the powerful icy winds dominating the battlefield.

Chase remembered what the plan was.

He and Lance knew that Chile would somehow manage to extinguish the flame.

Unless Lance shouted, "It's over!" indicating he had been successful in killing Chile from within the ring of fire, Chase's next move was to find a vantage point and wait for a large-scale explosion to occur from around the *hotel*.

Chase was stunned by what he was seeing. How did Lance know that Chile was going to target the hotel? And why *was* Chile attacking the hotel all of a sudden anyway?

But that wasn't important.

As soon as the hotel exploded into shards and shrapnel of ice and frozen concrete, Chase was to act, attacking Chile with another inferno, but this time, creating an inferno with a much smaller circumference, trapping Chile within it as much as he possibly could without directly attacking him.

Chase made sure to keep himself hidden from Chile but close enough that he could create the inferno without any issues.

The intensity of the wind increased as time went on, but Chase noticed that the storm that once stretched across the entire eastern shore retreated—and instead redirected its power *here*, focusing all of it on the hotel.

The way that Chile's Ice Risima and Ice spears lodged into the hotel reminded Chase of what Chile did to the meteor.

Once enough ice penetrated the meteor, the entire rock exploded with tremendous force, sending shards of ice out into the air.

This was identical to that. The first eleven or so floors of the hotel were encased in thick ice, segments of icicles protruding from and into the hotel from the walls on every side.

The way that Chile relentlessly unleashed wave after wave of attacks at the hotel, especially at one specific wing of the hotel, told Chase that perhaps *Lance* was inside there after all.

But Lance never told Chase what he planned on using the hotel for. He never even explicitly mentioned the hotel at all.

But Chase knew that when the hotel began to crack under the pressure and began to sway, allowing the sixteenth and above floors to begin toppling under the weight of the ice, that something was about to happen.

Chase readied his attack. After being out in the sheer cold for so long, Chase was growing immune to the sub-zero temperatures.

The only issue was the wind. With how fast and powerful it was, Chase would need to stay still and continue to pour Energy into the inferno in order to fuel it with as much Risima as he could concentrate on producing.

Chase's eyes quickly glanced to the hotel, noticing that as the structure began to collapse, that a figure had leapt out from one of the floors high up from the ground and disappeared as its body passed through another tall building across from the hotel.

Not even a second later, the upper half of the hotel collapsed under the pressure, falling in the same direction as the figure before it crashed into the second building, tossing dust and debris in every which direction.

Chase knew by now that the figure he saw was Lance.

And so Chase was on the move, preparing for the explosion.

As Chase carefully inched his way to the optimal point of attack, he could see Chile's Ice Risima quickly consume the rest of the hotel building and even parts of the second building Lance was currently in.

Chase urged Lance to hurry. Otherwise he'd be caught in a death box and killed by the Ice Risima Chile was prepared to discharge.

Chase used the fallen structures buried under the snow to climb to a higher elevation, using his speed to mount atop of what appeared to be a store or perhaps a restaurant that wasn't all that tall.

Chase slid his way across the slippery rooftop, anchoring his foot against the ledge of the roof, and crouched down.

Chase looked over the edge of the store and found Chile, not too far in the distance. But he was still focused on the hotel; he didn't even notice Lance had leaped from out of the building into another one!

This is perfect...! Chase thought to himself.

Not only was he close enough to create the ring, but he knew that he would be able to produce an even stronger inferno without having to risk being seen by Chile.

And then the explosion happened.

Chase's eyes widened, as right before the explosion rocked the hotel, sending a shockwave of Ice Risima throughout the sky, Lance's body emerged from the topmost floor of the office building, his body in the middle of the sky, right above Chile.

And then Chase knew *exactly* what Lance was planning.

*****

"Chase! Do it again! Now!"

Lance screamed at the top of his lungs, as his body began freefalling from eighteen stories.

At the same time, Lance's eyes flashed a dark-green color, radiating pure Earth Risima Energy. Ripping up loose particles in the ground, infusing metals, glasses, cement, and all the raw materials found on Earth, Lance's body became a beacon that began commanding the very Earth to obey Lance's mind.

Feeling immense resistance in his left hand, Lance clenched his fist and commanded the Earth Risima to obey his command, taking control of the *entire* office complex and ripping it free from its foundation.

It was a colossal-scale move, a perfectly executed plan that had only *just* begun.

The office building crumbled, the entire structure ripped free from the floor it rested on before the entire eighteen-floor building began to fall right over top of Chile's body.

Chase reacted perfectly, instantly igniting the floor around Chile's body with another powerful inferno.

But this time, Chile was on his guard.

With terrifying power, Chile's left hand produced Ice Risima and fortified the ground below his feet, instantly weakening the power and burning heat of the inferno.

Chile's left hand trembled as he lifted his right hand up toward the falling office building above his head.

Chile's Ice Risima turned the debris and ash into icicles, quickly freezing the entire building, connecting all the loose pieces in a wave of solid ice, stopping the falling building in time.

But Lance knew this would happen.

Chile had miscalculated something crucial—he forgot that he had never used his ice spears to penetrate the inside of the office building, which meant that his control of Ice and therefore his ability to freeze the office complex was limited to whatever he could *see*.

The eighteen floors of the office complex, still dislodged from Lance's Earth Risima, crashed into the frozen concrete and glass suspended in the air and sent even more pieces of rubble and glass toward Chile.

Panicked, Chile lifted his left hand, attempting to reinforce the office complex.

But as soon as he did, the Fire Inferno ignited, overpowering the Ice Risima around Chile's feet, engulfing Chile in intense heat once more.

Chile's body began seizing up. His throat began ringing before Chile yelled out with all of his strength, turning as much of the office complex into ice as he could.

Lance, still falling in midair, pushed out with his hands and forced Earth Risima to comply with his orders, clashing against Chile's Ice Risima.

The large piece of rubble began freezing in thick ice. But Lance forced it to continue falling, using his power to accelerate the velocity of the rubble and cause it to fly at Chile's body even faster.

Chile yelled out with insanity, both his eyes bleeding, whisking his hand with ferocity, flash-freezing the rubble in solid ice with all the Energy he could manage.

But Lance was still three steps ahead of Chile.

The inferno raging around Chile negated his ability to freeze large objects.

The rubble was quickly freed from Chile's control, both concrete *and* large amounts of *Water* now falling from the sky.

And Lance knew which one was more important for Chile to address.

But it was the *other* that Lance was planning on using to inflict a colossal amount of damage on Chile.

Chile, infuriated and seething with anger, directed so much force at the large piece of rubble with his hands, that the wind before the movement *alone* chipped pieces of the rubble apart.

Chile directed as many spears of ice as he could possibly manage at the falling rubble.

But the inferno around his feet denied Chile the ability to do so.

"This damn Fire!" Chile screamed like a lunatic, watching the rubble hovering right above his body.

Chile, fatigued and dismayed, unwilling to die, closed his eyes, and cried out as he leapt *through* the ring of fire in order to avoid the large piece of rubble, which slammed into the ground at high speed, nearly crushing him to death.

Chile rolled around in excruciating pain, screaming like a maniac as his body was scorched by the intense Fire.

He tried his absolute hardest to produce Ice Risima to cool his body off, but the pain was unbearable—he couldn't even think properly.

Even the intense winds rampaging at –140 degrees Fahrenheit proved to be no match for Chase's powerful Fire Risima, and Chile learned that lesson in the most unfortunate way possible.

Falling to his knees, unable to feel his limbs, Chile cried out in pain before the same unknown power began trembling in his stomach.

Chile's body began to shake in a frenzy, a chaotic Energy surging of him, before he felt a strange, *Forbidden* Energy begin to consume his body and even his thoughts.

Chile tried standing up, his body aching and creaking as he fought off the intense pain.

But then Chile was met with one last merciless attack.

In only a microsecond, Lance had determined that the diameter of the rubble had spanned 150 feet and had been moving over 80 feet per second. With this in mind, Lance knew that Chile would attempt to freeze the rubble and manipulate it to attack an exposed Lance falling out of the sky, using his instincts to turn an untimely situation into a powerful counterattack.

But Lance had negated all of Chile's advantages in one fell swoop.

As soon as Chile even managed to turn the rubble into ice, Lance's plan had succeeded.

Calculating the surface area of the rubble and using this same equation to determine the volume of the ice that Chile would create by multiplying the rubble's surface area by the average depth of Chile's ice-based attacks, Lance predicted that once the ice on the rubble melted, he had a volume of *twenty-two metric tons* of water falling from out of the sky.

And with this amount of Water in the air, untamed by Risima, Lance realized...

Chile looked above him, as one giant wave of kinetic water crashed into him with the force equivalent to *thirty-two million* PSI, generating a monstrous wave, which turned into a vortex of rapid-moving water, sucking oxygen and Risima away from Chile entirely.

Chile's body went limp, his senses unable to understand what had just happened.

Instinctively, Chile took a knee, bracing himself, his body thrashed by the vicious torrent of Lance's *Tsunami Flash*.

In an instant, all of Chile's bones and muscles were crushed under the insane pressure of Lance's *Tsunami Flash*, able to increase the pressure of a single metric ton of water upward of 3,500 times with *minimal* application of his mastered Water Risima Energy.

With this much water, at this much force, Chile had been struck by an attack that more than *quadrupled* what he would have gotten if he simply allowed the rubble to plummet on top of him instead.

Chile couldn't even cry out.

Although the excruciating sensation the fire left on his body was gone now, Chile's body was thrashed and battered constantly with torrents of water, constantly switching in direction as Lance continued to exert Risima Energy on the water, turning any body of water into his own *pool* of water.

Lance created a tsunami, his masterful control of Water Risima manipulating the world by creating an intense quaking sensation and generating terrifying power simply by expressing thought over it.

He was determined the destroy Chile with the tsunami, rendering his powers null by shattering his connection with Ice Risima while incapacitating his body.

After only three or four seconds of this brutal attack, Chile had nearly suffocated within the tsunami, his legs, arms, and ribs shattered by the monstrous power of the *Tsunami Flash*.

But Lance wasn't finished.

Lance held his sword up above his head, now only twenty-five feet off the ground and falling fast; Lance infused his last remaining bits of Risima Energy into his sword, straining as his eyes turned yellow.

A flash of Electricity lit up Lance's sword, and after gathering its magnificent power, the entire sky lit up, fuming with the sound of electricity running wild, like a generator spinning turbines to the max. Lance charged Risima up to his body's content, lightning bolts streaking out from his body—jolting across the sky.

No one could survive what was coming next. There was a very crucial reason almost no Rasrim in existence could use both Water and Electric Risima at the same time.

After Lance had accumulated as much Energy as he could possibly manage, he yelled furiously. It was a war cry so loud that it rivaled the howling screeches of the snowstorm.

With a powerful slash and the determination of a warrior, Lance unleashed a Lightning Bolt of powerful Electric Risima at Chile that was so fast and potent in force it produced an explosion that wiped out and cleared the city of all the snow and ice plastered on the streets and decimated entire buildings in the vicinity, sending streaks of lighting coursing through the entire city, obliterating everything in its path.

The strike was so destructive in force that it cratered the ground around Chile, puncturing the Earth through its core and shifted the tectonic plates.

The aftermath of the strike didn't stop there. The lightning streaking out into the ground had left a giant crack in the Earth's crust that spanned for several miles which split and leveled the ground of the entire city!

The blowback from the attack cleared the sky. The snowstorm had vanished.

The intense winds subsided. Sunshine began to peer through the thick clouds above.

Lance could hardly think straight.

He plummeted into solid concrete hard, nearly faint, having fallen eighteen stories without once stopping to think about how to break his fall.

Lance's bruised, broken, and fatigued body, quaking and shaking with discharging Electric Risima, could hardly move as the pain from the fall took its toll on Lance's body.

Lance gagged out, coughing up blood, somehow managing to roll to his side to spit it out but not before wincing out in awful pain.

Lance's shoulders and hands twitched. He tried his hardest to place his hands on the floor and move, lifting himself off the floor, hoping that his back wasn't broken.

After convincing himself that his body wasn't broken into pieces, Lance sat up, gagging on his own breath before he gasped, sucking in air hard before he reeled in pain, his chest sore and lungs nearly punctured from Chile's attack and battered from the eighteen-story freefall into solid concrete.

Lance held himself upright, trying to pull himself to his feet before he stumbled, nearly blacking out.

But he had been caught, held up by his arms and brought up to his feet.

"C'mon, stay up, Lance! Stay awake! I think it worked! It-it's getting warmer! The windstorm is even slowing down. Your plan worked!" Chase called out, holding Lance upright, determined not to let him fall or lose consciousness.

"W-where is he?" Lance called out, unable to think clearly.

"Lance, it's all right, it's over!"

"Is he...is Chile—?"

But they had both had their answer not even seconds after that. It was impossible to miss.

Chase and Lance stopped, their feet hanging over a massive crater in the ground. It must've been half the size of a football field, and at least thirty feet deep.

"Holy crap, dude," Chase said. "Is *that* why you wanted me to stay long-ranged and out of the way?"

Lance's head bent over. He had been laughing but soon reeled in pain. It hurt even when he laughed.

"Yeah. Kinda." He winced as he tried joking without reeling in pain.

Chase hoisted Lance up as his leg began drooping, keeping him on his feet.

"But this...this is a power on an entirely different level. I wasn't even thinking—I just charged and unleashed. I wasn't planning on the destruction being *this* massive!"

Lance pulled free from Chase's arms, the Risima in his legs and shoulder beginning to numb the pain.

"I'm fine now, Chase. You can let me go."

Lance limped on the ground, allowing his body to recover, thankful for Chase in every way imaginable.

Chase didn't say anything right away. He couldn't help but think about all the senseless violence and destruction the people of this poor city had witnessed.

"Imagine if there were people still nearby. This would've been a massacre..." Chase sighed, the emotional pain and remorse clearly present in his tone.

"And Chile *still* managed to do that!" Lance hissed. "We have no idea how many innocent people were caught in the storm. Imagine what he would've done after he had his way with us..."

The two continued sliding into the crater, noticing just how large and wide it had been. Rocks had been tumbling into the depths of the crater from all sides. The area had simply looked deserted— like the apocalypse had arrived.

Lance stopped. He saw something in the depths of the crater, lying at the bottom.

"Stop, look at that!"

Lance anchored his feet into the crater, finding a good position to stand up without tripping over.

The crater was steep. But seeing that there was nothing but dirt and rocks within it, Lance was able to stand up straight within it.

Chase placed his arm on Lance's shoulder, getting closer so he could get a better look, careful not to trip over any rocks or uneven grooves in the ground.

When Chase got next to Lance, he immediately saw what Lance was referring to.

Chase's eyes settled on the sight. He didn't even show any emotion. He didn't even say a word. He just looked, incapable of producing any real reaction. His mind was completely empty.

"Is that it then? Did we really kill him?"

Lance looked at Chase and then at the body of Chile. His face buried in the ground, his left arm mangled and broken entirely.

But before Lance said anything, he stopped for a moment, unsure about something.

"I can't say for sure if I feel sorry for him," Chase said, a tired look on his face.

Lance agreed, but he was deep in thought, focusing on something. "Yeah. I don't know either, man, but—"

He shifted his foot backward, a hesitant look in Lance's face, causing Chase's eyes to swell up with a look of trepidation as well.

"No! What now? What is it, Lance?!"

Lance tensed himself, on the cusp of breaking out into a sweat.

"H-he isn't dead, Chase! His heart's still beating, I-I can feel it!"

And then Chile's body twitched, dust and rocks clattering in the crater.

Chase was mortified, clearly in disbelief. "What, how?"

But even though Chase was in shock, he was prepared to act.

"W-well, we need to act right now!"

But Lance shot out and grabbed Chase's arm, pulling him back.

"Wait! You remember what happened last time, just hold on! We can't fall for that again!"

Chile's right hand opened, his palm lying against the floor of the crater.

Chase nearly roared, pulling free of Lance's grip.

"Just stay down, dammit! I don't want to do this anymore!"

But the words fell on deaf ears. Chile pushed his chest off the ground. His movements were slow and demonic. It was as if he were taunting the two.

Did you really think that I was dead? Did you really think that the two of you could take me down?

Chase and Lance stepped back, out of options.

Lance couldn't believe his eyes. There's no way *anyone* could have survived an attack like that! Was Chile more than a Rasrim?

Chile turned his face toward Chase and Lance.

Chase and Lance's faces were stricken with fear. Chile's entire face was covered in blood. And just like before, his eyes were *red*.

Steam surrounded Chile's body, the blood on his face slowly evaporating into thin air.

Lance noticed that a crimson-red aura light was glowing underneath Chile's shirt.

Lance tugged on Chase, directing him to what he was seeing in the crater.

"Do you see that light?" Lance asked, backing out of the crater cautiously, not daring to take his eye off of Chile for even a second.

Chase saw it but ignored the question, terrified at everything *else* he was seeing. "Dude's eyes are red. That's creepy, man!"

"Chase, you see that light on Chile's face?"

"Yeah, and I'm seeing a lot more than I wanted to!" He was referring to the burns stretched across Chile's neck and face and his exposed ribcage.

But both of the boys also noticed the dim red light illuminating Chile's body. It slowly began to fuse within Chile's body, slowly closing up Chile's wounds and removing the burn marks on his body.

Chase's heel touched flat ground once again, and his eyes lit up. "We need to aim for his heart, where that light is glowing the most! Either that or we—"

Lance gulped, looking at Chile's eyes.

"Or what?"

"You know what? How else do you kill a zombie?!"

Lance closed his eyes, trying not to imagine it.

But Chase was right. Lance had already tried to do it *twice* now.

Chile pushed himself to his feet. Chile grabbed his left arm with his right hand, holding it tightly—

Lance watched closely, his body feeling sick. He had to be dreaming.

And snapped each bone back into place like it was a puzzle.

The crimson-red light glowing in Chile's chest had suddenly taken the form of strange, ceremonial-looking lines and tattoos and stretched from Chile's chest to his shoulder and down his left arm.

Lance noticed the lines were no more than a few inches thick, but they weren't there before! Were they scars? But why were they *glowing* red?

Chile's bones cracked, before he stood up straight, his body completely healed. The holes left in his clothes showed there were no scars, bruises, or blood anywhere on his body whatsoever.

It was surreal, truly like watching a zombie resurrect from the dead.

Lance watched in terror; his eyes unable to process what he had been seeing. "What is that light? That isn't Risima!"

"He's healed himself completely!" Chase whimpered in fear. "How is that possible? How can you heal wounds like that? It isn't possible!"

"It *is* possible!"

"W-well, not that fast, even with Risima!"

Chile took a step forward, his sinister, tortured eyes hellbent on watching the two.

He never blinked. He didn't so much as move his eyes. He just walked forward, lurching with every step.

The marks on Chile's arms and chest glowed intensely, the red light so bright it was almost blinding to look at Chile's body. The more his body healed, the brighter the lights became—a signal that life was returning back to Chile's body and fueling him.

Lance pulled Chase away from the crater, suspecting they only had a few more seconds left.

"Chase, listen! I have *one last* idea!"

*****

Chile had felt more powerful than he ever had before.

The power coursing through him had made him feel more than alive.

He truly felt *reborn*.

In fact, this wasn't the first time that Chile "died."

His heart had stopped for the first time when he had first been subjected to the Rasrims trials conducted on him years ago. His body hadn't been suited for such torture, and his body gave up shortly after, his heart stopping for over two minutes.

But for some damned reason, Chile opened his eyes *again* that day!

And when he did, he noticed that the five scientists that had been experimenting on him had been dead, lying in a pool of blood.

He remembered looking at his left hand and noticed two distinct things that day.

One, his hand had been drenched in blood. His hand even had what looked like a Human heart in it.

Two, bright red marks had covered his left hand, tracing back to his chest.

These were the same marks covering his body now.

However, this was the first time he was seeing them again since *that* day...and this was the second time he had died.

Chile remembered something Melterai had told him. He remembered being told about the existence of powers and abilities one could receive only after encountering "death."

Chile walked through the crater, several voices screaming in his mind, calling him a demon.

Among one of them, however, was an entirely new voice he had never heard before. Chile didn't even think the voice was Human.

Kill them all. Satisfy your lust for vengeance. Kill everyone connected to the Division. You are a demon reborn now.

Chile had always ignored the voices in his head. He never understood what or who these voices were.

But this one appeared to be much louder than all the others.

Was Chile really reborn? Had he received these Forbidden Powers that Melterai spoke of?

Chile stepped out of the crater, looking around. He looked down at his hands, noticing they were trembling with power. All his muscles quaked with new Energy. He felt faster, stronger, and even that his Ice Risima powers had increased dramatically.

After looking around for a little longer, Chile opened his mouth. "Chase, Lance. Let's talk."

Chile waited, his eyes scanning the area.

He heard a noise from behind him. His eyes moved as far in that direction as they could, but he didn't move his head to look. He didn't move so much as a muscle.

Chile stood still, deeply listening to his surroundings.

"What's there to talk about, Chile?"

Chile didn't see anyone out in the open. He could only suspect that Chase and Lance were watching him from afar.

Chile turned his head around, looking through different buildings and down alleyways.

"I want to talk about my plans." He spoke.

"Your plans? Don't they just involve destroying property and killing innocent people?" Lance's distant voice called out.

Chile smirked, slowly nodding.

Kill him, Chile.

Chile lifted his head, his appearance that of a demon from hell.

413

"After I kill you and Chase, I want to kill the individuals responsible for my existence in the first place. The Division."

Hidden behind cover, Lance squinted, but he forced himself not to feel any emotions. Chile was playing mind games.

Lance's body was still recovering. He needed to stall to regain as much Energy as he possibly could before engaging with Chile again.

And then Lance saw Chase creeping up on Chile from behind, his eyes pulsating with Energy.

Chile took a step toward Lance's hiding spot, extending his hand out. He looked as if he were about to say something else. But before he got a chance, Chase rushed Chile from behind, his body engulfed in fire.

Chile didn't even react. He barely felt the burning sensation.

Chase was astonished. The same fire that put Chile on his knees just moments ago suddenly seemed to have no effect on him at all!

With tremendous force and patience, Chile retained his balance, and with a swift blow, he drove his elbow into Chase's stomach with colossal strength.

Chase felt powerless as Chile lifted him over his shoulder and hurled his body toward Lance.

Lance's eyes widened.

As Lance tried to help break Chase's fall, Chile's red eyes lit up, thunder erupting from overhead. White Energy flowed into Chile's body.

Lance caught Chase, keeping him upright before he yelled, "Run!"

Chase and Lance took not even two steps.

Chile released his Energy once more, and once again, the *Polar Vortex* was unleashed.

*****

Chile had kept his body still when he released *Polar Vortex,* unsure of how his body would respond to it now that he had been using Stellar Riora.

But to his surprise, he had felt *nothing*. He didn't lose any Energy. He didn't feel fatigued.

Chile walked forward, anger in his eyes.

This has gone on too long. You should have killed them on the beach. Chile's head twitched, the voice in his head diluting his focus.

Around Chile's body, gigantic ice structures resembling fortresses formed, completely consuming the town's architecture.

Massive palaces of ice filled the sky, blocking out the sky overhead. Shadows cast over the tiny trees left standing, and the roads felt claustrophobic and nonexistent next to the gigantic ice structures riddling the city—all created by Chile's delusions and warped perception of the society *he* believed Humans wanted to create.

In essence, he had been manifesting the very thing *he hated* but covered it up with the only thing he knew—Ice Risima.

Huge walls of thick ice with stalagmites protruding from their surfaces, creating crevices, turning the city of Rockdale into one large *glacier*, the streets and alleyways embedded within the city nothing more than cave systems wrapped within the developing glacier.

After a few minutes, this glacier would grow to become taller than the Eiffel Tower.

From there, after a couple of hours, the glacier would reach the stratosphere.

And from there, in a matter of a day, the glacier would become so large it would penetrate *space*, permanently blocking out the sun on Earth, effectively killing *everything* on the surface.

And once he discharged Ice Risima at that scale...

Chile opened his hand, a sharp ice spear forming in his hand.

Once again, the raging windstorm had consumed much of the environment, spreading thick ice and snow over virtually everything around Chile.

Chile walked quickly, tossing aside the snow accumulating in front of him.

He spun the ice spear round and round in his hand, reinforcing it with extreme amounts of Risima over and over.

Before long, Chile reached a point where his spear was sharp enough to pierce *diamonds*, which weighed over eighty pounds.

But Chile could wield it with one hand effortlessly, as if it were a pencil.

Chile walked through the wasteland in the direction he saw Chase and Lance freeze up in, before after another few seconds of walking, he came across a person hunched over in the snow.

Chile smirked to himself. It seemed not everyone enjoyed the cold.

Chile raised his spear in front of the body. With attitude and a cocky grin, he rammed the spear into the person's skull.

He placed his foot on the person's head and kicked off as he pulled the spear out of the person's head, surprised to see the entire thing was ice, and shattered, pieces of ice dropping to the snow as it cracked.

Chile was confused for a moment. He inched closer to the ice lying in the snow.

Chile's body tensed up in sheer frustration. *"This again?"*

Without any hesitation, Chile Ice Risima instinctively took control over Chile's body and forced his neck to duck down, a sword crossing over Chile's head and missing by only inches.

Lance swung again, putting more power into each attack.

Chile chuckled as he parried each of Lance's attacks, not losing even an inch of ground in Lance's relentless attacks.

Lance shifted his position, spreading his feet and lowering his center of gravity.

Chile raised his elbow and thrusted his spear at Lance—a nasty maneuver but Lance countered Chile's attack by assuming a low-guard stance and swept his sword upward, nearly knocking Chile's spear out of his hands.

Chile launched on the offensive—deciding it was time to change his attack style entirely.

Chile raised his spear and quickly slammed it against his wrist, splitting the spear in half, and raised the new weapon up in front of his body.

Lance scoffed. He couldn't believe his eyes.

Chile had effectively created a sword himself, a thin blade of ice with two sharp edges.

Things just got interesting.

But the fate of Humanity rested on Chase and Lance's shoulders, and they were racing against time for control of who got to decide Earth's fate.

Barely half a second later, Chile rushed forward at blinding speed, attacking Lance with monstrous intent.

Lance and Chile traded blows with one another, pivoting their positions, changing their angles and footwork and even switching their lead hands.

Chile slashed at Lance with an overhead swing.

Lance parried, timing the release of his counterattack by dropping his guard low and spinning, slashing Chile horizontally across the chest.

Chile blocked the attack, holding his sword sideways. He blocked a second attack, a third, and even a fourth from Lance.

Chile lifted his leg and launched a roundhouse kick across Lance's chin. Lance blocked with his shoulder, pushing against Chile before slipping to his right and dodging a thrust attack aimed in between his eyes.

Lance slammed his shoulder into Chile's chest before turning with an upward slash, catching Chile from his chest up to his chin.

Chile made some hideous sound as his chin and lower lip had been slashed. He kept his eyes trained on Lance and, for just a moment, acknowledged his speed and skill. Chile spat out blood, his eyes unfazed. Steam flowed out of Chile's wound before closing entirely.

Lance took notice of the amount of steam Chile's body released when healing different wounds.

At once, he began to have an idea of how to put Chile's madness down for good.

Lance pressed on, continuing the assault by wielding his sword aggressively. He knew he needed to overload Chile's healing factor.

But Chile didn't play on the back foot. Instead, he came charging ahead as if he were saying, "That was nothing!"

Their swords clashed against each other once more, Lance being sure to continue streaming Stellar Riora into his sword as best as he could, giving his sword the hardness of Earth Risima with the speed and sharpness of a sword ignited with Electric or Water Risima.

Lance swung his sword horizontally. Chile brought his sword straight down the middle. The swords clanged, sending intense shocks through each other's bodies. They had been countering each other perfectly.

Chile whistled as he sidestepped in an instant, dodging a Fire attack from Chase.

Up until now, Chase had been creating several rings of Fire, chipping away at the iceberg's sheer size and diameter and giving Lance a fighting chance. This had been part of the plan—but much of it had gone terribly wrong.

Even so, with the environmental advantage—even if only in this one area—Chase joined the fight to initiate phase two.

But Chile was ruthless and cunning. His strength and speed proved to be overwhelming as Chile took on both Chase and Lance fearlessly. With each passing minute, Chile was countering their attacks, blocking their strikes and blows with his sword, and dishing out precise, lightning-quick counters that slowly whittled down Chase and Lance's stamina.

Chase bombarded Chile with dozens of flaming orbs of Fire Risima, but Chile had grown fast enough to dodge it entirely.

He somehow managed to slip *underneath* the blast, throwing a heavy punch into Chase's stomach.

Chase coughed up blood, winded, putting up his arms as Chile spun round, bringing his sword around for the finish.

But Lance had pivoted around Chile in the nick of time, countering Chile's sword attack before throwing two powerful kicks at Chile's legs: one at his knee, and the other at his thighs, causing him to stumble forward and take a knee.

Chile was quick to recover, on his feet with his guard up in only a matter of seconds. But he didn't have time to react as he had been caught by Chase, pummeling Chile's body with a series of explosive punches at his shoulders and face, powered by Fire Risima.

Chile took the punch like it was nothing. Chase threw another punch at Chile's side, his ribs, and his chin, all of which landed in quick succession, knocking Chile's head back.

But it was a front.

As Chase came in for one last attack, Chile swung his head down *hard*, bringing his hands and sword down with him.

Chase panicked and fell backward, quickly spreading his legs, the sword crashing into the ground, missing him by inches, leaving a nasty crater in the ground.

Lance's eyes flashed Green. The ground underneath Chile's feet ruptured.

Chile blocked his face as from underneath the ground, large chunks of the street bludgeoned Chile from every direction, tearing his jacket to shreds.

Full of Energy and rage, Chile grabbed one of the chunks of Earth and flung it in a random direction, finding it increasingly hard to see with rocks and dirt in his eyes and face.

Chile stumbled backward, overwhelmed by the assault from Lance's Earth Risima before he crashed into a wall of rocks behind him.

Chile slammed his left elbow into the wall of Earth while he continued to swat at the debris in front of him with his right.

Lance rushed in, his body evading all the debris before throwing a full-force Electric punch at Chile, his movement speed amplified by Risima.

Chile's Ice Risima warned him of an incoming Energy surge, taking his last opportunity available to duck underneath what his instincts were telling him to avoid.

Lance's punch grazed the left side Chile's head but passed overhead and knocked a solid hole into the wall. Blasting Fire Risima into his hand, Lance angrily ripped his hand out of the Earth wall and focused even more Risima into the ground, quickly shifting his Energy to begin streaming Earth Risima, not allowing the taut resistance of the Risima to interfere with his movements.

Chile's body swayed, tumbling to the ground as he tried to stand.

Chile gasped as Lance had suddenly been in front of him, covering the distance in a blink.

Before Chile had time to finish exhaling, Lance ripped a blow into Chile's gut, sending shockwaves through the ground, and forcing Chile to gag.

Lance had even cracked one of Chile's ribs, blood spurting from his mouth.

Lance spun on his back heel, generating torque, using the momentum to infuse Electric Risima into his legs, before with a well-timed execution, unleashed a fast-spinning tornado kick into Chile's temple, shutting the lights in his eyes off completely.

"You're *done*, Chile!"

But with some unforeseen display of willpower, Chile held on to his position, the marks on his body taking control of his body.

Instinctively, Chile fired a spear of Ice Risima at Lance at point blank range, retaliating without even giving time to think straight while the marks on Chile's body desperately worked to heal his wounds.

But Lance had seen all of Chile's tricks and gimmicks at this point. He could see it coming before Chile finished *thinking* about it.

Inches away from Lance's eyes, the spear of ice was sliced clean in half by his sword.

Noticing a movement behind Chile, Lance changed his attack pattern. He rushed forward, using the sparkling crystals and shards of ice in the air as cover as he drove his sword into Chile's chest.

Chile dug his heel into the ground and launched himself backward. He brought his arms together as the tip of Lance's sword drove into Chile's chest, instead finding itself striking a solid piece of ice instead.

Lance pivoted forward, finessing his way to crouch under the block of ice before popping back up with an underhand slash aimed upward at Chile's exposed neck.

Chile lifted his arms and maneuvered his body backward, evading the tip of the sword. But Chile's heart sank as he suddenly lost his balance, almost swept off his feet completely.

Chase followed up with his attack, switching into a high guard throwing a roundhouse into Chile's shoulder, turning his off-balanced body entirely.

Chile huffed, clearly fatigued by Chase and Lance's coordinated strikes and merciless Risima attacks.

But Chile didn't falter.

He dodged Lance's sword, took a spinning-back kick from Chase, clashed briefly with Lance, spun, and slashed at Chase, dodged another attack from Lance, drove his sword to fend Chase off, and placed the palm of his hand on the face of his blade to block another sword attack from Lance, parrying his attack and forcing him to rethink his stance.

Chile held Lance to a standstill, and Chase had stayed low, building up Energy to continue fighting Chile from a distance with Fire Risima.

Chase and Lance were *exhausted*.

Thunder boomed over overhead as Chile stood uncontested in front of Chase and Lance. Lightning streaked across the sky in a furious display of might, and the snowstorm gained in intensity, the wind growing uncontrollably.

The ground continued to rumble as the two witnessed the entire city caving in and becoming an enclosure of solid ice—the iceberg growing larger and taller by the minute as Chile fed it Energy.

Chile had grown tremendously in strength and speed and showcased that by ditching his Ice powers entirely, instead resorting to fighting in a completely physical and offensive style of combat, that he had skills on par, if not greater than Chase and Lance.

Even without any training, Chile's vastly superior strength and conditioning with Risima posed a serious threat to Chase and Lance.

Chase panted as his knees began to grow sluggish, bleeding from his arms and one of his legs. He had been caught by one of Chile's ice attacks.

Lance wiped his mouth with his right hand, clutching his sword tightly in his left.

"Was *this* what you meant by pain?" Lance whispered to himself.

"Can we truly beat Chile? How many have already died because of him? Thousands? Millions? How much more will he kill if we can't stop him now? How much longer can we allow him to torture humanity? Will he purge the entire planet?"

Lance raised his sword in front of his body.

"Chase," Lance called out, his tone impatient and dramatic. He had been analyzing the entire fight in real time, keeping track of Chile's movements, fight pattern, recovery time, and even the size and speed of his ranged attacks.

Everything had gone according to plan.

Chase and Lance began circling Chile, who had surprisingly kept his action limited and disciplined, relying on counter attacking with his new Ice Blade.

"Phase Two! Wreck him!"

Chase's eyes quickly glanced over to Lance.

Here? Right now?

But Chase stood up, amassing as much strength as he could to stand straight.

"Yeah. Let's do it."

Chile smirked. He raised his arms in triumph, certain that no matter what the two ants had tried, he had what he needed to bring death to the entire planet en masse.

"You two can't be serious!" Chile chuckled, the red marks in his body suddenly glowing once more.

Chile stood still, glancing over at Chase and Lance with a sly look on his face, steam rising from around his body.

Aim for the chest or neck, a voice said in Lance's head.

One all-out attack with Stellar Riora. Even if it drains me completely. Even if it leaves me vulnerable at the last second and kills me. This is the only way.

Chase and Lance rushed forward.

Chile bent his legs, preparing to move—*fast.*

As soon as Chase and Lance were right in front of Chile, ready for an all-out attack, way past ready to end this nightmare, the steam from around Chile's body shrouded him in thick smoke, producing a massive breeze in the sheer coldness of the street that caused the wind speed to kick up dramatically, pushing Chase and Lance backward.

And don't hold back for any reason.

"Don't stop! Hit him hard!" Lance cried.

Lance slashed into the smoke.

Chase blasted the entire area with enough firepower to destroy a tank.

The wind caused the smoke from the attack to brush past the two, the area becoming clear as soon as a few moments after the attack.

Lance stepped into the smoke, raising his sword for the finishing blow but stopped.

"Stop! He's gone, move back!"

Chase skidded into the area Chile had last been, nearly yelling out in anger.

And then, for some reason, Lance's instincts told him to look up. His heart instantly sank to his stomach. All of the color in his face disappeared.

Lance grabbed Chase and yanked him hard, knowing something fearsome was coming. "He's in the air! Move, fast!"

About ten feet in the air, Chile had come crashing down in front of them, positioning his body to hit the ground *fast*.

Lance poured Energy into his body, sensing something *crazy* was coming, grabbing onto Chase and flashing away as hard as he could.

Chile tensed his right arm, yelling at the top of his lungs, his roar no different than that of a barbarian or perhaps even a demon— an enraged monster who was about to unleash hell upon *everything*.

When his body made contact with the floor, Chile *slammed* his fist into the street as hard as he could.

The entire world instantly felt Chile's absurd power. The entire planet rocked hard, almost as if God had struck it in anger. Everything, for just a breath, had been frozen in time before it *all* experienced the power that threatened everything that was.

Not even a millisecond after Chile struck the ground, a terrible screeching sound tore Lance's eardrums as a behemoth of *millions* of

Ice spikes and spears spread from the area Chile had struck. The Ice Risima he streamed into the floor turned into a ravaging avalanche of Ice, unraveled across the entire city.

The stampede of Ice spikes tore into *everything, shredding* buildings down to size, tumbling trees, and ripping through the floor beneath it.

The ground rocked with such fearsome, devastating power. An earthquake bombed the city, rupturing the streets and crumbled buildings as Chile's powers flowed through the channels of earth underneath the ground.

The Ice Risima in the ground piled up and multiplied, fusing together to produce massive displays of sharp ice that protruded from the ground some three or four *miles* away from where Chile hit the ground, a massive iceberg sticking up in the air where the Energy colluded together.

Chile stood up, moving back from the attack, admiring the work of art in front of him.

Chile's attack had spread *thirty miles* in total, devastating the city, turning it unrecognizable as it had been buried in ice and snow.

But Chile winced out in pain. He had then noticed he was also breathing hard and that his eye was throbbing in pain.

Chile held his fist into the air, allowing blood to drop from his fist and trickle down from his eyes onto the floor.

He had overdone it. First the iceberg and now this skyscraper sculptor of ice.

But Chile had most definitely succeeded. The damage he unleashed on Earth in only a few hours would leave a horrific scar on humanity for centuries to come.

The red marks on Chile's body produced more steam, causing the cuts on his fist to make a wet-squishing sound as the scars closed and healed.

Chile smiled to himself. It didn't matter.

Chile's head flowed back, the feeling of pure joy in his body. He began to walk, traveling alongside the palace of Ice Risima that invaded and destroyed the city. Chile lifted his right hand, marveling at how powerful he truly was.

This is the kind of power Melterai has. This is what I have been searching for.

And then Chile gasped out as a quick bullet of air slashed across his face, in the direction of the stampede of Ice spikes.

Chile's eyes glossed over the ice structure, examining the gaping hole toward the bottom of it which ate away from the rest. Where did it come from?

The horde of a small section of ice spikes rumbled, as a *mountain* of Fire erupted from the Ice, before a laser of Energy penetrated through the structure entirely, crashing into Chile's chest, tearing straight through him.

Chile gagged out, spitting blood on the floor as his body was sent hurtling backward, Energy coursing through him and frying his insides.

Chile hit the floor and skidded across it, bouncing and tumbling backward before he crashed into a frozen light pole far from where he had been struck.

Chile hissed in anger, allowing the Forbidden Energy inside him to roam free, steam pouring from every corner in his body.

Chile spun around as Lance had suddenly appeared behind him, holding a sword in his hands.

Chile spun hard, slamming the back of his fist into Lance's head. But water poured from the body, splashing onto the ground. "What?!"

Chile then cried out, screaming in agony as he was suddenly struck hard by a scorching-hot and sharp piece of metal was thrown at him at max speeds, piercing his leg knee.

Chile fell to the floor, smacking his face against the floor, howling in unspeakable pain as the metal bar lodged in his knee, preventing him from moving his leg.

Chase, hovering in the air above him, engulfed two more pieces of metal to its melting point before chucking the poles at Chile as hard as he could. He wasn't the only one allowed to fight dirty.

Chile was hyperventilating. If his body was unable to heal the wound quickly, he'd be paralyzed.

But he had enough stamina to lift his hand and focus more Energy.

His entire face squeezed up, clearly in his pain.

As Chile attempted to create a shield of ice in front of him, his head twitched as the floor around him began to rise into the air, carrying his body straight into the pieces of metal flying at him.

Chile's eyes widened when he began to understand what was going on.

Taking no time to ponder his options, Chile dodged one of the two metal poles by using his hands to throw his body to the side, scraping his arms and shoulder against the pointed stones in the floor.

Chile managed to dodge the first pole, which pierced straight through the platform of rock rising into the sky, leaving a perfectly round hole in the platform.

But Chile wasn't as lucky with the second one. It caught Chile's cheek and gashed his face, tearing a clean line from the side of his head down to his chin, causing his skin to boil.

Seething in pain, Chile threw himself off the floating island of asphalt, using the time he had been free falling to rip the iron pole in his leg out.

Chile froze the iron pole before his body burst with Forbidden Energy, giving him a temporary boost in strength. With a quick flick of the shoulder and wrist, Chile flung the iron pole back at Chase at near unrecordable speeds, hitting Chase in his shoulder, piercing straight through it.

Chase cried out and fell backward in the air, unable to control himself any longer.

Chile turned and raised his left shoulder, crashing back into the street below, breaking his arm.

Chile sucked in air hard, infusing as much Risima as he could while his body worked to heal the hole in his chest and leg. But the cut on his face had been wide and deep. It would take minutes to heal that completely.

"D-dammit!" Chile exploded. His heart rate began increasing dramatically as he began to lose pints of blood.

He heard a loud thudding sound behind him.

Chile turned and whipped his hand in the air, manipulating the Ice Risima in his hands to form a new sword.

Chile limped forward, practically dragging his left heel.

To hell with this!

Chile huffed and moaned painfully, a loud electronic-like sound sizzling as his leg healed. The pain had been immense. Chile's body had a hard time dealing with the Fire Risima Chase's attacks had marked him up with.

He reached Chase's unconscious body and raised his sword, going directly for Chase's heart. It was time to end this senseless bickering. Chase and Lance had no chance at stopping Chile any longer.

With no hesitation, Chile drove the sword into his target.

Chile stopped—inches above Chase's chest.

The sword was gone. It had evaporated into gas. The sky above Chile had begun clearing—the snow and hail that had rained relentlessly from the sky ceased.

The streets and sidewalks full of ice began to melt.

Chile watched as the city around him began transforming, reverting into its original state.

"What? Why?" Chile growled like a wild beast as he tried deciphering what had gone wrong.

Chile's eyes slowly fixated on Lance emerging from the icy-mist that covered the battlefield.

A bright, powerful white aura surrounded Lance's body, causing space around him to glow, static-like Energy spiraling marvelously, spinning and swirling around in the air with every step Lance took.

But Chile had noticed something else about Lance's appearance.

Chile began to feel unnerved. His instincts told him to *run*.

Lance's eyes were *cold*. His unwavering deep-blue eyes set on Chile had told him that Lance was ready to *kill*.

To Chile, they looked like they belonged to a demon, perhaps even the devil himself.

Chile had never seen what his hideously dubious appearance looked like. He had never seen what true intimidation had looked like before now.

Chile stopped moving, turning his shoulder to Lance, noticing that nothing had separated them except for the ruins of a blood-stained city.

And for just a mere moment, Chile had been *terrified*. Lance had traversed the battlefield with a sense of *hatred* and vile *disgust* as if he were prepared to slay Chile in cold blood. He saw exactly what he had done to Chase.

Chile could hear his heart beating. A single chill ran down his spine.

Faster than the blink of an eye, Chile burst into action, his body overflowing with power. His entire body had been engulfed with Forbidden Energy—the insignia of death that had gifted individuals with powers beyond reality.

Chile *could not* lose. He would not let his emotions gain the better of him.

Lance had felt nothing inside. He wouldn't even allow himself to think over what he was about to do.

Once he had seen Chase's body crash on the floor, Lance's mind *shut down* entirely.

Lance slowly picked up his sword, producing massive shock-waves of Stellar Riora around him, absorbing even the Ice Risima in the sky and in the city.

And then Lance took off, his body moving faster than *lightning*, his timing *perfect* and with no sign of *hesitation*.

Chile's red eyes flourished with power, charging up and releasing everything Chile had in him into manifesting one last spear of ice—one that was infused with enough Risima to destroy the entire continent. He was determined to pummel into Lance with everything he had, taking his heart right out of his chest. It would become the symbol of the world Chile would create—*heartless creatures with no heart, period.*

Lance swung his sword across the air, his cold, mean eyes never once leaving his target. He hadn't even bothered to look Chile in the eyes again.

Lance had been focused on Chile's *neck*. And this time, he wouldn't look away until he knew his blade met his target.

Chile opened his mouth and yelled as hard as he could as he drove his right hand into Lance's chest, unleashing every ounce of Risima and Forbidden Energy he could muster.

Lance's eyes flashed white. He focused *godlike* power into his sword.

Thunder roared. Waves crashed. Volcanoes erupted. Wind howled. Mountains collapsed. Entire galaxies collided.

And Lance's body had felt *all of it at once*, accumulating and infusing the power of all the world's most destructive Energy forces— and directed it into one last godlike attack.

The two Rasrims clashed.

The force of the collision had been stronger than anything Earth had ever witnessed in its entire history.

The sky temporarily lit up completely, a beam of light penetrating into space.

The force ripples throughout the city, and a ground tsunami fueled by Risima flipped over and decimated everything in its wake. It annihilated parks and trees, crumbled bridges and roads, evaporated the dirt in the ground, and even obliterated the clouds in the sky all at *once*.

It had even sent shockwaves into Osamos.

While Lance felt the powers of Divine Energy coursing through him, which nullified all his senses, it wasn't long before he also felt a sharp pain tear through his chest—piercing through his heart.

But Lance ignored the pain, putting his back into the slash, and drove straight through until he knew he couldn't anymore.

The pressure on Lance's body had been immense. He could hardly see. His mind had fogged up, and he felt blood rushing up through his chest and into his mouth.

The explosion cast a shadow of destruction across the city, a wave of wind billowing throughout the atmosphere, into space.

Lance's body quickly hit the ground hard and rolled several times. He didn't even have the energy to cry out in pain.

Lance's body stopped moving.

He breathed heavily, his body discharging Energy, several elements being released from his body at once.

Lance tried to move, but he couldn't. He struggled, trying to push himself to his feet. His arms and legs were paralyzed.

Lance barely had enough energy to force himself to sit up.

He looked down at his chest and noticed the spear of which had been stabbed through him, sticking out his body.

He winced, blinking hard as he then forced his body to move to the right, allowing blood to drip from his eyes.

Lance gripped his sword and drove it into the ground, pushing his entire weight into the blade to hold himself upright.

And then Lance's eyes slowly narrowed.

His body became heavy, and his vision began to dim. Darkness clouded his vision almost entirely. He couldn't hear anything except a muffled ringing in the back of his head. With every half breath he could even take, blood poured from his chest and arms and trickled down his face. Right before Lance collapsed, his expression and pacing mind sat still and settled when his eyes focused on a headless body lying in the street, Red Energy and what looked like Ife Risima slowly disappearing around the body.

Lance watched as all the ice and snow around the body disappeared into ash, no longer having a source of Risima to sustain it.

Lance let go of his Risima-infused sword, blood pouring from his mouth and chest.

His eyes began to fade from White to Blue and then finally Black.

Lance blacked out and collapsed.

His sword, however, had remained stuck in the ground.

It had been lodged in the ground in the same exact place that the Earth Rasrim that attacked the city of Rockdale had died.

The battle here would be lodged in history forever. It was the third time humanity witnessed it.

What had begun two years ago—and ended only after a bloodbath caused by three champions of life and death—was what was known as *the Apocalypse*.

And ones who saved the world from an untimely and inevitable fate were the ones responsible for it to begin with.

But they would never know.

CHAPTER 14

The Souls That Rule

A mysterious figure sat atop a building, watching overhead, curious to see the commotion brewing in space. He had seen clusters of light, fast-moving projectiles, and glimmers flashing from beyond the atmosphere.

He watched closely, peering and focusing his vision far in the sky.

He could see it all clearly—even from this far away.

The man shook his head. The Humans were so damn flashy!

A satellite from space shook ferociously, unleashing a large beam of light toward the Earth, the heat of the beam turning the satellite red, nearly melting its tungsten muzzle.

The man turned to another direction in the sky.

He watched as a dozen or so Thunderbirds, all modified with high-tech weaponry, fired a barrage of powerful, high-speed missiles into an iceberg that had miraculously begun forming over the city of Annapolis and several others. The man had guessed that the iceberg had been about thirty-two thousand feet tall.

Finally, the man's attention spun to something else far out in the distance in an ocean off the coast of Maryland.

He could feel the vibrations from underneath his feet, shaking even the building he was on.

The man squinted, and he could make out a large machine that began to rise from the Atlantic Ocean, some eighty miles away from where the man had been.

He continued squinting, his eyes studying what he had been seeing, gazing upon every detail of the machine.

He could see a cannon-like object mounted on the face of the machine. It had a large barrel on its front and was anchored to a platform that rose from the depths of the ocean, most likely from a secret underwater base.

The man watched as the cannon rotated downward and spun counterclockwise, now positioned *west* in the direction of the iceberg.

"Well, this one looks rather interesting," the man acknowledged.

Suddenly, a light brewed in front of the cannon, a high-pitched frequency charging as the cannon gained power. At once, it fired a massive red and purple-like Energy at the iceberg that screeched as it moved through the sky at supersonic speed, almost as fast as light itself.

And then the man turned his attention back before the laser had reached its target, watching as all three forms of attacks all met their target at a strategic spot of the iceberg located above a quarter of the way of its total height calculated from the base.

He had been impressed. He knew it would work. He could *feel* the Energy radiating from the various attacks.

In a beautifully timed symphony, the barrage of missiles, lasers, and cannons directed their fire at the growing monster of an iceberg before it exploded entirely, leaving nothing but sparkling, tiny shards of ice the size of grains of sand.

Melterai stood from the building, throwing his arms into the air. "What a buzzkill! I *could* have done that!"

Melterai watched as the glimmer of ice lit up and reflected light from the moon trickling down from the sky. It had been completely harmless.

"But for an attack led by Humans...I *suppose* it wasn't too shabby. The timing was spot-on," he mumbled.

Melterai turned his head into a city in the north.

He had felt a sudden depletion of what he knew were live sources of Risima.

Intrigued, Melterai went to investigate.

In only a second, a black aura had transported him from Annapolis to Rockdale in a fraction of a second, his body dropping down on a street below.

The city had been completely vacant.

Melterai turned, scanning the city from where he had been standing. He had a look of discomfort on his face.

It reeked of blood and foul air. It would take years to completely repair this city. It had seen far better days.

Of course, Melterai didn't care about that. He had been used to bustling communities of species suddenly turned into wastelands. It was all too common near *Kuro*, he told himself.

Besides, Melterai only cared about two things here. Everything else was a give or take.

Melterai started walking, strolling through the ruins of the city as if he were a tourist or something, taking in the scenery, comparing it to what the city had looked like just weeks before. He had been estimating the power needed to account for the damages he was observing.

Melterai walked for what appeared to be hours, strolling through streets riddled with debris, roads, and sidewalks beyond repair.

He looked to his left. Several buildings had been flattened and glass scattered all over the street and in nearby parks. Entire areas of trees and grass were missing and instead were just piles of dirt.

He even found a mound of dirt and concrete piled up in one corner of the city.

He looked to his right. There had been huge puddles of water flooding the streets with loose wires and other dangerous things floating in them. Perhaps a large amount of Ice had *suddenly* melted in the street?

Melterai sighed to himself.

He continued walking, coming across several holo-boards in front of storefronts that were malfunctioning, the screens flickering and playing distorted images of pictures and graphics on their screens.

The windows on stores and offices were missing sections of glass, the inside of the buildings flooded with water. Some have caved in completely, leaving chairs and desks out on the street. Others were on fire and burned, putting thick black smog in the air.

Such recklessness and destruction.

Melterai stopped walking when he came to a large hole in the middle of the street.

He was certainly intrigued.

"Oh, and what could've caused this?"

Melterai peered into the large crater where an intersection of a large area of the city had normally been. There had been pebbles tumbling to the center, and a pipe sticking out from the ground, leaking water, which trickled into the depths of the crater below.

Melterai slowly walked around the crater, gazing into it as he did.

Melterai thought to himself, *Even if they couldn't stop that meteor, this is more than enough power I was expecting. Minus the meaningless destruction and collateral damage, well done, you two.*

Melterai continued examining the city's ruins, evaluating destroyed structures, holes in the street, and even sections of the ground that looked as if fire had scorched the rocks and sand underneath.

And then, after around thirty minutes of wandering and observing, Melterai frowned as he came across the body of a boy, steam rising from around his limbs.

"Oh."

Melterai had suddenly felt remorseful. It wasn't an emotion he felt often.

He knelt to the ground and placed his hand on the boy's heart.

"You fought diligently and proved your point today. I wasn't there to see it all, forgive me."

Melterai closed his eyes.

"The world can no longer tolerate the ruse that the worst threats to humanity come from outer space, can it?"

Melterai opened his eyes, his movements and voice somber.

"'The true monsters are always closer than we think.' Isn't that right? Isn't that what you once told me, Chile? Isn't that the saying that stuck with you since your days in captivity? How pitiful and ironic."

Melterai's body began glowing with red Energy. His entire palm became infused with this bright, potent Energy before it found its way into Chile's body.

The marks on Chile's body began to react.

Melterai slowly lifted his hand from Chile's chest, but thought to himself, carefully, fighting something in his mind.

Finally, he came to his senses and exhaled deeply.

"No. I won't interrupt your slumbering soul, Chile. I won't allow you to suffer any longer. You've done your job. Your death will pave the way toward victory for the Universe. I swear that on my life, my lost friend," he whispered.

Melterai softly placed his hand back on Chile's chest before his body slowly disappeared, turning into pure Risima Energy, drifting away in the wind like twinkling shards of ice.

Melterai stood still for a moment, pondering, challenging his rampant mind.

"But what if I *could* have rescued Chile from his despair? Why does the universe tell me that Chile's survival would have threatened the fate of the universe? Why does his life enable the work of the damned and not us mortals fighting against the *truly* evil forces, lurking in the shadows? Wouldn't *they* champion Chile for what he attempted to do here on Earth?"

Melterai stood up, his body tensed.

"Perhaps there's even more I must learn. I've studied Greek mythology closely, their lessons ring true. If *they* truly exist in this Universe, they *must* be found and eliminated."

Melterai tensed his body, his mind suddenly flooded with memories of when he was younger.

"I've only killed *one*, that trifling bastard *Decrecious*, but even his memories do not prove whether the *Pantheon of the Divinia* exists or not."

435

Melterai held out his sword and aimed it at the sky, directly at Osamos.

Suddenly, he yelled into the sky, somber from one moment, enraged at the next. "The gods! Their souls be damned! They *are* real, and I *will* destroy them all! Once I finally acquire the power to eliminate them down to their roots, to ascend beyond all the gods, all that is left is for me to—"

Melterai stopped, his mouth still open, a new thought crossing into his mind full of swarming ideas and voices.

His eyes moved from one corner to the other corner of his mind as he listened to the voices playing in his mind—all from different sources.

These, however, were *not* voices of the minds he could read.

These were the voices of the *damned*—souls trapped in oblivion for all of eternity inside Melterai's soul, forced to feed their knowledge and wisdom to Melterai *forever*.

Melterai slowly dropped his sword down to his side before the sword disappeared entirely, fading into a different realm.

"No," he simply told himself, "the gods aren't watching *me*. They're watching *them*."

Melterai relaxed his muscles, feeling his presence in the openness of the calm, settling Earth wind, which had returned now that the calamity was long gone.

"But that means I'm still *hidden* from the majority of them. I understand that this won't remain true forever. But *that* is what I and the universe are counting on..."

Melterai turned his head back to the sky.

And then he laughed to himself derisively, his blood beginning to boil on the inside as anger swelled up in his body.

Finally, he yelled back into the air.

"They'll find you soon enough, won't they? They deserve to learn the truth before they *die*, don't they, Arreson? Will you lead them astray too? Will you pray to the very source of this universe's calamity and force it upon your sons, as you once did to me?" Melterai roared, his anger persistent, penetrating through the sky into a boundless Universe that acted as if it were unaware.

But Melterai *knew* the Universe had been listening.

Melterai snapped his head away, forcing himself to remain calm.

He took a deep breath, the image of a particular person soothing him, relaxing his mind.

He mustn't lose sight of what was important.

Melterai finally turned into a direction behind him, in a direction he knew *she* had been.

"And as for you, Olivia—"

*****

Lance opened his eyes.

He had been lying in a bed, bandages wrapped tightly around his chest.

He began to suspect the worst. He wasn't still outside in the street but in some building. Even if he had been in a hospital, that spelled terrible news.

Lance winced as he sat up, afraid that something was wrong, and ready to fight once more.

But he gasped, his eyes clearly deceiving him.

"Am I in my house?"

A head was placed on Lance's head, slowly pushing it back to the bed.

"Don't move just yet. Just rest for now," a familiar soothing voice said.

Lance closed his eyes and sat back.

"Miss E! I mistook you for someone else."

He heard Miss E scoff, but in a good way.

"You two came back like a hot mess for Christ's sake! I'm just glad you're okay!"

Olivia placed the back of her hand on Lance's forehead.

"I'm sorry I wasn't out there with you all. I...well, I was working on some things."

"I know. You were trying to destroy the meteor."

"Turns out the world needed me to destroy an *iceberg*. I can only imagine why."

Lance opened his eyes, pain slowly overcoming his face.

He sat up, unbothered by the jabbing pain in his chest.

"Chile—!"

Miss E placed a hand on Lance's shoulder.

"We'll get him. Don't worry about—"

Lance shut his eyes tightly. "He's dead, Miss E. I killed him. I did it. I did what you told me to do."

The words were spoken with such remorse and regret. Lance had sounded so tired, so weak. It made her feel a type of disdain she had long since done away with.

She didn't offer an answer back, not so much as an expression. Her light in her eyes began to dim, her pupils shrinking. "I see now."

Lance began to look around, remembering something awful.

"Chase, where is he?"

Miss E tried to calm Lance down.

"He's upstairs." Olivia's eyes slowly trembled.

"But I now understand why he hasn't said a single word to me. He's just been in his room. He hadn't even come out to eat."

"But his arm—!"

"His arm? What about it? *You* were the only one with injuries. Chase was completely fine. He just seemed drained and maybe a little shocked. I wouldn't have guessed that was because…no, I'm sorry."

Lance buried his face in his hands.

"Chase and I…we shouldn't be alive right now!"

Lance's body began to rock. His breathing became irregular. "We fought him with everything we had. It seemed like we had lost all hope."

Olivia grabbed Lance's hands and hugged him, brushing the back of his head.

"It's okay, Lance. It's over now. You don't need to worry about it any longer."

Lance's body slowly began to tremble again, but he wrapped his arms tightly around Miss E's body. He didn't want to let go.

"I didn't want to kill him, Miss E. I know what you said—it was just so hard to control myself! I, in the heat of the moment, I felt Stellar Riora, and the next thing I knew, I—"

"You did what you had to do. I know, Lance, I completely understand."

"*Completely*," she added.

Lance felt relieved.

He couldn't exactly understand why he had felt bad, but there was something about the fact that he knew he had been responsible for the death of another person that made him feel awful inside.

In the heat of battle, there was only the idea of survival in Lance's mind.

But in the aftermath, the prospect of death was even worse— even though he had survived and won in the end.

Lance felt like he should have died instead.

"The pain in my chest is gone," he said, attempting to get out of bed.

Miss E didn't stop him. Instead, she gave him the space he needed to move. He needed that. He had matured.

As Lance made his way out of the bed and over to the elevator door, Olivia called out to him one last time.

"Lance."

He stopped and turned to face his caretaker.

"Yeah?"

Olivia smiled. "Thank you for protecting Chase. He looks up to you in more ways than you'll ever know. Never forget that."

Lance nodded. "I know."

"I'm very proud of you, Lance. You've grown remarkably."

Lance smiled back at Miss E. Her sudden pleasantries had been warm and unexpected but not unwarranted.

Before Lance entered the elevator, he asked one last question.

"If I wanted to go to Osamos, would you help me?"

Olivia opened her mouth, but the question hit her much harder than she had anticipated. Her eyes slowly dropped to the floor for a moment.

She pondered. She thought the question over *seriously*.

Then when she had her answer, she looked back up to Lance.

"I won't prevent you from going anywhere you want, Lance. If you want to go to Osamos, I'll support you."

Lance nodded, turning away from Olivia.

"Thanks, Miss E." And when Lance stepped into the elevator, the doors promptly shut behind him, and began to move up.

Olivia sat back in her chair. She bit her lower lip.

"I can't protect them there," she whispered to herself.

She slowly bent over and rested her head on the desk.

"I couldn't even protect them today."

"But they protected themselves, Olivia."

Olivia's head shot up from the Center Console, her hand reaching for something underneath the desk.

But then she slowly relaxed. She couldn't believe her eyes.

Trying to make a statement, Olivia tried her best to seem annoyed. "Oh, it's *you*." Olivia's tone was shortsighted and brash.

"After nearly twenty years, you finally show yourself again."

She had been looking at a boyish individual. He had stood at five foot, ten inches and was wearing a modern outfit for most young adults: a stylish brown and black jacket that wasn't zippered and black jeans. He had curly brown hair and wore jewelry, an earring on the left ear, a crimson-jeweled ring on his right pinky finger, and a necklace with a strange pendant hanging down by his chest, resting over a black T-shirt tucked away behind his jacket.

"Lome, right? What do you want?"

The man known as Lome leaned against the counter of the Center Console, a look of confidence in his eyes.

"Chase and Lance seem to have gotten powerful in such a short time. They fought against and even *beat* one of the protégés of a man who goes by the name 'Melterai.' But that all should sound familiar, right?" Lome asked sarcastically, looking around the room.

"Even this room looks identical to the one I predicted all those years ago. That means everything you've done has gone according to plan. Huh, I think you've outdone yourself, Olivia. You should congratulate yourself."

Olivia remained calm, but deep down, she felt a certain disdain for the boy standing in front of her. She secretly wished that the boy would end up dead somewhere in another galaxy, far, *far* away from where she and her boys were. Regardless, she kept her mind empty on purpose and changed the subject, focusing on what he had said instead.

"The boys mentioned that name before: Melterai. I didn't realize this was the same person you mentioned twenty years ago. Is he someone who I should be aware of?"

Lome looked around restlessly and suddenly became a little cautious.

"So he isn't an acquaintance of yours? Why do I find that hard to believe? You Humans have always been so damn *sneaky*."

Olivia looked offended.

"A man who willingly took a murderous psychopath under his wing and almost killed my boys? Are you being serious?"

Lome scoffed. "Please, Olivia, let's not forget for a second what type of person *you* are. All those innocent people you murdered across the Pacific—including children—and for what? Resources. Sure. I guess I didn't realize you would suddenly have empathy for two Rasrim boys who don't even know who you really are."

Lome pointed at Olivia, taunting her.

"You'll have to tell me of the story where you made their mother disappear before she even got the chance to hold them. I never got the full details."

Olivia's eyes began burning.

She used every muscle and every lesson she ever learned in her life and prevented herself from killing the smug bastard right then and there.

Lome continued, "You need to understand how clever those who wish to undermine the grand calculus of Time can become, given the opportunity to do so. Now that you're one of the good guys, you'll begin to truly understand just how ruthless those on the other side are. And forgive me for the crude assumption I made earlier," he said sarcastically.

Lome leaned his elbows on the counter.

His eyes were suddenly analyzing every part of Olivia, his eyes telling her that he didn't trust her.

"Melterai is a *menace* to the universe as we know it and is one of these individuals I'm speaking about. He must be destroyed with no mercy. He runs a group of mercenaries known as the 'Galactic Elemental Forces.' Their goal is to bring about destruction to everything as we know it."

Lome stepped back from the counter and put his hands in his pockets.

"His actions here on Earth prove that. He's wiped out about a tenth of humanity with a snap of his finger. But the death that Humans witnessed on this planet is benign compared to the other planets in the universe who have become victims of his unspeakable acts."

Olivia looked disturbed. "So the rumors are true then. Millions of people died in those attacks…"

Lome whistled.

"And the death was widespread. Seems like your group was responsible for minimizing the damage. The, uh…Division, was it? Anyways, they've been busy! They have some guy running around providing protection for the masses anywhere from the Midwest to here in the east. Surely, you're aware of this?"

Lome looked around, observing the facility. "Without him, the numbers in this country alone would have skyrocketed."

Olivia looked intrigued. "A man in the Division you say? Are you sure?"

Lome lifted his chin up. "I know the future, Olivia. Provided, there were some loose ends I needed to tend to before *everything* became clear to me. But yes, his name is, uh, what was it again?"

Olivia's face turned dark. She knew exactly who it had been.

"Troy."

Lome snapped his fingers. "Yeah! That's the one!" He clicked his teeth. "So this Troy guy's been making a mad dash between Nevada and Washington for some reason. My guess is he's building some army down in the Midwest, but you know I could care less about what happens on this planet. You know anything about that, though?" His sly, cocky voice almost unbearable to listen to.

Olivia answered him, but she wasn't sure why.

"Troy practically runs Area 51," she said in a low voice. "Not even I know what he's been doing down there. I can only assume the worst. It's only a matter of time before he takes control of the Division and formally declares war on Osamos and any country who decides to recognize the prospect of coexistence with the Rasrims."

Lome looked surprised.

"Unless Melterai does so first, of course. And that'll give you two a common enemy!"

Olivia suddenly felt suspicious.

That was a loaded suggestion, especially coming from a man who could predict the future. Was Lome hoping that Olivia and the Division would begin targeting Melterai?

But instead of questioning the man, she allowed him to continue talking.

"If Melterai gets his way, he'll start a war on both Osamos and Earth and wipe out millions, perhaps even see genocide spread through the cosmos in order to 'lure' out what he believes is a 'true evil.' He's deranged—using his sword 'Exeridon' to gain the abilities of others and to acquire what many consider to be 'Forbidden Knowledge,' drunk on the powers of the Divine and the Damned alike."

Olivia cringed, immediately recognizing that phrase. She first learned of it on Osamos. And that was when she became grateful for all the weapons and technology the Earth had. Nothing could stand up to those who had access to *Forbidden Knowledge*. It was all but suicide.

Lome noticed Olivia's discomfort. "So I assume you're aware of what happens to an individual who becomes obsessed with such powers, aren't you?"

Olivia couldn't answer that question.

She had known too well. But instead of revealing any weaknesses or signs of doubt, she continued to look at Lome in a way to show she didn't completely trust him.

And the truth was that she didn't. She never did.

Something about the way he spoke didn't seem right. It was as if he acted like he owned *everything* and never needed to acknowledge others beneath him.

The only reason she valued him as an individual was his uncanny ability to manipulate Time.

"Needless to say," Lome began, filling in the awkward silence, "we can't allow that to happen. You need to get this Troy guy under control first, and see that Chase and Lance get to Osamos."

Lome leaned into the counter again.

"But they need to master Awme *first*, remember?"

Olivia scoffed. "Of course. You said after their trial involving Risima, which I can only assume was this *shitstorm* that involved Chile, that their next goal was to master Awme."

Olivia folded her hands, staring directly at Lome. She couldn't be any less kind to a man who claimed to know when tragedies would occur and yet refused to intervene themselves. It was a cowardly thing to do.

"So exactly how am I supposed to do that?!"

Lome shrugged, as nonchalant as anyone could possibly be.

"That's up to you, Olivia." Lome turned from the counter, leaning his back against the counter.

"All I can say is, you'll need to get them out of their comfort zone. Have 'em learn a bit more about history and Human culture, maybe."

Lome stretched his arms as if he were bored.

"In any case," he yawned, "they'll naturally gravitate to discovering Awme on their own no matter the path it is that you decide to take. *That's* all I can see, for now."

"So your infamous future sight is limited? That's ironic."

Lome laughed. He clearly thought otherwise.

"If only you knew what *I* know, Olivia. I think *anyone* would be able to predict the future, if they did."

Before he left, Lome gave Olivia one last, damning piece of information.

"I can also tell you that your *parallel* copies living in other universes were never as lucky as you are in *this* particular timeline, Olivia. Sleep tight knowing that you won the lottery—*factorially.*"

Lome walked away from the counter, hands in his pocket.

"But of course, since my future-sight is limited, who knows? Maybe you'll end up exactly where all the other versions of you do: *dead*. Killed by the thing you've always feared most—and keep this between us, *but it never ends well even if you tried to avoid it.*"

Lome waved his left hand in the air before he disappeared into the air, a golden flash of light evaporating into the air, before nothing of him remained.

Olivia sat, frozen stiff.

She balled her hands up, closed her eyes, and nearly screamed at the top of her lungs.

*****

Lance's head popped into the upstairs bedroom, a smile on his face.

"Yo! Why so down? You know I hate sad, pouty cheeks!"

Chase's head shot from up in his bed, stopping himself from bursting out in laughter.

"Dude, that's my line. C'mon."

"But today *you're* the one moping around!"

Lance sat on his bed, directly across from Chase.

Chase sighed, a smile still on his face.

"I mean..."

"We did it, man. It's over."

"It's really over? Seriously?"

"It is."

Chase looked down at his feet.

He lay back in his bed, his arms behind his head. "I was never worried."

That put a smile on his face. "We pushed through, Chase." Lance sat back in his bed, looking out his window.

Even though the hill had been left untouched by most of the destruction, Lance could clearly find where the site of the catastrophe had been. It was almost maddening he would wake up to this view every day, for now on.

"Maybe we should volunteer when the city begins rebuilding, whenever that is," Chase mumbled.

"Imagine how much we'd be able to do. Yeah. That would be a good idea," he added sarcastically.

Lance turned back to face him.

"No, seriously. Powers or not. You're right. Whatever it is, we should help."

Chase opened his eyes. "You serious? Wouldn't that be risky?"

"Of course not! Afterward, we could start school too."

Chase moaned, rubbing his eyes.

"Yeah. You must've had your head thumped harder than I thought."

Lance laughed to himself, lying back in his bed.

A moment of silence filled the room. It was deafening.

While the two seemed to be in high spirits, they knew how each other had felt.

"Chase," Lance began, "I feel bad for him. I didn't want to kill him. Not one second goes by when I don't think about the struggle—that feeling in my arm and chest when I knew that I had just… how can I sleep at night—now? How could I ever get over that?"

Chase sat back in his bed, eyes facing the ceiling.

"We had no choice. It was either him or the entire planet. He was going to kill billions."

Lance's eyes wandered out of the window once more.

His eyes constantly rolled over the destruction—the cleared fields of trees and crumbled buildings.

But even in the midst of all the damage and destruction, Earth had once again found *peace*.

The wind breezed, blowing through the restless leaves on the trees, rolling over the grasses. Animals, including deer grazed out in the grasslands, feeding on plants and berries. Birds chirped and swam in the puddles left by the melting snow and ice. Even though it had been mid-November, the average temperatures were in the fifties. And for those who thought it was bizarre, it most definitely was better than the alternative.

Lance watched as the grass flowed peacefully on their backyard lawn.

"Chase, would you do it again?"

Chase sounded like he was caught off guard. "What? Do what again?"

"If another Rasrim attacked the city like that, and you knew that the only way to stop him was to risk your life or watch the entire world be destroyed, would you do it again?"

Chase rolled over and faced Lance, a confused and sarcastic look on it.

Lance noticed him from the corner of his eye.

"Dude, Lance, of *course* I would!" He shuffled in his bed, trying to sit up. "That's what we signed up for in the first place, isn't it?"

Good, Lance smiled to himself.

But he didn't let Chase see it.

After a second, Lance turned back to Chase, lying sideways in his bed.

"I was just making sure we were on the same page. That's all."

Chase frowned.

He threw a pillow at Lance's face.

"You better be happy that pillow wasn't on *fire*!"

"Or what? You get hit with a bunch of lightning bolts? Maybe you fall in a crater or something?"

"How about you get hit by a spear while falling from fifty feet in the air?"

Lance laughed aloud.

"Oh, better yet, how about with a sword, huh? When'd you figure out how to do all that?"

"Oh *that*? I dunno, want me to teach you how?"

"Hell, yeah! Let's go now!"

*****

In the very end, it never really mattered what Chase and Lance wanted to do.

But they were just boys. And while they were and always would be Rasrims, Chase and Lance considered themselves Humans just as much as 'aliens.' They spoke English. They enjoyed similar activities. They are similar foods. They even looked like the average Human.

So why did it really matter what it was they actually wanted to do, and who truly had the right to make that decision for them? Why did they feel like they had this obligation to protect humanity? Because they could? Because they were raised that way? Because the alternative was extinction?

Perhaps Chase and Lance didn't know what they wanted out of life yet. It seemed like just yesterday that Lance was reading his book on what Risima was like. It felt like destiny was at the end of an everlasting corridor, expanding as fast as Lance ran down its endless hallway.

What was even at the end of that corridor? Was it a title? Was it status? Was it power? Was it love? Was it what they were raised for or what they would ultimately decide was best for them?

It was likely they couldn't even grasp the full extent of what being Rasrims on Earth truly meant. They *were* superbeings, whether they felt that way or not. They didn't have friends. They didn't have family. They only had each other and the world in front of them.

Were Chase and Lance heroes? What would all those who perished during the attack think? What did Olivia and the Division think?

Were they simply visitors? How did other Rasrims feel? Would they accept Chase and Lance back as their own? Would be they allowed to navigate between the two planets as members of each? And if not, what would happen as a result? What did their figures have in store for them?

But as Lance contemplated the complexities of life—the questions that would take the events of his entire story to answer completely—he decided that for now, it didn't matter where their adventures took them. As long as they believed they were doing the right thing and helping whoever they could, it didn't matter how much pain or how many lessons they had to endure.

After all, Lance couldn't help but truly feel alive, excited through the events of it all. No matter what obstacle was in front of him or what opponent he faced, he would never step down from the challenge. It was part of *his* way of fulfilling his own personal destiny.

But Lance could never stop feeling like all of this was nothing more than an experiment, that he and his brother's lives were nothing more than complex lies, that the real battles were being fought in some invisible world they had no comprehension of.

That someone, somewhere, perhaps close, perhaps eons away, was watching their every move; controlling everything behind the scenes.

And if Lance's hypothesis was true, he had an overwhelming feeling he would come face to face with this individual at some point.

And if he ever did, he would eliminate that person. No matter who he was or why he was doing it. He had already crossed a line he never wanted to; he had already witnessed thousands of individuals lying dead in front of his feet and even was responsible for the death of another person.

He could never forgive the person who set him up to do this.

And he would risk everything to find this person and put a permanent end to him.

But until Lance could fulfill that goal, Chase and Lance would always have each other's backs through the thick and thin alike. They would build each other up and see to each other's happiness.

And when they came together, Chase and Lance would always risk their lives to save innocent lives from the threats lurking within the shadows. Perhaps they were beginning to understand the real dangers were much closer than they expected.

But no danger was a challenge for the twins, and Lance's explanation for that was rather simple: It was because Chase and Lance Kolorio were the *souls that rule.*

Printed in the USA
CPSIA information can be obtained
at www.ICGtesting.com
JSHW020510280823
47302JS00001B/2